The Australian's Bride

ALISON ROBERTS
MEREDITH WEBBER
MARION LENNOX

Published in Great Britain 2015
by Mills & Boon, an imprint of Harlequin (UK) Limited,
Eton House, 18-24 Paradise Road, Richmond, Surrey, TW9 1SR

THE AUSTRALIAN'S BRIDE © 2015 Harlequin Books S.A.

Marrying the Millionaire Doctor, Children's Doctor, Meant-to-be Wife and *A Bride and Child Worth Waiting For* were first published in Great Britain by Harlequin (UK) Limited.

Marrying the Millionaire Doctor © 2008 Alison Roberts
Children's Doctor, Meant-to-be Wife © 2008 Meredith Webber
A Bride and Child Worth Waiting For © 2008 Marion Lennox

ISBN: 978-0-263-25207-1
eBook ISBN: 978-1-474-00386-5

05-0315

Harlequin (UK) Limited's policy is to use papers that are natural, renewable and recyclable products and made from wood grown in sustainable forests. The logging and manufacturing processes conform to the legal environmental regulations of the country of origin.

Printed and bound in Spain
by CPI, Barcelona

MARRYING THE MILLIONAIRE DOCTOR

BY
ALISON ROBERTS

Alison Roberts lives in Christchurch, New Zealand. She began her working career as a primary school teacher, but now juggles available working hours between writing and active duty as an ambulance officer. Throwing in a large dose of parenting, housework, gardening and pet-minding keeps life busy, and teenage daughter Becky is responsible for an increasing number of days spent on equestrian pursuits. Finding time for everything can be a challenge, but the rewards make the effort more than worthwhile.

CHAPTER ONE

THIS was...*weird.*

As though reality had become a dream. Of course, Wallaby Island usually had that effect on new arrivals. The largest of a collection of tropical islands off the coast of North Australia, it was a picture-perfect mound of exotic rainforest greenery, bordered by white sandy beaches, surrounded by a warm turquoise ocean and almost always bathed in brilliant sunshine.

Susie Jackson was not a new arrival, however. This environment was reality for her and the anticipation created by watching the privately chartered seaplane come in for a smooth landing and taxi to the pontoon at the end of the jetty was due purely to an empathy with the young girl standing by her side. Pressed close enough for the tremor to feel like her own. She tightened the arm around the girl's shoulders with a quick, reassuring hug.

Figures emerged from the small aircraft. The pilot stayed to secure the mooring and it was a single figure who began to walk down the timber slats of the narrow jetty.

That was when it happened.

When the edges of reality began to blur.

So much for the generic 'parent' figure she had expected to greet. Any last-minute words of encouragement for the girl beside her died on Susie's lips and she could only stare as the man striding towards them turned the jetty into a catwalk.

Modelling the latest Armani suit, perhaps, with an appropriate aura of elegance and power. Beautifully tailored dark trousers. A dark tie that had been loosened and a pristine white shirt with the top button undone. The suit jacket slung carelessly over one arm and a slim, black briefcase dangling from that hand. A mobile phone was in his other hand, held to his ear.

Was it the way he was walking? A mixture of casual grace but purpose with an unmistakable air of being very accustomed to attracting a spotlight. *Demanding it*, almost.

OK, maybe the man *was* a highly acclaimed neurosurgeon from Sydney and maybe he was a key figure in tomorrow's opening ceremony because he had donated enough money to help make the new, fabulous medical facilities on Wallaby Island a possibility in the wake of Cyclone Willie, which had devastated the area six months ago, but this wasn't about him right now, was it?

It was about Stella. The girl nervously standing beside her. *Without* the aid of her crutches. Waiting for the most important person in her life to applaud what was, quite literally, a huge step forward.

The nerves were contagious. Or maybe it was a trickle of apprehension that made Susie's stomach tighten and her mouth feel dry as Alex Vavunis strode closer. The phone was snapped shut and he was close enough now for Susie to take in the clearly defined lines of his face, the jaw softened slightly by heavy shadow and far more by a charming smile. Dark hair, dark eyes, olive skin. Lines on his forehead that suggested this man was used to frowning.

Not that he was frowning right now. Susie was invisible, standing outside a kind of forcefield created by the palpable bond between this father and daughter. What would it feel like, she wondered a little wistfully, to be so important to a man like this?

But then the lines deepened, confirming Susie's impression, and the smile of pride and delighted greeting faded as he focused intently on his daughter's face. For the briefest moment he looked taken aback. As though he didn't quite recognise the person he was looking at. Almost as though he was seeing a ghost.

'Stella! What's all this?'

Stella's tentative smile widened hopefully. *Look at me, Daddy*, it said. *Tell me it's OK to feel this proud of myself.*

Susie's smile widened, too. *She did this by herself*, it said. *Isn't it wonderful?*

But Alex Vavunis didn't even seem to notice the absence of the crutches. He was staring at Stella's face. Susie watched, transfixed by the changing expression on his face, not wanting to believe what she could see happening. Pleasure giving way to a blink of readjustment. Pride being tarnished by what could only be interpreted as disappointment. Surely not. How crushing would that be?

'You're...' Alex paused, and the transformation from loving parent to authoritarian figure appeared complete. 'Are you wearing *make-up*?'

Stella's smile wobbled. 'I... It's the camp disco to-night. I told you...'

'And what are you wearing? Whose clothes are they?'

'Mine.'

Her father made a faint sound—of irritation perhaps. As though he knew every item of clothing in his teenage daughter's wardrobe and didn't recognise these.

Maybe he did, in which case Susie might label him as a control freak rather than a caring parent. It was possible to give him the benefit of some doubt, though. What Stella was wearing at the moment was very different to anything she had brought with her to camp but, then, variations on a theme of denim jeans, oversized T-shirts and baseball caps were hardly what a girl would want to wear to her first disco, were they?

'There's a shop at the resort,' Stella was continuing bravely. 'You said I could buy anything I needed and put it on your room account.'

'Yes, but...' Alex took another look at his daughter's attire and sighed.

The sigh seemed to hang over them. The sound of a man who was capable of dealing with any amount of stress and decision-making in matters of life or death but who had not expected and certainly did not welcome having to deal with this particular issue.

Stella didn't sound so brave now. There was uncertainty in her voice. 'What's wrong with what I'm wearing?'

'Nothing,' Susie muttered.

The skirt was gorgeous. Layers of brightly coloured gypsy ruffles that ended at mid-calf. The perfect length and shape for making the first public appearance of that prosthesis discreet.

The lacy white camisole top was also perfect. Just what most teenage girls wore, and while the shop hadn't run to much in the way of lingerie, Susie knew Stella had been secretly thrilled at the boost from the lightly padded and underwired white bikini top.

'It looks like underwear,' Alex Vavunis decreed. He shook his head in a single, incredulous movement. 'Good Greek girls do not appear in underwear in public, Stella.'

'But…'

Susie could feel Stella's confidence draining. All the excitement and anticipation from revealing her progress and new, grown-up look was evaporating like the hiss of air from a pricked balloon. She glared at Stella's father. How could he *do* this? Did he have any idea how hard it had been to get to this point? How fragile his daughter's self-esteem was?

A degree of disapproval would have been understandable. Acceptable even. She had been prepared for that after more than one reference from Stella about how strict her father could be, but Susie had brushed aside the warnings. She had heard enough to convince her how proud Stella was of her famous father and how much she loved him. Any parent who inspired such loyalty had to be doing something right and it had been easy to convince herself that he would be as thrilled as she was at the extraordinary progress Stella had made this week.

Oh, Lord! This was *her* fault.

Susie still had her arm around Stella's shoulders and she could feel the gathering tension. Any second now and her arm could be shrugged off as blame was apportioned. There would be tears, no doubt. What should have been a joyous reunion would be a scene of misery and confrontation for everybody concerned.

'Charles Wetherby was supposed to meet me and arrange transport,' Alex said. 'We'll go straight to the hotel and you can get changed.' He frowned at his mobile phone then looked over Stella's shoulder.

Susie followed the glance. Sure enough, there was Charles in his wheelchair a little further up the path that led to the medical centre. How long had he been there? How much had he overheard?

Enough, she suspected, aware of a wash of relief. The medical director of Crocodile Creek Base Hospital had earned his position as the heart of this community. He never ceased to keep his fingers on the pulse of his realm. Not just the running of a large base hospital that provided a rescue base for the whole of far North Queensland. Or its satellite and now considerably upgraded facilities on Wallaby Island that meant they were able to expand the camps run for sick kids and their families. He also seemed to know anything important that was happening in the lives of his staff.

Susie sent a smile in his direction. A probably unnecessary plea for assistance in defusing this situation. Charles had been the point of contact for the neurosurgeon two years ago when Alex Vavunis had been checking out the possibility of a respite for his daughter who had been undergoing intensive chemotherapy for a type of bone cancer. He would know more about the man's personality than Susie did, so he would be aware of the undercurrents.

And everybody had seen how Susie had been drawn to this prickly teenager in the first week of this current camp. Charles had commented only yesterday about the extra hours Susie was spending on the island this time, but the twinkle in his eye had been approving.

He had seen what Stella's father was apparently blind to. Susie's smile suddenly felt crooked. Maybe Charles had also seen that the project was helping Susie as much as Stella. That she'd been drawn to the teenager because some of the events of this week had left her feeling just as forlorn and left out of the good things in life as Stella clearly did.

Charles rolled onto the planks at the land end of the jetty. The seaplane pilot had finished securing the moorings and was walking towards them from the other end, carrying a suitcase. She and Stella were a little island of femininity getting closed in by men. No wonder Stella trembled and seemed to lose her balance. Standing unaided was new enough without this sense of threat. That was why Susie had the elbow crutches clutched in her free hand. Hidden behind her back.

Amazingly, though, Stella straightened. Regained her balance. Susie loved the way her chin rose defiantly.

'No,' she told her father.

'No?' The echo was dumbfounded. 'What do you mean, "*No*"?'

'I'm not going to the hotel.'

'It's all arranged.' The words were impatient. 'We have a suite. You didn't want to stay in the dormitories with the other children, remember?'

Of course she didn't, Susie thought angrily. She has to take her prosthesis off at night, doesn't she?

'You refused to even come to camp this year,' Alex continued. 'You only agreed because I'd already gone to considerable trouble to create a window so I could attend the opening of the medical centre.'

Charles raised an eyebrow. It had been an invitation to a major sponsor, the gesture suggested. A courtesy, not an edict intended to create inconvenience.

'You *liked* the idea of the luxury suite,' Alex concluded firmly. 'And that you could fly back with me on Sunday instead of staying for the second week. It's all arranged, Stella.'

And that was that.

Or was it?

'I've changed my mind,' Stella said. She gulped in a breath of the warm tropical air. 'I *like* the dormitory now… And I like my new clothes…and…and I *can* wear make-up if I want to. I'm nearly *fourteen* and Susie said—'

'*Susie?*' The interruption was a snap. A low and dangerous sound. 'Who the hell is Susie?'

'Me,' Susie said. Oh, God, did it have to come out like the squeak of a cornered mouse?

For the first time Alex looked directly at her and Susie felt the eye contact like a physical blow. Sharp and penetrating. She felt like a bug pinned for inspection, and she couldn't escape. Couldn't—for the life of her—tear her gaze away.

Not that she really wanted to. Stella needed an ally here and *she* was it. She would just have to ignore the way her heart had begun hammering and the odd, prickly internal sensation that felt horribly like fear.

'Susie Jackson.' It was Charles's voice. Calm and strong. A reassurance all by itself. 'Our esteemed physiotherapist, Alex. She and Stella have made a formidable team this week.'

'Charles!' Alex slipped his mobile phone into the pocket of his trousers and extended his hand to greet the man now beside Stella. 'Good to see you.'

'And you, Alex. We're delighted you were able to make it.'

'Good timing, having the opening on while Stella's here for camp. It's about time I saw the place that's made such a difference to my only child's life.'

'Not to mention meeting the people.' Charles's smile drew Susie into the exchange. 'We're lucky there were no last-minute emergencies to keep you in Sydney this time.'

The pocket holding the cellphone got patted. 'There are always emergencies, Charles, as I'm sure you know only too well.' A determined intake of breath suggested resolution. Had he been dealing with difficulties in his unit even as he'd been taking his first steps onto the jetty? 'This time I told them they'd just have to cope without me.'

The charming smile was back but it had no effect on Susie. She wasn't prepared to make allowances for professional hassles. She was getting a rather clear picture of how important this man considered himself and his career and, in her opinion, Stella should be a long way further up his list of priorities.

It was, quite simply, not good enough.

'I might even turn my mobile off,' Alex said.

Susie almost snorted.

'Good thinking,' Charles said mildly. He swivelled to look over his shoulder. 'There's a cart on the way to take you to the resort but if you're not too hot, I could give you a quick tour of the centre.'

Susie found herself nodding agreement. Disappear for a while, she encouraged silently. *Let me see if I can repair the damage here.*

No such luck.

'We'll go to the hotel first,' Alex said crisply. 'I can't have my daughter out looking like—'

'Like *what*?' Stella's voice rose and there was more than a hint of tears in it. 'What's so wrong with the way I look, Dad? *Susie* said…' Her voice trailed away. Was it too hard to utter the notion that she looked gorgeous?

'Susie said *what*?'

Alex flicked another glance at his daughter's physio-therapist. His gaze dropped from her loose, shoulder-length hair, which always went a bit too curly with salt water and sunshine, to take in the soft singlet top she wore beneath an unbuttoned shirt, the sleeves of which were rolled up past her elbows. Dropped again, to denim shorts with frayed hems that did nothing to hide the length of her well-tanned legs—

Susie flushed. It wasn't a particularly professional-looking uniform but things were never overly formal in Crocodile Creek, and she was on an island right now with a bunch of kids who were having a holiday. A break from lives that centred around debilitating and sometimes fatal illnesses.

They were here to have fun and her role was to help them only as much as necessary. To encourage severely asthmatic children to keep up their breathing exercises. To provide maintenance therapy to those suffering from cystic fibrosis and cerebral palsy. And, yes, she had stepped over the boundary of maintenance therapy with Stella, but if she hadn't, Stella would have stayed on the outskirts. Hiding from the other children. From life. From having any fun at all.

And her father wanted to send her back into that dark space? Susie's chin went up the same way Stella's had.

She cleared her throat and was pleased with how firmly she spoke.

'I said she looked absolutely gorgeous.'

Her defiance was clearly infuriating.

'She looks,' Alex hissed, 'like a *tart*.'

Stella gasped. 'That's a *horrible* thing to say. How *could* you?'

Alex closed his eyes for a moment. He took a deep breath. When he opened his eyes again, his expression had softened. He raised his hand in a gesture of apology. 'I'm sorry, *latria*, but you're thirteen years old and I find you wearing underwear in public and with your face plastered with make-up. What did you *expect* me to think?'

It wasn't plastered. The make-up was discreet and enhancing. The result of rather long girly time in Susie's cabin that afternoon. She opened her mouth to protest but Stella got in first.

'I wish you hadn't even come.' The girl twisted under Susie's arm, having either not registered or not accepted her father's attempt at an apology. She was fishing for her crutches.

Should Susie try and hang on to them? Let Stella show her father she could now manage to walk on her prosthesis—something she had refused to even attempt until this week?

No. Stella was far too upset to remember how to keep her balance. To fall over now would only make her humiliation unbearable. Susie helped her fit a crutch to each arm, which took only seconds.

Tears were streaming down Stella's pale face as she looked up at her father.

'Go *home*,' she shouted. 'I *hate* you.'

With that, she turned deftly and manoeuvred herself past Charles, heading towards the end of the jetty.

'*Stella!*' The word was a command.

One that was blatantly ignored. Stella was picking up speed now that she had reached the path. She was running away as fast an anyone could with a pair of elbow crutches and a below-knee amputation. The state-of-the-art prosthesis that looked so wonderfully realistic wasn't touching the ground. It was back to being what it had been since its procurement. An aesthetic accessory.

Susie rounded on Alex.

'How *could* you?'

His face emptied of an expression worn many times by any parent of a teenager. That baffled kind of look that asked how on earth things had got so out of hand. As he focused on Susie, his face became completely neutral. 'Excuse me?'

'Your daughter walked nearly fifty metres this morning without using those crutches. She couldn't even *stand* without the crutches a week ago and we've worked incredibly hard to get this far.' The words were tumbling out. A release of all the hurt and disappointment she felt on behalf of Stella. 'That's exactly what she was doing when you arrived and *that's* what you should have noticed. Not the bloody *make-up*!' Susie gave an incredulous huff and put all her own fury into the glare she was directing at Alex. 'How *could* you?' she repeated.

There was a long moment of stunned silence. Susie had seen him flinch. She knew her words had found a target. Clearly, he was considering how to deal with such a personal attack.

The pilot had stopped approaching some time back,

obviously disconcerted by the sound of angry voices. He was peering at something over the edge of the jetty with studied interest.

Tiny sounds became magnified. The lap of gentle waves breaking on the nearby beach. The cry of exotic birds in the rainforest. A distant shout and then the laughter of children.

The heat was intolerable.

It wasn't a tropical sun that was burning Susie right now, however. The heat was emanating from the man in front of her. His sheer energy was overpowering. Not simply anger. Anyone could get angry, especially a parent who had been publicly defied and then criticised. No. The power here came from anger underlined with a heady mix of intelligence, position and...and the most potent masculinity Susie Jackson had ever encountered.

She had never met anyone like this in her entire life.

What the hell did she think she was doing?

His voice encapsulated every lightning impression she had just catalogued. It was a low, dangerously calm rumble.

'Stella is my daughter, *Miss* Jackson. I have raised her alone since she was three months old.' A tiny pause for effect. 'I don't think I need *anybody* telling me how I *should* be doing it.'

Obviously he did, but the defiant response refused to come out. Susie's mouth was too dry and she felt alarmingly close to tears herself. It was tempting to turn and run, as Stella had done, but she wasn't going to.

No way!

A purring noise broke this silence and it came from

the small, electrically powered vehicle that chose that moment to arrive. Slow moving and environmentally friendly, these island vehicles had two seats and could tow a small trailer for luggage.

'Ah…my transport.' Alex turned away, giving Susie the impression that she was a nuisance that had now been dealt with. He sounded slightly less sure of himself when he focused on the new arrival, however.

'What in God's name is that?'

'Garf,' Charles told him succinctly. 'The camp mascot.'

As was often the case, empty space in a cart or trailer had been gleefully occupied by the large, woolly dog.

'But what *is* he? I've never seen anything like it.'

'Labradoodle. Labrador poodle cross. Hypoallergenic. We had to be careful with pets and avoid anything that could trigger asthma attacks. He's still on parole as far as close contact with some of the children.'

Garf didn't know that. He had obviously been waiting for the cart to stop. As soon as it did, he bounced off the seat and loped off in the direction Stella had taken. Susie smiled. Garf had an inbuilt antenna when it came to unhappy children and he was probably the best medicine for Stella right now.

Alex gave a satisfied nod as the dog vanished up the track. 'I'll meet you back here in half an hour if that suits,' he said to Charles. 'Now, where is Stella's dormitory?'

Susie opened her mouth and then shut it again as she caught the flicker of Charles's eyebrow.

'Let me offer you a nice cold drink,' he said to Alex. 'I don't know about you, but I could do with one.' He smiled. 'Don't forget we're on island time here.

Nobody's going anywhere and nothing needs to be rushed.'

Diplomatic, Susie conceded. Far more so than she would have been in suggesting that Stella needed some time to herself before seeing her father again.

And Charles was not someone who could be dismissed. He might be in a wheelchair but that did nothing to diminish this man's presence, and he had the upper hand right now. They were on *his* patch.

Alex had the grace to concede at least a reprieve. He inclined his head. 'Wouldn't say no to a cold beer. I have to admit it's been rather a long and difficult day already.'

Was that some kind of backhanded apology? Inferring that Susie's earlier impression might have been valid and his reaction to Stella's appearance had been the last straw on a stressed camel's back?

Charles was gracious enough to assume something along those lines. 'I'll bet,' he said sympathetically. 'Let's send your luggage off to the resort and we can see what the fridge in my office has to offer.'

'Lead the way.'

'We'll go via the centre if you don't mind. I need to pop in on Lily.'

'Lily? Your daughter?'

'She's not very well.'

'I'm sorry to hear that.'

'Nothing too serious but you know how young children can go down in a heap with a virus. I'm keeping her in the medical centre this afternoon so we can keep a close eye on her.'

The voices of the two men faded as they moved away. The pilot took it as a cue to finish his journey along the jetty.

'Bloody suit,' he muttered. 'Thinks he's God's gift, doesn't he? You OK, Susie?'

'I'm fine, thanks, Wayne.'

'Poor kid.'

'Hmm. I might just go and see where she is.'

'You do that.' Wayne hefted the smart black suitcase onto the back of the electric cart and greeted the driver. 'There's a couple of dead birds floating under the jetty, mate. Those noisy shearwater things. Someone might need to do something before they wash up on the beach or the kids go swimming or something.'

The driver unhooked a radio from the dashboard. 'I'll call it in but I think the rangers are still out with the kids on some forest trek.'

The rainforest buggy ride was actually over, Susie realised as she walked back towards the camp facilities. Already groups of children and their parents or carers were heading to the beach for a late-afternoon swim. She waved at Benita Green, a nurse with a small group of her cancer patients in tow, and then found herself returning the wide grin of little Danny, who was still completely bald from his chemo.

It was hard to stay angry in this environment. Hopefully Stella had found a private spot and the island was working a similar magic on her. Or would she be angry at Susie for orchestrating the confrontation, albeit unwittingly? More likely, she was simply feeling utterly miserable.

Unloved and unlovable.

Where would she have gone?

Not to the dormitory with the others returning and racing in to get their togs and towels. The older ones would be looking forward to the disco this evening and probably discussing it, and that would certainly rub salt into Stella's wounds.

Would she have gone to the cabin Susie had been allocated because she was staying for the opening ceremony tomorrow and the gala dinner the five-star resort restaurant was hosting later? Stella knew the location because that was where they'd excitedly taken the purchases of new clothes and make-up for the styling session that afternoon. But she also knew that Susie was going to be sharing the cabin with other staff from the base hospital. She would hardly want to explain herself to strangers if they had already arrived.

No. Susie turned off the wide track that led from the beach, one fork going to the camp dormitories, dining hall and activity rooms, the other leading to the newly built eco-cabins in the rainforest. She doubled back towards the beach on a much smaller track, confident she knew one of the best thinking spots around.

Sure enough, hidden between the overturned timber hulls of a couple of ancient dinghies, Stella was sitting. A hunched figure scraping a meaningless pattern in the sand with a piece of driftwood, oblivious to the view of the ocean and small islands that advertised their presence in paradise. Beside her, with big brown eyes peering anxiously beneath golden dreadlocks, sat Garf. Close enough to cuddle but respectfully keeping his distance for now. The dog seemed, in fact, to be enjoying the view Stella was ignoring.

Susie slid down the side of a dinghy to a squat rather than a sitting position, being as careful as Garf not to intrude too forcefully into Stella's space. She couldn't assume she was welcome. Maybe it was only on her side that the relationship had become so much more than that of therapist and patient.

'Hey,' she said gently. 'You OK, hon?'

The only answer was a sullen sniff.

Susie picked up a handful of the fine white sand and let it drift through her fingers. 'Dr Wetherby's taken your dad off to see the medical centre. He thought you might want a bit of time to yourself.'

'I do. Go away.'

'I think your dad's had a stressful day getting here,' Susie offered. 'He got a bit of a shock seeing you all dressed up, that's all. He'll get over it.'

'No, he won't.'

'We won't let him stop you going to the disco.'

'I don't want to go.'

She didn't really expect Susie to believe that, did she? Maybe she didn't realise that her exchange with fourteen-year-old Jamie had been overheard that morning.

'You going to the disco?'

'Dunno. Maybe.'

'You should. It'll be choice.'

'Yeah… OK…'

'Cool. See you there, then.'

Even if she had been aware of Susie listening, Stella wouldn't have known that, in the wake of Jamie's grin, her face had been the picture of every teenage girl in existence who was experiencing her first crush.

And Susie had used that secret as an emotional key to get through the last barrier and get Stella walking properly. The day had snowballed from then on. The hugely successful physio session, the shopping and the make-over. A crescendo of excitement that had just been shredded.

A flash of anger resurfaced.

'Your dad's wrong,' Susie said firmly. 'He only said that about how you look because he doesn't realise you're growing up. It's not what the other kids will think, believe me.' Not what Jamie would think, but she couldn't say that.

Stella hunched into a tighter ball. 'It doesn't matter. I don't *care*.'

Using the side of the other dinghy as a climbing frame, Stella clambered upright awkwardly. She picked up her crutches without looking at Susie. 'Who wants to go to a stupid disco anyway?'

The hunched shoulders, resentful tone and total lack of eye contact was achingly familiar.

They were right back to where they'd been at the start of this week.

Back to square one.

Susie watched miserably as Stella moved slowly over the sand.

Something wonderful had been happening in the last few days. Something that had filled a lonely space with magic and created more joy than she had known her career could provide, but that new, hopeful space had just exploded, thanks to a human bomb. Even Garf's head on her knee wasn't enough to comfort her.

Susie straightened her legs, giving Garf a quick scratch under his chin as she stood up. She watched as two boys ran onto the beach, past Stella. They weren't camp kids but Susie had seen them hanging around in the last day or two and she didn't like the look of them at all.

'Hey, Zach, look!' One of them shouted. 'It's one of those cripples from the kiddie camp.'

'Crip-ple!' His mate taunted loudly. 'Hop-along! Go back to the forest with all the other freaky frogs!'

Laughing, the teens in their designer board shorts kept loping onto the beach, oblivious to the hurt they might have caused.

Susie's hands bunched into fists. She started moving, intending to intercept the boys and give them a piece of her mind, but from the corner of her eye she could see another group of young people arriving. These were camp kids and Jamie was leading them.

He must have heard the taunting and Stella would have to know he'd heard it, which would only have made it even more cutting. The tall, lanky body of the teenager, bronzed by so many hours in the surf, was gathering speed. Tousled, blond-streaked hair bounced. Susie could see why he was catching the attention of the girls.

And not just the girls. With a delighted woof and an apologetic glance up at Susie, Garf abandoned her to join the fun.

She watched the way Jamie bent to welcome the dog by ruffling his soft coat. Should she try and enlist the boy's help in boosting Stella's self-esteem? Could she do it without making it look contrived? Should she even try? Susie knew the answer to that one but desperation might have tipped the balance if her thoughts had not been interrupted by the ringtone of her mobile.

It was Charles.

'Could you spare a few minutes to come to my office?' he asked. 'Alex would like to talk to you.'

'I'm not at all sure I would like to talk to *him*.' Susie was still watching Jamie. He had caught up with the strange boys and was clearly saying the kind of things Susie had been planning to say. She smiled. Stella knew how to pick them, didn't she?

'Susie!' Charles's tone had a glint of amusement. Understanding. But it was also a reprimand. Charles wouldn't have suggested the meeting unless he thought it would benefit the people he cared about.

Like her.

And Stella.

Susie sighed. 'I'm on my way.'

CHAPTER TWO

'IT's the perfect solution.'

'I agree.'

The latest arrival in the office wasn't looking quite so convinced.

'Let me get this straight,' Susie said slowly, still looking at Charles. 'You want me to spend the weekend in the penthouse suite at the resort that was reserved for Stella and Mr Vavunis? And Mr Vavunis is going to use my cabin?'

'Call me Alex.'

He hadn't noticed how astonishingly blue Stella's physiotherapist's eyes were but, then, he hadn't taken much notice of her physical appearance at the jetty, had he? Or was it because they were now tucked away in the neutral décor of this air-conditioned space in the new medical centre and the competition from the vast blueness of the sky and ocean had been removed?

Whatever. The expression in those eyes was not impressed and she made no acknowledgement of the invitation to use his first name. Dammit! He knew he'd been rude earlier but it could hardly be considered unprovoked and he certainly wasn't going to jump through hoops in order to call a truce.

'It's the closest eco-cabin to the girls' dormitory,' Charles said calmly. 'A compromise that would allow Stella to spend time with her dad but still be close to her mates.' An eyebrow quirked. 'It's also the last available two-bedroomed cabin.'

'But what about Mike and Emily?'

Alex suppressed a sigh. He had anticipated a delighted acceptance of the plan he and Charles had come up with over their beer. What woman wouldn't want to exchange a simple hut in a forest for the ultimate in luxury? But no. Miss Jackson was going to be difficult.

Again.

He tapped his fingers on the arm of his chair. 'Mike and Emily?' he queried.

'Mike's one of our helicopter pilots,' Charles supplied. 'Also a paramedic. Emily's an anaesthetist at our base hospital.'

'My best friend,' Susie put in.

'And?' Alex couldn't see the relevance but he couldn't miss the note in Susie's voice that spoke of fierce loyalty to the people she called friends. He could approve of that.

'And they're coming over for tomorrow's opening,' Susie continued. 'They're going to be sharing my cabin.'

'Already sorted,' Charles told her. 'Don't worry.'

Even, white teeth appeared as Susie chewed her bottom lip. 'But the resort's right down at the south end of the island. It's a long way from the kids' camp.'

'Precisely,' Alex said with satisfaction. If Stella was determined to stay at the camp, it would effectively put him on a different planet, wouldn't it? Perhaps he was already as far as his daughter was concerned. What the hell *had* happened on this camp so far?

'It's not as far as the mainland,' Charles reminded

Susie. 'And you've been trekking back and forth all week. How about I organise a cart for your personal use?'

Susie flashed him a grin. 'A bicycle would do.'

Alex let out his breath. 'Thank you very much, Miss Jackson. I appreciate your cooperation.'

The corner of her mouth twitched but it wasn't a real smile. Not like the one she'd given Charles. It was more like a subtle putdown of his formality.

'Call me Susie.'

'I will.' He could go even further in cementing this new accord. He could offer a new beginning. Alex stood up and extended his hand. 'Pleased to meet you, Susie.'

She followed suit, standing as she put her hand into his, but the response was tentative. As though this formality was also out of place. Her hand was warm. And soft. The grip was surprisingly firm.

Why was she still not smiling? Blue eyes were regarding him with mistrust. She may be conceding a truce but he wasn't going to be given the benefit of a completely clean slate. He would have to earn any respect.

Alex Vavunis was not used to being mistrusted.

Quite the opposite, actually. Most women didn't even wait for an invitation to get closer. They used whatever means they could to attract his attention.

Including, on more than one occasion, his daughter.

It should be refreshing that someone was prepared to antagonise him on Stella's behalf, but Susie was not the only one capable of mistrust. What was it Charles had said? That Susie and Stella had made a formidable team this week? Alex had yet to gauge the strength of the relationship between this woman and his daughter and, given the unfortunate family spat on his arrival, it might be prudent to avoid any further antagonism until the emotional lie of the land became clearer.

If what Charles had been telling him was true, he owed this woman rather a lot and he was not a man to leave debts unpaid, but he would need to satisfy himself regarding motivation first. To make sure nobody was being used.

The vow may be years old now but nobody was ever going to use Stella like that again.

'Can I leave it to you to show Alex where the cabin is?' Charles was saying now. 'Jill's wanting to come over to help look after Lily. It's too late for the usual ferry or seaplane transfers but I said I'd try and sort out some transport.'

The black suitcase had already been whisked away to the resort hotel.

'I'll have it sent back,' Susie told Alex. 'As soon as I can tear myself away for the champagne and caviar.'

He didn't smile. He turned away, in fact, to stare at the ocean view as they began their walk towards the cabin. Did he think she was being critical of such an affluent choice of accommodation? Or, worse, that she was being serious?

Maybe the man had no sense of humour.

Not that he really needed one with his looks. Women must fall at his feet in droves, even without the additional attractions of vast wealth and an international reputation as one of the best paediatric neurosurgeons in the southern hemisphere.

Susie gave her head a tiny shake. It wouldn't be enough for her. A large part of the sheer joy to be found in being alive came through laughter.

On the other hand… Susie stole a quick glance at the man walking alongside her. It was a little too easy to imagine the kind of female response the sight of Alex would generate. She could actually feel an odd frisson of something herself.

Something she hadn't felt for a very long time.

Good grief!

She was *attracted* to him?

Susie flicked her hair back with a far more vigorous shake of her head. Not possible. Not when he had made Stella so miserable. And particularly not when she remembered that unpleasant emphasis in calling her *Miss* Jackson that first time. He'd been so sure she was unmarried, and why was that? Because he'd judged her appearance and personality and decided that nobody would have been interested?

At least he couldn't possibly know how well the barb had found a target.

The faint bars of a piece of classical music came from nowhere. It wasn't until Alex stopped that she realised the sound was coming from his pocket.

'Excuse me for a moment,' he said, extracting his cellphone. The phone he had said he was going to switch off. 'I'd better take this,' he added, after a glance at the tiny screen. 'It's my registrar.'

Susie took another pace or two before she stopped, and she didn't turn around. Her back could be a silent protest that he could still allow priorities other than Stella to claim his attention.

A rapid exchange of medical terminology was easy to ignore but then the tone of the conversation suddenly changed and Susie found herself eavesdropping.

'Do the parents want to speak to me again?' A heavy

silence as Alex listened. 'Please, tell them how sorry I am.'

He *sounded* sorry.

Sincere. And caring.

Susie tried not to let her opinion of this man take a U-turn. Why hadn't he sounded like that when he'd been speaking to his own daughter?

It was hard to ignore the heavy sigh she heard. Then a silence that seemed to speak volumes. But then Alex cleared his throat and it seemed to be business as usual.

'Can you give me a quick update on Melanie? I'm going to be unavailable by mobile for a while. What's the ICP looking like?'

There was another exchange of medical information, a farewell and then Susie heard the phone give a blip that suggested it was, indeed, being switched off.

'Sorry about that,' Alex murmured. He moved to catch up with Susie. 'It's been a day from hell in the unit.'

'Has it?'

Susie was only being polite. She didn't really expect Alex to start talking to her about his professional life. The silence around them was welcome rather than uncomfortable. Then it became *too* quiet. Where were all the children? All on the beach, perhaps, or rounded up to participate in some pre-dinner activity.

The shade of the patch of forest they were in had also been initially welcome but seemed to become oppressive. It was hot and there was no hint of any sea breeze reaching them now.

Or did the feeling of oppression come from her companion? Susie looked sideways and was startled to catch Alex's gaze. He was frowning again and Susie felt as if she was under some kind of new evaluation.

'I operated on a fourteen-year-old boy in the early hours of this morning,' Alex said abruptly. 'He and his brother got collected by a drunk teenager who lost control of his car last night. The brother died instantly. We did our best with Sean but we knew by this morning there was no point in continuing life support. There were potential organ recipients in the wings. I was talking to the parents again as I was arriving here. My registrar tells me they've just decided to have the ventilator switched off…and they've agreed to donate Sean's organs.'

'Oh…' Susie didn't know what to say. How glib had she been in considering that his day might have been stressful? Nobody could have missed the pain in his voice when he'd relayed his sympathy to the parents of that boy. Alex cared about his patients. A lot. How much of his mind and heart were unavoidably involved elsewhere at present? Beside a bed in an intensive-care unit where a family was gathered to say a final farewell to a child they should not be losing.

For the second time Susie was trapped by her eye contact with Alex. This time—incredibly—it seemed even more powerful. This wasn't any kind of surface inspection, however. Perhaps he was trying to gauge the effect his words had had. Did Susie understand why he might have been so horrified at the sight of his daughter having been transformed into a teenager in the space of a few days? That these years were enough of a minefield for any parent to contemplate, let alone someone in Alex's position who got to see the worst of what could happen?

Of course she understood. And she could respect anyone in the medical profession who cared that much about his patients. But Stella was his daughter. His only child. On top of what was almost always a difficult life stage, she was having to deal with things that, fortunately, most teens didn't have to face. A life-threatening illness. Stella was…special, and if a line in the sand was being drawn, Susie was not about to allow herself to get tugged onto Alex's side. She didn't know this man. Maybe he was clever enough to know how to manipulate people around him.

That could also explain why he had gone over the top when confronted by Stella's apparent misbehaviour.

Susie dampened the warmth that had started to thaw her opinion of Alex. She looked away, helped by the change of scenery as the track veered to the edge of the forest and afforded another spectacular view of the horseshoe-shaped bay to their right.

'Who's Melanie?' she enquired eventually, her curiosity getting the better of her and providing a means to end another awkward silence.

'Another patient. An only child. She's ten and she had her surgery this morning. We discovered her brain tumour was inoperable. Unless we can shrink it with chemo, it'll be a very short space of time before it invades her brain stem. She's not doing as well as I'd like post-op, either.'

The first of the eco-cabins came into view on their left. On short stilts to protect their inhabitants from some of the wildlife and made from well-weathered timber that blended into the surrounding rainforest, they looked like dolls' houses. Small and inviting. A fantasy that was a world away from the grim reality Alex had been relating.

Two of the cabins looked half-derelict, with their

windows unglazed and no netting around the verandas, but the third was clearly inhabited. A red-and-white canvas chair stood beside a table made from half a barrel. An old couch with brightly coloured cushions dominated the rest of the space, and the barrel top and veranda railing were decorated with shells and driftwood. A windsong made a tiny sound in appreciation of the puff of sea breeze reaching them again.

Alex stopped, turning slowly to take in the view of the sea and then to take another look at the cabin.

'How lovely!' he exclaimed. 'It looks as if it's been here for ever.'

'That's Beth's cabin,' Susie told him. 'She's the permanent doctor for the medical centre now and she fell in love with that cabin. It's the only one of the original cabins that was left intact enough to use after Willie. The others are just shells and we use them for the messy activities like pottery. See?' She pointed at another veranda which was covered with lumpy-looking, as yet unglazed bowls made from coils of clay.

'The cabin you'll be using is brand-new,' she continued. 'But they've been careful to use the same kind of materials.' She smiled at Alex, a concession that their relationship might be on a better footing now, thanks to his communication. 'The mosquito netting will probably work a lot better, as well.'

'I hadn't thought about mosquitoes.' Alex sounded irritated. Did he really expect to keep on top of what was happening so far away in Sydney and still be aware of every potential issue in this environment? 'How much of a problem are they?'

'Generally well controlled,' Susie responded. 'And you'll find eco-friendly insect repellent in the cabin.'

'What about mosquito-borne disease? Like Dengue fever and Ross River virus?'

'There hasn't been a case of anything nasty for years.'

'Complacency is never a good safety net.' Alex increased the length of his stride. 'Another good reason to make sure Stella keeps herself well covered.'

He was forging ahead of her now so he couldn't see the way Susie shook her head. Or hear her resigned sigh.

Much to Alex's relief, Stella was in the cabin Susie led him to.

He could hear the sound of her voice as they stepped up onto the veranda, part of his brain registering the fact that this was going to be a much nicer place to stay than a penthouse hotel suite. The netting overhead and around the sides of the veranda was so fine it was virtually invisible, and the surrounding trees were so close that sitting out here would be like sitting in the middle of the forest.

The larger part of his brain, however, was hearing the sound of his daughter's laughter and feeling the tension of his arrival and everything he'd left behind in Sydney fading.

When had he last heard her laugh like that? *So* long ago, it had probably been before her cancer had been diagnosed, and that was just over two years now. Was this part of what had been happening on this camp? If so, the donation he'd made to kick-start the rebuilding process had just paid for itself tenfold. And the staff needed to know how appreciative he was.

Alex turned his head, intending to catch Susie's gaze

and say something to that effect, but she was moving ahead to enter the main room of the cabin through the open ranch sliders that led to the veranda. She had a huge smile on her face.

'Mike! Em! What are you guys doing here?'

'We were looking for you,' a feminine voice responded.

Alex stepped into a spacious, open-plan living area to see Susie hugging another blonde woman. His gaze flicked past the man beside them, who was grinning cheerfully to where Stella was sitting on a cane couch. *Her* smile was fading rapidly as she watched her father's entrance and she looked disturbingly—and inexplicably—nervous. Then her gaze shifted and Alex understood.

He glared at the boy standing at the other end of Stella's couch. Trying to look nonchalant, with a towel slung casually over one shoulder that did nothing to cover his bare chest or disguise the way his damp board shorts clung to his hips.

'G'day,' the boy said. 'You must be Star's dad.'

'What? *Who?*'

Susie broke away from the hug. 'This is Alex,' she said to the group in general. 'Stella's father. Alex, this is Mike and Emily, whom you've heard about already.'

'Hiya!' Mike extended his hand. 'Pleased to meet you, Alex.'

Emily had a sweet smile and was nodding agreement. Susie was beaming at the boy.

'Hey, Jamie! Did you have a good swim?'

'It was awesome.'

Alex pulled his hand free of Mike's grip and stopped smiling at Emily. He frowned at the boy again. 'What *was* it you called my daughter?'

Jamie went red. He started to say something but his voice cracked and he went crimson. Stella glared at her father but Mike was still grinning.

'Star,' he supplied. 'It's what Stella means in Greek.'

'Yes,' Alex said dryly. 'I was aware of that.'

'I wasn't,' Stella said. 'You never told *me*.'

'Mike's Greek, too,' Susie said hurriedly, clearly trying to avert another father-daughter confrontation. Did she really think that he and Stella did nothing but fight?

'Mike Poulos,' Mike added helpfully. 'My parents run the best Greek restaurant you'll find in North Australia. The Athina. Just over the way in Crocodile Creek.'

'Spitting distance,' Emily said. She exchanged a glance with Mike and they both gave the kind of smile that indicated a private joke.

One that excluded Alex. The ceiling fan didn't seem to be doing much in the way of air-conditioning. He put down his briefcase, dropped his jacket over the back of a cane chair that matched the couch, rolled up his shirt-sleeves and gave up any pretence of feeling social.

He wanted a shower. A chance to change his clothes and spend some time with his daughter. Instead, his accommodation was crowded by strangers who seemed to find Greek superstitions a joke, his daughter was still wearing that scanty clothing, and she was currently being ogled by a prime example of testosterone on legs. It was infuriating.

Worse, having caught Susie's glance, it appeared that she knew exactly how he was feeling and—in her opinion—his discomfort was well deserved.

Then he saw the way she caught her bottom lip between her teeth. It may only have been the second time he'd seen her do that, but he knew a decision of some kind had just been made.

'Hey,' Susie said to her friends. 'You did know you're not staying here anymore, didn't you?'

Emily nodded. 'That's why we came to find you, to make sure you'd had a chance to talk to Charles.'

'Your dad's having the cabin,' Susie explained to Stella. 'We're moving to the hotel. There's two bedrooms here so you can stay, too.' She smiled encouragingly. 'It's really close to the dormitory and I'll bet the bed's a lot more comfortable.'

Stella looked mutinous and Jamie edged towards the door. 'I'd better go,' he said. 'See you at the disco, Stel—' He grinned. 'I mean, Star.'

Alex groaned inwardly. The new nickname made his daughter sound like something from a Hollywood gossip column, but it wasn't worth a battle. Not when Stella was staring at him, clearly expecting one.

'Am I allowed to go to the disco, Dad?'

It was a challenge. It was also an easy way to defuse any tension between them. It wasn't the disco that Alex had a problem with, was it?

'Of course,' he said.

Stella looked surprised. Pleased but wary. 'And I can wear my new clothes?'

'But I'll have to find another top!' Emily groaned in mock despair. 'We can't be there looking like twins.'

'Why not?' Susie was also staring at Alex and her gaze was just as challenging as Stella's had been. 'It's a gorgeous top.'

'I reckon.' Mike nodded. 'What do *you* think, Jamie?'

But Jamie just grinned again and disappeared with a wave.

Alex was now the focus of everybody's attention. They were confidently expecting his agreement—even Susie and Stella, who had to know how it would be contradicting his principles. He sighed.

'Maybe,' he said. 'I'll have to think about it.'

It was too hot to be making decisions that could have unpleasant personal ramifications. He needed a shower. And another beer. And some peace.

'I'll get my stuff,' Susie said into the silence. 'Why don't we head over to the resort and give these guys some time to themselves?'

'Thanks.' Alex tilted his head towards his briefcase. 'I've got a speech to get written before the opening ceremony tomorrow.'

'Maybe you could get it done while Stella's at the disco tonight.'

She wasn't going to miss an opportunity to tell him how to handle his daughter, was she? Did she really expect him to stay in the cabin and let Stella wander around in her underwear? Dancing with *boys?*

Except that she couldn't dance, could she?

Alex moved to go and sit down beside his daughter, the sudden tightness in his throat making it difficult to smile.

He barely noticed the others leaving the cabin.

The camp disco was aimed at the older children and wasn't due to start until 8:00 p.m. when it would be dark enough for the light show to be appreciated on the beach. One of the rangers, Ben, was an amateur disk jockey. He had his own sound and light system and, like many of the staff on the island, was only too happy to use his skills to provide something the kids would enjoy.

There were plenty of adults who were also looking forward to a spot of dancing, including Susie, Emily and Mike, but their bicycle ride back to the north end of Wallaby Island that evening was interrupted by first Mike's and then Susie's mobile phones ringing.

Mike finished his call first and was talking to Emily as Susie flipped her phone shut. Emily was frowning.

'Charles wants you to fly back to Crocodile Creek? At this time of night? Just to pick up Jill?'

'There's no other way she can get here before tomorrow morning. Lily's sick.'

'How sick?' Emily asked with concern.

'I heard Charles say it was just a cold this afternoon,' Susie put in. 'It can't be too serious.'

'Doesn't sound as if Charles thinks it's too serious,' Mike agreed, 'but apparently he couldn't persuade Jill about that. I think *he* thinks Jill's overreacting, but it sounds as though Beth's on his case now—telling him that any kid who's feeling miserable needs her mother.'

'Oh…' Emily nodded. 'He's got a point. And we do owe Charles.'

'Do we?'

'Of course we do.' Emily gave her husband a shove. 'It was thanks to him that we sorted ourselves out, if you remember. Come to think of it, that involved a helicopter ride, as well. To Wallaby Island, no less.' She grinned. 'Just think of yourself as Charles Wetherby's personal pilot. I can dance without you.' The grin got turned in Susie's direction. 'I've got my best friend to dance with.'

'I'm afraid not,' Susie said apologetically. 'Not for a while, anyway. My call was from Miranda Carlisle. You met her the other night, didn't you? She's a respiratory physician and the coordinator of the camp kids. She's worried about one of the boys with cystic fibrosis who's picked up this bug that's going around. I'll have to drop into the medical centre and see if he needs help with some extra physio to clear his chest. I'll try and get there before the dancing finishes.'

'Me, too,' Mike promised.

Emily shrugged philosophically. 'No problem. You guys go and do what you need to do.'

Surprisingly, for this time on a Friday evening, the new medical facilities on Wallaby Island were humming.

There seemed to be people everywhere and the distinctive shape of Charles's wheelchair was at the centre of a knot blocking a wide hallway Susie needed to use to reach the inpatient rooms.

Even though it was obvious they were trying to have a private discussion, the high-pitched voice of Lauren Allandale's mother, Kirsty, was also familiar. Lauren was another of the camp children who suffered from cystic fibrosis. The pretty, fragile-looking teenager had been in here only yesterday, having a nasty gash on her chin sutured, but that didn't seem to be what was upsetting Kirsty at the moment.

'We've got to evacuate her, Dr Wetherby,' she was saying urgently, still trying to keep her voice down. 'For God's sake, she's on the waiting list for a lung transplant. Any kind of chest infection could be…could be…' The woman turned, allowing her husband to wrap his arms around her, burying her face in his shoulder to cry silently.

Rick Allandale may not be as overprotective as Lauren's mother but his determination to look after his family was obvious in the stare he was directing at Charles.

'She's not showing any signs of infection,' Charles said.

Kirsty's face appeared again. 'She almost collapsed! Her hands went all numb!'

'Hyperventilation.' The calm voice came from Miranda, the respiratory physician standing beside Charles. 'She's feeling absolutely fine again now. I suspect it was simply due to the excitement of getting ready for the disco.'

'She can't possibly go to that disco,' Kirsty declared. 'All those children together when there's a flu bug going around.'

Judging by the way a nearby door swung open at that point, the subject of the conversation had been eavesdropping. Susie could only hope she hadn't heard the entire exchange but Lauren certainly looked less than happy.

'I'm going to the disco,' she announced. 'You can't stop me.'

Lauren was the same age as Stella but so far the only thing the two girls had in common was a crush on Jamie. Rebellion against parental edicts could now be added, Susie thought with a wry smile. Maybe the girls would end up being friends after all.

'Susie!' Miranda had spotted her arrival. 'You helped Lauren with her airway clearance this morning. What did you think of her condition?'

'No change from yesterday,' Susie responded. She smiled at Lauren. 'I think her technique's improved this week, as well. She's been trying hard.'

'Dr Wetherby?' A large woman, wearing an impressive selection of gold jewellery, came from behind

Susie. 'Please, could you come and see Eddie again? He's been sick and he says the pain in his chest is getting worse.'

The wheelchair swivelled. 'Is Dr Stuart with him?'

'She did tests. The electric whatever it was.'

'Electrocardiogram?'

'Yes. And she took a lot of blood. I think she's gone somewhere with all the test tubes.'

Charles was moving towards Susie. He paused for just a moment as he left the Allandales. 'It's your call,' he told Miranda. 'We've certainly got the space to keep Lauren in the centre overnight and I'm sure a flight out could be arranged tomorrow if necessary.'

'No!' Lauren's face crumpled. 'You can't make me go home. I want to stay here.'

'It's too dangerous, darling,' her mother pleaded. 'There's all these bugs!'

'I don't care! I've never been to a disco. Please, Mummy! What if…?' Lauren's eyes widened theatrically. 'What if it's the only chance I ever get?'

'Oh, darling… Don't say *that!*' Kirsty's arms went round her daughter.

Miranda closed her eyes for a second.

'Where's Jack?' Susie asked her. 'If I get his therapy done, I can go to the disco myself and keep an eye on Lauren.'

'Room 4,' Miranda responded quietly. 'I'll join you as soon as we're sorted here.' She raised her voice slightly. 'I've got Jack started on a hefty antibiotic regime but his chest isn't sounding great.'

Rick was frowning. 'You know, they say the worst place to pick up bugs is in a hospital. Fresh air on the beach might not be such a bad idea.'

'Is it?' Kirsty looked fearfully over her shoulder, as though someone was about to pop out of a room and infect them all.

'I'd better go and see Jack,' Susie told them. 'He really *is* sick.'

That seemed to settle it for the Allandales. 'Let's go,' Kirsty suggested hurriedly. 'We'll talk about the disco when we're outside.'

Jack Havens was twelve and quite independent. He had happily come to camp without any family support and usually managed his own airway clearance techniques by himself, but right now he was feeling rotten.

'My head hurts,' he told Susie. 'And I feel all hot and everything aches.'

'Sounds like flu, you poor old thing,' Susie commiserated. 'Is it feeling harder to breathe?'

Jack nodded miserably. 'Dr Miranda said I had to stay here tonight. For medicine and oxygen and stuff.'

'We'll look after you,' Susie promised. 'I'm here to see if I can help you clear your chest a bit. If we get rid of some of the junk in your lungs, it means there's less places for the bugs to hide and grow. Do you feel up to bit of percussion? I'll be gentle and it might make you feel a bit better.'

'OK…'

'Good boy. I'll just go and collect some nice big pillows.'

This time the corridor showed a change in activity. The Allandales had disappeared but Beth Stuart was there, showing Charles a sheet of pink paper.

'No sign of an infarct,' she was saying. 'I suspect the chest pain is due to his viral infection.'

'Sounds as if there are a few people at the resort down with it.' Charles sounded tired. 'Couldn't be happening at a worse time, could it, with the camp going on?'

'We'll cope.' Beth smiled at Susie. 'How's Jack?'

'Not feeling the best. I'm going to see how clear I can get his chest. I'll try and make it a quick session.'

But it took a lot longer than usual. The boy was tired and each change of position that assisted the drainage of different lobes of the lungs was slow. Susie kept her percussion as gentle as she could, tapping her cupped hands carefully on the small chest and back. Coughing was also painfully slow and not particularly effective.

'Try huffing,' Susie told him more than once. 'Like making a mirror steam up, remember? Sometimes it works better than coughing.'

Miranda came back and the session was interrupted for an examination and medication. Nebulised antibiotics were administered at the end and Susie stayed to help the nurse settle Jack into a comfortable position for sleeping.

By the time Susie had put away the equipment she'd used, it was half past nine. She left the medical centre and hurried into the warm darkness outside. She was far later than she'd intended being, but a dance or two was just what she felt like and Ben wasn't due to stop the music until 10:00 p.m. She could hear it now, the upbeat strains of something that could lift her spirits even from this distance.

Except that another sound could also be heard. Susie answered her mobile reluctantly.

'Sorry to disturb you…' The voice on the other end of the line must have picked up on her reluctance.

'Charles gave me your number. It's Alex Vavunis speaking.'

Susie had known that from the first word he'd uttered. Like everything else about Stella's father, his voice was a new experience. Authoritative. Dark. A distinct hint of a foreign accent. She had to pull in a new breath.

'No problem. What can I do for you, Alex?'

'It's Stella.'

'What's happened?'

'I…I don't know.' He cleared his throat. 'She… ah…won't talk to me.'

Susie looked down the beach to where she could see bright lights changing colour at regular intervals. 'Isn't Stella at the disco?'

'No. She's…ah…locked herself in the bathroom.'

They must have had another argument. Probably about what Stella wanted to wear to the disco. But that should have been sorted a couple of hours ago. Just how long had Stella been locked in the bathroom? And why was Alex calling *her?*

'Susie?' The voice was softer now. It had what she could only interpret as a faintly bewildered air. 'I think I might need your help.'

CHAPTER THREE

THE distance between the beach and the cabin took very little time to cover at the speed Susie moved, but it was quite long enough to think the worst.

Why was Stella locked in the bathroom? Was she injured? Unconscious, even? Had her father been so preoccupied with writing an impressive speech that he hadn't realised how long she'd been absent?

Or had he climbed back on that paternal soapbox and told his daughter what kind of morals her chosen outfit was advertising? If he had, he was going to get an earful of how clueless Susie considered him to be.

He would also get an eyeful of her own choice of attire. She had picked the soft, clinging, low-cut top deliberately and teamed it with hip-hugging, pale denim jeans that he would probably disapprove of more than a skirt. Not that she had expected to come across Alex at the disco. This had been more of a statement of support for Stella.

It was tempting to put her hands on the band of those jeans that marked her hips and tap her foot impatiently as she waited for Alex to open the ranch slider for her. He looked so calm, dammit! Crossing the room with the same kind of casual grace she had noted when he'd walked down the jetty that afternoon. As though he was in complete control of any space he entered.

His smile and greeting were as courteous as if nothing untoward was happening.

'Thank you for coming,' he said.

Accusations of provocation or neglect tumbled around Susie's brain, vying for utterance, but as she stepped inside and looked up, the words died on her lips.

That aura of control was an illusion. He may still be wearing his white shirt but the careful rolling-up of the sleeves was coming unravelled and the cuffs were hanging loose. Another couple of buttons at the neck were undone and his feet were bare. Eyes that she remembered as being dark were positively black right now. Bottomless pits she could fall into if she wasn't careful. Muscles in his jaw were bunched tightly enough to make day-old stubble very obvious, and how many times had Alex pushed stiff fingers through his hair to make it stand up in spikes like that?

She was looking at a parent who was worried sick. At the end of his tether.

Helpless, even.

It was the last impression she had expected and Susie could actually feel her early judgement of this surgeon split wide-open. She could move through the channel created and establish a connection if she wanted, and she had to make a conscious effort not to reach out and touch him.

Alex would hate that. This was not someone who was used to asking for assistance and instinctively Susie knew that stepping even a fraction over a professional line would be deemed patronising. Making that telephone call to ask for help had probably made him feel disturbingly vulnerable. It had also given Susie the power to either antagonise him irreparably or get a lot closer.

A choice that was made instantly. With her heart, not her head.

'What's happened?' she asked gently. 'How can I help?'

'She went into the bathroom, oh…' Alex flicked his wrist to glance at his watch. 'Two hours ago. I thought she was doing something with all that make-up you saw fit to provide.'

Susie opened her mouth but then snapped it shut and merely raised her eyebrows encouragingly.

'When she didn't come out after half an hour, I knocked on the door and asked if she was all right.'

'And?' Susie didn't like the cold trickle that ran down her spine. '*Is* she?'

'She told me to…' Alex's face twisted into an expression of extreme distaste and then he demonstrated exactly how he'd managed to spike his hair so effectively. 'Let's just say she let me know my presence in the near vicinity was less than desirable.'

Susie dragged her gaze away from the way some of the soft black spikes were settling. But she couldn't help the way the corner of her mouth twitched. She could be quite confident that Alex wouldn't be used to being sworn at. Then the embryonic smile faded. Had he got angry and shouted back? Hammered on the door and terrified Stella? Anyone that could exude the kind of power Alex did *would* be terrifying when really angry. It took rather a lot of courage to even ask her next question.

'Is the door locked?'

'You think I didn't try it?' The tone was scathing. Susie's heart tripped but then her hackles rose. There was no reason for this man to have any power over her and any emotional involvement she was feeling came from the notion that he needed her. Maybe he wasn't so helpless after all.

Then Alex shook his head wearily and his expression squashed any doubts. 'Sorry, but I've tried everything. The window's closed and too opaque to see through. The door bolts from the inside so it's no use sending for a skeleton key. Short of breaking the damn thing down—and, yes, I did consider that—the only thing I've been able to do is try talking to her.'

'And she's not answering?'

'No.'

'You don't think she's hurt herself, do you?'

'No. She's been crying but it doesn't sound as if she's in physical pain.'

'Have you got any idea what's upset her so much?'

Alex sighed heavily, spreading his hands in an eloquent gesture of frustration. 'I have absolutely no idea. I'd told her she could wear what she wanted to the disco.' His gaze travelled over Susie, as though only just registering what *she* was wearing. She saw him swallow with what appeared to be something of an effort. 'I said I hoped she was going to have a great time. And that… that if that boy didn't think she was stunning, he had rocks in his head.'

Susie grinned. 'You *said* that? Really?'

'Really.' Alex returned the smile and the heavy lines of his face softened. 'She…I…I feel as if I've stepped onto a new planet here, Susie. I sent a little girl away to camp and I came here to find a young woman. One that seems to think I've suddenly become the enemy.'

Susie was still smiling. 'I do understand, Alex. Don't worry. You're feeling like every parent of every teenager has felt at some point.' She turned towards the closed door on the far side of the living area. 'Right. I was a teenager myself once. I'll see what I can do.'

'She was so happy when she went in there.' Alex stayed where he was, still close to the ranch slider, watching Susie. 'I simply don't understand this.'

Susie tapped on the door. 'Stella?'

No response.

'It's Susie,' she continued. 'Are you OK, hon?'

Stupid question. No wonder it provoked a muffled sob.

'I can help,' Susie offered, hoping fervently that the statement was accurate. 'Whatever it is that's bothering you.'

Silence again but Susie had the feeling that Stella might be listening.

'It's just me,' she added. Turning, she flapped her hand at Alex and he hesitated for only a moment before giving a curt nod and stepping out onto the veranda, sliding the door shut behind him. 'I'm not going anywhere, Stella. You can talk through the door if you want, but it might be better if you let me come in.'

Susie had to bite her lip to allow the next silence to continue long enough for Stella to think it through. Finally, when it seemed she might have failed already, she heard shuffling sounds and then an odd thumping on the door.

'What's happening? You haven't hurt yourself, have you?'

'I'm using my crutch.' Stella's voice was thick. She

had been crying long enough to make it sound like she had a heavy head cold. 'To open the lock.'

Another thump then a bang and then Susie heard the metallic clink of the bolt moving. She tried the handle of the door and it opened.

'Lock it again,' Stella ordered.

'OK.' Susie obliged after a quick glance at the girl sitting on the floor in the space between the toilet and the bidet in the well-appointed bathroom. She looked exhausted and upset but not injured.

Having locked the door, Susie closed the lid of the toilet and sat down, leaning forward to try and make eye contact with Stella.

'What happened, sweetheart?' she asked carefully. 'Why didn't you go to the disco?'

Stella burst into tears again and Susie reached out automatically. And then Stella's head was in her lap and all she could do was stroke the sparse dark hair under her hand as the teenager sobbed uncontrollably.

'It's awful,' she choked out finally. 'My new skirt is *ruined*...'

'What's wrong with it?'

'It's...it's...' Stella's voice dropped to an almost inaudible groan. 'The *blood!*'

Susie's heart skipped a beat. Stella *had* hurt herself. Then something clicked into place. No wonder Alex hadn't been welcome.

'Is it your period, hon?'

Susie's jeans were wet from tears and now Stella's nose was being rubbed on her leg as she nodded miserably.

'Your first one?'

'They said...it might not happen for ages because of

the chemo. I didn't think it would happen on camp. And not *tonight!*'

'No.' Susie went back to stroking. 'It sucks, doesn't it? I'm so sorry you missed the disco.'

'I bet *Lauren* was there.'

Susie smoothed back fine wisps of hair from Stella's face. 'It's *you* that Jamie likes,' she said.

'How do you know that?'

'He came here, didn't he? To check that you were going to the disco?'

Stella had stopped crying. She raised her head enough to give Susie a suspicious glance.

'I'll tell you a secret,' Susie continued. 'Boys only use a nickname for girls they *really* like…Star.'

'He won't like me now.'

'He'll be disappointed that you didn't make it tonight but he'll get over it.' Susie smiled. 'Playing hard to get isn't always a bad move, and at least he got to see you wearing your new clothes.'

Stella pushed herself upright. 'You reckon he'll still talk to me?'

'Go to the beach in the morning. Smile and see what happens.'

'But I can't!'

'Why not?'

'Because…of…*you* know.'

Susie shook her head. 'Periods are a nuisance but they don't need to stop you doing anything you want to do. Let's get you sorted.' She eyed the vanity unit. 'These bathrooms come stocked with just about everything. I wouldn't recommend trying tampons this time round but there'll be something else. And why don't I go and find your pyjamas? You can give me your skirt and knickers and I'll get them washed and back to you tomorrow as good as new, I promise.'

'Thank you so much.'

Susie accepted the glass of red wine and sank back onto the comfortable veranda chair. 'My pleasure. I'm just happy I was *able* to help.'

'Which is probably directly attributable to the amount of time you've spent with my daughter in the last week.' Alex was pouring himself a glass of wine. 'You've obviously built up quite a rapport.'

'She's a great kid. You must be very proud of her.'

'Of course.' Alex put the wine bottle down. 'You sure she's all right now?'

'She's sound asleep. I'll check in on her in the morning but we've had a good talk about everything.' Susie's smile escaped as she tried to make it sound as though she had tackled the situation in a professional manner. 'She has an action plan.'

Alex folded long limbs to sit down on the adjacent chair. 'It didn't even *occur* to me that it could be something like her period.'

'Why should it? You're a bloke.'

'That's no excuse. I'm a single parent. I'm supposed to think of everything.'

'You get more than your fair share of things that need thinking about. Don't beat yourself up, Alex.' It was getting easier to use his name. Nothing like a bit of a crisis to get to know someone. 'Even if you *had* thought of it, Stella would probably have been excruciatingly embarrassed. Maybe even more than she already was.'

'Is it always like this? The first time, I mean?'

'Depends.' Susie took a thoughtful sip of her wine. 'Mine wasn't great. It was one of the only things I beat my twin sister Hannah at, but we were on a school camp at the time. I was only twelve and didn't have anything with me and it was a girls' school. There was this weird philosophy that only losers went to ask the teachers for help.'

'What did you do?'

'Coped. With wads of very scratchy toilet paper.' Susie hurriedly took a larger swallow of her wine to try and wash away an inward cringe. Why on earth was she sharing a piece of history that personal with Alex?

'Not something teenage boys have to deal with, thank goodness.' Alex was sounding far more relaxed. He still hadn't combed his hair or changed his shirt or shaved but, instead of looking like a distraught parent, he now looked rather deliciously dishevelled. 'I guess the closest I got would have been my first—'

He stopped abruptly, his gaze flicking up to meet Susie's and his eyes widening enough to let her know he had spoken without thinking and was disconcerted, to say the least, at what he'd been about to confess.

She knew what it was. The jolt into puberty that a boy's first wet dream represented.

The unspoken words hung between them, creating the most astonishing sexual awareness Susie had ever encountered.

Oh, help! The heavy tropical darkness surrounding them was suddenly devoid of oxygen. Closing in on them like a blanket.

Wrapping them up.

Both of them.

The loud night song of the frogs, the rustle of small creatures and the flap of wings from owls and bats vanished. Susie could hear a faint humming sound.

The sexual energy crackling around her?

More like the pulsing of her own blood, which had quickened rather noticeably. That would also explain the flush she could feel colouring her cheeks. Thankfully, it was too dark for Alex to have noticed.

She drained her wineglass. 'I'd better go.'

Good grief! She had to clear her throat to get rid of an embarrassingly obvious huskiness. She scrambled to her feet. 'It's a big day tomorrow, with the opening and everything. Did you get your speech written?'

'No.' Alex followed her example and stood up. 'I'd better get on with it now.' He also cleared his throat. 'Sorry,' he murmured. 'I didn't mean to…'

What? Embarrass her by talking about things normally kept private?

Or make her achingly aware of just how attractive she found him?

Susie shook the thought away with a flick of her head. 'It's fine,' she interrupted dismissively. 'Not a problem.' She stepped back as Alex took a step towards her. An unconscious reaction, as though her body knew there was some kind of magnetic pull going on and the only sensible thing to do was to stay out of the danger zone.

'Good luck with the speech.' Susie headed for the steps. 'I'll see you tomorrow.'

The sighting didn't come as soon as she might have expected.

Or hoped for?

Susie had to give herself a good mental shake due to the level of disappointment she experienced on finding the Vavunis cabin deserted at 8:00 a.m. the next morning.

Even being careful not to make any new assumptions about Alex, it seemed unlikely that he would have chosen to share the noisy, crowded camp dining room in order to have breakfast with Stella. More likely, they had taken a cart back to the hotel to sample the astounding array of food available in the main restaurant or something simpler in one of the cafés that had provided the superb cup of coffee Susie had indulged in.

They could easily have gone past her unnoticed. Susie had left her bicycle in the rack outside the medical centre, choosing to walk along the beach, carrying her sandals so that she could enjoy the wash of the gentle waves. She'd been careful not to wade out too far and dampen the only really decent pair of shorts she owned.

The denim cut-offs of yesterday had been discarded in favour of these sand-coloured cargo shorts that came almost to her knees. No skimpy singlet top, either. In order to look as professional as possible, Susie had donned her brand-new 'official' Crocodile Creek Camp T-shirt. It was white and featured a picture of the latest camp mascot—a brown toy dog that had arrived with Beth a few weeks ago. It had spaniel's ears, a top hat, black boots and a white-topped cane. With the flick of a switch, he could tap dance to the tune of 'Putting On The Ritz' and he never failed to make children laugh. The real camp dog, Garf, was in danger of being toppled from his position of leading the popularity stakes.

Susie had hoped it would make Alex smile. It certainly made a lot of the children smile when she went into the dining hall.

'We want Ritzy,' a small girl told her. 'Can he dance on our table today?'

'That depends,' said the aide in charge. 'He will if our group is the first to finish breakfast and we all remember to put our dishes onto the trolley.'

Susie was scanning the room. There were lots of adults—parents who were here with their children, camp leaders, instructors for special activities and medical personnel like the nurse Benita Green, who was here with the group of children suffering from cancer.

There was no sign of Alex but Stella was at a nearby table. Sitting beside Jamie, no less.

'Hi, Stella!' Susie was deliberately casual. 'What have you done with your dad?'

'He's gone to meet some guy from the medical centre. That one in the wheelchair.'

'Dr Wetherby.'

'Yeah. They're having breakfast and a meeting. I'm supposed to go and have lunch with him at the hotel.'

'That's cool. We'll have finished our session well before that.'

Stella shook her head. 'I don't want to go to lunch. I'm going to the beach.'

'I'm helping with surfing lessons for some of the older kids,' Jamie said. 'Not that there's anything like a real wave up here, but they can practise trying to stand on the boards and maybe catch a tiny wave. Hey, Star, you could have a go. Body-surfing, anyway.' He spoke as though missing part of a limb was simply an inconvenience rather than an obstacle. Susie beamed at him.

'I might just watch,' Stella muttered. 'Dr Miranda asked if I could help judge the sandcastle competition the little kids are having later.'

'Let's get your session done now,' Susie suggested. 'I need to get back to the medical centre myself soon and see how the sick kids are getting on.'

Stella was using her crutches as they left the dining hall but Susie was pleased to see she wasn't putting much weight on them. An insurance policy, perhaps?

'I like the way you're walking,' she said. 'And that you came to breakfast and sat with Jamie. You really are a bit of a star, aren't you?' Susie smiled at the girl hopping beside her. 'I think I might start calling you that myself.'

'Jamie came to sit with *me,*' Stella confided. 'He said he was worried I was getting flu or something, like the other kids, and that was why I hadn't shown up last night.'

'What did you tell him?'

'That I just had a guts ache.' Stella sounded defensive.

'True enough. Did…um…your dad say anything this morning?'

'No. He was really good.' Stella sounded surprised now. 'I thought he'd be mad at me for swearing at him. Did you tell him not to be?'

'No. He probably understands more than you think. Or maybe he's just a nice guy.'

Stella snorted. 'He's just Dad. Hey, what's the hotel like?'

'Gorgeous. The bed's so big I could sleep sideways.'

Not that Susie had slept much at all. Far too much of that odd energy had stayed with her and made for a wakeful night haunted by images of Alex. Of his black eyes and tousled hair. The sound of his voice and—most of all—that appealing vulnerability she'd seen for the first time.

A glimpse of a real man under the image and reputation. A man that clearly blew every other male on the planet out of the water as far as being attractive went.

'There was champagne in an ice bucket and a big bowl of tropical fruit,' Susie continued. 'Chocolates on my pillow and brochures about all the cool stuff you can do at the resort.'

'Like what?'

'Ooh, luxury stuff. Like day spas and personal trainers in the gym. Scenic flights in a seaplane or helicopter. Paragliding, scubadiving, private picnics on a deserted island. You name it, they'll make it happen. Oh, and a really good laundry service, too. Your skirt's in a bag on the veranda chair at your cabin.'

'Thanks.'

'No sweat.' They had reached the part of the administration building Susie used for her physiotherapy sessions. The equipment was minimal but adequate and included a set of parallel bars for standing and walking practice. 'How about leaving those crutches by the door, Stell—I mean, Star. If you can do as well as yesterday, we might head out and try the track. Maybe even some steps or sand.'

'You've done the right thing, admitting her.'

'Not… We're not overreacting?' asked Jill Shaw. She was the woman responsible for the little girl on whom Alex was just completing the neurological examination Beth had asked him to do. Charles's partner. Apparently Lily was their ward. Jill had a sticking plaster on a reddened cheek, which looked odd, but this was no time to ask her what had happened.

'Not.' Alex put down the reflex hammer but kept

Lily's leg bent at the hip, supported by his arm. 'Can you straighten your leg for me, Lily?'

She could and that was good. A negative Kernig's sign. Alex put the leg down and pulled the cover back over the sick little girl, whose eyes were closing again.

'She started showing these symptoms yesterday, is that right?'

'Yes.' The word was almost a growl from Charles, whose wheelchair was positioned right beside the bed that was in what passed for the medical centre's emergency room. 'But it looked like any run-of-the-mill viral illness. She had a bit of a temperature. She was a bit sniffly. That's all.' He sounded defensive.

Jill said nothing. She was standing at the head of the bed, holding Lily's hand. Alex caught the look she directed at Charles. Tentative. There was an undercurrent of tension between these two. Understandable, of course. They were worried about Lily and Alex was only too aware that he might not be able to allay those fears. Not yet, anyway.

'Beth says she was having nightmares.'

'More like hallucinations,' Jill whispered.

'It *was* a nightmare,' Charles interrupted Jill. 'I told you she was upset by that dead bird she found the other day.'

'But she saw it flying around the room.'

'She's running a temperature. She's in a strange place.'

Lily had opened her eyes again. She looked from Jill to Charles and back again. Her bottom lip wobbled. 'I want to go home,' she said plaintively.

Alex leaned closer and smiled at the frightened child. 'We've got you here so we can all take extra-special care of you,' he said. 'Do you remember my name, Lily?'

She shook her head. The over-brightness of her eyes and the two red spots on her cheeks were indicating the high temperature she was now running. It was the listlessness and drowsiness that was more of a concern right now, however. Alex had the impression her level of consciousness was down a point or two.

'How's your neck, poppet?' He slipped his hands behind Lily's head. 'In here.'

'It hurts.'

'It's just her glands,' Charles said sharply.

Alex caught his gaze. They both knew better than that. 'Let's not take that as read,' he said mildly as he straightened. 'Let's step outside so we can let Lily go back to sleep,' he suggested. 'Marcia, can you stay with Lily, please? She could have that dose of paracetamol now.'

The nurse, Marcia, nodded, moving closer to the bed as everyone else filed out.

'Beth's right,' Alex said, as soon as the door closed behind them. 'On the positive side, we've got no rash and a negative Kernig's sign, but we can't rule out meningitis without a lumbar puncture.'

There was a moment's silence as the implications sank in. Meningitis was a scary word, even to the kind of highly trained medical professionals these people all were.

Charles broke the silence. 'I'll do it.'

'No.' Beth spoke firmly. 'You can't. You know you can't. You have one of the country's top paediatric neurosurgeons right here. How many lumbar punctures have you done on children, Alex?'

'I can't say. A lot.'

'I'd be guessing it's a lot more than Charles or I have done,' Beth said. 'I'm sorry, but it's a no-brainer. You're her daddy, Charles. You get to hold her hand.'

'I'm staying with her,' Jill said quickly.

For just a moment Alex's attention was being diverted. Further along the corridor they were in, Susie was entering the medical centre. She looked almost prim this morning, with her hair tied back in a ponytail. And she was wearing long shorts and a demure T-shirt with a silly picture on it.

No hint of those endless tanned legs, blonde curls brushing bare shoulders or the lace-covered cleavage that had taunted him as he'd tried, unsuccessfully, to sleep last night. Curiously, the way she was covered up this morning only seemed to spark an even more noticeable ripple of attraction.

Especially when she smiled.

Alex caught himself staring at Susie's mouth. Fortunately, *her* attention was on Beth.

'Sorry to interrupt,' she said, 'but have you seen Miranda?'

'She's in with Jack,' Beth told her.

Susie was looking at Charles now. And then at Jill. 'Is everything all right? What's happened to your cheek?'

'It's nothing. But, no, everything's not all right.' For a second it looked as though Jill might lose the extraordinary control she seemed to have. 'Lily's sick. She's about to have a lumbar puncture.'

'We could use your help, if you're free,' Alex said to Susie. 'We might need extra staff to help position her.'

'Oh…' Compassion made her eyes an even darker

blue, but Alex couldn't afford any further distraction. 'Not our Lily.' She hugged Jill.

'Let's get on with it,' Alex said brusquely. He didn't want to stand there watching Susie hug people. No wonder Jill was looking ill with worry. Reminding her that Lily would have to be restrained to make the procedure safe hadn't exactly helped, had it? He gave her a sympathetic smile.

'Don't worry,' he said. 'Let's assume this is a needless test, taken to be on the safe side. I'll use plenty of local and make it virtually painless. With so many people around who know and love her, she'll be just fine.'

A few minutes later Alex was gowned and gloved. So was everybody else in the now crowded room. Lily stared at them all, wide-eyed and frightened. The tension was palpable and the sooner they got this over with, the better.

'What gauge needle have you got there, Beth?'

'A twenty.'

'Does the stylet fit the barrel?'

'All checked. We're good,' Beth assured him.

'Right. Lily, let's get you lying on your side, sweetheart. We're going to do a test on your back that'll help us find out what's the matter with you. It'll tell us which medicine is right for you. OK?'

'OK…'

'Jill, you stay close to her head and hold her hand. Charles, can you keep a hand on Lily's hip and the legs? Marcia? Legs for you, too, and Susie, I'll get you beside me with extra support for Lily's chest and arms.' He gave them all a significant nod. They would be responsible for holding the child absolutely still.

Beth swabbed the area of Lily's lower back with disinfectant and Alex pressed along the spine, counting carefully. He knew Susie was watching him.

'I'm looking for the space between the third and fourth lumbar vertebrae,' he told her. 'Have you seen a lumbar puncture before?'

Susie shook her head.

'It's not too major.' Alex spoke very quietly, and Lily was turned the other way, listening to something Jill was saying. 'The local's the worst bit.' He raised his voice. 'Small scratch,' he warned Lily.

He felt the girl stiffen as he injected the local anaesthetic and he heard her whimper. He could also feel the change in the firmness of the hold of his assistants. Jill was still talking to Lily but he couldn't hear what she was saying.

Alex picked up the needle and stylet. Angling the needle in the direction of the umbilicus, he advanced it slowly, withdrawing the stylet often to check for the drip of any cerebrospinal fluid. He knew precisely when he was in the right place, however, with that familiar decrease in the resistance to the needle. Clear fluid dripped easily and Beth had the required three serial tubes ready. Then the stylet was replaced, the whole system withdrawn and a sterile swab pressed to the puncture site.

'All over,' Alex said. 'You were a very brave girl, Lily. Well done.'

'Well done, you,' Susie murmured. 'I barely heard a squeak.' She helped Jill roll Lily over again. 'You're a wee champion, Lily, aren't you?'

'What about blood tests?' Charles asked.

Alex stopped watching Susie smiling. 'Let's get an IV line in and collect the bloods at the same time.'

'Antibiotic of choice?'

'Benzylpenicillin. IV. She's going to need half-hourly neurological checks. Response to light and verbal commands, hand grip on both sides—you know the drill. Fluid restriction for the moment, as well, until we get a better idea of what we're dealing with.'

'We'll get the samples away on the next ferry or flight,' Beth confirmed.

'Mike can take them now.' The command was issued with a vehemence that made everybody look at Charles, and his grin was a little embarrassed. 'I know. But this is my kid. I help fund the service—it cares for my kid.'

Beth was smiling. 'That's great. It'll mean we should get the first results back later today.'

Susie was still helping Jill settle Lily so Alex got her to keep the girl's arm still while he slipped a small IV cannula into place. Again, Beth had the tubes ready. Lily barely noticed the procedure and seemed to be listening to what Beth was saying to Jill.

'It's so good you got over to be with Lily. Poor little Robbie Henderson's come in with a bug and his mother's a single mum and there's no way she can leave four other children to be here.'

'What's wrong with Robbie?' Lily asked. 'Is he sick like me?'

'Kind of. Susie, do you know Robbie? Is he one of your patients?'

'Robbie? Ten-year-old with dark hair? Cerebral palsy?'

'That's him.'

Alex had the line secure and the giving set attached. The necessary blood samples had been drawn and the antibiotics started. There was no reason for him to stay and listen to this conversation but he didn't want to leave quite yet. Was that because of the sound of Susie's voice? The way her ponytail swung when she shook her head?

'I do know him,' Susie said. 'There were no requests for any special programme for him. He did join in with my swimming pool group once but camp activities have been enough to keep his joints mobile. Has he got flu?'

'He started vomiting in the night. He's running a temperature and complaining of a headache and sore eyes.'

'I've got sore eyes,' Lily said. 'But I haven't vomited.'

Charles was moving away from the bedside. 'You probably won't,' he reassured her. 'I'll see you later, Lily. I've got to go and get things ready for our big opening this afternoon. Jill's going to stay with you, aren't you, Jill?'

'Of course.'

Alex had been listening to the exchange about the new inpatient. 'Maybe it's the same thing. You want me to take a look?'

'If it gets any worse, yes, please,' Beth responded.

'If you have an influenza virus doing the rounds, it's not that uncommon to get meningoencephalitis. It should be self-limiting and only require supportive measures.'

'But I want to know straight away if we have any more cases,' Charles instructed. 'There's been a couple of staff off colour over the last two days. If there's a flu bug…'

'The last thing we want is for it to spread to our sick kids,' Beth added.

Alex nodded at the array of samples Marcia had finished packaging. 'We've done everything we can to find out what this is. It's a matter of waiting and watching for a while.'

But Charles didn't seem to be listening any longer. He rolled over to the bed, gave Lily a kiss and whispered something to her.

Susie followed Charles, Alex and Beth out of the room a minute later.

'Perhaps I should see Robbie now,' Alex said. 'While I'm here.'

'Busman's holiday,' Susie commented, but Alex could see approval in her eyes.

He liked that. Almost worth giving up a morning on a glorious tropical beach for.

'Leave it with me at the moment,' Beth decided. 'Hopefully I won't need to call you but at least we'll give you a party tonight to make up for it if I do.'

Alex was careful not to look directly at Susie. To make his query general. 'Is everybody going to the gala dinner?'

'Of course,' Susie said. 'We never miss a good party in this neck of the woods, do we, Charles?'

'No.' But Charles sounded as though enjoying himself was the last thing he was thinking about, which was hardly surprising given Lily's illness. 'And that reminds me, I've got a meeting with the restaurant staff to talk about seating arrangements. You want to have a look around the resort, Alex?'

Alex shook his head. 'I'll see it at lunchtime. I might go and see what Stella's up to as soon as I've got a free moment.'

'I think she'll be on the beach,' Susie told him. 'She's been roped in to help judge a sandcastle competition later.'

'Oh!' Beth checked her watch. 'Are you going in to see Jack, Susie?'

'On my way. He needs a good physio session to get his lungs clear.'

'Remind Miranda of the time. She wants to go and admire Josh's sandcastle.'

Alex paused for a moment as he left the medical centre, pulling his sunglasses off his head to cover his eyes and enjoying the touch of sunshine on his bare legs and arms. Funny that it didn't seem remotely unprofessional to be dressed in casual summer clothing here, even when seeing a patient.

The warmth was as sensuous as the heady smell of some tropical flowers growing nearby and Alex found himself stretching, letting his muscles go as he took a deep, appreciative sniff before setting off on what felt like a lazy ramble.

The spell of island magic had caught him. This was a place where senses were heightened and the ones he normally relied on, like sight and sound, were strangely less important than taste or smell or touch. A seductive environment that stirred all sorts of desires to explore those senses further.

Alex let his breath out in a contented sigh as he entered the shade of the forest walk. He had a few minutes to himself, which was a rare pleasure. He had most of the rest of the day to spend focused on the most important person in his life—his daughter. For the duration of this walk, however, there was no harm in letting his thoughts drift back to where they were being irresistibly drawn, was there?

No.

It couldn't hurt to think about Susie.

As he had been, rather a lot, since last night.

She couldn't have known how desperate he'd been. Desperate enough to ask for help for the first time in his adult life.

He'd never done it before. He hadn't done it when his world had turned upside down with his young wife dying so suddenly and tragically, leaving him with an infant daughter. Help had been offered, of course. Too much help, but Alex had needed to deal with his grief by taking control. Using instinct and sheer willpower to learn to care for a baby and to try and put his life back together.

He hadn't asked for help even when a second, potentially lethal blow had been delivered by fate and his beloved daughter had been diagnosed with cancer. It had been easy to take control then. To use his knowledge and contacts to put together the best possible medical management.

But last night he'd lost it. There had been no way to win by force or willpower, and instinct had completely deserted him. He'd had to ask for help from someone he wasn't sure he could trust. He'd handed an alarming amount of power to a woman who could have used it to pay him back for his rudeness on their introduction. Or to strike a cruel blow to his confidence as a parent. But she hadn't used that power for anything other than the benefit of Stella.

In fact, Alex was quite sure Susie would be incapable of cruelty. He had seen her concern. Her understanding. Her willingness to help.

Somehow, magically, as they'd shared that glass of wine, she'd slipped through a barrier he'd considered impenetrable. Mistrust had evaporated and it was possible to see her as a genuine person with no personal agenda. A very beautiful person.

Yes. Susie was part of the magic.

A temptation to his senses. All of them. She was beautiful to look at. The sound of her voice and laughter a pleasure. If he, say, *kissed* her, he would know what she tasted like, wouldn't he? Whether her hair or skin smelt of any tropical scents. At the very least, if there was any dancing involved with this gala dinner tonight, he could take her in his arms and he would know what it felt like to touch her…

Alex changed direction abruptly, taking a fork of the track that had to lead to the beach.

A dip in the ocean was what was needed here.

He could only hope it would be cool enough.

CHAPTER FOUR

'MORE champagne, Susie?'

'Go on, then.' Susie held her glass out. 'It's not as if I have to walk home, is it?'

'You don't even have to ride your bike. We can just pour you into the lift. Star's dad did us a favour, really, didn't he?'

'You and Mike should have had the penthouse suite. It's ridiculous having me rattling around in there by myself.'

'We've got a room that opens into the pool complex. It's perfect. We went swimming in the dark last night. Very romantic. There was no one else around. We could have swum naked if we'd wanted to.'

'And did you?' Susie gave her best friend a suspicious glance and then her jaw dropped. 'You *did!* You're a wicked woman, Emily Poulos.'

'It was Mike's idea.'

Susie felt the need to change the subject from romantic midnight swimming. 'This place is enormous, isn't it? We must have a hundred people at this function and it's completely separate from the rest of the guests.'

'I hear a bit of juggling went on. This room is the hub

of the convention centre and there's a medical conference on this weekend.'

This was a nice, neutral topic. 'Anyone from
Crocodile Creek at the conference?'

Emily shook her head. 'It's very specialised.
Epidemiology.'

Susie smiled. 'Skin…right?'

Emily laughed. 'No. Causes of diseases and stuff.
Hey, you made a joke!'

'What's so unusual about that? You trying to tell me
I'm no fun to be around?'

'No.' Emily touched her arm in a gesture that spoke
of long familiarity and close friendship. 'It's just…I
don't know…I got the feeling something was bothering you yesterday. You were very quiet when we were
coming over to the resort.'

'I was still steaming over the way Alex had been
treating his daughter, that's all. I thought he was a complete jerk.'

'Was?' Emily eyed her over the rim of her water
glass. 'Past tense?'

Susie shrugged. 'I guess I was wrong. He's OK.'

Emily's eyebrows shot up. '*OK?* He's gorgeous!'
She turned her head to give the top table a deliberate
stare and her sigh was wistful. 'Maybe it's being Greek
that does it. They do the tall, dark and handsome thing
so well, don't they?'

'Hmm. Don't try and set me up, Em. The man lives
in Sydney. If he's not already spoken for, he probably
has every single socialite in the city after him. And he
already has a family. I want my own kids, remember?'

Emily made a sound that suggested she understood.
She would, too. Susie knew she had spent her share of

time considering all the reasons why nothing would happen between herself and Mike. Plus, she was a woman. What was it about being a woman that could make you feel attracted to a man and then get a sudden insight into all the pitfalls a future together could produce? It was crazy.

Mind you, it had worked out rather well for Emily and Mike, hadn't it?

The two women were silent for a minute, watching the gathering. The other people at their table were all engrossed in their own conversations and the noise level was growing steadily as coffee and exquisite petits fours were being served to mark the end of the dinner. Around them, people were leaving their allocated table seating and starting to mix. A five-piece band was setting up at one side of a small dance floor.

The subdued lighting did nothing to dampen the glitter of this occasion. Silverware and crystal caught the light and sparkled on the white linen tablecloths. The women sparkled in their gorgeous dresses and jewellery and the men were all in black tie, which always seemed to automatically increase their attractiveness. Or maybe it was the champagne. Whatever. Susie couldn't help sneaking another glance at the front table herself.

Charles was there, of course. So was the mayor of Crocodile Creek, their member of parliament and George Poulos, who had spearheaded the huge support that had come from local businesses for the building of the new medical centre. Partners were also present…or supposed to be. There was an empty seat beside Charles.

'Where's Jill?' Emily wondered aloud.

'She'll be with Lily. Did you hear she had to have a lumbar puncture this morning?'

'Yes. I flew back to Crocodile Creek with Mike when he took those urgent samples.'

'I thought you didn't like helicopters?'

'I don't.'

Susie grinned. 'But you like Mike enough to get over it, right?'

'Right.' But Emily's smile faded. 'Lily couldn't really have meningitis, could she? It's too awful to imagine.'

'I hope not. Alex seemed to think he was just being careful and doing the test to rule it out, but she looked pretty sick.'

'You've seen her?'

'I had to help with the lumbar puncture. Alex asked me to.'

'Did he, now?'

Susie had to steer the conversation away from Alex. Why did everything seem to get pulled back to that man? 'Did you know that Jill and Charles are officially engaged now?'

'Sophia said something but she's always trying to marry people off. I didn't take too much notice.'

'She's got this gorgeous ring. Really unusual. An opal instead of a diamond.'

'I'm really pleased. Just a bit surprised, I guess.'

'Why? I think they're perfect for each other.'

'Yes, but do *they* think that?'

Susie sighed. 'Charles did say it was just a marriage of convenience. For Lily's sake.'

'Maybe they think it's the sensible thing to do, seeing as they're practically living together.'

Susie drank another mouthful of her wine. 'God, I hope I never get married because it's the "sensible" thing to do.'

'You won't,' Emily promised. 'The right guy is going to come along and you'll get married because you're hopelessly in love. You'll see.'

Susie's gaze strayed back to the top table again.

Alex, like Charles, was alone as far as female companionship went.

Alone… *Available?*

Susie drained her glass of champagne and eyed the bottle in the silver ice bucket. It was still more than half-full. She looked at Emily's glass. The flute didn't appear to have been touched.

'You're not keeping up with me, here, Em. What's the story?'

'I just don't feel much like drinking alcohol tonight.'

The sinking feeling in Susie's gut was too intense to ignore. 'Oh, my God…you're pregnant, aren't you?'

'I'm not sure.' Emily's eyes shone with joy. 'Maybe. Hey, what's the matter?'

Susie shook her head, trying to blink back stupid, stupid tears. She had got this out of her system the other night, hadn't she?

'I was going to tell you.' Emily was frowning now, her joy replaced by concern for her friend. 'Honestly, you were going to be the first person to know. It's just that I haven't even done a test yet. I'm only a couple of days late and…'

Susie blinked harder. She tried to smile. 'It's great news, Em. I'm so happy for you.'

'Could have fooled me.'

Susie tried again, stretching her smile. 'You're not going to believe this, but Hannah's pregnant, too. She rang the other night. Tuesday it was…' Susie sucked in a breath to try and stop herself babbling. 'She'd only just done the test. You'll probably be due at the same time. They'll be like…like twins…' The effort of sounding happy was too much. Susie picked up the starched linen napkin that matched the tablecloth, screwed it into a ball and pressed it against her mouth.

Emily had been listening quietly, her eyes huge. Then she put her arm around Susie. 'Oh, *hell!* I didn't even think. *You're* the one that's always wanted a family. Hannah's the career girl. And now it's me.' Her arm tightened. 'Do you want to escape for a bit? Go for a walk or something?'

'No. I'm fine.'

'Your nose is dripping. Have you got a hanky?'

'No.' Susie sniffed inelegantly.

'Use the napkin.'

'Ooh, gross!' But it made Susie smile. 'I'm OK, really,' she said a moment later. 'I just feel a bit left out, that's all.' She took another deep breath. 'OK, so I'm jealous. I'm sorry, Em.'

'Don't be stupid. It's me who should be sorry. It'll happen for you, you know. Like I said, some gorgeous guy is going to come along and before you know it, you'll be knee deep in nappies.'

'Ha! I haven't even met anyone I'd want to date in months, let alone marry.'

'Alex looks perfectly datable to me.'

'There's no point in dating when it's got no chance of going anywhere. I'm getting too old for games like that.'

'What's happened to that girl who persuaded her twin to have her first-ever one-night stand—to see what having the best sex in her life might be like? To try a playboy because they're the ones who've had the most practice?'

'She's grown up,' Susie said sadly.

Or maybe she'd just been hurt too many times. You got carried away by physical attraction and the next thing you knew you were in love with some guy who had never had any intention of making a relationship permanent. Or even long term. No wonder she had a personal crystal ball that revealed the future so easily when it came to men. Especially men like…Alex.

'Best thing that Hannah ever did, though, wasn't it?' Emily persisted. 'She let herself go enough to have a fling with someone she fancied, and look where she is now. Married to him. Having his baby.'

'Don't remind me. I'm going to be everybody's aunt. They'll all come to visit mad Aunty Susie who lives all by herself with a zillion cats.'

Emily's nudge was not gentle. 'Get a grip,' she instructed. 'Distraction is what you need, and don't try and tell me that Alex Vavunis couldn't distract you. I've noticed how often you've been looking at that table.'

'I've been watching Charles. He's looking a bit stressed, don't you think?'

'Liar!'

Susie had to smile back but it was disturbing to think it might have been so obvious. She'd tried to stop but her eyes had simply refused to obey instructions and kept travelling to catch another glimpse. Eye candy.

And this particular variety seemed to be addictive.

Had Alex noticed? The thought made her cringe. It also made her drag her gaze away from Emily to look over her shoulder. To her horror, Alex was a lot closer than the last time she'd seen him.

'He's coming over.' Emily's stage whisper was delighted. 'The music's started. I'll bet he's going to ask you to dance.'

It was the last thing Susie needed right now.

Or was it?

With every step he took towards her, she could feel the curl of that overwhelming attraction increase. By the time he was ten feet away, it was hot enough to be melting something deep within her. If she danced with Alex, she would be closer than she'd been to him so far. Dancing involved touching. A lot of touching.

Almost as much touching as…

Oh, *help!*

Susie didn't need to consider using the starched napkin as a handkerchief any more. She needed a fan!

The threat of tears was long gone. So was any thought of feeling sorry for herself. Maybe Emily had been right and she needed the distraction that dancing with Alex would provide.

It would be fun. Exciting. A chance to remind herself how much pleasure life had to offer instead of crying in a corner, feeling as if it was all passing her by.

Susie found herself rising to her feet.

Smiling at Alex.

Wordlessly taking his outstretched hand in her response to the invitation to dance.

Letting him lead her, hand in hand, onto the dance floor.

He'd been waiting for this moment for what seemed like for ever.

Alex had spotted Susie the moment she'd arrived for this function. Somewhat to his surprise, the whole room full of people hadn't stopped enjoying their pre-dinner cocktails and introduction session and turned to stare at her. She certainly looked stunning enough to stop traffic.

Soft waves of golden blonde hair, loose and shining under the artificial lights. A delphinium blue dress that was a perfect match for her eyes and made of some soft, clingy fabric that emphasised every delicious curve of her body. Tiny shoulder straps looked like blue spaghetti and the hem of the dress was uneven. It had pointy bits that hung below her knees, but when she moved it swirled, revealing tantalising glimpses of those long, tanned legs.

He couldn't get near her, dammit! At first he'd been stuck in an excruciatingly boring conversation with a self-important politician.

'The cyclone damage was in the millions. Made sure I got out and inspected every bit of it myself. Plenty of photos in the papers to prove that.'

Alex had caught a hint of blue between the black suits surrounding him. He'd put a finger under his bow-tie and loosened it just a little.

'I saw pictures of what happened to the medical centre here,' he'd murmured. 'Devastating.'

'Nearly destroyed the old bridge and cut the main hospital off from the town and the rest of Australia, for that matter. I've made a pledge to the people to get a new bridge built. Have to see if I can get old George on side. His business would go down the drain if the bridge went west.'

The mayor of Crocodile Creek was still wearing his gold medallion, although he'd discarded the rest of his official robes in the wake of the ribbon-cutting ceremony and speeches of the afternoon. He seemed to want to repeat his speech, verbatim, to Alex.

'We might be in the far north and outside the location of what many people consider civilisation, but if you're unfortunate enough to get sick or injured in these parts, you can be sure of getting the best care that medicine has to offer. Even if it happens when you're on a tropical island holiday.'

People were starting to move towards their allocated tables. Susie was going with her friends, Mike and Emily and another two couples. It seemed like one of the only tables with an uneven number. Was she here alone? Was she, in fact, single and...*available?*

Was it too soon to consider taking his jacket off? Did anyone else in this room feel that it was far too warm despite the air-conditioning?

Introductions to his other table companions, George and Sophia Poulos, spelt the end of any chance in the very near future of getting near Susie. Sophia was in transports of delight on discovering his nationality.

'My boy!' she cried, reaching up to pat his cheeks. 'Come. You must sit beside *me*. Tell me about your village. Your family. You must come to the Athina before you go home. As our guest, of course. Greek food. Greek music. It will be just like home....'

It was alarmingly like home already. Sophia could have been one of his mother's sisters. Or any woman in his home town. Hellbent on organising his life. Raising his child. Telling him exactly what he should be doing and how he should be feeling.

Well intentioned, of course, but totally suffocating and tiring to control. Claiming independence by moving as far away as he could had been the best thing Alex had ever done. The only way forward.

He could see Sophia now as he led Susie towards the dance floor. The older woman was tugging excitedly on her long-suffering husband's arm. Pointing in Alex's direction and talking non-stop. Delivering a verdict, no doubt, on his choice of partner. He could almost hear it. She would lament the fact that Susie was not a 'nice Greek girl' but within a breath or two she would be cooing about the beautiful babies that could eventuate.

It was almost enough to take away the pleasure of finally satisfying his desire to touch Susie.

Almost.

As they reached the dance floor, Susie turned and came into his arms. There was a question in her eyes as she looked up and caught his gaze. An expectation. That it was simply curiosity about his ability to dance felt too shallow. The chemistry going on here was far more powerful than that. Alex felt as if he was standing on the edge of an emotional precipice.

Where was the self-control he prided himself on so much in such areas of his life? Sucked into the ether somehow. Non-existent. Gone to the same place as that barrier that should have kept Susie from getting this close. It was too late now. There was no way he could step back.

He didn't want to. He wanted to dance. To touch this woman and move with her, the music flowing around them. And the moment they started moving, a whole new dimension opened. Susie was either naturally gifted or she had taken more than a few dance classes. The way her body moved was like touching the music he was hearing. As they grew more used to each other, he found it effortless to lead her. To provide the foil to let her interpret the music exactly the way she wanted to. To step and twirl and dip until she was laughing from the sheer joy of it and the hem of her dress was swirling high enough to reveal glimpses of smooth brown thighs.

Dancing was not going to be enough. They could dance until dawn and it still wouldn't be enough. How soon would this function wind up?

How soon could Alex offer to escort Susie back to her suite?

Why hadn't it occurred to Susie that Alex would dance as well as everything else he did in his life?

Or how dangerous it had been to accept that invitation?

Dancing was a revelation. It could tell you so much about the person. About their finesse, consideration of others, self-confidence. Even the need to control. It could be an exploration of someone's personality that could tell you far more than you might consciously recognise.

It was also a potent fuel. Dangerously inflammable. It was probably one of the fastest routes to falling in love ever invented, and Susie was, quite literally, being swept off her feet.

Falling in love with a man who made her feel like no man had *ever* made her feel.

Beautiful. Talented. Something to be cherished.

Experience had shown her that a man's talents on the dance floor could be correlated rather closely to his talents in the bedroom. By the end of the evening, hesitating for more than a moment when Alex offered to escort her upstairs required enormous self-control.

She did try a little harder when they reached the door of the penthouse suite.

'Is someone with Stella? Are they expecting you back?'

'No.' Alex was standing very close as Susie fum-

bled with the room card. 'She's staying in the dormitory tonight. They were having an evening of ghost
stories and she said she didn't want to sleep in a room
on her own after that. Here, let me do that for you.'

The door swung open but Susie didn't move. She
looked up at Alex.

She didn't want to sleep in a room on her own, either.

In fact, sleeping wasn't on any desirable agenda.

For the longest moment, their gazes were locked.
Slowly—with infinite care—Alex reached up and
brushed a strand of hair from Susie's cheek. Having
completed their task, his fingers hovered for a heartbeat.
And then another. And then those fingers went into the
hair at the back of Susie's head. Cradling her skull as
he bent and touched his lips to hers.

A brief, gentle kiss. Just enough to make every nerve
ending catch fire with a heat that was white hot. His
eyes closed for only a second. Susie knew that because
her own flew open in response to the intensity of the
heat being generated and she found herself looking into
black pools like the ones she had seen last night.

Pools she knew it would be easy to fall into.

She *wanted* to fall. No. She already had.

This was it. A wordless question, and she had no
words with which to answer it.

None were needed. Alex saw exactly what she
wanted him to see. He took her hand and led her inside
the suite, pushing the door softly closed behind them.

CHAPTER FIVE

CONCENTRATE!

This had to be important. An urgent staff meeting for every available medic on Wallaby Island would not be called for something that wasn't of major significance.

Susie tried to catch the anxiety she could see on the faces around her as she walked into the lecture theatre that was part of the convention centre at the resort. It wasn't easy. She felt as if she was floating above the scene. The way she had already floated through the first part of today—on autopilot, as she'd helped Jack and other children through their airway clearance sessions.

The way she had floated, early this morning, from the bed she had shared with Alex last night.

Part of it would be due to fatigue, she realised, climbing the steps to slip into one of the tiered seats. You couldn't indulge in mind-blowingly *incredible* sex for an entire night without being left a little on the tired side.

Another part was due to Susie being in a mental space she'd never discovered before. A space that felt alarmingly perfect. As exciting as the most thrilling roller-coaster ride imaginable but, at the same time, as secure as a trusted shoulder to cry on. A wild ride that was, paradoxically, soft and comforting.

Was this what being on cloud nine was all about?

The area at the base of the seating featured a lecturn and people were positioning themselves. Charles was there. So was Beth Stuart, talking to a tall man Susie didn't recognise. Beth took a seat and the buzz of speculative conversation in the room died down. Late arrivals found spare seats.

Miranda sat beside Susie, who noticed that Nick—the father of one of Miranda's young asthma patients—was accompanying her. The look and smile the couple exchanged as they settled hurriedly into their seats made it very clear they were together in more than a professional sense. Goodness, when had that happened? It was enough to prompt Susie to scan the rest of the room more carefully.

Where was Alex?

He'd gone back to the cabin to shower and change and had been planning to have breakfast with Stella. Had he not got the message about the meeting?

Yes!

Susie missed the first words Charles spoke because the side door opened again to admit Alex, and a wave of sensation rippled through her body with unexpected ferocity.

Just the glimpse of his hand as he pushed the door shut behind him was enough to make her skin tingle with the memory of his touch. As he turned, her glance went to his face and she could see he had shaved recently but that dark shadow outlining his jaw would always be there. Would always remind her of the deliciously rough sensation that stubble had given her last night. On her breasts. On her thighs…

A small sound must have escaped her because Susie earned a quick, surprised glance from Miranda.

'Are you OK?' she whispered.

'I'm fine,' Susie whispered back.

'Fine'. Such an innocuous word. It could be a cover for not feeling good at all. Or, in this case, a cop-out from an inappropriate attempt to search for a word that could encompass feeling *this* good.

Was Alex feeling good?

Susie hadn't expected to find the surgeon staring in her direction. For a moment, across all the heads turned in Charles's direction, her gaze locked with Alex's and the connection was enough to make her toes curl and that ripple of sensation kick back in.

'Angus Stuart,' Charles was saying in the background. 'An epidemiologist who's here for a conference. Angus has a particular interest in pandemics and has been involved in government think-tanks set up in the wake of the bird-flu scare we all heard so much about a couple of years ago.'

Stuart? The name finally sank in and Susie dragged her gaze away from Alex. She wasn't the only person to search out Beth, who was now sitting in the front row of seats. Were they related? She took another look at the man beside Charles. He was quite proper looking. Distinguished even. Very serious and unsmiling at the moment, which made him seem an unlikely relative for the friendly and outgoing Beth but, then, how much did she really know about Beth?

'As you will all be aware,' Charles continued, 'we're having an outbreak of an influenza-type illness here on the island. Currently we have two adults from the resort and three children from the camp as inpatients in our medical centre. None of them are critically ill but we're monitoring them carefully. Influenza is never something to be taken lightly and we have the additional concern of having a large group of children here, some of whom are already compromised healthwise.'

Susie stole another glance at Alex but he was totally focused on Charles and he was frowning. As though he had assimilated something that hadn't yet been verbalised and he either did not like or disagreed with the information.

'Dr Stuart's opinion was sought because an unusual number of dead birds have been discovered on the island over the last few days.'

Everybody was focused now. Silent and still.

'One of our inpatients is known to have been in direct contact with one of those birds last Tuesday. She started showing the first symptoms of her illness on Friday.'

'Lily…' Susie murmured. 'Oh, my God!' This was possibly worse than a suspected diagnosis of meningitis. *'Bird flu?'*

'Shh,' Miranda cautioned.

'One of our rangers who collected birds from the shoreline on Friday afternoon is also showing the first signs of a viral infection, with a raised temperature, headache, photophobia and arthralgia.'

The audience was not so silent now. Whispered conversations were breaking out. Alex stood silently, still frowning at Charles, his arms now folded. Someone else raised their hand.

'How many others are sick? That haven't been admitted yet?'

The 'yet' struck a note that increased tension. Already they were assuming that the viral infection was going to be a serious illness for everybody who caught it.

'Unknown,' Charles responded. 'That information is something we're going to ask all of you to help collate today. We want you to check the groups of children you're responsible for and report any symptoms, however mild they may be at present.'

The nurse who had accompanied the cancer children stood up to voice the fear everyone was now sharing. She had to raise her voice to be heard.

'Are you saying we've got an outbreak of bird flu on Wallaby Island?'

'No.' It was Angus Stuart who answered. 'And that's something we need to make clear to everybody. There's no cause for panic. What we *are* saying is that the coincidence of finding dead birds with an influenza outbreak means that further investigation is prudent.'

'What kind of investigation?' Miranda asked. 'Are you wanting us to collect blood or sputum samples?'

'We've started that with our inpatients. A series of specimens is needed over several days if we are going to rule out an infection with H5N1.'

'H5N1?' Susie whispered to Miranda.

'Avian Influenza A,' she responded quietly. 'A specific strain of bird flu.'

'At the moment we just need to get a handle on how many potential cases we might be dealing with,' Angus continued. 'And get an idea of demographics. Parts of the island these people have visited. Whether they've touched or seen any dead birds.'

'Everybody needs to be warned not to touch any and to report any sightings,' Charles added.

'But we're on an island,' someone said. 'We're a world away from any known cases.'

'We have migratory birds that travel long distances. The fact that this is an island is to our advantage. In the worst-case scenario, it means we can isolate this virus.'

'As of now,' Charles said clearly, 'Wallaby Island is quarantined. Until we know what we're dealing with, nobody will be allowed to leave.'

'What?' The single word broke from Alex into the stunned silence. 'That's impossible. I've got a full operating list waiting for me in Sydney with a 7:00 a.m. start time tomorrow. I *have* to be off this island today.'

Susie had known that he was due to leave this afternoon. She had known all along that last night had been a one-off, never-to-be-repeated experience. Still, it was disturbing how hollow it made her feel to have it confirmed so vehemently. And a bit humiliating to see that Alex couldn't wait to get away.

'I'm sorry,' Charles said firmly. 'It's now out of my hands. Angus has been in touch with the appropriate authorities and the quarantine has been notified. Disease investigation and control experts are coming in to take over but no one is going to leave. There will be no exceptions.'

'But people have already left,' someone objected. 'I saw the seaplane taking off early this morning.'

'Steps have been taken to intercept those people. And to contact everybody else who's been on the island in the last week. They will be kept under observation and isolation, if necessary, in their homes. Guests at the resort will be receiving a written bulletin shortly, outlining the situation. The staff will be doing their utmost to reduce the inevitable inconvenience and they will, of course, have free accommodation until this is over.'

'What about anyone who gets critically ill?' Miranda asked. 'Some of our children might need intensive-care facilities if they get a bad dose.'

'We're flying in extra supplies,' Charles told her. 'Antiviral medications, among others. We're already set up with one bed capable of intensive monitoring and ventilation. We've got another ventilator on its way. Just in case. If the situation deteriorates, we'll review it on a case-by-case basis.'

Miranda got to her feet. 'Have you got some free time, Susie?'

'I think so. Why?'

'I want to check every child in the camp with asthma or cystic fibrosis—the ones most likely to get into trouble if they get sick. I don't want to alarm the parents or the children, though. Nick wants to help. Have you met Joshie's dad?'

Susie shook Nick's hand.

'You know more of the kids than we do,' Miranda continued. 'I thought that, between us, we could reassure everybody while we're assessing them.'

'Sure. I'll do whatever I can to help.'

'Not that there's any point in not telling the truth,' Miranda added. 'You can bet this quarantine will hit the news big-time and there's no way they're going to shut down Internet or television reception at the resort, is there?'

'No.' There was no way Susie was going to get anywhere near Alex, either, as the group began to disperse. He had moved forward with a determined expression on his face and was now in earnest conversation with Charles. No doubt trying to persuade him that his hospital in Sydney couldn't cope without him.

They would cope, though, wouldn't they? There must be other paediatric neurosurgeons available for emergencies and elective surgery could always be postponed. It wouldn't be for more than a few days.

Some people were pushing towards Angus and she could hear him talking as she followed Miranda through the door.

'No sustained human-to-human infection documented so the World Health Organization's global preparedness plan is still at Phase 3....'

A final glance over her shoulder revealed frown lines on Alex's face like the ones she had seen when he'd first arrived. Stress lines.

OK, so this was inconvenient and potentially scary, but it was so unlikely that this could really be the flash point for a pandemic. Susie was worried for the sake of the children who might get sick, but she couldn't be frightened for her own sake. She was young and healthy and this did have a bright side, didn't it?

How long had it been, if ever, that Alex had had a few days that he could spend with his daughter uninterrupted?

Days with Stella. Just a few, but they could provide memories that would last a lifetime.

Susie hurried out into the bright, tropical sunshine.

Days turned into nights, didn't they?

If Stella was getting quality time with her dad during the days, Susie could enjoy his company during the nights maybe. She could collect her own memories to treasure for *her* lifetime.

Yes. No matter what else the cloud of anxiety hanging over Wallaby Island had in store, there was definitely a silver lining in there somewhere.

* * *

Lunchtime provided an ideal opportunity to assess the remaining children Miranda and Susie had not caught up with after the briefing. Charles and Angus had also been busy, talking with parents and camp staff, and although there was an undercurrent of anxiety, things seemed to be running normally. Parents may be conversing quietly with each other but the dining hall was as noisy and cheerful as ever when the two women entered.

Malcolm, the camp chef, emerged from the kitchens before dessert was served to demonstrate his skill at playing spoons. More than one scuffle was generated as children snatched each other's cutlery and tried to emulate the talent. Parents started smiling as the sound of clattering spoons was interspersed with shouts of laughter.

'They're not worried, are they?' a mother said to Susie.

'We shouldn't be, either,' she responded. 'We'll get on top of this. We're going to separate all the children who are even a bit sniffly.'

'But what if it *is* bird flu?'

'If it is, then human-to-human transmission is even less likely,' Miranda said reassuringly. 'The fact that we've got so many people getting sick is probably a good indication that it *isn't*.'

Susie could see Stella. She was watching Jamie, who had two spoons held back to back in one hand and was managing to make them clink as he hit them on his other palm. His fan club of younger children were standing close, crowding Stella's view. Susie went over to her table.

'How's it going?'

'Boring,' Stella replied gloomily. 'There's been nothing to do all morning. All these people have been here and everybody's been getting their temperature taken and stuff.'

'It's this flu bug. We need to know who's caught it.'

'Yeah. Jamie said it's bird flu and Stephen said that means we're all going to die.'

'Not true,' Susie said firmly. 'On either count.' She wanted to steer the conversation in a more positive direction. 'What's on for this afternoon?'

'There's pottery and stuff. Someone's reading stories on the beach. There's a group that's going to collect shells for making necklaces and there's swimming-pool soccer or kayaking.'

'What are you going to do?'

'Dunno.' Stella flicked a glance in Jamie's direction. 'I might just go to the beach.'

'You could go somewhere with your dad. If you got a cart, you could go up into the rainforest—up to that lookout on the top of the mountain even. He should see that before he goes.'

'He's not going. He's stuck here for days and days. He's really cross.'

'He's worried about his patients back in Sydney, that's all.'

'He's *always* worried about his stupid patients.' Stella's head hung as she picked at a small stain on her T-shirt. 'He never worries about *me*.'

'Not true,' Susie repeated. She gave Stella a gentle nudge. 'He was really worried the other night when you shut yourself in the bathroom.'

'He didn't even want to talk to me before.' Stella's voice was a low mutter that Susie had to strain to hear over the noise of the children around them. 'He's been on his phone all morning.'

'So he's probably finished making all the arrangements he needs to for not getting home on time. I bet he'd love to spend the afternoon just with you.'

Stella shook her head. 'He didn't even *look* at me before. Not really. I was just being a nuisance and I don't want to go back to the cabin.'

'Hmm.' Susie remembered the way Alex had dismissed her as a nuisance on that first meeting. How small and insignificant it had made her feel. 'What if I thought of a way that would make him *really* notice you?'

Stella's suspicious glance was hardly a surprise. It had been Susie's idea that she dress up in her new clothes to impress her father when he arrived, and look how that had backfired. But this idea was much better. Susie leaned over to whisper in Stella's ear.

The girl shook her head again. 'I can't do that.'

'You could,' Susie encouraged. 'I know you could.'

Stella thought about it for a minute. Then she sighed in acquiescence. 'Will you come with me? In case I can't?'

'Sure.' Susie was smiling, already anticipating results. 'Let's go, Star.'

Alex was still on the cabin veranda. An open laptop sat on the table in front of him and he was talking on his mobile phone, his gaze sightlessly encompassing the broad, gently sloping track that led towards the camp complex.

Susie stayed near a large tree at the bottom of the slope but she was only half-hidden. She needed to watch to make sure Stella didn't get into difficulties and lose her confidence as she walked—without her crutches— towards her father.

The moment Alex became aware of what he was seeing was obvious. He became very, very still. The conversation he was having was abruptly terminated, the phone slowly put down and abandoned. Alex sat, riveted by what he was watching. Poised to rush in and offer assistance if necessary but holding back—willing the miracle to continue.

Which was exactly how Susie was feeling. The grip on Stella's crutches became loose as her palms got sweaty. The tight feeling in her chest was what reminded Susie to breathe. From either end she and Alex were walking every slow, measured step right along with Stella.

Susie could see the limp but she could also see every correction for balance.

'Go, Star,' she murmured aloud. 'You can do it.'

She could feel the tension in Stella's body as she concentrated hard on her task. Being a gentle uphill slope was helping. It would have been much harder going downhill. But there were steps at the end of her journey to get to the veranda. They had only practised steps once. Would Stella risk undermining her triumph by attempting something that could be too difficult?

Stella's face was hidden but, from behind, the angle of the girl's head suggested that her gaze was firmly on her father. She certainly had *his* undivided attention. He was half standing now, and even from this distance Susie could see the play of emotion on his face.

Amazement.

Pride.

Love.

It was impossible to swallow past the lump in her throat as Susie watched Stella reach the steps and barely hesitate. The grip on the handrail was tight but only one-sided. Would Stella remember which foot to lift first? Could she transfer her weight and lift her prosthesis and then position it well enough to transfer her balance?

Yes.

One slow step. And then another. It took for ever to get to the top but Alex, bless him, didn't step forward to offer help and break the spell. He stood, his face raw with emotion, his arms held wide to welcome his daughter.

Susie could barely see the embrace through her tears. She turned away to give them a few moments' privacy then she followed the route Stella had taken. Her reasoning for intruding was that Stella would need her crutches back, but the reality was that she wanted to share the moment.

More than that. She may be drawn to these two people for very different reasons but the pull from both father and daughter was way too powerful to resist.

It didn't seem like an intrusion once she reached the veranda.

'I did it, Susie! I *did* it!' Stella pulled herself from her father's arms to hug Susie.

'I knew you could.' Susie returned the fierce hug and this time she didn't bother to try and blink back her tears. A big fat one trickled past her nose. 'I'm so proud of you, hon.'

As proud as her father was?

Susie glanced up to share the pride and was unsurprised to see an identical tear to her own rolling down Alex's cheek. He seemed oblivious, reaching out to touch Stella's back as she hugged Susie. Connecting the three of them, his gaze still on his daughter.

On Susie.

And that was when she fell completely into the moment. Into an equal share of what felt like a victory. The first steps—literally—into a future that was, finally, full of hope.

In a flash of insight Susie could feel everything Alex had been through in the last couple of years. The pain and despair. She could feel the power of the love this man had for his child. The need to protect, the pain of not being able to shield her from suffering and the fierce determination to make things as good as they could possibly be from now on.

A tiny moment of time in her life. Just one of millions of heartbeats, but it was enough.

Enough for Susie to know that she loved this man. That the strength of how he felt about his daughter was mirrored by how she could feel about him.

No, not 'could'.

Did.

It was true. You could fall in love with the speed of a lightning bolt and you could know, with absolute certainty, that this was it. That this person was the one you wanted to spend the rest of your life with.

Did Alex feel any of this? Was it possible to feel such a connection if each side wasn't completely in tune with the other?

This wasn't the time to seek an answer. This was Stella's moment, but if even a part of the love she could see shining in Alex's eyes was available for *her,* then she would happily wait to discover how much.

And she would have to wait.

The voice they could hear from the direction of the track, beyond the tree Susie had waited beside, was urgent.

'*Help!* Someone! Anyone! Please, I need *help!*'

CHAPTER SIX

'IT'S DANNY!' Stella had moved with speed on her crutches behind Alex and Susie as they raced up the track towards the cry for help. 'What's wrong with him?'

'He's having a seizure.' Alex dropped to a crouch beside Benita, who was holding the young boy on his side. 'You're doing a good job keeping the airway open,' he told the nurse. 'How long has this been going on for?'

'Too long,' Benita answered worriedly. 'I thought it would stop in a minute or two. I sent Cameron to get help from the medical centre and one of the girls took the younger children back to camp, but it's just gone on and on. Must be nearly ten minutes now—that's why I was calling for help.'

'What's his history?'

'He's a few weeks post an autologous bone-marrow transplant.'

'For what reason?' Alex held Danny's bald head as the boy's muscles continued to twitch and jerk.

'Intensive chemo post-surgery. They saved his bone marrow to put back afterwards.'

'What was the surgery for?'

'A neuroblastoma.'

'Any secondaries?'

'No. Or not that they know about. He had a really good result from the last round of tests.'

'History of seizures?'

'No.'

'He's very hot.' Alex's hands were gently cradling Danny's head, making sure he wasn't going to injure himself on the rough surface of the track.

'I noticed he was looking flushed,' Benita said. 'But I thought he was just running around too much in the heat. He got really excited because we were off on a frog hunt.'

'No flu symptoms? Did he get checked with the other children this morning?'

'Yes. His temperature was up just a point or two but he seemed fine and it was still within a normal range. He said nothing hurt but, then, it takes a lot to slow Danny down.'

'He looks *awful*,' Stella whispered to Susie in horror. 'Is he going to die?'

Susie put her arm around the girl. 'No,' she said. 'The seizure makes it hard for him to swallow, which is why he's got all that saliva on his face. It's also a lot harder to breathe and that's why his lips are getting a bit blue. He'll be OK. He's got your dad here to look after him now.'

Alex glanced up at her words. 'Could you intercept whoever's coming from the clinic? Make sure they're carrying some oxygen and diazepam? Otherwise we'd better find a way to transport Danny pretty quickly.'

Susie didn't have to go far before she met Beth

coming in their direction in a cart, a large first-aid kit on the seat beside her and Garf riding in the trailer.

'What's happening?' Beth queried. 'Has the seizure stopped?'

'No.' Susie did a U-turn and trotted beside the cart. 'Do you have oxygen with you? And diazepam?'

'Yes. Who's with Danny at the moment?'

'Benita. And Alex—Stella's dad. He asked me to check what you were carrying.'

They were back at the scene now and Susie could only stand beside Stella and watch as the two doctors treated little Danny.

'How old is he?' Beth asked.

'Nearly six,' Benita told her. 'He's just very small for his age.'

The nurse held Danny's small arm as still as possible as Alex slipped a cannula into a vein. Susie could see what a difficult task it had to be, but Alex made it look simple. Beth calculated his weight and drew up the required dose of sedative.

Finally, the seizure stopped. Alex picked up the still unconscious child. 'I'll carry him,' he said. 'Let's get him back to the clinic.'

'Has he got any relatives with him?' Beth asked Benita.

'No. He's one of the unaccompanied ones. My responsibility. I should come with him, shouldn't I? But I sent the rest of the group back to the camp and I'll have to make sure someone's looking after them.'

'We can do that,' Susie offered. 'Can't we, Star?'

Stella's nod was surprisingly eager.

'Cameron went to find Beth,' Benita continued. 'But he knows to go back to the younger ones. There should be five of them waiting on the steps by the dining hall.'

'We'll find them,' Stella said. 'I can take them for a walk to look for frogs.'

The reminder of just how capable she was of doing that made Susie catch Alex's gaze. He had seated himself in the front of the cart now, with Danny in his arms and the oxygen cylinder between his legs. Beth was putting the first-aid kit into the trailer.

'Shove over, Garf,' she instructed. 'Make room or you'll have to run behind.'

Alex looked as if he did things like this all the time, Susie thought. As though it was completely normal to be cradling a sick child and caring for him no matter how unusual the circumstances. Her heart twisted with another shaft of the astonishing depth of the new emotion she was feeling for this man, and she knew her smile was wobbly.

Alex smiled back. Calm and confident but apologetic as he shifted his gaze to his daughter.

'Sorry about this, chicken. I'd better help Beth get Danny settled and assessed, but I shouldn't be too long. We'll do something special together later, yes?'

'Sure.'

It wasn't Susie's imagination. Stella was standing taller. Looking somehow older and far more mature. Where was that slightly sullen teen she had spoken to just an hour or so ago? The one who had been muttering about getting less attention than her father's patients?

'It's OK, Dad,' Stella added. 'Danny needs you more than I do right now.'

Susie wasn't the only one to notice the change. A flash of the pride Alex had shown earlier returned, and Stella was clearly soaking it up. Her smile was almost smug as she turned to Susie.

'Let's go,' she said.

Susie followed, still amazed at the change she could feel. That moment of victory she had engineered for Stella had opened new doors within relationships, it seemed.

For all of them.

An hour or so later, Alex was trying to find his daughter.

The camp seemed deserted but in the dining hall he found staff setting tables in preparation for the evening meal.

'Try the pool,' a young woman who was arranging trays on a table suggested. 'Or the beach. It's so hot, I think everyone wanted to swim. Which one's your daughter?'

'Stella. Wears a baseball cap and she's got crutches.'

Maybe not for much longer, though, on both counts. Her hair was growing back and the prospect of seeing his girl walking confidently—even running or dancing—without her crutches was now a real possibility in the near future.

Thanks to Susie.

'I know her,' the camp worker nodded. 'She's not sick?'

'No.'

Not any more. The aggressive therapy and even the amputation had been the right thing to do. As far as they were able to tell, Stella was cured of her cancer. She could go on and be free of the dreadful disease for the rest of a long lifetime, thank God.

'That's good. Only there's a bunch of them in one of the dormitories. It's been turned into a giant sick bay and we're doing special meals that they'll have in bed.'

She pointed at the trays she was setting. 'Shame, isn't it? Having a bug like this going around when these kids are supposed to be having such a good time.'

'It is,' Alex agreed. 'Thank you. I'll go and find Stella.'

He cast a glance towards the dormitories as he headed for the swimming pool. Hopefully, Stella was finally robust enough to ward off a dose of flu but even if she didn't, it was highly unlikely that this viral illness was really dangerous and the camp had still been worthwhile.

And thank goodness he had made the effort to get here himself. To have the opportunity to witness those early—unaided—steps that Stella had taken.

Now that arrangements were in place to cover his extended absence from Sydney, Alex could see the bonus this quarantine represented, even though he still considered it to be an overreaction.

Unexpectedly, he was being given time to get to know the young woman his daughter had suddenly morphed into. He could get used to the idea that she was no longer a little girl and actually appreciate the glimpses he was getting of the adult she would become.

Like the way she had put someone else's needs ahead of her own and accepted that Alex had to look after Danny. More than that, the way she had been prepared to take responsibility for the care of other children in Benita's absence.

It should be easy to find her because she would be with Susie and a group of younger children. Alex could see Benita near the pool, sitting in the shade of a fig tree, a child wrapped in a fluffy towel on her lap. He scanned the whole area but, disappointingly, neither Stella nor Susie could be seen.

'I got back here a while ago,' Benita told Alex when he approached her. 'I left the medical centre while you were off talking to Dr Wetherby. Stella was doing a great job with this lot but she looked a bit tired. I told her and Susie they should go and chill out on the beach.'

Alex nodded his thanks. 'I'll catch up with you later and give you an update on Danny. I said I'd go and check him again in a couple of hours.' He tapped the pocket of his shorts. 'I've got my mobile on and Beth knows to call me if she's worried.'

Halfway down the track leading to the beach, Alex figured out why this search seemed an odd thing to be doing. He never went looking for women. They were always just there—waiting for *him*. Following him even. Nurses, nannies, housekeepers. Even Stella.

Susie was different, wasn't she?

And, maybe thanks to her influence, Stella was becoming different.

Alex liked that.

He liked it a lot.

He thought back to those first minutes of meeting Susie. To what he had perceived as an unprofessional-looking, difficult woman who had seemed intent on telling him how he should be bringing up his daughter. Ready to stand there and fight on Stella's behalf, no less. Prepared to antagonise him right from the start. No hint of using Stella as a means to get closer to him. Quite the opposite.

And if he'd harboured any doubts about her sincerity, they had blown away when he'd seen those tears this afternoon. Her sheer *joy* in sharing Stella's victory. Joy that spoke of a real understanding of what his daughter had been through in the last couple of years.

What *he'd* been through.

That moment had touched something very deep within Alex. Deep enough to have been hidden even from himself. For the first time he had realised what he'd missed in not having someone close enough to share those dark times. Someone he could trust enough to lean on. He'd been so sure he hadn't needed that. He'd proved he hadn't needed it.

Catching Susie's gaze at that poignant moment of triumph had shown him how much easier it would have been to have had someone like Susie by his side.

No, not someone *like* Susie.

Only Susie.

The idea that there could be some way to keep her in his life was new. Startling enough to make Alex pause as he reached the beach. To stand and watch the gentle surf rolling in instead of searching the shoreline for the people he was trying to find.

What the hell did he think he was doing? He'd sworn off ever thinking like this again. He needed a moment to remind himself why. To remember the betrayal that had been intolerable because it had involved someone more important than himself.

Stella.

Strangely, the bitterness associated with summoning Greta's image into his head had lessened. So much that it was difficult to find it and, by association, hard to resurrect the mistrust for any woman that automatically precluded the idea of a meaningful relationship.

He had loved Greta. Stella had loved her. Perhaps it had been the girl's conviction that she had finally found the mother she'd been desperate for since she was old enough to notice what was missing in her life that had persuaded Alex to take that relationship to the next level.

To—almost—propose marriage.

Thank God he hadn't. The pretence of her love for Stella had been unmasked with astonishing ease. From the moment the cancer had been diagnosed, Greta had backed away from hospital visits, unable to disguise her distaste for hair that had come out in handfuls and the inevitable vomiting from the chemo.

Susie wouldn't have been like that. She would have been there, holding a distressed girl's head. Finding something prettier than a baseball cap to hide the hair loss. Ready for when Stella felt well enough to show her how to use make-up to help her feel better about the way she looked.

Alex had seen more than the tears of joy at Stella's success today. He had seen where they had come from. Not simply the comprehension of the struggle to get to that point. The depth of Susie's involvement in that moment could only have come from the way she felt about Stella.

The bond she had already demonstrated when she had so willingly and effectively dealt with the bathroom crisis the other night.

Real caring.

Love.

Yes. Alex took a long, deliberate inward breath and let it out very slowly. It might take time to get used to feeling this way but new determination was being born. Determination to continue this journey with Susie Jackson and to see where it might lead them all.

It wasn't because of the way Susie felt about his daughter. That had simply opened a door he had considered locked. Made it a possibility that he could trust again. Allowed him the undeniable thrill at the prospect of more of what he had shared with Susie last night.

He wanted her.

He wanted her more than he had ever wanted any woman and allowing himself to consider the possibility that it could work was fuelling a spark of passion that felt as if it could become…huge.

Big enough to last a lifetime?

He would be stupid not to make sure he found the answer to that question.

Susie had been for a swim. A gloriously refreshing, cooling swim out beyond the breakers. The stresses of the day were pushed to one side for the moment and now, blissfully, she lay on her towel, letting the warmth of the afternoon sun dry her body. So relaxed she was half-asleep.

When she saw Alex approaching, the image misted by the lashes of her almost closed eyes, Susie thought she was slipping into that delicious, pre-sleep state where you could trick your mind into making fantasy seem real. Then desire kicked in and she pushed herself up onto her elbows. Her body knew this was no fantasy. Alex was walking towards her.

Smiling.

With an expression that made her feel as though she was the only person he was interested in.

As though the only thing on his mind was taking her into his arms and kissing her senseless.

Susie twisted into a sitting position, reaching for her T-shirt with the intention of shaking out the sand and putting it on, despite the fact her bikini was still wet.

Funny how she felt so exposed when Alex had seen far more of her body last night.

Seen it. Touched it. *Tasted* it.

Oh, *Lord*! The T-shirt was caught under Stella's crutches and Susie's tug made them rattle. Glancing up, she found the sound had diverted Alex's attention.

'Where's Stella?'

'Walking.'

'On sand? Without her crutches?'

'She's got some help.' The T-shirt was forgotten as Susie pointed down the beach to where Stella was walking, slowly, on the damp sand left by the receding tide.

'It's that boy again.' Alex's stare was intent. '*Theos*! They're holding *hands*!'

'To help her keep her balance,' Susie said serenely. 'That's all.'

Alex made a growling sound and Susie's lips twitched. 'It's OK,' she said. 'They like each other, Alex. Stella's going to do more to impress Jamie than she would for me. Or even you, I suspect.'

'She's far too young for that sort of carry-on.'

'She's nearly fourteen. How old were you when you thought you were in love for the first time?'

'Oh, God!' Alex groaned, folding his long frame to sit on the edge of Susie's towel. 'I was fourteen.'

'There you go, then.' Susie wrapped her arms around her legs and grinned at Alex. 'Runs in the family. Memorable, isn't it, that first love?'

'Yes.'

'You wouldn't have been too impressed if your father had told you *you* weren't old enough. Or, worse, forbidden it.'

'He tried to.'

'And what happened?'

Alex shook his head but he was smiling. 'I married her a few years later. When I was eighteen.'

'Oh…' The answer had been unexpected. It was hardly the adolescence of someone who had all the hallmarks of being a skilled player. 'Was that…Stella's mother?'

'Yes. Helena. The girl next door. Or from the next village, anyway.' Alex was still staring at the slowly receding figures of the teenagers. 'Where does that boy live?'

'I don't know.' Not that it would make much difference these days, anyway, with the way mobile phones and the Internet made it so easy to stay in touch. 'But right now he's here and Stella thinks he's wonderful and…life has suddenly become rather different for her. Better.'

'Yes…' The words were almost a sigh. 'For me, too.'

And me, Susie thought. *Big time*. She couldn't say it out loud, though, could she? She barely knew Alex. If she confessed she thought she was in love with him, she probably wouldn't see him for dust.

On top of that, she needed a little time to get her head around the fact that he'd married his childhood sweetheart. To push aside the ridiculous jealousy she felt towards someone who had captured his heart so completely.

Stella had told her she couldn't remember her mother, who had died when she'd been a baby, but Alex obviously remembered. Was some of the poignancy she could hear in his voice now because Stella was maturing virtually before his eyes? Did she look like her mother had at the same age? When Alex had fallen in love with her? Was he thinking about finding—and losing—the love of his life?

Changing the subject seemed like a very good idea. 'How's Danny?'

'Still very drowsy, but that's hardly unexpected.' Alex clearly had the ability to put aside anything personal and focus immediately on a professional matter. 'He's post-ictal after the seizure and he's had a sedative. I'll go and check him in an hour or so and will try a more comprehensive neurological examination then.'

'Has he got flu?'

'Seems likely. He's running a temperature of just over forty degrees centigrade, which is quite high enough to explain a febrile seizure.' Alex paused, and then continued as though thinking out loud. 'I'm not that happy about him.'

'How come?'

'It's very rare for a six-year-old to have a febrile seizure and there are other, worrying possibilities.'

'Like his history of cancer? Could he have secondary involvement of his brain?'

'It's possible. Meningitis or encephalitis is also on the list. I don't want to do a lumbar puncture on him until I'm satisfied his ICP isn't raised.'

'ICP?'

'Intracranial pressure. It goes up if there's swelling of the brain or extra fluid or something happening inside the skull. It's like a box and there's no room for too much of anything like that. A rise in pressure could be another explanation for the seizure.'

'Why can't you do a lumbar puncture?'

'If the pressure's high enough, removing spinal fluid can precipitate movement of the brain. Coning.'

'Oh…' Susie knew that wasn't good.

'Mmm.' Alex echoed her tone. 'It could be catastrophic. It's why I don't feel happy being this far away from the kind of diagnostic and monitoring facilities I'm used to. Like CT or MRI scanning. The nearest paediatric ICU is in Brisbane and Charles says we can't transfer him unless he's critical.'

'You disagree?'

'No, I wouldn't say that. Charles is quite right. Danny could well be exhibiting the symptoms of the viral infection that is the precise reason this island had been put under quarantine. We could be endangering a lot more people than young Danny if we evacuate him.'

'Do you think this flu is really dangerous?'

'Influenza should never be taken lightly. Especially in people who have other health problems. Or with the very old or young.'

Susie shivered, despite the warmth of the sun. 'Not what you expected when you came for a weekend at a tropical resort, is it?'

'No.' Alex seemed fascinated by the goose bumps that had appeared on Susie's arms. He reached out and touched her lightly. The frisson of fear vanished—the chill suddenly replaced by burning heat. Susie's gaze was locked on Alex as he raised his eyes. 'I've found a lot of things I didn't expect here,' he said softly.

His hand moved. A slow stroke that drifted down her arm until it reached her knees. Knees that were bent to provide shelter for breasts that hadn't received the cover of that T-shirt. Susie could feel her nipples tighten so dramatically it was painful. Alex leaned closer and her lips parted in expectation of his kiss.

'Dad!'

The voice was a distant shout but it was close enough

to be audible. Susie could see the way Alex's intent drained from his eyes. She could almost imagine a degree of the same disappointment she was feeling. His hand lingered in the space between her knee and her breast for just a second longer. And Alex smiled. A smile that was just for Susie. A promise that whatever had been ignited was still glowing. It could be fanned into life later. And then he turned, moving smoothly so that he was simply sitting beside Susie. Facing his daughter. That moment of connection and desire had been screened, Susie realised. Stella didn't need to know there was anything between her therapist and her father.

Did Alex not want her to know?

Why not? Was it too soon or did he protect her from any relationship he might have so that it didn't impact on her life when it was over?

Susie fought the stab of disappointment. This was crazy. She was expecting too much. *Hoping* for too much. She drew a deep, steadying breath as Stella and Jamie got closer.

She was in way over her head here.

'Jamie's cool, isn't he, Dad?'

'He seems like a very nice boy.' Alex was actually watching Susie as she left the beach. Her T-shirt was covering her top but those endless legs moved under a very neat bottom with an action that was mesmerising. The boy just happened to be walking beside Susie.

'Wait till he comes back with his surfboard. You should see him surf, Dad. Not that there's real surf here. Jamie say it's a millpond, whatever that is, but he can still stand up for ages. He's awesome.'

'I've got a cart up on the track. Didn't you want to go for a ride up into the rainforest?'

'Not *now*!' The prospect was clearly not a contender when the opportunity of feasting her eyes on the sight of the boy riding baby waves was on offer, but Alex just smiled as Stella turned to face him.

He'd never seen her looking this happy.

He could feel almost envious of that pure joy. The kind of trust and devotion that you could only experience once in your life because, when it was broken, you knew that being hurt again was always a possibility.

'OK if I hang out here with you for a while, then? I don't have to go back to check on Danny for an hour or so.'

'Sure.'

They both lounged on the sand, watching the surf and a group of children playing well down the beach. The silence was companionable and Alex didn't try to engage his daughter in conversation. The secret smile he caught pulling at the corners of Stella's mouth on more than one occasion was evidence of what she preferred to be thinking about.

Susie was right. Trying to interfere would only push Stella away, and that was the last thing Alex wanted. Especially now, with this new—wonderful—adult-type closeness growing between them.

It was only for a day or two. Let her enjoy the thrill of her first experience of being a couple. If he didn't push her away, he could be there for her when she was separated from the boy by circumstances. He could be understanding. Sympathetic. Deepen this new bond even further.

'You're not getting sunburnt, are you?' he asked eventually.

'No. Jamie gave me some of his sunscreen.'

Had he put it on for her, too? It was an effort to suppress outrage. It was none of his business. Not really. Even if the boy *had* been brave enough to offer to cover the difficult areas like her back, it would have been an innocent experience.

Yeah…right! Alex couldn't help imagining how it would have been to smooth sunscreen onto Susie's brown skin, the feel of which was branded into his memory for ever. Not just the feel of it, either. She had smelt perfect. *Tasted* perfect. Responded in a way Alex had never encountered before.

He sucked in a breath that earned a glance from Stella, and he said the first thing he could think of.

'How about dinner with me tonight, sweetheart? Something special over at the resort. Five-star stuff.'

'Um…no, thanks, Dad. We're having nachos at camp. That's my favourite.'

'Is it?' Alex blinked. Since when had Mexican food become a favourite?

'Yeah. And it's movie night. We're getting the new James Bond movie and popcorn and everything.'

And she would get to sit next to Jamie, no doubt. Holding hands.

'Take Susie to dinner.'

'What?' Alex was even more startled. Had Stella seen something in their body language maybe before she'd called out to him earlier?

'She's really nice.'

'I'm sure she is.'

'She'd like dinner. And you don't have to come back early. I'll sleep in the dorm again.'

Was Stella trying to encourage him to date Susie or

was this a means of getting her father out of the way for the evening? Alex's hackles rose.

'I don't think that sounds like a very good idea.'

'It's a great idea,' Stella said firmly. 'Susie's been great. I wouldn't be walking like I am if it wasn't for her, and it would be a nice way to say thank you.'

'True. So you should come to dinner with us.' Alex raised an eyebrow. 'You could bring Jamie along if you want.'

'We want nachos. And the movie. Besides…' Stella's grin was impish '…if I'm there, you won't be able to talk about me and how well I'm doing. I might get a big head.'

The reminder of how well Stella was doing was enough to make Alex relax. To make a concerted effort to embrace the encouragement she was getting, rather than his suspicions of the boy's motives.

And he was a nice boy. Responsible. Caring. Plus, he must know after that first meeting that Alex would kill him if he did anything to harm Stella. The camp was well supervised and the dormitories were full of kids. It was perfectly safe.

'Fine,' he said with only a hint of resignation. 'I'll take Susie to dinner, then. By myself.'

'It's only dinner, Dad.' Stella's tone was soothing. 'I know she's not your type.'

'Oh? What *is* my type?'

'Dark and kind of brooding. Like those pictures of Mama. Like…you know…Greta.'

Yes. Dark and sultry. Or should that be sulky? Funny how that didn't seem remotely appealing any more.

'Susie's different,' Stella concluded.

'Yes. She certainly is.'

But Stella wasn't listening any longer. Jamie had reappeared, with a surfboard under his arm, and Stella's face was glowing—her eyes alight with joy. Starstruck.

Alex understood. Too well maybe. It might be totally hidden but there was a part of himself that was feeling the same way. Blown away.

Touched by magic.

And his daughter, bless her, had just ordered him to spend the evening—the whole night, in fact—exploring more of that magic.

CHAPTER SEVEN

AN EVENING with Alex.

Dinner at the elegant resort restaurant—the Rainforest Retreat—a vast conservatory that blended into the rainforest behind the hotel. With huge indoor palms and ferns blurring the transition even further.

Dancing.

And Alex had said Stella intended staying in the camp with her friends. Why would he have told her that unless it was an invitation to spend the whole night with him?

'It sounds wonderful,' was all she'd said.

Could he have guessed what a mastery of under-statement her response had been? Anticipation was an astonishingly powerful drug running through her veins now. Having a physio session to get through with Jack Havens before she could shower and change and indulge in the luxury of thinking of nothing but the evening ahead was doing little to dull the underlying thrill.

How could it, when Alex was in the same room, doing an examination on young Danny? The curtain between the beds was pulled but Susie could still hear the clear sound of Alex's voice.

'Wake up, Danny! Open your eyes for me.'

Susie kept her voice down so she wouldn't be a distraction to the medical team on the other side of the curtain. 'You can turn on your side now, Jack.' She bent to pick up one of the large, extra pillows she had brought with her. She could see Alex's feet. They weren't the only set of feet around Danny's bed and it wasn't unusual to see a doctor wearing sandal-type footwear, but those were *Alex's* feet.

Bare toes. Impossible not to remember the sight of him discarding his clothes last night—the hard, lean lines of his naked body illuminated by the soft light of the moon coming through the unshuttered glass wall of the penthouse suite. Maybe it wouldn't be quite so overwhelming tonight. She could take the time to savour what she saw. Tease them both by helping him undress…slowly…

Susie shut her eyes for a second, clutching the big, soft pillow in her arms.

'Bright light, Danny,' she heard Alex say. 'Keep your eyes open and look at my nose.'

'It hurts…' Danny's voice was uncharacteristically pathetic, but at least he was talking now.

'What hurts, buddy? Your eyes?'

'No. My head.'

'Whereabouts? Can you show me?'

'No. Can't. It's inside.'

'All over inside, or just in one place?' Susie could hear the smile in Alex's voice and it made her own lips curve as she tucked the pillow behind Jack.

'All over.' Poor Danny sounded miserable.

'OK,' Susie whispered to Jack. 'Turn back over now, sweetheart.'

Jack flopped, ending up at a forty-five-degree angle because of the cushioning. Automatically, he lifted his arm on that side and tucked it over his head, well used to the position that gave his therapist good access to the middle lobe of his left lung. She cupped her hands, conforming the shape to match the chest wall and trapping a cushion of air to soften the impact as she began the rhythmic percussion.

'Squeeze my hands, Danny,' Alex said behind her. 'Good boy. And this hand?'

'Danny had a fit,' Jack told Susie.

'I know. I was there. He's not very well, poor wee guy.'

'He's been really sleepy since he came in here. I heard the nurse talking to one of the doctors. They think there's something wrong with his head.'

'Just let your leg go floppy,' Danny was being instructed. 'I'm going to tap it with my special hammer. Don't worry, it won't hurt.'

Susie stopped the percussion and flattened her hand to shake the lung segment and try to encourage the movement of mucus.

'Big, deep breath,' she instructed.

The action started him coughing and Susie waited until he had finished.

'Excellent! You're doing really well, Jack. Do you remember what the next position is?'

'Pillow between my legs and I put my arm down.'

'Cool. Let's go.' Susie moved the pillow. 'You're sounding a lot better.'

'My temperature's down. I'm going to be allowed to go back to camp.'

'That's great. Did they say when?'

'Tomorrow.' Jack twisted to look up at Susie hopefully. 'They might let me go back tonight if you said it was OK. They're having a movie.'

'It would be fine by me. As long as you take things quietly. You might not be able to run around too much for a day or two.'

'I don't mind. I'd like to see the movie, though. It's been really boring in here. I thought I could play with Danny but he's just sleeping all the time.'

'He's sick.' Susie started percussion on the lower lobes of Jack's lung, staying quiet to try and hear what Alex was saying to his medical colleagues. Was it unprofessional and selfish to hope the little boy would be well enough to give them an uninterrupted evening? She may not know Alex very well but Susie was quite confident that personal pleasure would be postponed if he was needed by one of his patients, even out of hours.

'Where are those baseline recordings we did?'

'Here.' There was rustle of paperwork and a moment's silence as Alex scanned the information again. 'I'd like another full set,' he said. 'Including a head circumference. I'm not happy with this blood pressure, either.' He had moved to the foot of the bed and his voice was lowered. Danny was quiet. Had he fallen asleep again?

'Systolic pressure's stable enough.' It wasn't really a surprise that Charles hadn't been content to leave Alex with nursing staff to share the consultation. Did anything happen in his domain that he didn't involve himself with?

'Yes, but the diastolic pressure's dropped. Widening pulse pressure could be sign of rising ICP. It needs watching. I'd like thirty-minute recordings. Have we got a cardiac monitor available?'

'Yes.'

'Pulse oximetry and automatic BP?'

'Of course.'

Alex still didn't sound happy. 'GCS is down at least a point. He's still drowsier than I'd expect. He hasn't had another seizure since being admitted, has he?'

'No.'

'Has someone been with him all the time?'

'Not every minute. We've been flat out with another three admissions. We're calling in extra staff but until now we've been run off our feet.'

'I want someone with Danny at all times,' Alex decreed. 'It's possible he's had another seizure that was short-lived enough to go unnoticed.'

'Jack's been here.' That was Marcia's voice.

The curtain was twitched back. For a split second Alex caught Susie's gaze and his look of intent focus softened. Susie's hands stilled as she felt the delicious tingle of being noticed.

Acknowledged.

'Hey, Jack?' Alex tilted his head, his attention on the boy now lying on his stomach with the pillow under one side. 'I'm Dr Vavunis. You haven't noticed Danny doing anything strange, have you?'

'He's just been asleep.'

'Not twitching or making funny noises?'

'You mean, like having a fit?'

'A seizure. Yes.'

'Nah.' Jack shook his head, caught his breath and then started coughing, which ended the exchange. Alex turned back and Susie held Jack's ribs to support him because he was beginning to sound tired.

'We're almost done,' she encouraged. 'You'll feel a lot better when we've got your chest clear.'

Alex was almost done, too, it seemed.

'It would be good if we can get Danny's temperature down a bit further,' he said to Marcia. 'Tepid sponge bath, perhaps. And a fan. When's the next dose of paracetamol due?'

'Fifteen minutes.'

By the time Susie was moving Jack into his final position on his stomach with the pillow under his hips, Alex was leaving the room.

'I want to be called if there's any change,' he said. 'Marcia? If you're monitoring him, I'd like a full GCS check with the vital-sign recordings.'

'You mean, wake him up and talk to him?'

'Yes. I need to know if his level of responsiveness drops any further. At least ensure that he's easy to rouse.'

It was torture.

Exquisite but almost unbearable.

If anticipation was a drug, Susie was in danger of falling victim to an overdose.

Could Alex not feel it? Or was he enjoying this? Doing it deliberately, in fact? Drawing out this public part of their evening together as a kind of foreplay?

The way he was looking at her certainly seemed deliberate. Susie couldn't hold that gaze for more than a few heartbeats at a time. It was so…intense.

'*Interested*' was too pale a word for it. He seemed fascinated. *Smitten* even?

Wishful thinking, perhaps, but it would be far too easy to fall into that dark gaze. To lose herself and any control over what she might say. And that would be dangerous. Susie didn't want to change the way Alex was looking at her. How awful would it be to see a hint of alarm or a cloud of doubt dulling that fierce approval? Or, worse, a gaze that slid over her shoulder to scan other women in the room.

There were plenty of them. The resort was full to capacity thanks to the quarantine trapping the guests. Many of the people using the restaurant were dressed up for the occasion and Susie was sure she was the only one wearing the same outfit as she had the night before. She hadn't expected to be going out on a date, though, had she?

And she could never have expected Alex. Not in this lifetime. He was too good to be true and that gave a sense of urgency to this dinner. Any moment now he would wake up and realise how beautiful the other women in here were and wonder what on earth he was doing, sitting here so intent on Susie Jackson.

Or his phone would ring and he'd be called back to see Danny or some other patient. He'd work all night and by morning daylight would make him see clearly and realise that Susie wasn't *this* special.

His touch contradicted her fears. Even more deliberate than his gaze, the way he rested a forefinger lightly beside her elbow and then traced the curve of the muscle all the way to the pulse at her wrist. A pulse that had to be telling him just how arousing his touch was, which made it even harder to hold his gaze. Susie had to use her tongue to dampen suddenly dry lips and she saw her own flare of desire mirrored in those dark eyes.

Yet he still appeared to be in no hurry to finish the meal. He picked up his fork again, speared an asparagus tip then added a shred of the braised lamb shank beside it, put it in his mouth and chewed carefully, his gaze barely leaving Susie's face.

Her own fork felt as if it was made of lead and her appetite was waning rapidly. For food, at any rate.

'So...' Alex swallowed, put down his cutlery and reached for his glass of red wine. 'You know about my early love life. Tell me about yours.'

Susie opened her mouth to protest that she didn't know very much. He had married the girl next door—the love of his life. A marriage marred by tragedy. OK, maybe that was enough. Knowing more might be too scary.

'Did you start early?' Alex prompted. 'Like my Stella seems to be doing?'

'I got interested,' Susie admitted, 'but there were... ah...technical difficulties.'

Alex looked startled. 'Sorry?'

'I had a clone,' Susie explained. 'Still do, actually.' She had to take pity on Alex's deepening expression of bewilderment. 'I have an identical twin sister. Hannah. Boys were either scared of us because they thought we were playing tricks on them or they went too far the other way and thought they could get both of us—at the same time.'

'Oh...' The slow smile of comprehension was gorgeous. Susie watched his lips curve and wanted to lean over the small table and kiss him. 'Two of you,' he murmured. The smile widened. 'Yes, I can understand the attraction.'

'We're only alike to look at,' Susie added firmly. 'Quite different in other ways. Hannah's the assertive one. She's a kick-ass A and E specialist who works in a big city hospital in New Zealand. She recently married another ED doctor and...and she's just found out she'd expecting her first baby.'

Oh, Lord, how had that slipped out? And with that edge of wistfulness that Alex surely couldn't miss. Good grief—how to scare a man off in one easy move.

'So I'm going to be an aunt,' she finished—hopefully brightly. 'It's very exciting.'

'Hmm.' Alex was loading his fork again. Cutting his food with a precision that reminded Susie what he did for a living. Reminded her also of how skilful those long fingers were in other, more personal arenas. Hurriedly, she dropped her gaze to her own plate and stirred the wild mushroom risotto she had chosen for a main course.

Change the subject, she ordered herself sternly. *Fast*!

'You would have been proud of Stella today.' Good choice of topic, Susie congratulated herself. Appropriate and distracting.

'I'm always proud of Stella.'

'She was wonderful with the children in Benita's group. She knew quite a lot about rainforest frogs and she's a natural teacher.'

'Is that so?' She had definitely caught his interest.

'Yes. Even when she was really sick in hospital, she took an interest in the younger children. It's a shame she never had any siblings.'

Susie was grateful she had a mouthful of risotto that precluded a response. Was Alex suggesting he might want more children in the future?

'Teaching wouldn't be a bad career for her if that's something she wants to do,' Alex said. 'Challenging but not necessarily too physically demanding.'

'I don't think anything is going to hold Stella back. She had a major hurdle to get over in accepting her prosthesis, but I think she'll go from strength to strength now.'

'Thanks to you.' Alex discarded his fork and caught Susie's hand, covering it with both of his. 'I am very, very grateful for what you've done for my daughter.'

'It's been a pleasure.' Susie loved the feeling of her hand being enclosed like this. It felt safe. Protected. A miniature version of what it would feel like to have her whole body held in Alex's arms.

She wanted to be held. *So* much.

'You're very fond of Stella, aren't you?' Alex seemed to be watching her carefully.

It rang a warning bell. What was the real question being asked? Whether she could see herself being Stella's stepmother? Surely not. Scared of reading too much into the query, Susie simply nodded in response. And smiled.

'And you're going to become an aunt.' Alex let go of her hand to return his attention to his dinner. 'Do you see yourself having your own children one day?'

Oh, help! The was getting heavy. A question as loaded as a shotgun. Susie tried to remember how he'd worded his comment about siblings for Stella. He'd used the past tense, hadn't he? That meant he wasn't considering the possibility.

'I love kids,' she said cautiously. 'And, yes, I guess I did always see myself being a mother, but...'

'But?' Had Alex noted the way she had also used the past tense?

'It would depend,' Susie floundered. Somehow she had to avoid slamming doors. She also had to avoid putting Alex under unreasonable pressure by hinting how strong her feelings were. He couldn't possibly share them. It was too soon. Too much the stuff of fairy tales.

He wasn't going to let her off the hook, however. 'On what?' he asked.

'On the partnership I was in.' Susie abandoned her food in favour of her wine. She also gave up any mental gymnastics. This was important and she couldn't be less than truthful.

'I'm thirty-three,' she said bluntly. 'It's quite possible that someone I meet will already have children and not want any more. Yes, I'd be sad not to have a child of my own, but if I meet the man I want to spend the rest of my life with, I'm not going to let that get in the way. It's the partnership that's the most important.'

Strangely, Susie was finding it easy to hold Alex's gaze as she spoke words that came straight from her heart. 'It's the feeling of never being alone,' she said softly. 'Even if you're miles apart. Knowing that someone is there for you, no matter what.'

'Trust.' Alex nodded. 'Two halves of a whole.'

'Yes.' Susie still hadn't looked away. Hadn't even blinked. 'And finding that is like the end of the rainbow. Anything else…*everything* else…has to be negotiable.' She smiled, hoping to lighten the odd intensity surrounding them. 'Whew! Does that answer your question?'

'Indeed.' But Alex wasn't smiling. He was looking very serious. Digesting what she had said? Planning an early escape from a crazy woman who was planning to snare some poor man for a lifetime?

The waiter's approach to their table was well timed. 'Would Sir and Madam like to see the dessert menu?'

'Would we?' Alex raised an eyebrow at his companion and Susie had to lick her lips again and reach for her wineglass. Her whole mouth felt dry now.

Alex cleared his throat. 'I think,' he told the waiter, 'that we might avail ourselves of room service if we require dessert.'

'Very good.' The waiter took their plates and moved away smoothly.

'Is it?' Alex stood up, dropping his linen napkin onto the table and extending a hand to Susie. 'Very good, that is?'

'Oh…yes.' Susie put her hand into his. She had been looking forward to dancing with Alex again tonight but, finally, he seemed to have caught the urgency she had been aware of all evening.

And it was, indeed, very good.

They left the restaurant in almost unseemly haste. Hand in hand. Susie was only vaguely distracted by Sophia Poulos's open-mouthed delight as she spotted them in the foyer.

The lift was, satisfyingly, instantly available but they had to share it with another couple. The grip on Susie's hand tightened until it was almost painful, but Susie made no complaint. When the strangers got out, they waited, unmoving until they reached the top floor. Then Alex pulled her from the lift, somehow opened the door of the suite and then Susie found herself with her back to the wall, grateful for its support under the onslaught of Alex's kiss.

But then—disturbingly—the urgency was flicked off like a switch. Alex broke the kiss, moved his hands away from Susie's hips and placed them on the wall on either side of her head. He took a deep breath and let it out slowly, and his gaze seemed fastened on where Susie could feel her pulse hammering on the side of her neck.

'Tonight,' he said softly, 'we take our time.'

It was as though they had agreed on a destination last

night and located the maps and the most direct route. Tonight was about exploring detours. Finding every delight that might otherwise have been hidden. Knowing where they would end up but making the most of the journey.

Potential interruptions from a phone call were forgotten.

The idea that she might not be special enough had been long since vanquished for Susie.

She had never felt so desirable.

So…worshipped.

'You're beautiful,' Alex told her more than once as he moved to caress and kiss a new patch of her skin. '*So* beautiful.'

And Alex was…

Alex.

Perfect.

Susie learned the pattern of the dark hair that was a butterfly shape on his chest. She traced it with her tongue, revelling in the hard pebbles of his nipples and way his skin became so soft as the hair trailed off. The sound of raw need being heightened when she took him in her mouth and the way he breathed her name so much later in the moment of ultimate release.

Tonight they slept. Locked together with Alex's arm cradling Susie. Her head on his chest, one leg curled over his. When she woke, a little before dawn, she watched him sleeping and waited for the moment when his eyes would open and he would see her. Expecting to see the truth in his eyes.

She didn't have to wait long. Alex took a deeper breath and stirred. Then long, dark lashes lifted and his eyes opened. For a split second he looked startled but then Susie saw something melt in those dark eyes. A liquid warmth was released that enfolded her even before his hands reached to touch her.

He was smiling but Susie couldn't return it. Emotion threatened to overwhelm her and she had to remain still and blink back the prickle of tears. All she could do was welcome Alex with everything she had to offer.

Her body and mind.

Her heart and soul.

She saw them coming along the beach.

Holding hands.

They probably thought it was too early for anyone to notice them. Or maybe they didn't care. They looked like nobody else in the world was important. Only them.

They were only small, distant figures in the shadowy, early light so Stella turned her gaze back to what she was supposed to be watching. From her vantage point under the tree, she could see the main camp buildings, as well as the beach. She'd got up really early, leaving the bunkroom she had shared with three other girls last night. The objective had been to watch one of the other bunkrooms. To wait until Jamie had gone in for breakfast. Then Stella was going to walk in. Without her crutches.

Jamie would notice. Like her dad had yesterday. He would watch her with *that* look. The one that told her how amazing she was.

Stella wanted Jamie to think she was amazing. He did already, kind of, or he wouldn't have held her hand during the movie last night. Not when he didn't need to, to help her walk or anything.

It had been really hard to get to sleep after that. Not because the movie had been scary but Stella couldn't

stop thinking about how it had made her feel, having
Jamie holding her hand like that. It was the most incredible feeling ever. Warm and tingly but so *exciting*.

What would being kissed be like?

Stella touched her lips with her fingers, the way she
had in the dark, private space of that bed in the bunkroom. Aware of her lack of privacy now, Stella shifted
her gaze quickly, but there was still no one else about.
Just that couple on the beach.

They had stopped walking. They were locked in a
passionate embrace. Doing the kind of kissing Stella's
imagination had been playing with.

Weird. Like she had sent a message telepathically
or something.

A twist of emotions Stella couldn't identify properly
jumbled for dominance. Envy of people grown up
enough to be doing that stuff? Fear of taking that big a
step towards *being* that grown up? Sadness, even, knowing that being a little kid was going to be lost for ever.

The figures started walking again, this time with
their arms around each other. They were getting close
enough to see how tall the man was. The shine of blonde
hair on the woman. The familiarity…

Oh, my God!

Stella's mouth dropped open and any thought of watching the first arrivals at the dining hall was forgotten.

That was her *dad*!

And…and…Susie!

He'd taken her to dinner. He was coming along the
beach right from the end. He must have spent the whole
night with her.

'No!'

Stella startled herself by saying the word aloud.

She gulped in a big breath. It wasn't that she didn't *like* Susie or anything, but this wasn't supposed to be happening.

Not now. Not when her dad actually had time to notice *her* for once. When he was so proud of her.

It was too late for this. Stella was over that kid thing of desperately wanting a mother. She and her dad didn't need anyone else in their lives. He'd told her that when Greta had left.

He'd told her that it hadn't been her fault because she'd got sick. That it wouldn't have worked out anyway. That she—*Stella*—was the most important woman in his life, and always would be.

Through narrowed eyes Stella watched the couple turn towards a track that led away from the beach. Susie would probably go to the dining hall and that tarnished the attraction of having breakfast with Jamie.

Her dad would go to their cabin. He'd probably pretend he'd been there all night. That nothing with the potential to change their lives was happening.

Stella reached for her crutches and jabbed her hands through the loops to grip the handles. No way she was going to walk without them this time. She needed to move faster than that.

She needed to find out just what the hell was going on. And what she was going to do about it.

CHAPTER EIGHT

'I SAW you!' The words were breathless but still an accusation. 'On the beach. With *Susie*!'

Alex let his breath out in a sigh. His daughter's outraged face suggested he was about to face an uphill battle.

In the background, the sound of the early morning news broadcast on the television filled the short, tense silence.

'None of the patients admitted to the recently upgraded medical facilities are listed as critical. We cross now to the army base, where a helicopter is preparing to airlift a mobile biohazard laboratory and decontamination unit onto Wallaby Island…'

'It was nothing,' Alex said cautiously to Stella. Nothing for Stella to worry about, that was. He was more than prepared to take things slowly if he had to. As slowly as necessary to ensure Susie's place in his family. In his life.

'You were *kissing* her!' Stella shouted.

'Who's going to be using the laboratory?' An interviewer was asking someone wearing a military uniform. *'Are extra people going to be put at risk of catching bird flu?'*

'We like each other,' Alex told Stella. That was a safe

place to start, wasn't it? Surely Stella wouldn't feel threatened by him *liking* a woman? She had pushed him into having a date with her, for heaven's sake.

And what a date! Alex felt more sure about this than he ever had about anything. He and Susie were made for each other. He had never—*would* never—find anyone else he could feel like this about. Susie was perfect. Gorgeous. Intelligent. Compassionate. Trustworthy. The other half of his whole. The—

Stella snorted. 'It looked like a lot more than that. Did you sleep with her last night?'

'That, young lady, is none of your business.' They might be entering a new phase of their relationship and it might be a far more adult one, but there had to be limits.

Where had that little girl gone? The one with the shining eyes who had interrogated him about every woman he met in the hope he was choosing a new mother for her?

'*Angus Stuart,*' the military man was saying. '*By a fortunate coincidence, we happen to have an international expert on site already. He's planning an autopsy on one of the dead birds found on Wallaby Island. We should have a much better idea of what we're dealing with by as early as tomorrow....*'

'Of course it's my business. You're my father!' Stella was glaring at him ferociously, and she had never looked more like her mother. Helena. Furious with him. Unhappy. Trapped in a marriage that had started far too early in life.

'Are you going to *marry* her?' Stella was attempting contempt, but the sentence ended in a squeak that made it obvious tears were imminent.

Ah, *Theos*!

Alex picked up the remote and flicked the television into silence, cutting off the footage that must have been taken by one of the helicopters seen buzzing over the island yesterday. A disreputable-looking man with a sack was holding a dead bird up by its legs. Right now the whole quarantine emergency seemed far less important than what was happening inside this cabin.

The combination of seeing the genuine misery his thoughtless action of kissing Susie in public had generated, along with the memory of his own marriage that had faded so unhappily, was enough to make Alex push aside the extraordinary feelings he was gathering for the new woman in his life.

For something like doubt to be born. He was going to have to think carefully about the implications of where his heart was leading him. Later. Right now, Stella was the only person who mattered. He dropped the remote and closed the distance between them. Enveloped the rigid body of his daughter in a hug.

'Of course not,' he reassured her. 'I've only just met Susie, sweetheart. Yes, we like each other, but it was just a date. A…a holiday thing.'

'Oh…' He felt the stiff, hunched shoulders relax just a little, which was the best he could hope for, given that her hands were firmly gripping her crutches. 'I guess she is…kind of pretty.'

'Not my type, though,' Alex said lightly. 'Remember?'

'Yeah.' Stella's sniff sounded mollified. 'You need someone that looks like Mama.'

No! Although he remained silent, the word filled Alex's mind. Vehemently. Never again. Not that he'd ever taken that much notice of the colouring he'd been attracted to in the past, but it suddenly seemed like a revelation. Susie was light. Bright. Capable of filling his life with warmth and sunshine—the colour of those soft tresses of her hair that his fingers could remember trickling through. Those embryonic doubts were getting buried rapidly.

'But we don't *need* anyone, do we, Dad?' Stella pulled back but lost her balance and Alex had to keep a grip on her shoulders to steady her. His heart squeezed painfully on his daughter's behalf. This was so unfair, that she had trouble even taking a step backwards. The fall-out from the reminder of what Stella had had to face—what she still had to face—created a chill breeze that shifted the covering on those doubts. He could see them again. Feel their presence like a gathering storm.

'You said that when I was sick, remember?' Stella's dark eyes were fixed on his face. Huge and pleading. 'When Greta went away? You said it was just you and me and we'd manage. That we could get through anything if we stuck together.'

'I did say that,' Alex agreed, his heart heavy. 'And I meant every word of it.'

Stella gave a slow, single nod. She straightened and her balance was regained. Alex gave her shoulders a last squeeze and let go.

'How about we go and have a slap-up breakfast at the resort? Bacon and eggs. Or croissants. Something special.'

'Just you and me?'

Alex smiled. 'Just you and me, *latria*.'

Stella frowned. 'It's a long way.'

'I'll ring for a cart. Hey, you might get that funny dog coming along for a ride.'

Stella finally smiled. 'I love Garf. Can we get a dog, Dad? When we get back to Sydney? *Please*?'

This was more like the little girl he remembered. 'Maybe. Let's talk about it over breakfast. A dog is a big responsibility, you know.'

Stella nodded eagerly. 'I know. I could look after it, Dad. You wouldn't have to worry about it. And it would be good company.'

'I'll organise a cart. We'll talk about it.'

'I'm supposed to be back here by ten o'clock. Or do you want to call Susie and say I can't go to my physio session today?'

Alex shrugged. This wasn't the time to look enthusiastic about talking to Susie. Then he shook his head in a decisive, negative response. 'We've got plenty of time. You can be back by then. The physio's important.'

He picked up the phone to order their transport. He'd have to find a way to have a private word with Susie at some stage, though, wouldn't he? While he was satisfied he had reassured Stella, it might pay to suggest to Susie that they be a little more discreet. The relief the idea generated was surprising. Did he actually want to slow things down? Lose some of that incredible but now slightly alarming intensity?

Yes. Maybe he did. Maybe *he* needed time to get used to this as much as Stella did.

The session was going well.

'I'm going to increase the weight today.' Susie picked up a soft, flat weight that had wide Velcro strips. She fastened it around Stella's thigh. From the knee up this leg looked perfectly normal until you compared it with the other side. The muscle wastage made it half the size. Pathetic and weak looking.

It shouldn't be like this. Stella should have been having physiotherapy from the moment the amputation had taken place, but it was easy to understand why she had lost so much ground. Susie only had to think back to the sullen and uncooperative teenager she had started working with last week. They had come a long way in a very short time. A miracle, really.

Almost as big a miracle as having found Alex. The person she could see herself spending the rest of her life with. As he himself had put it—the other half of her whole.

'You'll find walking with your prosthesis much, much easier when you've built up this quadriceps muscle again,' she told Stella.

'Cool.' Stella lay back on the padded floor mat in this small gymnasium room that Susie used for indoor therapy sessions. 'I'm going to have to get good at walking 'cos Dad says I can have a puppy when I get home.'

'Really?' Susie beamed. 'That's awesome!' Good thinking on Alex's part, too. What better way to encourage Stella to really get moving? 'What sort do you want to get?'

'I want one like Garf.' Stella frowned, only partly due to the concentration of lifting and holding her leg. 'Only I don't know what he is.'

'I know. He's a Labradoodle.' Susie smiled at the girl, delighted to be able to help. To involve herself in what would be a major change for the small Vavunis family. A puppy would be so much fun.

Stella groaned. 'This is really hard.'

'I know. You're doing really well.' Susie held her hand under Stella's thigh for encouragement rather than support. 'Hold for five this time.' She counted slowly. 'Four…five… Good girl. Try and let it down slowly.'

Stella grunted with the effort and then lay still, catching her breath. 'What did you say Garf was again?'

'A Labradoodle.'

'What's that?'

'A cross between a Labrador and a poodle.'

'How do they do that?'

'One of the parents is a Labrador and the other one is a poodle. They're crossing poodles with all sorts of things these days. Designer dogs. They use poodles because they don't shed hair and it makes it a good choice for people with allergies or people that don't want their chairs covered with dog hair. I've heard of spoodles, which are spaniel poodle crosses, and schnoodles, which are schnauzer poodles, and—'

'But a Labrador's a big dog and poodles are tiny!'

Susie grinned. 'You get poodles in different sizes. A standard poodle is a big dog. Quite big enough to cross with a Labrador. Garf's quite a big dog, you know. Are you sure you want one that big? Have you got a big garden at home?'

'Pretty big,' Stella replied. 'And we live right on the beach. On the other side of the harbour from downtown.'

'Wow.' Harbourside properties in Sydney were some of the most expensive real estate anywhere. Susie hadn't really considered the implications of how wealthy Alex was. Would it make a difference? She could bet that, for a lot of women he met, it would be a very major attraction.

Not for her, though. She'd want Alex if he was a

waiter in a Greek restaurant or...or a professional surfer. But the pleasant notion of imagining Alex stripped to board shorts and striding into the waves with a board slung carelessly under one arm was the stuff of fantasies and hardly appropriate at the moment.

'OK, let's have another set of lifts. We'll go sideways this time and get those inner thigh muscles.' Conversation was a great distraction from the difficulty and boredom of these repetitive exercises. 'How much do you know about training puppies?' she asked Stella.

'Heaps. Jamie's got a dog and he's been telling me all about it. Did you know you can put a clock in the box with them when you first bring them home? It sounds like their mother's heart beating and it stops them being lonely and crying all night.'

'Sounds like a good idea. Puppies can get very lonely.'

'I think Dad might let it sleep in my room. For company, you know.'

Susie nodded but her thoughts had whirled off in their own direction. She could so easily imagine herself helping to train a puppy. Reminding Stella of her responsibilities regarding its food and exercise and house training. Helping out herself if Stella had better things to do—and what teenager didn't have better and much more urgent things to do once the novelty had worn off?

Yes. She could so see herself involved. With more than the adoption of a four-legged family member.

She could see herself as a member of that family herself.

For ever.

It wasn't until she became aware of the odd expression on Stella's face that Susie realised she was smiling.

That kind of secret smile that could only come from feeling…loved. Hastily, she straightened her face.

'Fabulous,' she congratulated Stella. 'Let me see how you manage with getting that prosthesis attached by yourself and then we'll do some walking with the rails.'

The smile sneaked back. Susie caught it herself in the large mirror that was positioned on the wall behind the parallel bars to help her patients with their posture. It was too hard to keep the smile bottled up when you were this happy, she decided. And it was hardly surprising that Stella eventually noticed.

'Why are you smiling so much?'

The smile widened. 'I'm happy,' Susie said simply.

'Why are *you* so happy?' The tone was a putdown— as though Susie wasn't important enough to be allowed happiness. Stella's expression settled into the kind of confrontational lines that Susie had thought conquered—at least, as far as she was concerned. They were friends, weren't they? Bonded by the success of the therapy, and more. By the girly fun of choosing clothes and playing with make-up and by that rescue from the trauma of Stella's first period. Why would Stella feel threatened by Susie being happy?

A faint warning bell sounded.

'I just am,' Susie said quietly. No big deal.

'Did you like having dinner with my dad last night?'

The warning bell grew louder. Susie chose her tone with care, keeping it casual. 'Yes, it was lovely, thanks.'

'It was my idea,' Stella told her. 'Dad wanted me to come but I didn't want to.'

Why not? Because the meal included *her*? Susie had to force a smile now. 'Fair enough. I guess it was more fun being at the movies with Jamie.'

Stella ignored the reference to the person they both knew was her primary focus at present, and that was when Susie felt the ground shift beneath her feet.

Stella *knew*. Had Alex said something at breakfast? She wasn't happy about it in any case. Any girly connection, like talking about a boyfriend, was clearly off limits. The bond Susie thought they had was being dismissed.

'I told him it would be a good way of saying thank you.' Stella had walked away from the rails now. She was picking up her crutches in a clear indication that she considered the session completed.

And it was—physically. Stella had been working hard for the whole of the allocated thirty minutes. It just didn't feel finished. Susie could sense a conclusion that wasn't far away, however. One that she just knew she wasn't going to like.

'That's all it was,' Stella announced as she headed for the door. 'Saying thank you.'

'Did your dad tell you that?' With a supreme effort Susie still managed to keep her tone light. Managed to pretend that her attention was on picking up the weights and tidying the room.

Stella opened the door. 'No.' She turned her head and met Susie's questioning gaze. 'He said it was just a holiday thing.'

A holiday thing?

Or had she said fling?

Did it make any difference?

No.

Susie actually felt physically ill. Hot and then cold. Her head was starting to ache.

Fresh air would be a good idea but Susie wasn't ready to face the world. She needed the privacy of this space and the time to try and make sense of the blow she'd just been dealt. Shutting the lid on the wooden box that housed the weights, Susie sat down on its lid.

It wasn't true!

She had seen the real truth in Alex's eyes that morning in that unguarded moment when he'd just woken up. She had felt it in the way he'd held her hand and matched his stride to hers on that walk along the beach. That lingering, gentle kiss with the sound of the soft surf behind them had only confirmed what she'd already known.

Not that he'd *said* he loved her. Not in words.

He *had* said he was grateful, though, hadn't he?

'Very, very grateful'.

Susie closed her eyes. Weird how an emotional blow could be making her feel so awful. Even her chest hurt as she forced herself to take a deep breath.

Maybe she'd been reading Alex all wrong. It wouldn't be the first time she had misinterpreted how a man felt about her. It wouldn't be the first time she had fallen in love with someone who had no intention of anything more than a brief encounter.

A…a…*fling*.

Oh, *God*!

Susie badly needed someone to talk to. Someone to help her organise thoughts that were fleeting impressions chasing each other. She wouldn't really know how she felt about this until she could corner them and have a proper look.

She shouldn't ring Hannah, who would be on duty in Emergency and probably busy, but Susie took out her mobile phone anyway. She could at least send a text and ask Hannah to ring her when she was free.

Except she couldn't because she had been with Alex last night and she'd forgotten she needed to recharge her phone. It was dead.

Emily wouldn't be available, either. She had taken off with Mike to walk the circumference of the island and have a private swim somewhere. It was a rare treat for neither of them to be on call. With no one leaving the island, Mike's helicopter was grounded and Emily was hardly likely to be needed as an anaesthetist for major surgery.

The more Susie tried to think about it, the faster the impressions moved and the worse it got. She had no one to talk to. Nowhere to go. As much as she would have liked to, she couldn't leave the island and go home and wait to see if Alex bothered coming to find her. She didn't want to go back to the penthouse suite. Even if housekeeping had already serviced the rooms, memories of those rumpled sheets and the hope that had been born there would be too painful.

Then again, maybe she was overreacting?

Would someone like Alex really confide in his teenage daughter to the extent of confessing to a holiday fling? Unlikely.

But what if Susie had been right and Alex had said something unguarded and then found himself facing Stella's disapproval? Would his feelings for her be strong enough to make him want to win his daughter over?

Even more unlikely. Alex had been solely responsible for Stella since she had been three months old. She had been the focus of his life. The pride and love she could see he had for his daughter wasn't something a newcomer would be allowed to dent. And Susie didn't want to compete for Alex's love. Not with his daughter. No way! Stella was a part of the picture here. It was either the whole package or nothing.

Her head was spinning enough to make her feel sick. She couldn't sit here for the rest of the morning. She had children who needed her attention. Like Jack. Was he still managing after being discharged from the medical centre?

Susie's legs felt stiff as she pushed herself to her feet. Her knees actually ached. When she opened the door to the treatment room, the light hurt her eyes.

Come to think of it, she had found the light overly bright on the beach that morning and her limbs had found the walk unusually tiring. She had been far too happy then to register the nebulous symptoms, however.

Not now.

Now it felt as if she was coming down with flu, which was no great surprise given her close contact with sick children like Jack and Robbie.

Susie's spirits plummeted even further. The prospect of a broken body to go along with a broken heart wasn't appealing.

But then the sound of children's laughter came from somewhere nearby and a young girl came tiptoeing past Susie. She had seen her before but couldn't remember the girl's name. She had almost no hair, like Stella, and stick-like limbs that suggested she was battling cancer. She grinned at Susie.

'We're playing hide and seek,' she whispered. 'Don't tell, if they come looking for me, will you?'

'I won't.' Susie smiled back.

Loud counting could be heard from another direction and then a gleeful, singsong shout. 'Coming! Ready or not!'

The girl slipped behind a flowering hibiscus shrub, crouching down with a giggle. Finding joy in a simple game. Pleasure in just being alive, with no thought of any misery life might still have to produce.

Something like shame twisted in Susie's gut. So she had a bit of a virus coming on. So what?

She had a man who was just using her for a few days of pleasure. Again, so what in the grand scheme of things?

Some cheesy little proverb she had once heard flitted into Susie's head.

Don't cry because it's over. Smile because it happened.

Her smile was gorgeous.

It had only been a few hours but Alex had missed seeing that smile so much. Not that he could tell Susie that, of course. Not with Stella sitting right beside him in the cart as he parked in front of the medical centre.

'We just picked up a picnic lunch that was delivered from the resort kitchens,' he told Susie. 'We're heading off for a ride up the mountain through the forest.'

He wished he didn't need to sound so distant. He wished he'd been able to talk to Susie before meeting her like this. To warn her that they needed to be careful in front of Stella. He'd tried to ring her on her mobile more than once that morning but it had gone straight to voicemail. She probably turned it off when she was busy with her patients. Stella had stayed close after her physio session. Had she sensed that Alex wanted to talk to Susie? And it had been Stella's idea that they did the rainforest ride and the picnic. She wanted his attention.

Why did he feel the need to apologise to Susie anyway? Or such a strong need to spend some time in her company? Being this close to this woman was not helping. He couldn't think straight. Any difficulties that a potential future together might present started shrinking. The desire to make it work seemed more and more possible.

Vital, even.

This was dangerous territory. He was here because of his daughter and he should be ashamed of having to remind himself of that.

'Father-daughter time,' he heard himself telling Susie, a little more crisply than he had intended.

She was still smiling. 'Sounds fun. Enjoy.'

Her gaze slid away from his almost instantly, which was unexpected. Disappointing. Alex was getting too used to that kind of prolonged eye contact that only lovers could have. That almost telepathic line of communication where so much could be said without words. Clearly, Susie didn't want that at the moment.

Why not? Had he been wrong in gauging her level of involvement? Was she not as blinded by what was happening between them as he was?

Another good reason to step back and slow things down. To think carefully. Not that he'd been doing much else that morning. His brain had veered from dreaming up ways he could encourage Stella to see how their lives would be enhanced by including Susie to trying to convince himself he wasn't being selfish in wanting this so much. Had it all been a waste of energy? Had he been plotting something that might upset Stella for no good reason?

The feelings were new. Powerful. Confusing.

Alex could feel a frown creasing his forehead as he stared at Susie's profile for a full second after she'd looked away. He was still frowning as he answered his mobile.

'Danny's had another seizure,' Charles told him. 'It lasted for twenty minutes and he's been vomiting repeatedly ever since.'

'GCS?'

'Down. He's not talking and he's only opening his eyes to painful stimuli.'

'What's his blood pressure?'

'He's hypertensive. Systolic's at 120. Diastolic's dropped, though. Pulse pressure is 15 degrees higher than it was this morning.'

'Heart rate?'

'Sixty.'

'That's well down, isn't it?'

'Yes. It was 96 on last recording.'

'Pupils?'

'Sluggish.'

This wasn't good. It sounded as though the pressure in Danny's head had rapidly increased for some reason.

'He needs intubation and ventilation,' Alex said tersely. 'I'm right outside the centre. I'll be two minutes, max.'

Both Susie and Stella were staring at him as he snapped his phone shut.

'Sorry, but I have to go. Danny's crashed.'

'That's OK.' But Stella didn't look happy.

Alex waved a hand at the cane basket in the cart as he jumped out. 'Maybe you and Susie could go and have that picnic somewhere.'

He saw the wary look that passed between them.

'I'm not really very hungry,' he heard Susie say as he turned away. 'And I've got some gear I need to pick up here.'

'I'm all right by myself,' Stella announced. 'I'll wait. You won't be that long, will you, Dad?'

Alex turned back briefly, shaking his head. 'No idea, sorry. Eat the lunch while you're waiting. I'll try to be as quick as I can.'

He also had no idea what was going on between Susie and Stella, but he didn't have time to think about why they might be avoiding each other's company.

Women! Old and young, they were a mystery.

It was a relief, in a way, to increase his speed and head towards something he *did* know how to deal with. Towards the kind of challenge he was well used to facing and—far more often than not—winning.

CHAPTER NINE

THE ODDS on winning this time were looking slimmer by the minute.

Tiny Danny was now deeply unconscious. Intubated and attached to the ventilator. The head of the bed was elevated thirty degrees and an infusion of mannitol was running. And he was still critically ill.

'We have to evacuate him. He can't be treated without appropriate imaging and monitoring.'

'I agree absolutely.' Charles was looking stressed, which was more than understandable. The quarantine would have to be broken when they still didn't know exactly what they were dealing with on Wallaby Island, but the ramifications of doing that were not the only problem.

The medical centre was short-staffed right now. Alex and Charles had dealt with the intubation and ventilation of Danny by themselves. Beth was having a day off and apparently she and Angus were off on an expedition that had something to do with Angus's interest in the local birds and mosquitoes.

The extra Crocodile Creek base hospital staff on duty were flat out, looking after new inpatients.

Dr Cal Jamieson was dealing with another adult from the resort who had come in, having fainted and not regained consciousness for a significant length of time. She was showing all the symptoms of a systemic viral infection but had to be investigated for other possible problems. Miranda was looking after one of the asthmatic children from the camp who had been rushed in after a severe attack secondary to a chest infection, and Ben, the ranger, was sitting miserably in a room, still waiting to be seen.

'I've got hold of another one of the rangers,' Charles informed Alex. 'He's going to try and locate Mike and Emily. We'll need the rescue chopper to transfer Danny, and Mike doesn't seem to have taken his cellphone with him.'

Alex adjusted the settings on the ventilator. 'Mild hyperventilation,' he said aloud. 'Controversial in greater amounts, I know, but this should be enough to give us some cerebral vasoconstriction and reduce the ICP. We'll run fluids to maintain normal arterial blood pressure and peripheral perfusion.'

'What else can we do?'

'If he was in my unit, I'd be looking at doing a ventriculostomy to drain some CSF but, then, I'd have the results of an MRI or CT and I'd actually have a good idea what was going on in his head.'

'Gut feeling?'

'ICP's through the roof. The increase in head circumference may be minimal and it's a crude parameter in any case, but with what else is going on with the GCS, blood pressure and heart rate, it's adding up to a pretty clear picture. How long before we can move him, do you think?'

Charles shook his head. 'Could take thirty minutes to find Mike. I'm guessing another thirty minutes to get the chopper ready for take-off, seeing as it hasn't been used for a few days.'

'And it's a thirty-minute flight to the base hospital?' Alex looked at the child lying on the bed. He scanned the screens of the monitoring equipment, reading the figures. 'It's too long. He's deteriorated even in the fifteen minutes since we intubated.'

'Could you do the ventriculostomy here?'

'I prefer to do them in the OR but they can certainly be done as a bedside procedure. Not ideal but it happens often enough in an ED.'

'What would you need?'

'Preferably two assistants. A twist drill with an 11/32 bit. Local with adrenaline. Scalpel, needle holder, suture materials and dressings. A drainage set-up and a sterile ventricular catheter.'

'I'm not sure if we've got something that specific but I'll check the head trauma kit. I'm pretty sure we've got a drill and I do know we've got chest drains, pericardial drains and lumbar-puncture cannulae.'

'None of those would be long enough. I need something closer to thirty centimetres.'

'I'll check.' Charles swivelled his wheelchair. 'And I'll find us some assistance.'

This was the last thing Susie had expected to be doing.

She wasn't prepared. Or competent, for that matter. She felt uncomfortable just being gowned and masked like this. Uncomfortable and unwell. Her chest felt tight and her head ached. She felt dizzy but that was probably partly from nerves.

'I'm not a nurse,' she warned Alex. 'I haven't been trained for anything like this.'

Alex had been scrubbing his hands. Now he was drying them carefully with a towel that had come out of the package containing a gown, mask and gloves.

'All I need is for you to stabilise Danny's head. You can stay at the side of the bed and you'll put your hand under the drapes to hold his chin. Don't worry, I'll talk you through it.'

For a second, dark eyes over the mask met Susie's gaze. She saw a warmth and confidence in her ability that she was far from feeling herself. She also saw a flash of connection. A faint echo of what she'd seen in Alex's eyes early that morning. The distance that had been between them outside in Stella's company had been closed.

It was confusing. Hope was being offered but Susie had no idea whether to allow herself to accept it. She couldn't begin to try and think it through, either. She needed every ounce of concentration right now. Alex thought she was capable of doing this and she was determined not to let him down.

'Could you tie my gown for me, please, Susie?'

Concentration was harder getting this close. Susie had to reach around Alex to find the tie. She was wearing gloves but she still had to be careful not to touch him. So close but not close enough to touch.

Maybe she would never touch this man again. The thought was a desolate one and Susie's feet felt like lead as she moved to her position on one side of the small boy.

It was Charles who picked up a swab, soaked in iodine solution, in a pair of forceps to swab Danny's bald head.

'No shaving needed. That makes life a bit easier for us.'

While the iodine was drying, Alex held his hands crossed loosely in front of his chest, looking over the sterile tray Charles uncovered.

'This is excellent,' he approved. 'We've got everything we need. Where did you find the catheter?'

'Burrhole kit for head trauma. We set this place up to cover every eventuality we could think of and we weren't short of funding, thanks to people like you.'

Alex ignored the tribute. 'I'll have that local now, thanks. Susie, could you push the bed out a little further from the wall, please? I need a good three feet of space to get in while I'm drilling.'

Susie swallowed a wave of nausea. 'Drilling?'

The glance she received was almost a reprimand. 'You not up to this?'

'I could hold the head,' Charles offered.

'I need the height and the elevation. It's going to be a lot easier for someone that's standing.'

He hadn't needed to snap like that. Susie caught Charles's gaze, trying to apologise for the put-down. They both knew he *could* stand and do this if really necessary. A tiny quirk of an eyebrow let Susie know it was up to her. Did she want to step aside? Admit failure in front of Alex? Susie had the strong impression that Charles was encouraging her. He wanted her to show Alex what she was made of. To be strong.

'I can do it,' Susie said quietly. 'I just wasn't aware of what the procedure involved.'

'I'm going to drill a small hole,' Alex explained. 'Here.' His gloved fingers began palpating a line across the middle of Danny's head. 'Kocher's point,' he murmured, as though running through his own checklist. 'The junction of the plane one centimetre anterior to the coronal suture in the mid-pupillary line.' He raised his voice. 'Charles, did you remember to ask Danny's mother whether he was left- or right-handed?'

'I did. He's right-handed.'

Alex nodded. 'I would have gone for the majority anyway so we would have got the non-dominant side.' He started injecting local anaesthetic into Danny's scalp. Susie looked away from the bulging of the fluid under the skin.

This was a little boy here. One who had been happily and enthusiastically involved in camp activities only a couple of days ago. Life was a fragile business, wasn't it? You had to make the most of every minute. She stole a glance at Alex.

Don't cry because it's over, she reminded herself. *Smile because it happened.* And it might not be over. Or did Alex always look at women like that? The women he invited into his life just for the odd, convenient times on holiday?

'It's lucky we've got you here, Alex,' Charles said.

Susie said nothing. Her life might be a lot easier in the foreseeable future if they hadn't had Alex here.

Charles was watching closely as the surgeon picked up the scalpel and made a very small incision. 'Even with the facilities at Crocodile Creek, we wouldn't have your expertise for this kind of procedure. It's not something I'd like to be doing blind.'

'It's a blind procedure, no matter what the imaging facilities are. It's a matter of using surface landmarks and aiming carefully. We get junior residents in neurosurgery doing this under supervision. A good ED physician should cope as well.' Alex's eyes crinkled a little at the sides. He was smiling. 'Experience never hurts, though, does it?'

Susie wasn't sure she would agree with that statement, either. Just as well neither of the men seemed to notice how silent she was. She watched quietly as Alex turned the drill. Slowly. Again and again. She drew in a careful breath, hoping to banish dizziness, and concentrated on holding Danny's head very, very still.

'I'm losing resistance,' Alex commented. 'We should be between the cortical layers. Not far to go now.'

'We'. Strangely, Susie did feel part of this small team. Important. To be doing this for Alex—by his side—made it special. Susie closed her eyes and willed Danny to get through this procedure. To get well again.

Charles was holding a syringe of sterile water that he was using to flush away the small fragments of drilled bone coming to the surface. Bleeding was minimal as Alex threaded the catheter into place and thankfully Susie didn't feel any fainter. She was able to hold her position and keep Danny's head still until the fine tube was sutured into place, the end finished with what looked like a complicated set of adaptors, stopcocks and a drainage bag.

'I'm only going to draw off two to three ccs at a time,' Alex said. 'Any more and the changes in intracranial anatomic relationships will be too rapid. I'll stay with him until we can arrange transport.'

Charles checked his phone. 'I've got a text message,' he reported. 'Mike's been located. He's on his way.'

'Good. Can we organise transfer to a neurological ICU? Brisbane, perhaps?'

'I'll sort it,' Charles promised. 'Can you go with him as far as the Crocodile Creek airport? We should be able to arrange a fixed-wing air ambulance with ICU staff to meet you there.'

'Of course. What about quarantine difficulties?'

'Isolation procedures will have to be put in place but that's not our problem. Danny has to be moved and I'm going to make sure that happens.'

Over the next hour, as arrangements fell into place, Danny's condition improved and stabilised. Various staff came and went and Alex was focused on his monitoring, but Susie stayed with Danny. Holding his hand even though he was unconscious. Talking to him and reassuring him just in case it made a difference.

It felt very odd going outside, finally, when Danny was on a stretcher and being moved to the helicopter pad. The light was far too bright and the air felt as if it held no oxygen. Susie walked just in front of Alex down the ramp that came out just beside the huge old fig tree that had a bench seat beneath it.

The back view of the figure on the bench was still easily recognisable, thanks to that backwards-facing baseball cap.

'Oh, no!' Alex groaned. 'I completely forgot to let Stella know what was going on. You don't think she's been sitting out here waiting all this time, do you?'

'I don't think she's minded.' Susie bit her lip. Being just ahead of Alex, she had the first glimpse of the other figure on that bench which Stella's back had screened. Under the shade of that lovely old tree, the two teenagers appeared to have taken their relationship to a new level. Surely this wasn't their first kiss, given the way they were oblivious to their surroundings?

Or maybe not so oblivious. Susie heard Alex suck in his breath as he saw what she could see and at the same moment Stella and Jamie became aware they were being observed. Two startled faces appeared and Susie could almost see the blood draining from them. Looking that scared made them look an awful lot younger. Young and terrified.

'Go back to the cabin, Stella,' Alex snapped. 'I'll talk to you as soon as I get back.'

A quick glance behind her at the fury on Alex's face and Susie could feel scared on Stella's behalf. And that new emotion was the straw that broke the camel's back. All the confusion of the morning—the joy of believing Alex felt the same way about her as she did for him, the despair in the wake of the bombshell Stella had dropped, the worry about Danny and the stress of having to watch such an invasive procedure at such close quarters reached bursting point. The maelstrom of emotion found release in a form Susie could never had anticipated.

Anger.

As they reached the bottom of the ramp, Susie stepped away. Alex and the other staff could manage the transfer of Danny from now on. She didn't want to be this close to Alex any more. It was all too difficult and she simply didn't have the strength.

'I'll stay here,' she said coolly. 'And don't worry, Alex. It's probably nothing.' She spoke through gritted teeth. 'Just a...*holiday thing*.'

Susie turned and walked away. Away from the stunned expression on Alex's face. Away from the pale, frightened girl still sitting on the bench. What she needed right now was space. Time out. By herself.

The way she had been before the Vavunis family had come into her life.

The way she would be again in the very near future.

'Susie! Wait!'

Susie kept going. She felt as if she was swimming

through the air. The beach was where she needed to be, with a cool breeze hopefully and some shade. A good thinking spot like that one between the old dinghies. How ironic that she was heading there again, angry with Alex. A lifetime seemed to have come and gone since she had last headed for that spot. And that time she had been trying to find Stella, not get away from her.

The track was further away than she remembered. It wasn't this far surely? No. There it was. Not far. It just *felt* like for ever.

'Susie! *Susie*!'

Stella crumpled onto the sand beside Susie and burst into tears. 'I'm sorry,' she sobbed. 'I know I was mean to you but…but why won't you *talk* to me?'

The wail was desolate. A frightened girl being abandoned. There was no way Susie could ignore the plea.

'Of course I'll talk to you.'

'Oh…' With a fresh outburst of sobbing, Stella threw herself into Susie's arms. 'What am I going to *do*? Dad's going to *kill* me!'

Susie patted her back. 'I don't think so, hon. Calm down.'

'He *saw* me…kissing Jamie! Of course he's going to kill me.'

Typical teen. It was all about her, wasn't it? But maybe that wasn't a bad thing. Susie didn't really want to have to think about herself. That would only make her feel worse.

'He might be upset,' she conceded, 'but you would expect him to be, wouldn't you, after that fuss he made about your clothes and our make-up?' Talking was making her feel breathless. Dizzy. 'He's having to adjust to you growing up, Stella. It's not something that's going to happen overnight.'

Susie could feel an odd crackling sensation in her chest and she knew what it was. She dealt with the accumulation of fluid in people's lungs all the time. She needed to cough and try to clear her airways but it was enough effort to just breathe at the moment. And talk. Stella needed to talk.

'You made it OK—about the clothes and the make-up.' Stella lifted a tear-stained face to peer hopefully at Susie. 'Can you talk to him about *this*?'

'Um…' Susie's head was spinning again. She still hadn't caught her breath properly.

'I can't go back to the cabin like he told me to,' Stella declared. 'I'll have to run away. Or kill myself or something.'

'Don't be ridiculous.' Susie was in no mood to put up with teenage melodrama. 'It was just a kiss.' She glared at Stella. '*Wasn't* it?'

'What? *Oh*!' Stella looked horrified. 'Of course it was just a kiss. I'm only *thirteen*!'

Susie had to smile. 'You sounded just like your father then.'

'And that was the first time I've ever kissed *anybody*.' A wobbly smile tried to shape Stella's lips. 'Nobody's ever wanted to kiss *me* before.'

Susie's smile twisted into something poignant. She could understand how special it made Stella feel only too easily. And it was important, wasn't it, that she learned she was still attractive? Something to be celebrated, really. 'You didn't pick a very good place, hon, did you?'

'I didn't know Dad was going to come out. I'd been sitting there for *hours*. Jamie saw me when he was on the beach and he came to keep me company and…and we started talking, you know, about liking each other, and…and it just happened.'

'As it does,' Susie murmured wryly.

'And now Dad's going to kill me and Jamie has to go back to Melbourne after the camp and I'll probably never see him again and…and I don't know how I'm going to live without him.'

'You'll survive.'

Stella's jaw dropped. A look of contempt flashed over her features and she drew away from Susie. 'You don't know anything,' she accused. 'You don't understand.'

'Don't I?' The dismissal angered Susie. Goodness, she was scratchy today, wasn't she? Not like herself at all. 'You think I've never been in love, Stella?' She sucked in a breath. 'That I don't know what it's like to… think that life isn't going to be worth living…if it doesn't include that one, special person?' Another breath. They weren't lasting very long. 'It's something that happens to us all. Welcome to adulthood.'

Stella was staring, still open-mouthed.

'You… Are you *in love* with my dad?'

Susie said nothing. Would a 'neither confirm nor deny' policy work with a teenager?

'You *are*! Oh…' Stella hunched into a ball, drawing her knees up and putting her head down. 'And I told you what Dad said…'

Susie shrugged. 'Best to know these things sometimes.' She had to draw in a breath to finish the sentence and she could feel the rattle in her lungs. 'Don't worry about it.' She still didn't seem to be able to catch a breath so she also leaned forward, using the side of the dinghy for support. Her head was turned sideways.

'Where are…your crutches?'

'Dunno. I dropped them up on the track somewhere.
I couldn't go fast enough to catch up with you.'

'You were…*running?*' Susie was amazed. Flattered.
Stella had wanted to talk to her *that* much? She was that
important to the girl?

Stella shrugged. She wasn't looking for praise so it
didn't matter. She sniffed and scrubbed her nose with
her hand, sitting silently for a minute. That was fine by
Susie. All *she* wanted to do was close her eyes and rest.

'I didn't like it when I saw you kissing Dad on the
beach this morning,' Stella said suddenly, the words
tumbling out. 'I thought maybe he'd think you were
more important than I was, and I liked that he's been
taking more notice of me. But he's only been doing that
because of you, hasn't he? And…and I didn't know, did
I?'

'Huh?' Susie was confused. 'Didn't know what?'

'About—you know…kissing. About…being in
love.'

'Oh…' She should talk to her, Susie thought hazily.
About being in love. Relationships. Safe sex. All sorts
of things.

Too many things. She was way too tired for this.

'I didn't think I wanted to have you around,' Stella
was saying, 'but I was wrong, OK? I *like* having you
around. I like talking to you. Maybe I don't need a
mother any more like I did when I was a kid but you'd
be a cool stepmother.'

Stella was doing something strange with her face.
Showing her teeth. It took Susie several seconds to
realise that it was a smile. The words were becoming
fuzzy. Like static.

'You'd be, like, a *friend*, you know? Or a big sister.'
The face loomed closer. 'What's the matter?' Stella
seemed to be shouting. The words hurt Susie's ears.
'You look really…weird!'

'I…don't…feel very good.' Susie could feel herself
slipping down the side of the dinghy. 'Hard to…
breathe…'

It couldn't have been coincidence.

Not to use the same, *stupid*, throw-away phrase that
had been intended only to reassure Stella.

Alex stood on the scorching tarmac of the apron of
Crocodile Creek's airport. Afternoon heat shimmered
around him and he could smell the tar. He watched the
last of the figures—dressed in full personal protection
equipment of splash suits, masks, goggles and
gloves—climb into the plane. A sombre reminder of
how serious this viral threat could still be. The side
door of the twin-engined plane was being locked shut.
Danny was now in the safe hands of an experienced
ICU registrar and nurse, about to be airlifted to a place
that could take good care of him. He had done all he
could and at least he had stabilised the little boy long
enough for transport.

He could, finally, turn his thoughts to more personal matters.

It should have been the shock of seeing Stella kissing
that boy that was foremost in his mind, but it wasn't.

It was Susie's face he could see. The misery and,
yes, anger in those blue eyes. The sound of her voice,
the words a complete dismissal of anything worth
having.

A holiday thing.

Did Susie actually believe that? Had she been upset earlier? Was that why she wouldn't look at him? Why she had sounded so offhand when he'd been telling her about the intended picnic?

A picnic that hadn't taken place. The day had been hijacked. He'd left Stella sitting, abandoned, outside the medical centre. It would have been worse to go outside and see her sitting all alone, wouldn't it? Instead of having a cuddle with someone who clearly thought she was special.

Special enough to kiss.

Like Susie…

He would have to talk to Stella, of course, and the prospect of that conversation gave Alex a hollow sensation. He'd never thought ahead to being the solo parent of a teenage girl, had he? All that tricky baby stuff, the childhood woes, even the cancer treatment seemed easy compared to what Alex knew he would have to contend with in the next few years.

How much better it could be if Susie was by his side.

'*No.*'

Alex actually said the word aloud. How much better it *would* be. He increased his pace, striding back to where Mike was keeping the helicopter rotors turning, ready to whisk them both back to Wallaby Island. He was going to sort this out. With Stella *and* Susie. He'd faced huge challenges in his life before so why should this one be any more daunting?

Because his life—or at least his happiness— depended on it?

The figures emerging from the terminal building were a surprise. One man had a large camera balanced on his shoulder. Another held a fluffy microphone on a long stick. A third person was a glamorous woman that Alex vaguely recognised. The front person for one of the news shows?

'Dr Vavunis!' The call was demanding. 'Stop! Please! We'd really like to talk to you.'

'I have nothing to say.'

More figures could be seen at a distance, emerging from within the terminal building, with more running from around one side. Whatever cordon the Crocodile Creek police force had put up had been breached, but not for long.

'We're here to cover the airlift of the mobile laboratory to Wallaby Island,' the reporter said hurriedly.

Alex turned his head automatically. He'd already noticed the vast Iroquois helicopters with their camouflage paintwork well to one side of the runway. Chains were being secured around the white box that was presumably the laboratory.

The police were almost here.

'Oi!' One of them yelled. 'Just what do you lot think you're doing?'

'We've since learned,' the reporter continued doggedly, 'that you've just brought a critically ill child over from Wallaby Island. Who gave you permission to do that? What kind of precautions have been taken to make sure this virus isn't being spread?'

Alex's cellphone started ringing. Mike was climbing out of the helicopter to see what was happening.

'Stay back!' he yelled at the television crew. 'Don't you know anything about safety zones around choppers?'

An argument broke out between the police and the television crew.

'Freedom of the press,' he heard the woman say furiously. 'If we want to take the risk, then we have every right…'

Alex looked at the display screen of his mobile. It was Stella calling. He answered it automatically, latching on to what had to be the most important thing happening around him.

'Stella?'

The sounds he could hear were incomprehensible for a few moments. Then he realised that his daughter was crying so hard she couldn't catch her breath.

'Calm down,' he said. 'It's all right…' Alex searched for some way to get through this wall of misery he could hear. 'Hey…Star! We'll get through this, OK?'

'Dad!' Stella finally got a word out. '*Help*. You've got to help.' The words were strangled and difficult to interpret. Alex had to concentrate. To block out the annoying buzz of the people around him. 'Susie can't breathe!' Stella sounded panicked now. 'I can't wake her up.'

'*What*? Where are you? What's happened?'

'I don't know,' Stella wailed. 'I was talking to her and she looked really sick and then she said she couldn't breathe and now she's just lying there. We're on the beach, beside the boats, and…and I don't know what to *do*.'

Alex was thinking fast. Or trying to.

The reporter was being hauled away by the police but she wasn't giving up.

'Dr Vavunis? We're on. Just in your own words.'

'Go away,' Alex growled. 'I've got nothing to say.'

'*Dad*?'

'Stella! Is there anyone else you can see on the beach?'

'No. Oh, wait. I think I can see Jamie. He's got my crutches.'

'Call him.'

The female reporter was standing with her back to him now. 'This helicopter has just been used to evacuate one of the flu victims from Wallaby Island,' she was telling the camera. 'Sydney neurosurgeon Alex Vavunis is refusing to comment on the evacuation. We can only assume this has been done without the relevant permission…'

'Hello?' The query was tentative. Alex spared a moment's sympathy for the lad who was having to talk to the father of the girl he had got into trouble with for kissing. He'd have to talk to the lad later, as well. 'Tell me what's happening,' he commanded. 'Are you close to Susie?'

'Yeah. She looks as if she's asleep.'

'Put your fingers on her neck. Tell me if you can feel a pulse.'

There was only silence to listen to now on the phone. On the tarmac, Mike was telling the television crew to get lost. Airport security was arriving.

'Trouble?' Mike asked Alex.

'It's Susie.' Alex couldn't believe how afraid this was making him feel. 'She seems to have collapsed on the beach. I—' His attention went back on his phone. 'What did you say, Jamie?'

'I can feel a pulse.'

'Is she breathing?'

'I can't… How can you tell?'

'Make sure she's lying on her back. Tip her head back so her airway is open and then— Are you listening, Jamie?'

'Yeah.'

'I want you to run faster than you've ever run in your life. Get back to the medical centre. Get help.'

Mike's hand was on his shoulder. 'Let's go, mate. Let's get you back where you need to be.'

Alex simply nodded. For once in his life he was happy to accept both the gesture of empathy and any help anybody could offer.

For the first time in his life he was feeling helpless. Lost.

As though he was about to lose something he knew he could never find again.

CHAPTER TEN

'ARDS? ADULT respiratory distress syndrome?'

'Yes.' Charles was positioned beside the bed that held the still form of Susie.

Alex hadn't expected that. He'd run through every possible cause of unconsciousness he could think of during the nightmare flight to get back here, realising how little he knew about the woman he loved. Was she epileptic? Diabetic? On some form of medication she might have inadvertently over- or under-dosed on?

History couldn't be repeating itself. The coincidence of Susie suffering an aneurysm like the one that had killed Helena was far too freakish to be conceivable, but the fear had been very real. Was it because he'd been through this before that made it so much worse? Or was it because it was Susie this time?

Seeing her like this—attached to the same kind of life-support equipment they'd had to use for Danny such a short time ago—was unbearable. A flash of what he'd done for Danny presented itself. Pushing the hard laryngoscope into place. Forcing a tube down the trachea. Choosing settings on a machine that were intended to keep someone alive.

This couldn't be happening. Not to *Susie*.

'Who intubated her?'

'I did.' Miranda was on the other side of the bed, drawing a sample from what appeared to be an arterial cannulation on Susie's forearm. 'She came in unconscious, Alex. Cyanosed. Pulse oximetry was below seventy per cent. CPAP wouldn't have been enough to bring it up.'

'What's the level now?' Would it help to try and stand on the professional side of this equation?

'I'm just going to run this arterial sample through.' Miranda looked up at the monitors. 'We're up to eighty-two per cent on the external oximetry.'

No. Trying to look at this as a clinician wasn't helping. The level was too low and inadequate oxygenation was incompatible with life.

'Chest X-rays are up there.' Miranda moved to the bench where the small machine that could instantly analyse the level of oxygen in arterial blood was positioned. She tilted her head toward the illuminated wall-boxes.

Alex looked at the images. At the evidence of fluid filling space that should be available for gas exchange.

'Pneumonia?'

'Presumably viral,' Miranda nodded. 'Relatively sudden onset.'

'Oh, my God,' Alex breathed. Susie must have already been sick when she'd been standing there holding Danny's head for him. She certainly hadn't looked happy but he'd assumed she'd been having difficulty being part of what must have seemed like gruesome surgery for her. And he'd been completely focussed on his young patient. He should have seen that Susie wasn't well.

She must have thought he didn't care. And all the time she'd been thinking of what Stella must have passed on to her. That he *didn't* care. That she was just a passing fancy to keep him amused on holiday.

Viral pneumonia. One of the few things that could kill a perfectly healthy adult within a very short time.

The hollow feeling inside Alex grew. He had the odd sensation that he might be falling into it.

'What are you doing for her?' The words came out gruff. Demanding. 'Apart from respiratory support?'

'There's not much else we *can* do, Alex.' Charles spoke gently. 'You know that. We've given her oseltamivir as an antiviral medication. We're supporting fluid balance and oxygenation as best we can.'

Alex covered his eyes with his hand for a moment. Then he pushed his hair back, taking his hand over his head to rub his neck. He had to think. To find a way through this.

'She might just need a few hours' support.' Miranda's expression was deeply sympathetic. 'She was exhausted when she came in. I suspect she's probably had symptoms for some time that she was ignoring.'

'We've kept sedation as light as possible,' Charles added. 'She can override the machine and breathe for herself any time. As soon as that starts happening and the oxygen levels are acceptable, we'll extubate her.' His gaze was understanding. 'Stay with her if you like, Alex. I'll make sure Stella's taken care of.'

'Stella will want to see her. She sounded distraught on the phone.'

'Yes.' Charles's face creased in sympathy. 'She seems to think this is *her* fault for some reason. I've got Marcia sitting with her in my office at the moment.'

Alex moved closer to the bed. He picked up Susie's hand. It was warm. Far too warm. 'What's her temperature?'

'Thirty-nine point seven. Down a bit from when she came in. Heart rate's down, too.'

It was still way too fast—130 on the digital screen and the audible beeping, along with the rhythmic hiss and click of the ventilator, made the atmosphere very tense. This was critical-care stuff. Susie should be in the best-equipped ICU the country had to offer. Not in a toy emergency room on a tropical island.

Charles had to be a mindreader. 'We're doing everything possible, Alex. Everything that would be done no matter where she was. There's no point trying to evacuate her.'

They couldn't, anyway. The potential disruption and stress could tip the balance into disaster.

Alex held the limp hand a moment longer. He moved his fingers, feeling the shape of that hand. Remembering, all too easily, the feel of those fingers when Susie was conscious. Touching *him*.

He bent down and put his mouth close to Susie's ear. 'I'm here,' he murmured. 'You're going to be all right.' Alex had to swallow past the painful constriction of his throat. She *had* to be all right. There simply wasn't an acceptable alternative. 'I've got to go and talk to Stella but I'll be back. *We'll* be back.' He was holding her hand too tightly. Reluctantly, he let it go and touched her cheek instead. A soft stroke with the back of his forefinger.

'*Agape mou*, Susie,' he said very quietly.

He looked up. Miranda was busy with the blood test. Charles was probably listening but what the hell did that matter? Alex hadn't felt this vulnerable since he'd lost Helena. Or since he'd been given Stella's frightening diagnosis of cancer. Maybe it was time to stop being proud of his ability to hide vulnerability. Time to be honest about what really mattered in life. What if he lost Susie and she'd never heard him say the words that were crowding his head right now? Drowning out every other thought? She wouldn't understand his Greek, would she?

'I love you, Susie,' he whispered, his voice catching. '*So* much.'

Straightening, he didn't even try to avoid Charles's gaze.

'I love her,' he said more steadily. Louder. Speaking the words he knew were true beyond any shadow of doubt. 'She doesn't know that yet. Stella doesn't know it yet but I'm going to marry this woman, Charles.'

Charles was smiling. As though *he'd* known it all along. As though he approved.

'Will you stay with her?' Alex asked. 'Until I've had a chance to talk to my daughter?'

'Of course.'

'Look after her.' It was another demand but it was tempered with an attempt to return the smile.

Not a very good attempt, mind you. Alex tightened every muscle in his face as he headed for the door. Showing vulnerability was one thing. He wasn't about to cry in front of anyone.

Stella was crying.

'It's my fault. It's *always* my fault.'

Marcia slipped out of the office and Alex took her chair beside his daughter. He took her hand in his.

'What are you talking about, *latria*?'

'It was my fault Mama died when I was born and Greta went away because I got sick with my leg and… and now Susie's going to die, and it's because I told her she didn't matter.'

Where on earth was all this coming from? Alex tried to focus on one thing at a time.

'What makes you think you had anything to do with Mama's death? That's simply not true.'

'But you always tell people she died when I was a baby.'

'You were three months old. Your mother died because a blood vessel in her brain had something wrong with it and it burst. It had nothing to do with you being born.'

Surely he had explained that more than once? Or had it been too long ago, when Stella had been too young to understand? Had she heard about some woman dying in childbirth and come to her own conclusion somewhere along the way?

'It's my fault,' he said aloud. 'I didn't explain properly. I've never talked to you enough, Star, and I'm sorry. I'm going to change that, starting right now.'

But Stella didn't seem to have heard the assurance. 'You…you called me Star!'

'You've become one,' Alex told her solemnly. 'Actually, I think you've always been one, but I've only just really noticed. Here. You've grown up so much all of a sudden. Hey…' He wanted to make her feel better. To smile, if that was possible. 'You've even got a boyfriend!'

Stella's face crumpled. 'I don't want one. Not if Susie's going to die.'

'She's not going to die.' Alex spoke as if it was the

truth because it *had* to be the truth. He ignored a twinge of something like panic that he might be wrong and grabbed something to change the subject.

'And it wasn't your fault that Greta went away. That was never going to work out.'

'But she left because I got sick.'

'She left because I wanted her to leave,' Alex said firmly. 'And, yes, part of the reason I wanted her to leave was because it was obvious she didn't care enough about you. And you, Stella Vavunis, are still the most important person to me. You come first.'

'More important than Susie?'

Alex couldn't read her tone. Weirdly, she sounded as though she wanted a negative response.

'Important in a different way. You're my daughter, Stella. My child. *Fos mou*. My light. You have a part of my heart that can never belong to anyone else. A very big part.'

'But not all of it?'

What was she wanting him to say? 'The human heart is extraordinary,' Alex said carefully. He wasn't sure what kind of reassurance Stella wanted but the intense gaze he was being fixed with told him that this was important. He had to reassure her but he also had to be honest. He had room in his heart to love more than one person. 'It's kind of elastic,' he added.

'So there's room for Susie?'

Alex swallowed. 'Do you *want* there to be room for Susie?'

Stella nodded, tears streaming down her face. 'I don't want her to die, Dad. I want…I want you to marry her.'

She didn't mean that, surely? She was overwrought.

Too emotional. She blamed herself and she'd been there when Susie had collapsed. It was way too much for a young girl to handle.

'Susie's not going to die,' he repeated. 'Dr Wetherby is helping to look after her. She needs some help breathing at the moment but you can come and see her. It's possible she might be able to hear what you say to her.'

'Can I tell her I'm sorry?'

'What for?'

'For telling her you didn't care. That you didn't love her as much as she loves you.'

'Susie *loves* me? She *told* you that?'

Stella hung her head. 'Not…exactly.'

The disappointment was crushing. Hope felt as fragile as Susie's hold on life was right now. Stella looked up as though sensing his despair and Alex could see something he'd never seen before. A very adult kind of expression. His daughter wanted to protect *him* and the knowledge that she'd grown up that much was poignant. He had never felt this close to Stella.

'But she didn't say she didn't, either.'

Alex squeezed her hand. 'Let's go,' he suggested. 'We can be with Susie. Tell her how important it is for her to get better. For both of us.'

Stella stumbled a little as she got to her feet but she shook her head when Alex offered the crutches.

'I can do without them,' she said. 'For Susie.'

This was blissful.

She was lying on a grassy hilltop. The wrong way so that her legs were higher than her head, which made her brain feel too full of blood, but she didn't want to move. The breeze here was so wonderful. Cool and refreshing. She could fill her lungs with the wonderful air. Again and again.

'She's breathing on her own,' someone said.

Of course she was. What a silly thing to say!

Susie wasn't alone on her hilltop, which was why she was feeling so happy. Alex was beside her. Holding her hand. Saying things she couldn't understand sometimes but she knew they were words of love.

Kardoula mou.

Hara mou.

Anasa mou.

Latria mou.

Susie's lips curved. It was all Greek to her!

'Susie?' Stella was here, too. Running through the long grass on the hillside. 'Are you smiling?'

Of course she was smiling. She was so happy. So proud of Stella.

Star. That was one word in Greek she would never have trouble translating.

Ouch!

Something hurt. She could feel it catching in her throat. She was choking! Struggling to get some more of that air.

'It's all right.'

Alex's voice. Soothing.

'They've taken the tube out. You can breathe by yourself now, Susie. You're going to be all right.'

Alex?

Good grief, he sounded close to tears. Where was the man with the world at his fingertips and everything under control? The man who had owned that jetty like a catwalk and had strode, unannounced virtually, straight into Susie's heart?

Something was beeping insistently, like an alarm

clock someone had forgotten to switch off. And something smelt strange. A hospital sort of smell that didn't belong near fresh grass.

She was dreaming.

Or was she waking up?

This was all too confusing so Susie let herself drift. Thinking only of the one thing she was sure about—that it was Alex holding her hand.

Both her hands.

How was he managing to do that?

It didn't matter. Alex was capable of doing anything. And Susie would do anything for *him*.

Anything at all.

The hill was long gone when Susie finally opened her eyes.

Somehow, finding she was in a hospital bed was not unexpected. Or frightening. The smell made sense. So did all the beeping noises. She'd been sick. She remembered now. She'd been on the beach and Stella had been crying.

Susie blinked. Alex was beside her bed. Her hand was covered by both of his but the grip was loose and his head was bowed. Was he asleep? Susie curled her fingers experimentally and instantly they were gripped firmly. Alex's eyes snapped open and his gaze captured hers.

'Hi…'

'Hi, yourself.' Alex closed his mouth. Then he opened it again but no sound came out.

'It's dark,' Susie said.

'It's the middle of the night, *kardoula mou*.'

She'd heard those words before, but where? Susie frowned in concentration as she tried to remember.

'It means *my little heart*,' Alex told her. 'You are my heart, Susie. My breath. My soul.' His smile was embarrassed and his inward breath sounded shaky. 'I've been…worried about you.'

He'd been more than worried. Susie could see the deep lines on his face. The rumpled hair. He looked even worse than he had that night when he'd been so upset by Stella locking herself in the bathroom. That dark light in his eyes spoke of vanquished despair. She had thought—hoped—he could care about her, but this much? She had never dreamed anyone could care *this* much.

Her lips trembled. 'I'm OK.'

'You are now, yes.' Alex's hands were moving over hers, feeling her fingers. Touching her skin and joints questioningly, as though reassuring himself that she was in one piece.

'Was I very sick?' She must have been, Susie realised. To look like this, Alex must have feared for her life. She would feel like that if *he* was very sick.

'You were,' Alex said sombrely. 'And you'll need to rest for a while yet. The drugs have helped you turn the corner but you've still got a little way to go.'

'What's wrong with me?'

'Pneumonia. Viral.'

'Bird flu?'

'No.' Alex smiled. 'We still don't know exactly what it is but I heard that Angus and Beth are onto something. I've also heard that Danny's doing well.'

'Oh…thank goodness.'

'You helped. Our little operation got him through the complications from the virus and the scans he's had show nothing nasty going on in his head so I'm hopeful he'll bounce back. He's a tough little cookie.'

'Me, too.' Susie tried to sound convincing. She wanted to get better. Fast.

'I'm sure you are.' Alex was still smiling. 'But we're still going to move you to Crocodile Creek Hospital first thing in the morning. To make sure you get the best of care while you recuperate.'

With an effort, Susie shook her head. 'I don't want to go.'

'Why not? From what I've seen and heard, you've got half the town worried about you. There will probably be a huge crowd to welcome you when Mike lands that chopper tomorrow.'

'But…you're here.'

He understood. A smile danced in his eyes. 'I'm coming with you. So is Stella. You don't think we're going to let you get away from us that easily, do you?'

'I don't want to get away.' The effort to talk was tiring so Susie stopped trying. She just smiled instead and gave herself up to free-floating under Alex's gaze.

It was the same feeling she'd had before, except that this time *she'd* been the one to wake up. Did that make it any less believable?

No. Susie basked in the look.

The *love*.

And she drew in a breath. This was as good as lying on the hill. Or was it? She had to make the effort to speak again.

'Where's Stella?'

'Sleeping. Charles let her have a bed in the room across the corridor. She totally refused to go back to camp. She sat here for hours, holding your other hand. We had to wait until she was so deeply asleep she didn't notice getting carried to bed. She loves you, Susie.' Alex leaned down and placed a gentle kiss on her lips. '*I* love you.'

Susie smiled again. 'I love you, too. You're not going to get sick, are you?'

'No.' Alex was smiling again. 'I've never felt better in my life. How could I not? You're going to be well again and you're going to be my wife.' He paused for just a heartbeat. 'At least, that's what Star is hoping. What I'm hoping—with all my heart.'

'My heart,' Susie echoed. 'Yes. That's what you are for me, too, Alex.' Her eyes were drifting shut.

'Sleep,' Alex whispered. 'I'm here with you. I'll always be here for you.'

Susie pushed her eyelids open again. 'Yes,' she said.

Alex looked startled. 'You're awake again. You need to sleep longer than that, *latria mou*.' His face came closer as he leaned towards her.

'But I had to say yes.'

He was going to kiss her. He was so close Susie could feel his breath on her face as he spoke. 'Why did you need to say yes?'

'Yes, I'll marry you.'

'Oh…' Alex bent his head a fraction further so that his forehead was resting against hers.

A connection Susie could feel right through her body.

Touching her soul.

She had no idea how long they stayed like that. Maybe she even slept again because the soft sound on her other side was unexpected. Quiet enough for it not to have disturbed Alex, who must have finally given in to exhaustion. A nurse, perhaps, here to take her temperature or something? Charles, checking up on another of his people?

No. It was Stella. Looking pale and tired but standing there without any aids. Looking at the way her father's head was sharing Susie's pillow.

'Are you OK?' she asked Susie.

Susie smiled and nodded her head gently. The sound and movement woke Alex, who jerked his head up. He blinked at his daughter and Stella smiled back.

'You asked her, didn't you, Dad?'

'Yes.'

'What did she say?'

'I said yes,' Susie said.

Stella looked taken aback. 'That's all?'

'It was enough for me,' Alex said.

'And me,' Susie said.

Stella looked at her father and then at Susie and then a smile lit up her face. 'Can I be your bridesmaid?'

Alex and Susie spoke together. 'Yes,' they said.

CHILDREN'S DOCTOR, MEANT-TO-BE WIFE

BY
MEREDITH WEBBER

Meredith Webber says of herself, "Some ten years ago, I read an article which suggested that Mills & Boon were looking for new medical authors. I had one of those 'I can do that' moments, and gave it a try. What began as a challenge has become an obsession—though I do temper the 'butt on seat' career of writing with dirty but healthy outdoor pursuits, fossicking through the Australian Outback in search of gold or opals. Having had some success in all of these endeavours, I now consider I've found the perfect lifestyle."

CHAPTER ONE

IT WAS, Beth decided as she helped other camp volunteers assemble the children for the night spotlighting tour in the rainforest, the best of all possible jobs. True, she was missing out on the gala evening that followed the official opening of the newly rebuilt and extended Wallaby Island Medical Centre, but to share the joy of a night drive in the rainforest with these kids meant so much more to her than dressing up and dancing.

With the extension of the Wallaby Island Medical Centre and the appointment of a permanent doctor—her very own self—to staff it, Crocodile Creek Kids' Camp had also been expanded, so now they could take up to twenty children at a time, providing a fun holiday with tons of different experiences for children who couldn't normally enjoy camp life. This week, the camp was playing host to children with respiratory problems and to a group of children in remission from cancer.

'No, Sam, I'll drive today with Ally in the front. You take care of Danny in the back. Remember he's not feeling very well so don't tease him.'

She settled the three children she was responsible for

this evening into one of the little electric carts that were the only mode of transport on the island, and guided the cart into line behind the slightly larger one that Pat, the ranger, would be driving. He had seven children on board with another volunteer, and he also had the spotlight.

Pat checked his passengers then wandered back to Beth's cart.

'You're a glutton for punishment, aren't you?' he said. 'Someone was telling me you'd just come off duty and you're volunteering for this job. Should be at the party, shouldn't you?'

He was just making conversation, Beth knew, but he was a nice guy and deserved an honest answer.

'I'm far happier out playing with the kids than partying,' she told him. 'And remember, this is an adventure for me, too. I haven't been in the rainforest at night.'

'Got your light?'

Beth held up the big torch he'd given her earlier.

'Now, your job is to shine it on the animal, so the kids see all of it. My light will hold the eyes and keep it still.'

'I think I can manage that,' Beth told him, although Sam was already asking if he could hold the torch and she knew they'd have a battle of wills about torch-holding before the evening finished. Sam might be slight for his eight years, but he had the fighting qualities of a wild tiger.

Pat returned to his cart and they drove off into the rainforest, taking the track that led to the resort on the other end of the island for about five minutes, before turning off towards the rugged mountain that stood sentinel over the rainforest.

The little carts rolled quietly along, the whirr of their

wheels the only sounds, then Pat stopped and doused his headlights, Beth pulling up behind him.

'Now, remember we have to be very quiet or the animals will run away,' Beth whispered to her charges as Pat turned on the big light and began to play it among the palms and ferns that crowded the side of the track.

'There,' he said quietly, and the children 'oohed' as the light picked up wide-open, yellow-green eyes. Beth shone her torch to the side of the eyes and nearly dropped the light. They were looking at a snake. A beautiful snake admittedly but still a snake.

Diamond patterns marked its skin, and though it was coiled around a tree branch, Beth guessed it had to be at least eight feet long.

She wasn't very good with snakes, so the torch shook in her hands while her feet lifted involuntarily off the floor of the cart. Ally, perhaps feeling the same atavistic fear, slid onto her knee.

Fortunately Pat's light moved on, finding now, fortunately on the other side of the track, a tiny sugar glider, its huge eyes wide in the light, its furry body still.

There followed a chorus of 'Ahh!' and 'Look!'

How could children keep quiet at the wonder of it, especially when the little animal suddenly moved its legs so the wing-like membrane between them spread and it glided like a bird from one branch to another?

Next the light was low, catching an earthbound animal, sitting up on its haunches as it chewed a nut.

'A white-tailed marsupial rat,' Pat said quietly, while Beth's torch picked out the animal's body and then the white tail.

The children's hushed voices startled the little animal, sending him scuttling into the undergrowth, so Pat changed lights, holding up another torch and shining ultra-violet light around until it picked up a huge, saucer-shaped fungus, the light making it glow with a ghostly phosphorescence so the children 'oohed' and 'ahhed' again in the wonder of it.

They moved on, Sam listing on his fingers how many animals he'd seen, soon needing Danny's fingers as well.

'You'll be onto toes before long,' Beth said to him, when Pat showed them the emerald-green eyes of a spider in his web.

'This is so exciting,' Sam whispered back. 'Isn't it, Danny?'

But Danny, Beth realised, was tiring quickly and, with a couple of children already in the hospital with some mystery illness, she decided she'd take him back to camp. Ally, too, had probably had enough.

'What if you go into Pat's cart and I take Ally and Danny back to camp?' she suggested to Sam.

'No, I'm Danny's friend so I'll stay with him.'

'I'll go with Pat,' Ally said, surprising Beth, although she knew she shouldn't be surprised by anything children did.

She shifted Ally into the bigger cart, found somewhere to turn her cart, then headed back, stopping when she heard any rustling in the bushes, letting Sam sit in the front so he could shine the torch around and spotlight the animal.

'Over there! I can hear a noise over there. Shine the torch, Sam,' Danny whispered, when they were close to the junction of the main track.

Beth eased her foot off the accelerator and Sam turned on the torch, finding not an animal or reptile but a human being.

A very tall human being.

A very familiar human being!

'A-A-Angus?'

His name came out as a stuttered question, and she stared at where he'd been but the torchlight had gone. Sam had taken one look at the figure, given a loud scream, flung the torch down into the well of the cart and darted away, heading along the track as fast as his little legs would carry him.

Danny began to cry, Beth yelled at Sam to stop, to wait, but it was Angus who responded first, taking off after the startled child, calling to him that it was all right.

Beth took Danny on her knee, assuring him everything was okay, driving awkwardly with the child between her and the wheel, hoping Sam would stay on the path, not head into the bushes.

'He got a fright,' she said to Danny, 'that's all. We'll find him soon.'

Fortunately, because Danny was becoming increasingly distressed, they did find him soon, sitting atop Angus's shoulders, shining Angus's torch.

'He's not a Yowie after all,' Sam announced, as the little cart stopped in front of the pair. 'I thought he was a Yowie for sure, didn't you, Danny?'

Danny agreed that he, too, had thought Angus was the mythical Australian bush creature, although Beth was willing to bet this was the first time Danny had heard the word.

As far as Beth was concerned, she'd been more afraid Angus was a ghost—some figment of her imagination conjured up in the darkness of the rainforest.

Yowies, she was sure, were ugly creatures, not tall, strong and undeniably handsome…

A ghost for sure, except that ghosts didn't chase and catch small boys.

Which reminded her…

'You shouldn't have run like that, Sam,' she chided gently as Angus lifted the child from his shoulders and settled him in the cart where he snuggled up against Beth and Danny. 'You could have been lost in the forest.'

'Nuh-uh,' Sam said, shaking his head vigorously. 'I stayed on the path—I wasn't going in the bushes. There are snakes in there.'

'And Yowies,' Danny offered, but he sounded so tired Beth knew she had to get him back to camp.

And she'd have to say something to Angus.

But what?

Not knowing—feeling jittery, her composure totally shaken—she let anger take control.

'I've no idea what you were doing, looming up out of the bushes like that,' she said crossly. 'You scared us all half to death.'

'Beth? Is that really you, Beth?'

He was bent over, peering past Sam towards her, and he sounded as flabbergasted as she felt.

'Who *is* that man?' Sam demanded, before she could assure Angus that it was her. 'And what was he doing in the bushes?'

Exactly what I'd like to know myself, Beth thought, but

her lips weren't working too well, or she couldn't get enough air through her larynx to speak, or something.

Fortunately Angus wasn't having any problems forming his speech.

'I'm Angus and I'm staying at the resort. Right now, I'm doing the same thing you're doing, looking at the animals at night. That's why I have my torch.'

He lifted it up, showing it again to Sam who took it and immediately turned it on and shone the light on Danny and Beth.

'Turn it off,' Beth said, finding her voice, mainly because the light had shown how pale Danny was. 'We've got to get back to camp.'

She wasn't sure who she'd said it to, the kids or Angus, but she knew she had to get away, not only because of her own fractured mental state but because Danny needed his bed.

She nodded at Angus—it seemed the least you could do with an ex-husband you found wandering in the rainforest at night—and put her foot on the accelerator.

They shot backwards along the track, Sam laughing uproariously, even Danny giggling.

'Little devil,' Beth muttered at Sam, turning the key he'd touched while they'd stopped to forward instead of reverse.

She accelerated again and this time moved decorously forward, passing Angus who was still standing by the track.

If the shock he was feeling was anything like the shock in her body, he might still be there in the morning.

Back at the camp, she left the two children with their

carers, explained that Ally had stayed with the larger group, then made her way to the medical centre.

Was she going there to avoid thinking about Angus?

She tried to consider it rationally, wanting to answer her silent question honestly.

Decided, in the end, she honestly wasn't. Little Robbie Henderson had been asleep when she'd come off duty and although Grace Blake was an excellent nurse and would page Beth if there was any change, she wanted to see for herself that he was resting peacefully.

And check on the other patients, of course.

And it *would* help her not think about Angus!

She parked the cart outside the medical centre, frowning at a dark shadow on the ground just off the edge of the parking area. A shearwater going into its burrow? She watched for a minute but the bird didn't move.

Hadn't Lily picked up a dead bird the other day?

And Ben, one of the rangers who was sick, had also been collecting dead birds.

'I was just going to page you.' Grace greeted Beth with this information as she walked into the hospital section of the medical centre. 'He slept quite well for an hour, then woke up agitated. Actually, I'm not sure he's even fully awake. Luke's here, but he's with Mr Woods, the man you admitted this afternoon with a suspect MI.'

Luke Bresciano was a doctor with the Crocodile Creek hospital and rescue service and, like all the Crocodile Creek staff, he did rostered duty at the medical centre. Officially he was the doctor on duty tonight, but Beth had admitted Robbie, talking to him about his family back home as she'd examined him, and the little boy had relaxed in her presence. If he was distressed, he might react better to her than to the other staff.

She went into the room where he tossed and turned feverishly on the bed, a small figure, his left leg and arm distorted by the cerebral palsy that had also affected his lungs, so even a mild infection could result in respiratory problems.

'Hey, Robbie!' she said quietly, sitting by the bed and taking his hand in hers, smoothing back his floppy dark hair from his forehead, talking quietly to him.

He opened his eyes and looked at her but she knew he wasn't seeing her, lost as he was in some strange world his illness had conjured up.

'Go to sleep,' she told him, gently smoothing his eyes shut with the palm of his hand. 'I'll stay with you, little man. I'll look after you.'

And holding his hand, she began to sing, very softly, a funny little song she remembered someone singing when she'd been very young, about an echo.

Had the song sprung from her subconscious as a result of seeing Angus—as a result of that echo from the past?

Surely not, but seeing Angus had unsettled her so she sang to calm herself as well as Robbie, changing to other songs, silly songs, singing quietly until the panicky feeling in her chest subsided and the peace she'd found on this island haven returned.

So what if Angus was here? She was over Angus. Well, if not over him, at least she'd managed to tuck him away into some far corner of her mind—like mementos tucked away in an attic. Could memories gather enough cobwebs to become invisible?

To be forgotten?

Not when they still caused pain in her heart.

'Bother Angus!' she muttered, then hurriedly checked that her words hadn't disturbed Robbie.

They hadn't, but what made her really angry was that the peace she'd found in this place—even in so short a time—could be so fragile that seeing Angus had disturbed it.

Here, working in a medical centre with a kids' camp attached, she'd thought she'd found the perfect job. Caring for the children, playing with them, sharing their experiences, she was finally getting over the loss of her own child—her and Angus's child. In the three years since Bobby had died and she and Angus had parted, this was the closest she'd come to finding happiness again. Ongoing happiness, not just moments or days of it.

At first she'd wondered how she'd cope with the kids, especially with the fact that many of the children at the camp had cerebral palsy, the condition Bobby had suffered from. But from the day of their arrival she'd known that didn't matter. Just as Bobby, young though he'd been, only three when he'd died, had fought against the limitations of his condition—severe paralysis—so these kids, whether asthmatics, diabetics, in remission from cancer or with CP, got on with their lives with cheerful determination, relishing every fun-filled moment of camp life, and drawing staff and volunteers into the joy with them.

Yes, it was the perfect job, in a perfect place—a tropical island paradise. What more could a woman want?

The L-word sneaked into her mind.

Pathetic, that's what she was!

Had it been seeing Angus that had prompted such a thought?

Of course it must be. Seeing Angus had raised all kinds of spectres, weird spectres considering Angus had never loved her—she'd known that from the start—although back then she *had* allowed herself to dream…

Not any more!

She pushed her thoughts back into the cobwebby attic. So what if he was on the island? He was at the resort at the other end, nowhere near the camp or medical centre, so there was no reason for them to meet again.

None!

Except that the island was no longer a haven, she admitted to herself in the early hours of the morning when Robbie slept but her own fears came to the fore, tiredness magnifying them.

She'd tried to tell herself she was unsettled because of the Angus incident—because of his escape from the attic of her mind—but, in fact, it was a combination of things that had her so uptight.

So desperately worried!

Seeing Angus had brought back memories of Bobby's death. Bobby had died of a massive chest infection they'd at first thought was simply flu.

With vulnerable children was there ever 'simple' flu?

And then there were the birds…

Her island paradise had become a place of sick children and dead birds!

The combination of words played again and again— like an echo—in Beth's head as day dawned, grey and wary, outside the window. Now, tired though she was, she tried to put aside emotion and just list the facts.

The celebration of the opening the previous day had been dampened by the fact that the ten-bed hospital attached to the medical centre was half-full. Sick adults were bad enough, but the sick children?

Lily, Jack and Robbie hospitalised here in the medical centre, Danny not well last night. For these children a simple cold was a big concern—flu was even worse.

Bird flu!

Not a fact but an inescapable thought…

The feared words hadn't yet been spoken but Beth imagined she could hear them murmuring on the soft tropical wind that blew across the island and whispering at her from the palm fronds. The worrying thing, as far as Beth could see, was that no one was doing anything to find out if this might be the flash point of a pandemic.

Charles Wetherby, head of Crocodile Creek Hospital and the prime mover in expanding the medical presence on Wallaby Island, would normally have taken charge, but he'd been distracted by the official events and the dignitaries attending them, to say nothing of the fact that his ward, Lily, was one of the sick children.

Distracted generally, it seemed to Beth, although she didn't know him well enough to be sure distracted wasn't part of his usual personality.

As far as the mystery illness was concerned, blood samples *had* been sent to the mainland for testing—that was a fact—but there were so many different strains of flu, would an ordinary pathology lab on the mainland think to consider bird flu or even have the facility to test for it?

In the pale dawn light Beth sighed, knowing she had to go through with a decision she'd made some time around midnight as she'd sat beside Robbie's bed, looking at the child but seeing a much smaller and younger child—not Robbie, but Bobby. *Later we'll call him Bob*, Angus had said, *it's more manly than Rob*.

But Bobby had never grown to be a man, and Angus?

She sighed again.

Angus was a short electric cart ride away, in the luxury resort on the southern end of the island.

Angus was a pathologist who specialised in epidemiology.

Angus would know about bird flu.

She had to go there.

She had to ask him.

Before another child got sick…

Before another child died…

Beth left the small electric cart in the parking lot at the edge of the resort.

'Stay!' she said firmly to Garf, the camp's goofy, golden, curly labradoodle, who considered riding in the carts the best fun in the world and had hurled himself in beside her before she'd left the clinic.

Garf smiled his goofy smile and lay down across the seat.

Not that he'd guard the cart for her—he'd be more likely to encourage someone to steal it so he could have another ride.

Smiling at remembered antics of the dog she'd grown so fond of, she walked along the path through the lush tropical greenery that screened the small cart park from the resort itself, and found herself by the pool. It looked a million miles long and she realised it had been designed to seem as if it was at one with the surrounding sea. At this end, there were chairs set around tables that sheltered under wide umbrellas, and closer to the pool low-slung loungers, where a few people were already soaking up the very early rays of the rising sun.

To her right, the resort hotel rose in terraced steps so in a way it repeated the shape of the rugged mountain beneath which it sheltered.

'Wow!'

The word escaped her, although she'd been determined not to be impressed by the magnificence of the newly rebuilt resort.

And possibly because she was so nervous over approaching Angus that she'd been concentrating on the setting to exclude Angus-thoughts from her mind, and talking to herself helped.

Then she remembered Robbie Henderson—and Jack and Lily and the other patients—and why she was there. With steady steps and a thundering heart, she made her way towards the building.

'You are not the wimpy twenty-five-year-old who fell for the first hazel-eyed specialist who looked your way—awed by someone in his position taking notice of a first-year resident,' she reminded herself, muttering under her breath to emphasise her thoughts. 'You're a mature, experienced woman now, a qualified ER doctor and head of the Wallaby Island Medical Centre. All you're doing is what any sensible medico would do—seeking advice from an expert.'

Who happened to be the love of your life, an inner voice reminded her.

'Past tense!' she muttered at the voice, but it had been enough to slow her footsteps and she needed further verbal assurances to get her into the resort.

'What's more, he won't bite you. He'll want to help. In fact, it's probably only because he hasn't heard about the kids being sick that he hasn't already offered. And he's kind, he's always been kind—work-obsessed but, once distracted from his work, very kind...'

She'd been telling herself these things all night, repeating them over and over again to Garf on the fifteen-minute drive through the rainforest that separated the camp and clinic area from the hotel, but the repetition wasn't doing much to calm her inner agitation, which churned and twisted in her stomach until she felt physically sick.

'He's not answering the phone in his room, but if you go through to the Rainforest Retreat, he could be having breakfast there.'

The polite receptionist, having listened to Beth's explanation of who she was and whom she wanted, now pointed her in the direction of the Rainforest Retreat, a wide conservatory nestled into the rainforest at the back of the hotel building, huge potted palms and ferns making it hard to tell where the real forest ended and the man-made one began.

Beth paused on the threshold, at first in amazement at the spacious beauty of it and then to look around, peering between the palms, her eyes seeking a tall, dark-haired man whose sole focus, she knew from the past, would be his breakfast.

Whatever Angus did, he did with total concentration—yep, there he was, cutting his half-grapefruit into segments, carefully lifting the flesh, a segment at a time, to his mouth, chewing it while he attacked the next segment.

'The kitchens in hotels never get it cut right through,' he'd complained during their weekend honeymoon in a hotel in the city, and from then on it had been her mission in life—or one of them—to ensure his grapefruit segments *were* cut right through.

Although Angus's morning grapefruit hadn't been her concern for three years now—three long years…

She was trying to figure out if that made her sad or simply relieved when she saw his concentration falter—his forkful of grapefruit flesh hesitating between the bowl and his mouth. Which was when she realised he had company at the table—company that had been hidden from Beth's view by a palm frond but was now revealed to be a very attractive woman with long blond hair that swung like a curtain as she turned her head, hiding her perfect features for a moment before swinging back to reveal them again.

Reveal also a certain intimacy with the man who'd returned his concentration to his grapefruit.

Beth's courage failed and she stood rooted to the spot, wishing there was a palm frond in front of her so no one would see her, or guess at her inability to move.

But she was no longer an anxious first-year resident overawed in the presence of a specialist—she was a competent medical practitioner, and Robbie and the other children needed help.

Now!

Legs aching with reluctance, she forced herself forward, moving like a robot until she reached the table.

The blonde looked up first—way past attractive! Stunning!

If Beth's heart could have sunk further than her sandals, it would have.

'I'm sorry to interrupt,' she said quietly, finally detaching Angus's attention from his grapefruit, pleased to see he looked as surprised as she felt nervous.

'Beth?'

The word croaked out, though what emotion caused the hoarseness she couldn't guess.

'I'm sorry I couldn't talk to you properly last night but Danny, the little boy in the back, he wasn't well and I wanted to get him to bed. How are you, Angus?' she managed, blurting out the words while clutching her hands tightly in front of her so he wouldn't see them shaking.

He stared at her and she wondered if he'd written off her presence in the rainforest the previous evening as a bad dream.

His silent regard tightened her tension and she forgot about maturity and experience and bumbled into speech again.

'I really am sorry to interrupt, but we've a crisis at the medical centre and I—'

She saw from his blank expression that he didn't understand, just seconds before he echoed, 'Medical centre?'

'I thought you'd have heard—there was an official opening yesterday, a gala evening last night here at the hotel. The medical centre's at the other end of the island— an outpost of Crocodile Creek Hospital on the mainland.

There's always been a small centre here on the island but it was extended because after Cyclone Willie the Crocodile Creek Kids' Camp was rebuilt and expanded, and with the extensions to the resort it seemed sensible to have an efficient and permanent medical presence on the island.'

The words rattled off her tongue, her apprehension firing them at him like bullets from a gun.

'Crocodile Creek—that's Charles Wetherby's set-up—has a rescue service attached—yes, perhaps I did hear something,' Angus said, not needing to add, to Beth anyway, that if whatever he'd heard didn't directly concern him or his work then he'd have filed it away under miscellaneous and tucked it into a far corner of his brain.

But now he was frowning at her, the finely drawn dark brows above hazel eyes encroaching on each other, indenting a single frown line above his long, straight nose.

'And what has this to do with you?'

The question was too sharp and for the first time it occurred to Beth she should have phoned her ex-husband, not run here like a desperate kid, seeking his help. For a desperate kid was what she felt like now, not mature at all, standing in front of Angus like a child in front of the headmaster in his office at school.

Had this thought communicated itself to Angus that he suddenly stood up, pulled out another chair, and told Beth to sit?

In a very headmasterly voice!

But her knees were becoming so unreliable, what with the lack of sleep last night and the strain of seeing—and talking to—Angus again, that she obeyed without question.

At least now she could hide her hands in her lap and he wouldn't see them shaking.

Angus sat down again, pushed his nearly finished grapefruit half away and turned his attention to Beth. Most of his attention, that was. Part of it was focussed on pushing back memories and totally unnecessary observations like how tired she looked and the fact that she always looked smaller when she was tired, and she'd lost weight as well, he was willing to bet, and why, after three years, did his hands still want to touch her, to feel the silky softness of her skin, to peel her clothes off and—?

'Start with why you're here,' he began, hoping practicalities would help him regain control, not only of the situation but of his mind and body. 'Not here in this room right now, but on this island—connected to this medical centre.'

'I work there. I'm the permanent doctor at the centre. I saw the job advertised and thought it would be wonderful, just what I needed, something different.'

Far too much information! Admittedly she was flustered—wasn't he?—but...

He shuffled through his mental miscellaneous file—the Crocodile Creek Kids' Camp was for children with ongoing health problems or disabilities. Had she chosen to work in a place where she'd be seeing these children because of Bobby?

Of course that would be a factor, though it went deeper than that. On a resort island people—especially these kids—came and went. She wouldn't have to become too involved with any of them, and if she wasn't involved she wouldn't get hurt—Beth's self-protective instincts coming into full play—the same self-protective instincts that had made her adamant about not having another child…

Although maybe he'd suggested that too early—too soon after Bobby's death…

'Angus?'

The woman's voice—not Beth's, Sally's—made him wonder if he'd lingered too long in his thoughts. He was usually better than this—quick on the uptake, fast in decision-making, focussed…

He turned to his companion—tall, elegant, beautiful, clever Sally. She was relatively new on his staff, but they'd been dating occasionally and he'd suggested she attend the conference with him thinking…

He glanced towards Beth, weirdly ashamed at what he'd been thinking then furious with himself for the momentary guilt.

'Sorry, Sally, this is Beth, my ex-wife.'

'I'll leave you to catch up,' Sally said, in a voice that suggested any chance of them getting to know each other better over the weekend had faded fast.

But though he knew she wanted him to tell her to stay— to touch her on the arm as he said it—he made no move to stop her as she stood up with her coffee and raisin toast and moved through the room to another table on the far side, where other conference attendees were enjoying a far noisier breakfast.

'I'm sorry, I didn't mean to upset anyone,' Beth said. 'I'll explain quickly, then you can explain to…Sally? I'm sure she'll understand.'

The words made no sense at all to Angus, who failed to see why Beth should be concerned about Sally. Although Beth did have a habit of being concerned about everyone—even in little ways. He'd remembered that, with a twinge of regret, as he'd wrestled with his grape-fruit.

'There's a bug going around on our side of the island that presents with flu-like symptoms but three of the children, Jack and Robbie from the kids' camp and Lily, Charles Wetherby's ward, are quite seriously sick, very high temperatures that we're having trouble controlling with drugs, and on top of that are the birds. There are dead birds, shearwaters I think they're called, all around the island.'

She glanced around and added, 'Probably not here—the groundspeople would clear them away—but over on our side. Lily picked one up and gave it to Charles, thinking he could cure it. We've vulnerable children in the camp, Angus, and although no one's saying anything, I'm sure in their heads they're whispering it might be bird flu.'

Her wide-set blue eyes looked pleadingly into his, asking the question she hadn't put into words.

Would he help?

As if she needed to ask—to plead! He felt a stab of an-noyance at her, then remembered that Beth, who'd had so little, would never take anything for granted. And cer-tainly not where he was concerned. Hadn't he accepted her decision that they should divorce and walked away without another word, burying himself in work, using his ability to focus totally on the problems it presented to blot out the pain, only realising later—too late—that he should have stayed, have argued, have—

But that was in the past and right now she needed help.

'Do you have transport?'

'Electric cart parked out the back.'

'Then let's go.'

He stood up and reached out to take her hand to help her stand—an automatic action until he saw her flinch away as if his touch might burn her. Pain he thought he'd conquered long ago washed through him.

How had they come to this, he and Beth?

CHAPTER TWO

SKIN prickling with awareness of Angus by her side, Beth led the way back to the cart, then sighed with relief when she saw Garf.

He could sit between them, they could talk about the dog and she wouldn't have to think of things to say.

'Good grief, what's that?'

Beth had to smile. Garf looked more like a tall sheep or a curly goat than a dog.

'That's Garf, he loves a ride. Move over, dog!'

Garf had sat up and yapped a welcoming hello. He was now regarding Angus with interest.

Was this a man who knew the exact place to scratch behind a dog's ear?

'He's a labradoodle, a non-allergenic kind of dog,' Beth replied. 'The kids love him and when they're all up and about he's usually with them. His other great love is riding in carts and it's impossible to tell him he's not wanted— he just leaps in.'

To her surprise, Angus and Garf took to each other like old friends, although Angus was firm about not wanting a thirty-odd-kilo dog sitting on his knee.

'He likes to hang his head out,' Beth explained apologetically, but Angus had already worked that, easing the dog to the outside of the seat and sliding across so his body was pressed against Beth's.

'I could make him run back—it's not far,' she said, thoroughly unnerved by the closeness.

'No, he's fine,' Angus said, so airily, she realised with regret, that he wasn't feeling any of the physical upheaval that was plucking at her nerves and raising goose-bumps on her skin. He might just as well have been sitting next to a statue.

A statue that kept thinking about a blonde called Sally.

'I'm sorry I interrupted your breakfast,' Beth said, and although she knew it was none of her business, she plunged on. 'You and Sally? You're a couple? That's good. I'm glad. I'm—'

'If you say I'm happy for you I'll probably get out and walk back to the resort!' Angus growled. 'For your information, Sally and I are work colleagues, nothing more. We're here for a conference. I'm giving a paper on Tuesday.'

'Oh!'

The relief she felt was so totally inappropriate she blustered on.

'But you're well. Busy as ever, I suppose?'

Angus turned and gave her a strange look then began to talk about the tiny finches that darted between the fronds of the tree ferns.

So, his personal life was off-limits as far as conversation went—Beth felt a momentary pang of sympathy for Sally who probably was quite interested in her boss and didn't realise just how detached from emotion Angus was. And personal issues like health and work had just been squashed; what did that leave?

Beth joined the bird conversation!

'The bird life's wonderful here,' she managed, her voice hoarse with the effort of keeping up what was very limp and totally meaningless chat.

'The night life's pretty surprising as well,' he said, ice cool, although he did offer a sardonic smile in case she hadn't caught his meaning.

'Well, it *was* last night,' she admitted with a laugh, remembering how strange she'd found it, in the past, that Angus, who was usually so serious, could always make her laugh. And with that memory—and the laugh—she relaxed.

Just a little.

'I nearly died to see a person standing there, then to find it was you.' She shook her head. 'Unbelievable.'

'But very handy, apparently,' he said, and she had to look at him again, to see if he was teasing her.

But this time his face was serious.

'Very handy,' she confirmed, although it wasn't handy for her heart, which was behaving very badly, bumping around in her chest as if it had come away from its moorings.

'How long have you been on the island?'

She glanced his way again and her chest ached at the familiarity of his profile—high forehead, strong straight nose, lips defined by a little raised edge that tempted fingers to run over it, and a chin that wasn't jutting exactly but definitely there. The kind of chin you'd choose not to argue with—that had been her first thought on seeing it.

Forget his chin and answer the question!

'Only a couple of weeks. I spent some time at the Crocodile Creek Hospital on the mainland, getting to know the staff there, as they—the doctors and the nurses—do rostered shifts at the clinic and, of course, the helicopter rescue and retrieval services the hospital runs are closely connected with the island.'

'Why here?' he asked, and she glanced towards him. Big mistake, for he'd turned in her direction and she met the same question in his dark-lashed eyes. Although that might have been her imagination! He had beautiful eyes, but if eyes were the windows of the soul, then she'd never been able to read Angus's soul, or his emotions, in them.

Except when he'd looked at Bobby. Then she'd seen the love—and the pain…

'It was somewhere different, a chance to see a new place, experience different medicine, meet new people.'

'Always high on your priority list,' Angus said dryly, but this time she refused to glance at him, keeping her eyes firmly fixed on the track in front of her.

'I've always liked meeting people,' she said quietly. 'I might not be the life and soul of a party, or need to be constantly surrounded by friends, but I enjoy the company of colleagues and patients—you know that, Angus.'

Did she sound hurt? Angus replayed her words—and the intonation—in his head and didn't think so. She was simply making a statement—putting him down, in fact, though she hadn't needed to do it because he'd regretted the words the instant they'd been out of his mouth.

For all her shyness, or perhaps because of it, she *was* good with people, knowing instinctively how to approach them, intuitively understanding their pain or weaknesses, easing her way into their confidence.

'And are you enjoying it? The island? The people?'

They were on a straight stretch of track, coming out of the thick rainforest into a more open but still treed area, and he could see cabins and huts nestled in private spaces between the trees.

Apparently more sure of the path now, she turned towards him before she answered, and her clear blue eyes—Bobby's eyes—met his.

'Oh, yes!' she said—no hesitation at all. 'Yes, I am.'

Then her brow creased and she sighed.

'Or I was until the kids starting getting sick. What shall we do, Angus, if it *is* bird flu?'

'Let's wait and see,' he said, touching her arm to reassure her.

Or possibly to see if her skin was really as soft as he remembered it...

He shook his head, disturbed that the strength of the attraction he felt towards Beth hadn't lessened in their years apart. Perhaps it was a good thing she had a problem at the medical centre—something he could get stuck into to divert his mind from memories of the past.

Although sick children were more than just a diversion—they were a real concern.

She pulled up in front of a new-looking building, the ramp at the front of it still trailing tattered streamers and limp balloons. The dog leapt out and began biting at the fluttering streamers, trying to tackle them into submission.

Was this the medical centre and these the remnants of the official opening celebrations? The building was certainly new, and built to merge into its surroundings—tropical architecture, with wide overhangs and floor-to-ceiling aluminium shutters to direct any stray breeze inside. Beautiful, in fact.

'Around the back,' Beth said, leading him down a path beside the building. 'The front part is Administration and a first-aid verging on ER room. The hospital section is behind it, here.'

They walked up another ramp and had barely reached the deck, when a woman with tousled curls and a freckled nose came out through a door, greeting Beth with obvious relief.

'Thank heavens you're back,' she said. 'I've called Charles, but you're the only one who can calm Robbie. He's babbling—hallucinating, I think—just when we thought he might have turned the corner.'

'I'll go right through,' Beth said, then, apparently remembering she'd brought him to this place, turned to Angus.

'Grace, this is Angus. Angus, Grace. He's the doctor I told you about, Grace. Could you take him around so he can see the other patients, introduce him to Emily if she's here and Charles when he arrives?'

The 'doctor' not 'ex-husband', Angus thought, feeling annoyed about the wording for no fathomable reason, though he did manage to greet the distracted nurse politely.

Beth hurried back to Robbie's room. The virus that had struck the camp had started off with drowsiness, and the children seemed almost to lapse into unconsciousness in between bouts of agitation. Right now Robbie was agitated, tossing and turning in his bed, muttering incoherently, his movements more violent than they'd been during the night.

Beth checked the drip running into his arm, then felt his forehead. Not feverish, she guessed, then picked up his chart to confirm it. The paracetamol she'd given him earlier must be working.

'Hush, love, it's all right, I'm here,' she whispered to the fretful little boy, holding his hands in one of hers and smoothing his dark hair back from his forehead with the other.

But even as he stilled at the sound of her voice, fear whispered in her heart. They were treating the symptoms the patients had without any idea if this was an aggressive cold or something far more sinister. Alex Vavunis, a paediatric neurosurgeon who was a guest on the island, had taken samples of spinal fluid from the sickest patients the previous day, but it was too early to expect results.

Beth knew her assurances could easily be empty—that everything might not be all right for Robbie.

'We've three children not feeling well, still in the camp, but Robbie and Jack are the most severely affected. My ward, Lily, was admitted yesterday and she's a little better today.'

Beth heard Charles's voice before she saw him, and turned to see he'd guided his wheelchair silently into the room, Angus seeming taller than ever as he stood beside the chair.

'How is he, Beth?'

Charles wheeled closer as he asked the question.

Beth shook her head.

'Agitated,' she said, 'although there is some good news. Jack seems a little better this morning. Lily?'

She heard Charles's sigh and knew the little girl must still be unstable.

'Jill has been with her most of the night. And Grace tells me you've been here all night. You should go home and rest.'

'I dozed between checking on the others,' Beth assured him. 'Emily's on duty today, but I'll stay now in case Angus needs some help with tests or information.'

She glanced towards the man who had moved to the chair beside Robbie's bed and was reading through the notes on his chart.

'You've how many sick?' Angus asked, looking at Charles who nodded to Beth to reply.

'We have the adult from the resort, one of the rangers and three children, making a total of five. There are another three children at the camp showing symptoms. We've moved those three to a cabin and the staff and volunteers there are entertaining them, keeping them as quiet as possible and making sure they take in plenty of fluids. Among the staff, the rangers, even people at the resort, there could be more who are simply not feeling well, people feeling the "beginning of flu" symptoms but who haven't said anything.'

'And you're how far off the mainland?'

This time Charles fielded Angus's question himself. 'A half-hour flight by helicopter—less by seaplane.'

'You've got to close the island, Charles,' Angus said. 'You must have had similar thoughts yourself, given the number of dead birds you say have been found. We have to quarantine the whole place—resort, national park, the camp and eco-resort—at least until we know more. It's a thousand to one chance it's anything sinister, but even that's too big a chance to take.'

Beth stared at him, sure her jaw had dropped in disbelief.

'You're serious? You think it *could* be bird flu?'

She looked at the little boy still twitching restlessly on the bed and pain washed through her.

'No!' she whispered, but she doubted whether the men heard her, Charles asking questions, Angus answering, Charles talking practicalities—how to enforce a quarantine, important people here for the opening who wouldn't like it, Health Department and Australian Quarantine Service concerns—

'It has to be complete and it has to start now!' Angus said in a voice Beth recognised as brooking no opposition. This was the focus Angus always brought to his work. 'It would be criminal of us to allow even one person who could be carrying a deadly virus to leave the island. And we'll have to get the police and health authorities to trace anyone who has left in the past week and to isolate those people as well.'

'That won't be hard. Most people here this week stayed on for the opening of the medical centre, and resort guests are usually here for a week, Sunday to Sunday. There'll be guests due to go today but not until later in the day. The helicopter pilots who do the passenger runs each day—they come and go more than anyone but rarely get out of their machines. Their manifests will tell us who's left so we'll have a list to give the authorities on the mainland.'

The two men had turned away, intent on putting their

quarantine order in place, as well they might be. It was going to be a complicated task, and more than a few people were going to be very annoyed about it.

Beth smiled to herself. Alex Vavunis, the self-important paediatric neurosurgeon, for one. He'd made life uncomfortable for several people, simply because he'd been upset to find his daughter, Stella, was growing up. Although being forced to stay longer might give him more time to spend with his daughter and to accept the new Stella—so good could come from bad.

And Nick Devlin, who'd stayed on longer than he'd intended already because his little boy, Josh, was enjoying the camp so much. But Josh was a brittle asthmatic and a lung infection of any kind could have serious consequences. Beth shivered at the thought of Josh picking up the infection, then felt a momentary pang of sympathy for Angus. He was the epidemiologist—he'd be the one coping with the fallout of the announcement.

Although Angus could handle that—work-related problems would never faze Angus. Only emotions could do that…

'We're definitely closing the island. Charles has been on to the quarantine people and the head of the state health department and she agrees it's the way to go in the short term but she doesn't want to go public with it and start a panic about a pandemic. Containing everyone on the island might help to keep the news off the front pages.'

Angus returned to Robbie's room alone, explaining this to her while standing in the doorway, his eyes taking in the small ward, and the child now lying quietly, seeming even smaller than he probably was because of the big hospital beds.

'In this day of e-mails and mobile phones, do you really think the news can be contained?' Beth asked. 'Besides, there were reporters and photographers here for the opening and though some went back on the last boat last night, I'm sure the local gossip columnist stayed on. Apparently she loves mixing with the rich and famous and the opportunity to spend time at the resort was too much for her to resist.'

Angus studied her for a moment and Beth could almost hear his brain working.

'Perhaps if we don't mention birds, just talk about a virus of unknown origin that has spread quickly, it might attract less interest from the press.'

'It won't work,' Beth told him. 'Most of the people on this side of the island know about the dead birds. And on top of that, you'll have to tell people to stay away from dead birds—maybe all birds—and the moment you say that, then the words "bird flu" will ricochet through everyone's mind.'

'You're right. We'll just have to ask them to keep quiet about it—maybe someone will have to speak directly to the local columnist. Explain we don't want to start a nationwide panic.'

'Or maybe we'll get lucky and some film star or other celebrity will do something dreadful that grabs the headlines and the quarantine of the island will go unnoticed,' Beth suggested, and Angus shrugged.

'Could we be that lucky?' he said, then he smiled and Beth felt a surge of emotion in her chest—a too-familiar reaction to an Angus smile. And just when she'd been doing so well—playing the part of the mature professional to perfection, though being in the vicinity of Angus was reminding her nerve endings of how good things had once been.

Physically…

'Charles tells me you're off duty, but he wants all available hospital staff, as well as hotel personnel, park rangers and eco-lodge management people, at a meeting in the lecture theatre at the convention centre at the hotel. Can you drive me back there?'

Beth hesitated, desperately seeking an excuse to say no. Even before the surge she'd known that the less time she spent with Angus the better off she'd be. But she'd asked for his help…

He'd come right into the room now, and stood beside her, looking down at Robbie, who was sleeping more peacefully now.

'You go, I'll keep a special eye on him.'

Grace must have followed Angus in, for there she was, flapping her hands at Beth as if shooing chooks.

She had no choice, standing up slowly, careful not to look at Angus, though every cell in her body was aware of his presence.

'Do you think it *is* bird flu?' she asked, and didn't need to hear Angus sigh to know what a stupid question it had been. 'Of course you don't know,' she answered for him. 'It's just that it's been in the forefront of my mind all night. H5N1, a seemingly innocuous grouping of letters and numbers, yet with the ability to make anyone who understands them very anxious.'

'From doctors up to heads of governments,' Angus confirmed, his voice deep with the gravity of the situation. 'But what we can't do is panic—or even become overly dramatic about it. There's a set routine for any disease outbreak—identify its existence, which we do by seeing how many people are affected—'

'Five in hospital, three segregated in the camp, and who knows how many who haven't sought medical attention.'

'Enough to cause concern in a relatively small population,' Angus agreed as they reached the cart Beth had used earlier. 'The next step is to verify the diagnosis.'

He sounded worried and she looked at him and saw the frown between his eyebrows once again.

'Problems with that?'

'Of course,' he said, climbing into the driving seat without consultation, but this was hardly the time to be arguing over who should drive. 'There is now a fast and definitive test for H5N1, a gene chip known as the MChip, but it's only been used in laboratories in the US. Out here we still use the FluChip, which is based on three influenza genes. It provides information about the type of virus but the lab then needs to run more tests to get the virus subtype—to identify H5N1, for example.'

'Clear as mud!' Beth muttered, although in the past she'd always enjoyed the way Angus had discussed his thoughts and explained things to her.

Or was it because of that past enjoyment—and the risk of enjoying it now—that she was feeling so narky?

'I'm saying tests take time,' Angus added, turning towards her so she saw his frown had deepened.

'I know,' she admitted. 'I must be more tired than I realised. Have you and Charles talked further than quarantine?'

Was she interested or just making conversation? Angus wondered.

Once, he'd have known—once, he'd have been sure it was interest, because that was Beth, always keen to learn.

Or had she been?

Had her interest been feigned because she'd known how much he'd enjoyed talking over his work with her? Discussing her work, too, until she'd taken maternity leave, then, with Bobby's diagnosis of cerebral palsy, hadn't worked after that, staying home to care for their fragile, crippled little son.

While he had lost himself in work, trying to dispel the fear love brought with it by focussing on genetic mutations of the flu virus—or had it been HIV at that stage? He could no longer remember, just knew he'd used work to escape the pain of seeing Bobby fight for every breath he'd taken.

Not all the time, not when Bobby had been well, and laughing with glee at silly things—but often enough, when things had got too tough…

He pushed the memories away—though not too far away—and turned to Beth.

'Was it hard, getting back into the swing of things at work?'

The question followed so closely on his thoughts he was surprised when she looked startled.

And puzzled.

'I was back at work before we parted, Angus,' she reminded him, and he had to smile, though it wasn't a joyous expression.

'You were putting on sensible working clothes and going to the hospital, and no doubt doing a very efficient job, but it was something to do, somewhere to go, somewhere to escape the emptiness—not something to enjoy or feel involved in.'

He stopped the cart and was about to get out, when he realised she hadn't answered him—not only hadn't answered, but was sitting staring at him as if he'd suddenly morphed into an alien.

'How do you know that?' she demanded, so obviously puzzled he felt pain shaft through him—pain that they could have lived such separate lives, that they had lost each other so completely in the thick emotional fog that had descended after Bobby's death.

Anger rescued him, blazing along the path the pain had seared.

'Do you think I didn't do the same? Didn't feel pushed so far off track by Bobby's loss that I wondered if I'd ever find my way back again?'

His anger eased as he watched the colour fade from her face and saw her ashen lips move.

'You never said,' she whispered. 'You never said…'

'We never talked it through, did we?' He spoke more gently now, shocked that she'd lost colour so easily. 'Not about the things that mattered. I don't suppose that's surprising, given we were two people who had grown up not talking about emotions.'

He reached out and touched her cheek.

'That made it very hard.'

He walked away before she could respond. Beth's eyes were on his broad back as she followed him towards the hotel building. He was there for a conference, he would know where the convention area was, and the lecture theatre.

But her thoughts were far from the upcoming meeting. How could she not have known how he'd felt?

He'd loved Bobby—she'd known that much—and had grieved after his death, but that Angus had been as lost as she had been, *that* was the revelation.

'*You never said,*' she whispered again, this time to herself, but even as she said it, she realised how stupid it was to be surprised. Angus was right. They had *never* talked about their emotions. After meeting Angus's father, the only family he had, she had understood why he couldn't. His father was an academic and conversation in the Stuart family ranged over many and varied topics—scientific, political, even religious, but never, ever emotional.

In fact, going to visit had always been an ordeal for Beth as the cool—no, cold—atmosphere of the house and her detached, unemotional father-in-law had intimidated her to such an extent she'd rarely said a word, while taking Bobby for a visit had always made her feel inadequate. Dr Stuart Senior had produced one perfect child, Angus, while Beth had produced one small boy, who through an accidental loss of oxygen to his brain during his birth, had been, in the eyes of those who hadn't known and loved him, less than perfect.

Angus had stopped by the steps leading into the hotel and she caught up with him, looking up into his face, wanting to apologise, though for exactly what—not knowing how he'd felt, Bobby's birth trauma, getting pregnant in the first place—she wasn't certain.

Not that she could have apologised anyway. The look

on his face was enough to freeze any words she might have said—freeze them on her tongue.

'This way.'

Her heart ached at his remoteness, which was stupid considering they'd been apart for three long years. Why wouldn't he be remote?

And wasn't remote part of Angus anyway? He might have been one of the best-looking men in the hospital—not to mention one of the sexiest—but one look from his eyes, one tilt of his head, and even the most desperate of women would back away.

Which, of course, had been part of his allure to every single woman on the staff, and probably a lot of the married ones as well...

Angus led the way through the lobby towards the wing that housed the convention area. He and Beth had been together less than an hour and already he—or they—had managed to put up impenetrable barriers between them.

Yet seeing her had thawed parts of him he'd thought frozen for all time...

Seeing her had heated other parts of him—parts the beautiful Sally had barely stirred...

How could it be? He looked down at the shiny hair capping Beth's head, feeling a certain contentment just to be near her, yet not understanding why he should feel that way.

Familiarity, that's all it was, he tried to tell himself, but he didn't believe it for a minute.

No, there was chemistry between himself and Beth he'd never understood, no matter how hard or how often, in the past, he'd tried to analyse it. And it was probably, if he was honest, his inability to analyse it—to dissect it, understand it and so rationalise it—that had led to him allowing Beth to push him away when Bobby had died.

He'd told himself she was like a drug that wasn't good for him—that was the closest he could come to an explanation. And though he'd craved the drug, he'd gone, separated from her, telling himself it was for the best, pretending to himself he was doing it for Beth because she wanted it that way, losing himself and his grief in work…

'The lecture theatre's through here,' he said, touching her arm to guide her through a door at the end of the passage, touching her skin, Beth's skin…

Charles beckoned them forward, indicating seats at the front of the hall, taking his place behind a lectern, waiting for latecomers to find somewhere to sit, waiting for silence before telling all those assembled that the island was now in quarantine.

CHAPTER THREE

BETH watched Angus as he spoke, introduced by Charles as an epidemiology expert, explaining the necessity for quarantine until the source of the virus had been isolated.

Someone at the back immediately asked if it was connected to the dead birds, and Angus gave Beth a slight nod as if in confirmation of her words earlier.

'It is highly unlikely to be bird flu,' he said. 'But because it is similar to a flu virus, we believe flu vaccine might stave off infection in people not already infected. A number of you are hospital staff or are in related medical fields so have already had flu shots for this year, but we are flying in more stocks and will vaccinate everyone on the island who isn't already covered. This will be a big task but, like any task, it can be broken down into sizeable chunks.'

Hands shot up in the air as people wanted to question Angus, but Charles broke in to ask those with questions to wait until Angus had finished speaking, then, if he hadn't covered all aspects, to ask questions then.

He waved his hand to indicate Angus could again take the floor.

'So, vaccination programmes will begin, testing is ongoing and we should get results within forty-eight hours, but in the meantime we must act as if bird flu is a possibility, however remote. We know that more than ninety-nine per cent of bird-flu cases have come from direct contact with infected birds. So it is imperative we warn guests and staff to keep away from all birds, whether alive or dead. We have already ordered full body suits with rebreathing masks to be flown to the island. As soon as they arrive, the rangers will all be rostered on duty to collect and dispose of any dead birds safely.'

He didn't say that the cull might include all birds, not just the sick ones, but Beth suspected that would be the case and her heart ached, for the abundant bird life—the constant chatter and cries of the birds—was part of the magic of the island. She was wondering how it could be done humanely, when an irritated voice broke into her thoughts.

'You tell people not to touch birds. If we were allowed to leave—if everyone was evacuated—there'd be no need to worry. Why can't everyone who isn't sick leave now? We're capable of watching our health, looking for symptoms and getting to our own doctor if we should feel ill. There's no need for all of us to be part of this crisis.'

Beth didn't know the man who was complaining—perhaps he was one of the hotel management people—and she could understand his concern. The tide of dissent was rising, people muttering and mumbling behind her, agreeing with the man.

'There *is* no crisis,' Angus replied, his quiet, measured voice contrasting with the loud, bullying tones of the guest.

'The quarantine is purely precautionary. We are isolating the people who are already sick and those who are showing slight symptoms. The fact that the illness struck so quickly makes it likely that the quarantine period will be relatively short. The normal process is to isolate a community for a set number of days after the last person becomes ill. In the meantime, if you wish to remain isolated from other people, that is up to you, and I'm sure the resort staff will help you facilitate it.'

Would the man accept this common-sense explanation? Beth turned towards him and saw him take his seat, although his lips were moving and she knew he was muttering at the people around him, no doubt still complaining, while around him rose a mumbling of rebellion that could easily slip out of control.

'Excuse me!' The man's voice silenced the pocket of conversation. 'You're talking about vaccinations for those who haven't had a flu shot this year and saying those who have had one should be all right, but aren't flu shots virus-specific?'

It was Mike Poulos, a paramedic helicopter pilot from Crocodile Creek, who asked the question, and the practicality of it didn't mask the concern in his voice.

Was his concern for his wife, Emily, the doctor now on duty at the medical centre? Of course it would be—Emily and Mike were not long married and so devoted to each other it always warmed Beth to see them together.

'They are developed each year for the specific virus experts predict will hit our shores, but viruses mutate so quickly that by the time the Australian flu season starts it is usually not the virus for which the vaccine was developed. But the vaccination will help prevent other flu strains, and in this case having some protection could be better than none.'

Angus spoke quietly but the undeniable authority in his voice quietened the muted whispers and Beth saw many people nodding in agreement.

Was it because he was aware he now had the full attention of his audience that he continued?

'But remember,' he said, 'that we're by no means certain it is bird flu or, indeed, any other type of flu. The vaccinations are purely precautionary and are not even compulsory. We shall make the vaccine available to anyone who wants it, and Charles will provide staff to administer it.'

Someone asked a question and as Angus turned his head to answer, Beth studied him, trying to see him dispassionately—as a doctor and an expert, not an ex-husband. It wasn't only his voice that suggested confidence and authority but his bearing—his whole demeanour.

And once again she wondered what on earth such a man had ever seen in a little snip of a thing like her—a fellow doctor, sure, but when they'd met she'd been a first-year resident—dust beneath the feet of most men like Angus, men who were already making their mark and heading inevitably towards the top of their chosen fields.

Sexual attraction, that was the only explanation—some chemical reaction between them, something neither of them had control over.

It was where it had led that had caused the problem.

Familiar guilt weighed heavily in her heart—guilt she

knew it was stupid to feel as her falling pregnant had been a two-way street.

And Angus hadn't *had* to marry her—she'd told him that.

Except, being Angus and with very clear views on responsibility, he had insisted.

He'd married her because of her pregnancy, not because he'd loved her—that was the part that hurt.

She pushed the past away, worried that it still had the power to affect her physically, and tried to concentrate on what was going on in the present.

'Programmes for vaccinations. Any of you who haven't had flu vaccine please put your name and cabin or room number on a sheet of paper here at the front of the room before you leave and we'll contact you regarding a time for the vaccination.'

Charles was talking again, adding that hotel staff and guests would be seen at the hotel, while those in eco-cabins and the camp could come to the medical centre.

'And what if it's not bird flu?' someone asked, and Charles nodded his willingness to take the question.

'Well, you'll all be inoculated against flu for the next season's outbreak,' he said, smiling reassuringly, although Beth knew he must be worried sick about both Lily and the situation. 'Seriously, though,' he added, 'we are looking into that. We've sent specimens to the mainland and should have some information back tomorrow, or the following day at the latest.'

More questions followed but in the end Charles called a halt, telling everyone they'd be kept informed with daily bulletins.

Was it chance that Beth found Angus by her side as she walked out of the hotel?

Surely it was. And why was he walking out anyway? Simply to upset her equilibrium, not to mention her nerve endings?

'Haven't you a conference session to attend?' she asked, as he accompanied her down the steps and turned towards the cart park.

'I'm giving a paper on Tuesday, I can't avoid that, but I can get notes for the rest of it.'

'But going to the sessions would be better than notes. I know I asked you to help but that was mainly because I was worried that it might be bird flu and you'd know what to do about quarantine and things—who to contact. It's not as if we're short of doctors. Half the staff of the Crocodile Creek hospital came over for the official opening and they're all stuck here with everyone else.'

Had she sounded a little hysterical that Angus had stopped walking and turned to look down into her face?

'Is that a practical protest or a personal one, Beth?' he asked, not smiling but not frowning either. 'Do you really believe I have nothing to offer over there, or is it that you don't want me around on your part of the island?'

She stared at him for a moment. Put like that, her comment seemed remarkably petty.

'I feel awkward,' she replied, opting for honesty. 'It was hard enough coming over here to ask for your help, Angus, and now—well, I don't know the "and now" part...'

She walked on, getting to the cart and climbing in— behind the wheel.

'I wouldn't think we'd have to see much of each other,'

he said, apparently unaffected by either her actions or her words. He simply took the passenger seat and kept talking. 'From what Charles said, you're off duty for a few days now, and even if you're called back to help with the vaccination programme, our paths don't need to cross.'

It's what you want, she told herself, starting the cart and turning it back along the road through the rainforest.

Liar!

What you really want is to be near him again, for whatever reason, and that is *not* mature. In fact, that is pathetic!

She stared fixedly at the road ahead, although the little cart moved so slowly a glance now and then would have sufficed. But because her attention was so focussed she didn't know he'd raised his arm until his fingers touched her cheek.

'Are you feeling all right yourself? No flu symptoms? You're very pale.'

Touch me again, her heart shouted, beating so loudly she was surprised he didn't hear it.

'I'm fine,' she assured him, still not looking at him, afraid now he'd see her reaction—the attraction that still fired all her senses—in her eyes.

'Well, you don't look fine. That little boy who was hallucinating—did you sit with him last night?'

Lie?

How could she?

She nodded.

'Because he looks like Bobby?'

She stopped the cart and turned to face him, then a demanding beep from the cart behind reminded her that most of the medical centre staff had been at the resort and were now returning to their side of the island.

Started up again, staring ahead as she answered.

'He does remind me of Bobby, but I spent the night with him because he's one of a number of children who came to the camp on his own. Part of the reason for the camp is to give the family respite from caring for a child with special needs. Give the parents time to do things with their other kids—things that are sometimes awkward when one child is in a wheelchair or can't go to places with flashing lights. Anyway, when Miranda, the respiratory physician who's in charge of the kids with lung problems, phoned his mother to tell her Robbie was sick, she was distraught, because she's a single mother with four other kids and it's impossible for her to get up here.'

'So you offered to be the replacement mum.'

Something in the way he said it—not sarcastically, but knowingly somehow—reminded Beth that even when she'd loved him most, he'd still been able to infuriate her.

'You've got a problem with that?' she snapped. 'Going to give me a lecture about keeping a professional distance between myself and my patients? Some worldly wisdom about not getting too involved?'

She heard him sigh and glanced his way, catching a look—surely not misery?—on his face.

'Would you listen?'

His voice was soft—gentle—and it coiled itself inside her, squeezing her lungs and winding around her heart, snaring her so effortlessly in the net that was her love for Angus.

'No!' she snapped again, because she didn't want to believe he could still do this to her—or admit it to herself if he could. 'And for your information, if I've bonded especially with any of the kids it's not with Robbie but with Sam—the little boy who ran away from the cart last night. He's the cheekiest little devil, in remission for the second time from acute lymphoblastic leukaemia, but with so much fight in him that if anyone will beat it, he will.'

Then she sighed, relaxed, and smiled at her passenger.

'Actually, I love them all. I love being part of their lives, even if it's just for a short time. They're so grown up somehow, kids who've had bad things happen in their lives—so mature for their ages in some ways, but still little kids in other ways.'

'Softy!' Angus teased, touching her cheek with the pad of his thumb, tracing a line towards her jaw. 'Of course you love them all.'

The wandering thumb edged towards her lips, brushed them briefly, then moved away, leaving Beth a silent, heart-skittering mess.

How could Angus still reduce her to this state?

Did he know the effect he was having on her or was he just being Angus?

And how could she allow herself to be reduced to a helpless puddle of desire from one touch of his thumb?

Pathetic, that's what she was.

Hopeless!

The maturity she thought she'd found in three long years, gone with a smile and a touch of a thumb...

She pulled up at the medical centre, where people returning from the hotel had already gathered, awaiting orders from Charles. Mike Poulos was on the deck, looking anxious as he spoke to his wife, Emily.

'You have to tell Charles,' he was saying, loudly enough for anyone to hear. 'If he knew you were pregnant, he'd be the first to tell you to keep away from here.'

'Husband and wife?' Angus asked, and Beth nodded, although this was the first she'd heard of Emily being pregnant.

'Will you introduce me to them?'

The question was unexpected, but Beth could see no reason not to, so she led Angus up the ramp. Doctor Beth and colleague Angus—exactly how things should be! Though Angus's wanting to meet the pair seemed to indicate an interest in their problems—something the Angus she had known would have avoided at all costs. It was tantamount to emotional involvement—the very thing he'd been teasing *her* about just now.

And he *had* been teasing, not lecturing...

'Mike, you were at the meeting so you know who Angus is. Emily, this is Angus Stuart, he's a pathologist and epidemiologist. He's working with Charles on the quarantine.'

'Angus Stuart?' Emily said, raising an eyebrow at Beth.

'My ex-husband,' Beth managed, although the 'ex' part sliced into her throat like a razor. 'Angus, meet Mike and Emily Poulos.'

She stepped back as Angus moved closer to the couple.

'We couldn't help overhearing your conversation,' he said, 'and you're right to be concerned, Mike, but if by some million-to-one chance it is bird flu, it's unlikely that it would pass from human to human. There has only been one possible example worldwide where that *might* have happened. In all other proven cases it has come from contact with infected birds.'

'It's still a risk for Emily to be working here,' Mike

said, his stubborn Greek genes pushing him to protect his woman.

'Not if she's careful. All staff will be wearing masks and double-gloving, although gloves should never take the place of hand-washing. Looking at the symptoms the patients are showing, if it's more serious than bad flu, it's likely to be some kind of viral encephalitis, which is very serious and very dangerous itself, but again, although the underlying infections that cause it—mononucleosis, herpes, even measles—are contagious, the encephalitis isn't.'

Mike nodded but didn't look any less happy and Beth guessed he wouldn't be unless he could wrap Emily in cotton wool for her entire pregnancy.

'Dr Beth, Dr Beth!'

Beth turned at the cry and saw Cameron, one of the little boys in the cancer group, racing towards her.

'It's Danny, he's sick. On the track near Stella's cabin.'

Angus, Emily and Mike were forgotten. Pausing only to check that the cart they used for emergency trips had its first-aid box and emergency gear strapped on behind, Beth climbed behind the wheel and spun the cart in the direction of the beach. Garf came flying from nowhere and landed beside her as she moved off.

Susie, the hospital physio, over here for the camp, came racing up the path as Beth neared the junction.

'Seizure,' she said. 'He hasn't come out of it. Alex Vavunis is with him—said to check you had oxygen and diazepam on board.'

'I've both,' Beth assured her as Susie turned and trotted by the cart. 'Who was there when it happened? Is someone timing it?'

'Benita, the nurse in charge of that group, was with him. She called for help when he didn't come out of it. Alex and I were close by.'

'Alex is involved in paediatric neurology, isn't he?' Beth said, remembering talk about the man. 'Best person Danny could have around,' she added, when Susie nodded.

She saw the group and drove close, stopped, then brought the oxygen bottle and first-aid box from the cart to where the child lay. Alex slipped the mask over the child's nose and mouth and started oxygen, then, while Beth guessed Danny's weight—he was very small for six—and calculated how much drug he'd need, Alex slid a cannula into the child's vein, making an often difficult task seem simple. Once he was satisfied the line was secure and the drug was flowing into Danny's bloodstream, Alex glanced at Beth for the okay then lifted the child, Susie carrying the oxygen bottle and holding it while Alex settled into the cart, the limp child in his arms, the oxygen bottle placed between his legs.

Beth drove steadily back to the medical centre, where it seemed even more people had gathered. But she went straight to the ramp at the rear, so Alex could carry the little boy into the closest room, the one where Jack Havens was recovering from the mystery virus.

'You're not on duty,' Charles reminded her, as she emerged from the room after settling Danny into bed. He was wheeling towards the room, no doubt having heard of the emergency. Angus was beside him, the two men looking as if they'd already bonded in some way.

Both work-obsessed, Beth guessed.

'I've asked all the staff not on duty to leave the medical centre,' Charles told her. 'Keep your mobile phones or pagers handy as we'll be contacting you about rosters for the flu vaccine as soon as Jill and I have that sorted.'

He turned to Angus.

'You'll be around? I want to check out this child then get straight onto these rosters but once that's done I'd like to talk to you about further measures we should take.'

'I came straight from breakfast and don't have my mobile on me, but I'll walk Beth back to her cabin. You can contact me there.'

Beth opened her mouth to protest but as most of her mainland colleagues were still hovering around the bottom of the ramp, she shut it again.

Why had he said that? Angus wondered. He could just as easily have waited here, at the centre, maybe sat with the little boy whose mother couldn't come, but—

'I just want to check on Robbie before I leave,' Beth said, and although he'd been thinking of the child himself, and Beth had denied any special bond, Angus was still concerned by her connection to him.

She slipped away, but he followed, meeting a harassed-looking woman on the way.

'Jill Shaw,' she said, offering her hand as well as her name. 'Director of Nursing at the hospital over on the mainland. I gather you're Beth's ex-husband. Good of you to help out like this.'

Angus shrugged off her thanks, taking in the shadows beneath her grey-blue eyes, and the lines of worry creasing her face.

'I understand the little girl who is sick is related to you.'

'Related to Charles,' Jill said, twisting a ring on the third finger of her left hand—an opal ring, the stone shooting fire as she moved it. 'She's our ward—well, sort of.'

Jill was so obviously distressed, Angus touched her shoulder.

'It's hard, watching a child you love suffer,' he said quietly, and the soft eyes lifted to his face.

She saw something in it that seemed to settle her. She found a smile and touched his hand.

'It's more than hard,' she said, 'but thank you for your understanding.'

She whisked away, leaving Angus with the feeling that he hadn't quite understood the conversation, and doubting, for all her thanks, that he'd helped at all.

But Beth was coming out of Robbie's room, and he forgot the worries of a woman he'd just met to concentrate on his own concerns, the main one being that he could still feel such a strong attraction towards his ex-wife.

He watched her as she stopped to speak to a nurse, studying her, thinking, as he always had, how this woman had caused such havoc in his life.

It had been three years—surely he'd moved on. Surely—inner wry smile—he'd beaten the drug!

What he'd actually done had been to lose himself in work and though that was normal for him, for the past few years he'd pushed harder, worked longer hours, leaving himself little time for thoughts not connected to whatever project he had in hand.

Going to the US had helped, working in Atlanta's Centers for Disease Control and Prevention. It had been an opportunity granted to few, and he'd relished it—and worked even harder over there…

'He's sleeping, and peacefully,' the woman he'd been pondering about said calmly, smiling at him so the tiredness disappeared from her face and her eyes shone with simple pleasure.

Of course he still felt attracted to her, he excused himself, she was the most genuine person he had ever met, and that, added to an undeniably sexy body, was irresistible.

At least to him—

Or any man?

She was chattering on about Robbie and the other little boy, Jack, while Angus tortured himself over the possibility of there being another man in Beth's life. A man who might even now be waiting for her in her cabin.

Although surely she'd have said something—objected to his suggestion of waiting there.

'You don't have to walk back with me,' she announced, so perfectly on cue he immediately assumed there *was* a man.

Which, contrarily, made him determined to stick by her side. She was an innocent for all she'd been married. Any man could con her. His protective instincts went on full alert...

'I have to wait somewhere,' he said. 'And I'd like to see where you live.'

She slowed her pace and turned towards him.

'Why, Angus?'

Such a simple question but the equally simple answer— because he still cared about her—would sound ridiculous.

'Just to see,' he said, aware of how lame he sounded, but, tired though she must be, she smiled.

'It's not so different from the flat I had when we first

met,' she told him. 'The kind of place that will make you reel back in horror. Junk everywhere—not all mine, because some was already there—but I'm still a magpie and beachcombing yields such unlikely treasures I hate to part with any of them.'

They were walking along a narrow path, in the dense shade of the huge soft-wooded trees that grew among the palms and ferns all over the island. Birds chattered above them, reminding Angus of the seriousness of the situation in which he found himself, but for the moment, walking with Beth through the cool shadows, it was hard to think of doom or disaster. He found instead a contentment he hadn't felt for three long years.

'See,' she said, as they came into a clearing and he saw a wooden hut, the timber silvered by time and sunlight, wide French windows open at the front so the deck and living room were one. A faded red and white canvas chair was pulled close to the edge of the deck, beside a table that appeared to have been made out of half a barrel. And on it were scattered shells, large and small, and pieces of driftwood in silvery, sinewy shapes.

In the far side of this deck a woven hammock, green and purple, hung temptingly, while inside an ancient old couch was brightened up with a rainbow of cushions. Angus felt a hand close around his heart.

Then squeeze!

Beside the couch was a little cane chair—child size— a colleague had given them for Bobby…

He shook away the memory of the little boy—his little boy—sitting in the chair and considered colour instead.

Beth's love of colour!

He thought back to his apartment in the city, the one Beth had moved into when they'd married. A very expensive interior designer had decorated it for him only a year earlier, modern, minimalist grey, white and black. Functional!

When Beth had first moved in she'd brightened it with soft mohair throws, magazines strewn across the coffee-table, or huge bunches of vivid flowers, but as time had gone on, she'd come to confine her love of colour to Bobby's room, although an orange throw she'd left behind when she'd moved out still hung over his black leather lounge.

Apart from her touches of colour, she hadn't changed anything in his apartment, and he hadn't needed to ask why. Beth's only desire had been that he be comfortable, and he'd accepted her unobtrusive way of making sure that happened without ever questioning whether she was happy or whether making him happy had been enough for her...

'Would you like a coffee? You didn't finish your breakfast. I've cereal and fruit if you'd like some, but I take most of my meals at the medical centre or the camp, so I don't keep much in the way of food here.'

'You're doing it again,' he growled, then regretted his tone of voice as her startled gaze fixed on his face.

'Doing what?'

'Thinking of other people—me—first,' he said, grumbling now rather than growling. 'You always do it! You've been up all night, you must be exhausted, and emotionally upset as well because you *have* connected to that little boy, yet you're offering to make me coffee. Worrying that *I* didn't have breakfast. I'm willing to bet you haven't eaten either. And you've lost weight—you're way too thin. This was a stupid idea, running away like this to an island—'

'Angus?'

It wasn't so much his name as the smile that accompanied it that stopped his grouching. The smile was soft and gentle, loving even, and it hurt his chest as if it had pressed against a bruise.

'You always get cranky when you're hungry. Sit down. I'll get us both some cereal, although I suppose it's closer to lunchtime, but it's all I can offer. And tea? I'm making a pot. And I *will* rest later, but I did sleep during the night. It's just not the same, is it, the sleep you get sitting up?'

Beth hoped it didn't sound as if she was prattling on but if it wasn't bad enough having Angus in her home—her sanctuary—here he was saying things that made her think he still cared about her, cared about her health and welfare.

Weird!

Although he was a very caring person once you got past his rather stern, remote exterior.

And when his mind wasn't on other things, like work.

Although surely his mind should be on work now—on this possible pandemic...

She poured muesli into cereal bowls, sliced pawpaw from the tree just outside her door onto it, added milk then made a pot of tea. Angus, who had mooched around her tiny, cluttered living room, picking up a shell here, a glass float there, was now in the nook that served as her kitchen, so close she bumped into him as she turned to get a tray.

'Sorry,' he said, grasping her elbow to steady her.

'That's okay, it's a bit cramped,' she managed, although her skin burned where his hand had been and it took all her willpower not to throw herself into his arms and lose herself and her tiredness and her worry over Robbie and the other patients, in the strength of his arms and the warmth of his body.

Really, after three years you should be doing better than this! she scolded herself. But she doubted if a thousand years—a million—would stop her feeling the way she did about Angus.

It's physical, she tried to tell herself, but she wasn't very convincing. The physical appeal was only part of it— loving him was the hard part. Loving him and knowing her love wasn't returned. Oh, he'd been fond of her, and he'd loved Bobby, but...

She fought the memories, managing to put the bowls, spoons, cups and the teapot on the tray. He picked it up and carried it, without asking, out to the deck, moving a few shells so he could set it down on the table.

Angus looked around, saw her other deck chair folded by the wall. He picked it up, feeling slightly smug, unfolded it and set it opposite the one she used.

Surely if she had a man living here, even overnighting occasionally, she'd have two chairs on the deck, Angus decided as he settled cautiously—he knew these darned things could fold up on you in an instant—into the chair.

Then he took in the surroundings for the first time and realised he could see the pure white sand and green-blue water of the lagoon through the fringed fronds of young coconut palms.

'This is a beautiful setting,' he said, shaking his head as he realised just how beautiful it was.

Beth was smiling at him, as if she could read his surprise and was pleased by it.

'Not a bad place to run away to,' she teased, and he shook his head again.

No one had ever teased him as Beth did—gently and lovingly, but still getting under his skin.

In fact, everything about Beth got under his skin—it had happened six years ago when he'd first met her, and it was happening again. Or maybe she'd just stayed there, and he'd pushed her deep inside, trying to pretend she wasn't there at all.

He had to be careful. He didn't want that to happen again. Losing his child had been something from which a part of him would never fully recover, but losing Beth had been worse. It had disrupted his life to such an extent he'd lost his joy in work, the one thing that had always been there for him, and though he'd continued working—had worked like a madman, in fact—he'd known he hadn't been getting the results he'd got when he'd been married. Known that he'd lost the ability to find that extra connection to produce brilliant results rather than satisfactory ones.

The invitation to go to the CDC had been like a lifeline. It had given him a challenge, a new focus—something big enough to stop him thinking, remembering…

Regretting…

CHAPTER FOUR

'WHAT'S next?' Beth asked when she'd finished her late breakfast and no longer had the excuse of eating to save her making conversation.

Angus, also finished, had been looking out at the view while he drank his tea. He turned back towards her, sipped again, then sighed.

Stop thinking, Beth…

Focus.

'I've been thinking about it. I'd like to autopsy one of the dead birds.'

'You can't do that!' Beth said, fear for him making her voice too shrill, too loud. 'That's exactly how those people in the laboratory overseas died before the virus was isolated. They were studying the dead birds and didn't realise just how deadly the virus was. And that was in a lab, with at least some containment facilities. To do it here would be suicidal, Angus.'

'I do have *some* sense,' he reminded her. 'Apparently there's a lab at the park ranger station, but I doubt they'd have a lamina flow room or chimney. But gowned and gloved—'

'It's still a risk,' Beth protested, but he quietened her with a touch of his hand on her arm.

'I don't think it *is* bird flu, Beth,' he said. 'The worst avian influenza outbreaks have been in China, where millions upon millions of birds are farmed, and it is in those populations that the worst outbreaks have occurred. Chickens and ducks in particular have been susceptible and other what we might call domesticated birds like geese and even swans have been found with the virus. Where it's passed to wild birds, it's passed to those species, not crossed to other species.'

His hand had remained on her arm and now his fingers stroked her skin—absent-mindedly she knew, and she should ignore it, but the touch was soothing and electrifying at the same time.

She couldn't let Angus do this to her again! Couldn't let herself be carried away on a tide of physical sensations.

Although—

Nonsense!

She focussed on her argument.

'But it could—in fact, you can't be certain that hasn't already happened. You've said yourself no one ever knows all the latest developments in any scientific process.'

He smiled at her.

'Quoting me, Beth?'

The smile and a softness in the words made her blood swoop along her veins, but she had to maintain her poise— maintain a pretence that this was just a normal conversation with a colleague. She would *not* be swept into a bundle of dizzy desire by Angus's smiles.

Not again.

'Only because it seemed to fit.' Very mature response, that. 'And the fact remains that birds are dying.'

Angus nodded.

'I've been thinking about that and I believe there could be a simple explanation—sad, but simple.'

Beth watched him, waiting for more, so ridiculously happy to be sitting here like this with Angus she knew she should probably have herself committed to a secure ward somewhere until the madness passed.

'Are you going to tell me?' she finally asked, when the silence had stretched between them for so long she wondered—more madness—if he might be as comfortable as she was.

Another smile.

'Not yet,' he said. 'But when I know, I'll explain it all. In the meantime, you should get some sleep. I'll see you later?'

It was such a weird question, asked as if he was taking it for granted that he would—no, more than that, that he *wanted* to see her later…

How likely was that?

When she'd suggested their marriage wasn't working, he'd walked away without a second thought. So swiftly, in fact, she'd known for sure that what she'd always suspected had been true. Angus had married her because she'd been pregnant, not because he'd loved her…

But that had been then and this was now, and if it had just been a casual remark, she had to respond in kind.

'I suppose so—if you'll be around the hospital, we probably won't be able to avoid each other.'

She was looking out towards the water as she spoke and

didn't see his reaction, so when he replied, 'I was thinking more of personal contact, Beth,' she had to swing around to look at him to see if she could make out what he'd meant from some expression on his face.

Impossible! It always had been that way when she'd tried to read emotions on Angus's face.

So she had to ask.

'Why?'

His eyes scanned her face and she wondered just what he was reading there.

Fear?

Apprehension?

Hopefully not excitement!

'Would you object?'

'That's not an answer,' she managed, although her nerves were now so taut that any movement might snap them.

He sighed and rubbed his hands across his face, the way he did when he was tired, or worried about something, then turned and looked at her.

'Seeing you again,' he said, so slowly she wondered if he was testing each and every word before he said it, or if reluctance was holding them back, 'I realise how much I miss you.'

The words stopped the swooping in her blood, replacing it with song, but this was worse than madness—this reaction was stupidity. She had to stay calm, stay focussed. She'd rebuilt her life and grown to be happy in her own way. Content…

Mature!

'It's been three years, Angus, and you've just realised that?'

He lifted one shoulder in an embarrassed kind of shrug.

'I've been busy with work. You must know I can do that—can get so involved with it, nothing else matters.'

'Yes, I know,' Beth said quietly, then she stood up, stacked the dirty dishes on the tray and walked away.

Angus watched her go and wondered just which occasion when he'd been too 'involved' had sprung into her mind. When she'd phoned to say her labour pains were down to three minutes apart and he'd suggested she get a cab to the hospital and he'd meet her there?

Even this long after the event, remorse and shame stabbed through him.

He *had* met her there eventually, though for an hour he'd used an important phase of an experiment at work as an excuse to not go, afraid that seeing Beth in pain might be too much for him to bear. Afraid of how he might react to her pain—afraid of emotion—that dangerous X factor he'd been trained by his father, and his own childhood experience, to not feel.

And by the time he had arrived, she'd been in trouble, the cord twisted around Bobby's neck, everyone too frantic for any talk, everyone intent on saving the infant.

Saving Bobby...

Beth rinsed the dishes and set them on the sink to wash later, then considered washing them now in order to prolong the time before she had to face Angus again. The problem wasn't her pathetic reaction to Angus's words—his admission that he'd missed her—although singing in the blood was bad enough, but why Angus would say such a thing?

Angus never said anything that might be even vaguely

indicative of his feelings. In fact, at times, early in their marriage, she'd wondered if he had feelings—if perhaps his extraordinary intelligence had somehow taken up the space where feelings should have been.

But then she'd seen him with Bobby—seen the gentleness in his hands as he'd held his little son, seen the way he'd smiled at the little boy, and stroked his head and cheek when he'd been fretful.

So, yes, he did have feelings.

But for her? Or did 'missing her' simply mean he missed the convenience of a wife—someone to cut his grapefruit in the mornings?

She was thinking she *had* to return to the deck, when the phone rang. Charles, for Angus. She carried the handpiece out to him then backed away, not wanting to seem to be eavesdropping, although the conversation, on Angus's side, was unrevealing. Two 'Right's and an 'Okay' before he stood up and brought the phone into the living room where she was sitting on the couch.

'I'm going back to the medical centre,' he said, hovering beside her, eventually taking a deep breath before adding, 'I'll call in here after I finish.'

Finish?

Beth was about to ask, when she remembered his talk of autopsying one of the dead birds. She leapt to her feet.

'You're not still thinking of looking at one of the dead birds, are you?'

Had she sounded too anxious—manic?—that he smiled?

'I'll take every precaution,' he assured her, 'but you must admit it might be the fastest and easiest way to allay everyone's fears.'

'But how? You'd still have to send samples from the bird to the mainland for testing. You can't tell just from looking at the inside of a bird what it died from—unless it was strangled and had petechiae or some other indicator of cause of death.'

'Exactly,' Angus said. 'Something like starvation—that should be obvious. Birds don't suffer from anorexia.'

'Starvation?' Beth echoed, but Angus was already crossing the deck, though he paused at the top of the steps, turning around and lifting his hand in a half-wave.

'I'll see you later,' he said, then leapt the two steps onto the soft sand, striding briskly away before Beth could again ask why.

It was useless to speculate on exactly what was prompting Angus's behaviour, so Beth focussed on the earlier conversation.

'Starvation?' she muttered to herself. Here on an island with abundant life all around it? Most of the birds lived on shellfish, of which there were plenty, so how could they possibly be dying of starvation?

She reached up to the bookshelf behind her and found her bird book, seeking the chapter on shearwaters.

Migratory, she knew that. It was because they were migratory, flying north for the Arctic summer then returning south to breed, that bird flu had loomed as a possibility in her mind. The birds' path took them across Siberia, Korea, China and Southeast Asia. Stopping to feed in any of these places, they could have picked up the virus.

Although according to Angus, ducks gave it to ducks and chickens to chickens, so *was* it possible for shearwaters to pick it up on their way south?

Realising she had no idea, or any way of finding out, she headed for her bedroom. Sleep would do little to clear away her confusion over Angus's behaviour, and certainly wouldn't provide answers to her bird queries, but it would make her better able to deal with whatever lay ahead of her on this confusing day.

Angus made his way back to the medical centre with long, swift strides—trying to escape the strange emotions that had come upon him in Beth's little hut. Had he really told her he missed her—revealed his confused emotional state to her?

He had, but was that all bad?

Wasn't it not talking about their emotions that had brought them to the end of their marriage?

Hadn't they already discussed this earlier?

So telling her must be good.

Mustn't it?

As he neared the new building, he realised he might be creating an impression of urgency which could panic someone watching him, and deliberately slowed his pace.

But taking shorter steps didn't make it easier to switch his thoughts from Beth to science, although now he'd mentioned starvation—thinking aloud as he'd talked to her—something was niggling in his brain, something to do with flight paths of migratory birds.

Focus.

Think.

Where?

Korea, he rather thought, teasing at the idea, sure if it was an article he'd read, he'd be able to recall it word for word as his memory was visual.

Had it been something he'd heard?

'So much for keeping it quiet,' Charles said gloomily as Angus, still trying to recall the snippet of information, walked into the medical centre office. 'The phone's ringing off the hook—journalists wanting a story. Next thing we know there'll be news helicopters hovering overhead, all looking to photograph dead birds. We're trying to contact all the parents of children who are at the camp without their families, so we can allay their fears before they hear or see a news report, but that's not easy, with so many parents at work.'

'Have you someone competent who can handle the press calls?' Angus asked, and Charles smiled.

'Fortunately, we have an excess of staff available. It might not have come from her training as a cardiac surgeon, but Gina Jamieson is a genius at using a lot of words to say nothing. *And* she's got an American accent so she sounds as if she really knows things. All the press calls are going to her.'

'And the vaccination programme?'

'Will get under way as soon as stocks of vaccine arrive. In the meantime, the Australian Quarantine and Inspection Service has contacted the army, who will fly in a mobile bio-hazard laboratory and a mobile decontamination unit to Crocodile Creek. An army helicopter will then airlift them to the island. Both units should be here tomorrow afternoon at the latest.'

'Are they sending personnel—scientists?'

Charles shook his head, then he smiled at Angus.

'They seem to think they've got one of the best on site.

You spent some time at the Centers for Disease Control and Prevention in Atlanta recently?'

Angus nodded. Like epidemiologists the world over, he'd jumped at the chance to spend time in the world's premier disease-control centre, and one of the things he'd studied there had been the genetics of the bird flu virus. But then his learning had been theoretical.

Putting what he knew into practice was different…

Testing without an MChip was different…

The bed was too hot, or maybe it was too soft. Beth tossed and turned, telling herself she had to sleep, knowing she wouldn't. In the end she forsook the bed and wandered out onto the deck, climbing cautiously into the hammock which had been known to tip her out if approached unwarily.

But there, with the salt-laden breeze cooling her skin and the smell of the reef in the air wrapping around her, she dozed.

And dreamt…

The raucous squabbles of a pair of sooty terns, fighting over a morsel of food, woke her, and she looked around blearily. Above the noise of the birds was another noise, also familiar, although why a helicopter should be circling overhead, she wasn't sure.

The small aircraft throbbed into view and tilted over the beach, then swung in a wide arc and the noise slowly faded into the distance.

Press, Beth realised. The island was already in the news. The now-familiar fear tightened her nerves, but Angus had said it probably wasn't bird flu and that the quarantine was just a precaution.

Angus!

The thought of him calmed her, and now she realised that, through the leaves of the pawpaw tree, she could see a tall figure on the beach—a bizarre sight on this tropical island, for the man was wearing a white business shirt, un-buttoned at the neck and with sleeves turned up to the elbows, and grey trousers, rolled up to just below the knees. And beside him a little boy—Sam?—running in and out of the water, splashing with his hands so the man's trousers were probably spotted with salt water.

She remembered back to what Angus had been wearing at breakfast this morning—not for him casual, tropical wear of baggy shorts and floral shirts. No, he was at a con-ference—working—and work wear was grey trousers and a white business shirt.

But Angus paddling? Splashing with a little boy? Angus?

She remembered thinking that morning that he'd changed, but paddling? For that was what the man was un-doubtedly doing. Sloshing through the shallow water at the edge of the lagoon, bending over to splash water at the child and looking, for all the world, as if he was enjoying it.

She tipped herself out of the hammock and went to join them, passing Angus's shoes set neatly by her bottom step, *her* bare feet enjoying the crunchy texture of the coarse coral sand on the path down to the beach.

'You were sleeping,' he said, as she drew closer, and Sam greeted her with a shout.

'You could have come in anyway,' she told him, uncer-tain now she was closer just why she'd come.

'Your little friend was heading for the beach. He tells

me he's supposed to be in the hall, having quiet time. I did check with one of the carers—Mrs Someone, an older woman—who said as long as he stayed with me and kept his hat on, he could play in the water. Actually...' He smiled as he added, 'The water tempted me as well.'

Ordinary enough words but something in his voice suggested a subtext in the phrase.

She studied him, then smiled back at him, certain he couldn't have meant anything more than he'd said—certainly not that seeing her asleep had tempted him in some way.

'And Charles? You're not wanted at the medical centre? You've given up the idea of autopsying a dead bird?'

'Until tomorrow,' he told her, and although he explained about the containment laboratory and the precautions they would put in place, her heart still filled with fear for him.

'So, are you free until then? Would you like a lift back to the hotel? Sam would come for a drive, wouldn't you, Sam? Or would you like to have a look around, see the camp and meet some more of the staff and kids? You could stay to dinner.'

Was she mad, suggesting this? Finding ways to keep him there, when every minute, every second with him reminded her of what she'd lost?

'I'd like to see the camp. Do I need my shoes?'

She looked down at his feet, narrow and white—feet quite unused to walking barefoot around an island, walking barefoot anywhere.

Aristocratic feet, she'd always thought.

As if aristocratic feet would look any different from ordinary feet! Feet were feet.

'Share the joke?' he asked, and Beth realised she must have been smiling at her foolishness.

'I was thinking about feet,' she offered, but didn't add whose feet, hurrying on to say, 'You should be okay barefoot. I get around that way all the time, except at work, of course. I doubt the patients would appreciate a barefoot doctor.'

Aware she was prattling, she led him towards the camp's main buildings, the dormitories, dining room and hall where discos, concerts and general fun took place, Sam darting ahead, then dashing back behind them, always on the move.

'Where is everyone, Sam?' she asked, taking his hand to stop the dizzying movement so now the three of them walked along the path.

'Hall! Listening to music, silly music—some old fellow who's dead. And watching some slides of the birds.'

'After lunch is quiet time,' Beth explained to Angus. 'They can go to their rooms or dormitories for a rest, or to the hall where they loll around, look at movies, listen to music or someone reads a story.'

She sighed.

'Poor kids—this is supposed to be a really fun time for them, going out on the reef, walking through the rain-forest at night, spotting the night animals—they came here for an adventure, not to get sick.'

'Those who are well can still enjoy the programmes surely,' Angus said, removing from Sam's hands a stick he had picked up before he could behead a bright flower from a shrub beside the path.

'Yes, they can,' Beth agreed, but she still felt the fun had been blighted—the joy of camp diminished somehow.

'Obviously there are competent support staff,' Angus said, poking his head into one of the older huts now used for arts and crafts. 'How many do they have? And who provides them?'

'The organisation sending the kids sends one person—we've got Miranda, who is a respiratory physician, with the chest group, and Benita with the cancer kids. Then Crocodile Creek Hospital supplies more support staff—Susie, our physio, and usually an occupational therapist as well. On top of that are local volunteers, people from Crocodile Creek who've been involved since the beginning—a guy who's a crocodile hunter—'

'Bruce, he's my friend and he's going to take me crocodile hunting before we go home,' Sam said, jumping up and down in anticipated excitement.

'A crocodile hunter? Surely crocodiles are protected,' Angus protested, and Beth flashed him a smile, shaking her head to warn him not to spoil Sam's fun.

'They are, but if you're a tourist from overseas and you want to see crocodiles in their natural habitat, do you want to go out in a boat with a guide or with someone who calls himself a crocodile hunter?'

She spoke quietly, but Sam had dashed ahead again, maybe in search of Bruce, entering a hall not much farther along the track.

Angus returned Beth's smile, reminding her of the folly of being close to him any more than was absolutely necessary. But it also made her feel warm and happy inside—almost complete…

And she'd missed him *so* much…

'So Bruce—that's hardly the name for a crocodile-hunter hero, is it?—is a volunteer, and I suppose the others are equally unlikely.'

'They are. There's the mayor and sometimes the CEO of the sugar mill—his son Harry is in charge of the local police station. Harry's married to Grace, the nurse you met at the hospital this morning.'

'And I've met Harry as well. He flew in this morning to ensure the quarantine order is carried out—he's the official heavyweight, from what I can gather.'

They'd reached the hall, carefully constructed to withstand future cyclones but looking as if it had grown among the palm trees, a building at one with its surroundings.

'The dormitories, girls' and boys', are over there.' Beth waved her hand to the two equally well-designed buildings. 'And the dining room is behind them. The paths here, as you can see, are compacted sand to make wheelchair access easier. I'm sorry, I'd forgotten that—is the surface rough on your feet?'

Angus heard the anxious note in her voice and wanted to shake her—gently—to tell her she had to stop worrying about other people quite so much. But that was Beth and nothing would change her, and his urge to shake turned into an urge to hug.

But hugs would lead to other urges that were already causing some concern, not in his body which was revelling in this contact with his ex-wife, but in his head, where images of Beth he thought he'd excised years ago were now flashing on a memory screen.

Beth serving him a hot, delicious meal at midnight

when he'd come in from work so tired and frazzled the last thing he'd wanted to do was eat. Yet he'd known he had to so he'd sat, and while he'd eaten, she'd massaged his shoulders and neck, her fingers easing out the knots of strain until, well fed and more relaxed, he'd been able to take her on his knee and feel the rest of the frustration of the day disappear from his body, lost in the softness that was Beth.

He watched her as she walked through the open door into the big hall, its walls decorated with huge posters showing coral and bright fish, reminders everywhere that they were in a national park and not to touch animals or plants in the water or on the land.

Inside, children and teenagers sat or lay in groups on the floor, some talking, some listening to stories. No dead person's music that Angus could hear, although Sam had attached himself to a man in a battered hat—so battered Angus suspected it had holes poked in it by a sharp knife to represent a tussle with crocodile teeth.

One of the older camp kids, a teenage boy with the blond-streaked hair of a surfer, saw them come in. Angus saw him prod the girl beside him, a pretty teenager, the baseball cap backwards on her head suggesting recent chemo.

'Here's Beth,' the lad called out. 'Dance for us, Beth.'

The girl clapped her hands, starting a movement that ran around the room.

'Dance, Beth, dance, Beth!' The kids clapped and chanted and though Beth smiled it was forced, while the look she sent to Angus was one of pure, anguished apology.

'I'm sorry. We shouldn't have come here—this is silly—but I can't say no, you can see that. The kids…'

Her shoulders lifted in a rueful shrug, and with a final tormented smile at Angus she made her way to the front of the hall, where Sam, deserting his mate, now joined her, a toy dog in his hands.

Without looking at it, Angus could have described the toy—a brown dog, dressed in a top hat and tails, its front paws holding drumsticks, a drum in front of it. And as Sam pressed the button to start the music, Angus felt his heart contract into a hard, tight lump. The first time he'd seen Beth she'd been in the children's ward at the hospital, dancing to the beat of a similar drumming dog, singing along with it. A year later he'd surprised her by buying another copy of the toy for Bobby and it had become his favourite, so he'd gone to sleep each night to the dog beating out the toe-tapping tune, 'Putting on the Ritz'.

Had Beth bought this particular toy for the kids' camp? Angus suspected she had, for it certainly wasn't Bobby's dog. Bobby's dog was—

'Start the music again, Sam,' Beth was saying. 'I'll only dance if all of you who know the steps get up with me,' she said, and a knot of small children scampered out to join her.

'Go on, Star,' the surfie-looking lad said to the girl beside him.

'Not yet,' she said. 'I will eventually because Beth's so patient, just not yet.'

And to Angus's surprise, the young lad reached over and took the girl's hand, whispering, though loudly enough for Angus to hear. 'I know you will!'

But familiar music at the front of the room diverted Angus's attention from the young couple.

And as Beth tap-danced across the front of the room, her hands clapping to produce the taps her bare feet couldn't, he understood her fractured sentences earlier and the worry that had stained her voice, but, watching, he thought not of Bobby but of the day he'd met Bobby's mother...

The day she'd tap-danced her way into his heart.

Except that he hadn't realised that's where she had been until it was too late and both she and Bobby were gone.

And he had been left with his work...

CHAPTER FIVE

HE WALKED out of the hall, making his way back to the beach, not wanting to see Beth—not wanting her to see him and divine the emotion the silly drum-beating dog had aroused in him.

A dead bird lay in the centre of the path, and he felt the scrunch of panic in his chest. It was well within the boundaries of the camp. What if one of the children had picked it up?

He felt in his pocket, sure there'd be a plastic bag, but, no, he was on a holiday island—at a conference—so why would he be carrying plastic bags? The dining room must be close—Beth had said it was behind the dormitories—but in the meantime there was the bird.

'Ah, another one.'

He turned to see an elderly man behind him. The man was dragging a large garbage bag and carrying a tool road-cleaners used to pick up rubbish from the verges. He pressed the handle so the jaws at the end of the long tool opened, then clamped them around the bird and dumped it into his bag.

Angus watched with a mix of horror and relief.

'The rangers are supposed to be collecting the dead birds,' he protested. 'And they're supposed to be wearing protective covering and masks. You should be, too, if you're picking up dead birds.'

'It's not bird flu,' the man said, and he sounded so sure of himself Angus was inclined to believe him, though for no scientific reason at all. 'They're falling out of the sky, the birds. I've been watching. It's not the birds that got here safely that are sick, but the ones still coming in. The fishermen out on the reef have seen it, too. Now, I'm no fancy scientist but it seems to me birds sick with bird flu would have died before they got this far. Say they got sick in China on the way, they wouldn't have had the strength to fly for another week to get here, now, would they? I reckon these birds aren't sick, they're exhausted.'

Again the memory of hearing something about birds and exhaustion tickled in Angus's head but he still couldn't grasp the significance of it. In the meantime, this man seemed to know what he was talking about.

'Do you live here on the island?' he asked, and the man shook his head, then extended his hand.

'Grubb's m'name but people call me Grubby—don't mind that they do. The wife and I, we work at the hospital over on the mainland—have done for more'n forty years. Met there when we were youngsters, got married forty years ago. Charles, he reckons we should celebrate the anniversary, gives us time off, and there's nothing for it, Mrs Grubb announces, but that we come over as volunteers for the kids. She loves the kids.'

Angus stared at the man who'd imparted a lifetime of information so succinctly, then backtracked.

'But you know something about these migratory birds?'

Grubby twisted the top on the plastic bag before answering.

'Been coming to the island for holidays since I was a kid. Was here when the university fellas tagged all the mutton birds and tracked them all the way back to Siberia in Russia—did you know that's where they go when they're not here? Funny, that, from a tropical place to snow. Course, people coming to the posh resort don't take kindly to a bird named common like a mutton bird, so they call 'em by their right name—shearwaters—now. But mutton birds they are here and always will be. Used to be a plant here that boiled them down for oil. Powerful stuff, mutton-bird oil used to be considered. Easy to catch because they burrow, you see.'

Hardly comforting news, Angus decided as Grubby departed, the sack now slung over his shoulder. How many dead birds might be hidden in the burrows? And just where was Grubby going to despatch his dead birds?

Hurrying after the man, Angus discovered he was going to the medical centre.

'I put 'em in the hazardous waste drums, seal 'em up and shove them in the freezer with the other contaminated hospital waste. Fly it out once a week because they've only got a small freezer unit here, and it's collected from the hospital on the mainland once a month.'

'Can you wait while I get my shoes? I'd like to see the process,' Angus said.

Grubby rested his sack on the ground by way of reply and waited until Angus returned, neatly shod and with his trousers rolled back down.

By the time he'd had a tour of the medical centre's disposal facilities and spoken to Charles about plans for the arrival and placement of the mobile units, it was late afternoon.

He should, by rights, return to the hotel and join his colleagues for dinner, but he found he had no desire at all for theoretical conversation when the containment of a possible epidemic was happening right here and now. He was also drawn to return to Beth's little hut, sure she'd be there now.

But that might look needy, and needy was a weakness his father had ruthlessly eliminated from Angus's nature. A man should be complete within himself, using the intelligence he had been given to programme his life to perfection. Yes, there were physical needs genetically wired into us for the survival of the species, but these could be satisfied by mutual agreement between a man and a woman. They did not have to be romanticised, or emotionalised—that way lay disaster.

Angus shuddered as his father's edicts rang so clearly in his head. How had he, Angus, an intelligent man, allowed himself to be so brainwashed?

Although he couldn't entirely blame the brainwashing. Hadn't he learned the truth himself, that day, aged seven, when he'd whispered those fatal words, 'I love you, Mum,' to his mother as he'd left for school, returning in the afternoon to find her gone…

He pushed away the memories, not wanting them hanging like a black cloud around his head, thinking he'd visit the little boy and the thick black clouds might be visible to a child.

Robbie…

The name was nothing more than coincidence, but when he entered the room and found Beth beside the little boy's bed, he knew she, too, felt the tie.

She turned at his entry, her eyes, above the blue mask she wore, dark with worry.

'No good?' Angus murmured, lifting a second chair and setting down noiselessly beside Beth's, lifting the mask that hung around his neck and fastening it into place.

'No good at all. He's lapsing in and out of consciousness, and then Danny, one of the other children who'd been isolated, has been admitted following a seizure. Then there's Lily—Alex, the guest who's a neurosurgeon, did a lumbar puncture on her yesterday afternoon.'

Robbie was tossing and turning on the bed, at times muttering feverishly then quietening, before the muttering began again.

'The earlier test results not back?' Angus asked, and Beth shook her head.

'Apparently there was some mix-up and they were sent to Brisbane rather than being done locally, then the containers were lost at the lab.' The words were muffled by the mask but the story familiar enough. Why was it always the important specimens or slides that went missing? 'Charles has spent hours on the phone this afternoon, trying to chase them down. I think he's found where they are and is pushing for a result asap. On top of that, he's desperately concerned about Lily.'

'Depending on the facilities in this mobile lab they're sending, I could do the tests here tomorrow.'

He sounded quite cheerful about it, but Beth couldn't

help feeling guilty. She was feeling a lot of other things as well, with Angus so close, but guilt was the only one she could consider right now.

'I'm sorry I got you into this,' she said. 'But you don't have to stay involved. I know Charles must have been enormously grateful to have someone like you to back him up over the steps he had to take, but now things are all under way, you could go back to your conference.'

Angus was watching Robbie, stroking the little boy's arm with the tip of his gloved forefinger. Beth waited for him to turn, to look at her, but when he answered, he kept his eyes on the sick child in the bed.

'I'll be needed here tomorrow when the lab arrives,' he said. 'So I may as well stay. Problem is, Charles tells me accommodation on this side of the island is fully booked. Am I right in thinking that old couch of yours folds out into a bed?'

Beth heard the words—and none of them were complex or difficult to understand—but taken together they didn't make a lot of sense.

Well, they did, but the sense they made filled her with apprehension.

'You want to stay here? On this side? It's only fifteen minutes in a cart from the resort where you've got a comfortable bed, yet you'd sleep on my old couch?'

'I'd rather be close to the action,' he said, still not looking at her, but Beth could feel it now, the physical attraction that had stirred between them from their first meeting. It was filtering beneath her skin, and teasing alert the hairs on her arms. It was heating tissues deep inside her, and making her breasts ache with wanting.

'Just close to the action?' she whispered, accenting the final word only slightly.

Now he looked at her, his hazel eyes meeting hers, a slight flush on his cheeks.

Sun-kissed from his walk on the beach or something else?

'No,' he said, but she'd forgotten what she'd asked, so caught up in the physical heat that had drawn her to Angus from the beginning, her mind was barely functioning.

'Mu-u-u-m!'

Robbie's tortured cry broke the spell, and Beth bent over the child, whispering to him, holding his shoulders until the convulsive thrashing stopped.

'That's the first coherent word he's spoken,' she said to Angus, her voice breaking with the pain she felt for the sick child. 'And his mum can't be here with him.'

'He's barely conscious and probably doesn't realise that,' Angus said, putting his arm around Beth's shoulder and giving her a comforting hug, while she used a damp cloth to wipe the sweat from Robbie's face. 'Why don't you take a break? I'll sit with him for a while.'

'No, you can both go.'

The voice made them both turn, and Beth smiled when she saw Marcia in the doorway.

'Angus, this is Marcia, one of the nurses from the mainland hospital. Marcia, Angus. But, Marcia, aren't you running the kids' camp trivia contest tonight?'

'It's been cancelled and they're having a movie instead—James Bond, especially for the older boys. Not to mention an excuse to have popcorn. So I'm here to tell you that Robbie's mine for the next few hours. Remember

I'm the one he came to when he felt sick—I'm the one who looks like his mum. So off you go. You can come back later, Beth, but you know he'll be in good hands if you actually decide to have a decent night's sleep.'

She glanced from Beth to Angus, seeming to focus on Angus's arm still around Beth's shoulders.

'Or not,' she added blithely, before hiding her smile behind her mask and coming farther into the room.

Would Beth tell him to return to the hotel?

Angus found he didn't have a clue how she would react, but then, growing up as she had, in and out of foster-homes all her life, she'd learned, too well, to hide her feelings.

Though she had shown them in her anxiety to please, in her quiet determination to do whatever she could to make others around her happy.

'The dining room will be closed but I can get some fish or steaks from the kitchen and rustle up a salad. Would that do you for dinner?'

The question told him she'd accepted his decision to stay and it was all he could do not to do a little tap-dance himself, except that, try as she had, Beth had never been able to teach him the steps.

'Do you have a barbeque? And do we get a choice when you're pinching things from the kitchen? I'm probably a better steak cook than a fish cook.'

She turned to smile at him.

'You're probably equally proficient with both,' she said, smiling at him. 'Apart from tap-dancing, I doubt there's anything you've ever set your mind to do and not succeeded.'

He shook his head, surprised to find their thoughts had been so in tune. Though it had often been that way—to such an extent he'd sometimes wondered if it was their mutual difficulty in expressing their emotions that had led to them communicating through their thoughts.

Though back then he'd dismissed such ideas as fanciful.

'Perhaps steak. I had fish last night.'

They'd reached the building behind the dormitories and although most of it was in darkness, a light shone above a door at the back. Beth produced a bunch of keys, selected a bright pink one and unlocked the door.

'It's like the corner store,' she said. 'All the staff have access. We write down what we take, and get a monthly bill. Far easier than trying to work out what food we want sent across from the mainland.'

She moved easily around the big kitchen, picking up a plastic carry basket and stacking her selection into it— plastic-wrapped meat from a cool-room, mushrooms, an avocado, some green leaves in a plastic bag, tiny tomatoes and, with a smile directed at Angus, a couple of onions.

'Can't have steak without onions,' she teased, quoting him again, the smile in her voice making him feel comfortable and confused at the same time.

Surely they couldn't be slotting so easily back into each other's lives—not after parting as they had, both of them lost in bitter grief they hadn't been able to verbalise or share.

And surely there was danger here, danger in the feeling of comfort into which he was sinking—as dangerous as quicksand, the sinking as inevitable. Yet the pleasure of simply being with Beth—being in her undemanding company—was too much to resist, so thoughts of danger were pushed away and the warning signals ringing in his head were ruthlessly ignored.

Back at her little hut, she produced not a regular gas-fired barbeque but a small, cast-iron brazier, with space for heat beads in the bottom and a grilling rack and hot plate combination on the top.

'The single woman's barbeque,' she said, putting it down on a side table and lighting the beads. 'Though it's big enough for two steaks. Do you want to slice the onions while it heats?'

The question surprised him, reminding him it had been three years since he and Beth had lived together. That Beth would have sliced the onions herself, protesting, if he'd offered, that she'd liked to fuss over him.

And as he followed her into the kitchen he wasn't sure just what he felt about this change—small enough but indicative that this Beth was a stranger, no matter how familiar she seemed.

Big mistake, suggesting he slice the onions, Beth realised as he followed her into the tiny space that was her kitchen.

She tried to stay as small as possible as she washed the salad leaves and whirled them dry, then cut the avocado into slices, but inevitably they brushed against each other and when, the onions neatly sliced, Angus swung around to wash his hands, they collided. His wrists—oniony hands held carefully away—caught her shoulders to steady her and their eyes met, then their lips, the kiss a question and a confirmation.

Was this what they wanted?

The magic was still there…

'Onion hands,' Angus said, breaking away.

'And I've squashed the avocado,' Beth managed, though she was sure she didn't sound as composed as Angus had. 'I'll have to make it into dressing now.'

She studied the solid back of her ex-husband as he, very efficiently, washed his hands at the sink. The kiss had suggested that he'd been feeling the same residual attraction she'd been feeling since they'd met that morning, but was that all it was—remembered physical delight?

Assuming it was, the best thing to do was to ignore it.

And maybe scrape the avocado off her fingers before she spread it all around the cabin…

'I'll put the onions on first,' Angus said, turning from the sink, her small pumpkin-shaped and -coloured hand-towel in his hands. 'A plate for when they're cooked?'

She pulled out a drawer where her assortment of crockery, mostly found at flea markets and antique shops, was kept and handed him one, wishing that particular one hadn't been on top—who knew what Angus would think of a Donald Duck souvenir plate from Disneyland via the farmers' market at Eumundi?

Not her, certainly, because, although he'd raised an eyebrow at her as he'd looked at it, he made no comment, simply carrying it, the bowl of sliced onions and the steak out to the deck.

How could she ever have believed their marriage would work? That plate was symbolic of the differences between them—Angus's crockery had all been perfectly matched, square white plates and square black plates, varying in size so they could sit on each other in black and white harmony or stand alone—a black dinner service or a white one. Not a Donald Duck plate in sight!

But when she carried the tray with the salad bowl, cutlery and two more plates out to the table, the sight of Angus bent over her small barbeque seemed so right that for a moment she forgot to breathe.

Beyond him the sky had darkened with the sudden tropical nightfall, and the paler blur of the sea was the only demarcation between the earth and the heavens. And Angus stood there, solid, concentrated, complete within himself. It had been the completeness that had fascinated Beth— and she, who'd been such a mess of insecurities, had been drawn to him as the ocean tides were drawn to the moon.

Inevitably.

Irresistibly.

'Still medium-rare?'

The man she'd been watching turned as he asked the question. She nodded her response, too afraid to speak, the secret heart of her wondering if this time it could be different—

There was no *this time*, she told herself crossly. This was ships-passing-in-the-night stuff, a chance encounter, nothing more. The crisis would be over and, like the mobile decontamination unit, Angus would depart— leaving no way to decontaminate herself if she was foolish enough to fall in love with him again.

Again?

Admit it—*still* was the word.

She still loved Angus…

No! It was attraction, nothing more. She was still *attracted* to Angus!

Liar!

The smell of the barbeque, meat and onions filled the night air, reminding Beth her meals today had been scanty to say the least. She shifted shells to make room at the table and set two places, a strange feeling of displacement settling over her as she considered she and Angus sitting down to dinner in this unlikely setting.

Though the setting was no more unlikely than her and Angus sitting down to dinner together somewhere else, given how far apart they'd been when they'd parted.

'Smells wonderful.'

The voice came out of the darkness but Beth recognised it.

'Doing some spotlighting, Jamie?' she asked, as the young lad came into the light of the deck, Stella Vavunis by his side.

'No, just giving Star some extra practice with her leg. It's easier for her to do it when the others aren't around. Although most of the others are encouraging, there are a couple of kids staying over at the resort who come to the lagoon to swim and they freak her out. And it's especially hard for her to walk on the sand, so we're going down to the beach.'

Beth smiled at the young couple.

'Nothing to do with the fact that the full moon will be rising shortly,' she teased, and Stella laughed.

'I think all Jamie knows about the full moon is that it brings good surf conditions,' she said, teasing Jamie in her turn.

'Well, have fun, the two of you,' Beth said as they moved away, Jamie with his arm around Stella's waist, presumably to steady her as she walked on her new prosthetic leg.

'Cancer?' Angus asked as he came to the table and divided the steak and onions between two plates.

'It was in the bone. She lost her lower leg. She's an example of how good the camp can be for kids—when she arrived she was determined not to use the prosthesis, insisting on wearing jeans and using crutches, but Susie, the Crocodile Creek physio, has been working not only on her muscle co-ordination but on her self-esteem, and she's done wonders.'

'I imagine young Jamie hasn't hurt her self-esteem either,' Angus said, nodding to where the pair were now heading for the harder sand at the edge of the water. 'He's some young man, to be prepared to help her the way he is.'

Beth nodded.

'I suppose, having been through cancer treatment himself, he has more understanding than a lot of kids his age. Or maybe he was always going to be a very special young man. Whatever, he's been great and Stella—he calls her Star—has blossomed under his friendship.'

'Young love!' Angus said softly, then he looked across the table at Beth.

'Did you ever feel it?'

She had just sliced off a piece of meat and balanced it and some onion rings on her fork, when Angus asked the question.

Only when I met you, didn't seem like an appropriate answer, for she'd been past young at twenty-five, but that had been exactly how she'd felt—like a giddy, dizzy teenager plunged into something she didn't fully understand.

She shook her head.

'I was moving around too much. I started my teens with a foster-family in Brisbane, then my grandmother in Gympie decided she wanted me, then I went back to a different foster-family. Moving around meant I missed school so I was always trying to catch up on schoolwork.'

'Yet you still qualified for medical school.'

Angus spoke so quietly Beth had to look at him to make sure she'd heard it right.

'Of course. I'm sure I told you some time that being a doctor was my only ambition. I was five when I had to have my tonsils and adenoids out and the doctor I was taken to was so kind and gentle I knew right from then that one day I'd be a doctor and be kind and gentle to little kids.'

Angus *had* heard the story, but hearing it again made something shift in his chest at the idea of a child so young deciding on an ambition because a stranger had been kind to her.

How little kindness must she have known that this had made such an impression?

She might talk about the benevolence of her foster-families and protest that she had never been ill-treated, but neither had she been loved.

And if anyone deserved to be loved, it was Beth.

Which, now he remembered, had been why he'd walked away from their marriage without argument. Because Beth, of all people, deserved more than a man who didn't know how to love…

Not properly…

Not the way Beth deserved to be loved…

He was eating and thinking about this, when the wail of a baby nearby stopped his fork on the way to his mouth.

'A baby? Do you have babies in the camp?'

Beth smiled across the table at him.

'That's the cry of the shearwaters. Now it's dark they'll start up—you'll hear them all night.'

'They cry like babies and burrow into the ground to nest—what else do they do, these strange birds?'

'Well, to me the marvel of them is that the adults migrate before the young are strong enough to fly all the way to Siberia, yet the young know where to go, and no doubt where to stop on the way to feed.'

'Ah! Light-bulb moment. Thank you, Beth. It's been bothering me all day, something I'd read or heard about our migratory birds, and you mentioning feeding places brought it back. Apparently there are tidal flats on the Korean peninsula where a lot of migratory birds break their journey to Australia, and recently the flats were closed off by a wall, millions of shellfish died and migrating birds were left without food for their migration. Maybe Grubby is right—the birds *are* dying of starvation.'

'Grubby? You've met Grubby?'

Beth sounded a little lost so Angus had to smile and touch her reassuringly on the hand.

And having touched her, surely leaving his hand covering hers for a short time wouldn't hurt.

'I have indeed, and now, if you've finished eating, why don't we, too, walk down to the beach—maybe not in the direction Stella and Jamie took—and watch the moon rise over the water?'

Beth stared at him, unable to believe Angus had suggested something so romantic.

Or why!

Though maybe it wasn't romance he was thinking of—
maybe the moon might help him remember more about the
feeding habits of migratory birds on tidal flats in Korea.

And although her head told her that walking on the
beach in the moonlight with Angus was little short of
madness, her heart assured her head it could handle it this
time. After all, Angus was no longer her first love. She had
changed, matured, become so much more sure of herself,
as a doctor and as a woman. She could handle a little
romance on the beach.

If that's what he had in mind...

She stacked the dirty dishes on the tray and carried them
inside, noticing the breakfast things still waiting to be
washed.

Do them now, common sense suggested, but Angus
had followed her inside with the salad bowl and when she
turned he took her in his arms and her last rational thought
was that they probably wouldn't see the moon rise this
particular night.

Kissing Angus was so familiar yet so different. She
recognised the taste of him, the texture of his lips, recognised, too, her body's reaction—the heat, sizzling deep
inside her, shafting downwards. Yet the way he held her,
gently, barely touching her, as if expecting her to pull
away at any moment—that was different.

But how could she pull away when the spell Angus had
cast over her from the first time they'd kissed still held her
firmly in its grip?

'Angus.'

She breathed his name against his lips and felt hers
whispered back. Just so had they always made love—

silently—nothing but their names confirming their iden-
tities as if in kissing, touching, loving they might lose
themselves and need to know again just who they were.

His arms engulfed her, wrapping her in the security of
his body, holding her close so all her doubts and fears and
uncertainties were kept at bay. This, too, had always been
the way. Safe in Angus's arms she'd lost the insecurities
that had plagued her all her life, living for the moment,
living, eventually, for him, and then for Bobby…

His lips were tracing kisses down her neck, then up
again, resting where her pulse beat—wildly and erratically
she was sure. They found her mouth again and claimed it,
a kiss so deep it drew all air from her lungs and left her
gasping, clinging, wanting more than kisses.

Could he still read her so well that he lifted her into his
arms, carrying her as easily as if she were a child into the
bedroom where she'd tossed and turned hours earlier?

He lowered her onto the bed and knelt beside her,
brushing back her hair, repeating her name, a note of
wonder she hadn't heard before in his voice.

But that short journey had brought doubts in its trail—
what was she doing? How could she think of rushing back
into—into what? It was hardly a relationship.

Soft kisses—exploratory—moved across her skin, her
name a mantra on Angus's lips.

She could barely think, and what was Angus doing?
Thinking Angus, who was so controlled.

Angus, who always thought things through…

Or nearly always.

Angus—the man she'd loved—

Still loved?

She supposed so, but that didn't mean…

Thoughts twisted in her head as she kissed and was kissed, thoughts doing nothing to stop the hunger rising in her like a king tide, threatening to lift her on its curling waves and carry her to a far-off shore.

His hands roved across her breasts, encountering nipples already peaking with desire, his fingers, thumbs teasing at the tight nubs, shooting messages of desire through her body.

Then her name became a question.

'Beth?'

His hands at the buttons on her blouse…

Instead of answering, she sat up and stripped it off, over her head, then began to unbutton his staid white shirt, pushing back the edges so she could touch his skin.

Thoughts befuddled now by wanting Angus, tiny messages trying to get through—whispering in the back of her mind.

Her fingers trembled, so great was her need. They fumbled with his buttons so Angus stood and stripped off his clothes, too, joining her on the bed as she wriggled out of shorts and knickers, needing to feel his skin on hers, to be close to him all over. Wrapped in Angus once again…

But he took his time, teasing her, letting her tease him, hands grazing skin as they explored and remembered, little touches, kisses, sensations Beth had totally forgotten, desire enhanced by waiting until it became greedily demanding, their kisses hot and hard, their hands frantic in their touching.

'I want to be inside you,' Angus whispered, voice hoarse

with the hunger they'd generated—had always generated between them.

For an answer Beth shifted, lifting her hips to ease his entry, clutching at his arms in an attempt to keep herself centred, then as his erection touched her—probed—some echo of the past returned, faint at first then yelling at her.

Yelling a warning about falling back into bed like this, as if there'd been no parting, no divorce, no Bobby—

Bobby!

'No, Angus, wait, it's not safe.'

She slid away from under him, so embarrassed she wanted to shrivel up and disappear, but Angus had reacted differently, sitting up and snapping on her bedside light, a look of fury on his face.

'Are you still obsessed about not having another child? Is that what this is all about? Do you lead other men on then pull away or do they come prepared with condoms? And why, in heaven's name, if you're so damned determined to remain childless, wouldn't you be on the Pill? You're a doctor—it isn't that difficult for you to get them.'

Beth stared at him, totally bewildered by his anger.

'Angus, we're not married,' she said, lamely pointing out the obvious. 'And I wasn't thinking of not having another child, but of repeating the same mistake I made last time—of getting pregnant and putting you in a position where you felt you had to marry me.'

Her voice sounded very small, even to her own ears, and perhaps Angus hadn't heard it, for he continued to pull on his clothes with a haste that suggested he couldn't wait to get out of her hut.

Holding his shoes in one hand, he headed for the door, muttering now, but words Beth couldn't hear. Then, just as she was resigned to him walking out and probably never talking to her again, he turned, glared at her, and said, 'I didn't *have* to marry you!'

CHAPTER SIX

ACCEPTING, after an hour of fruitless tossing and turning, that she wasn't going to sleep, Beth got up and headed for the shower. She'd go back up and relieve Marcia by Robbie's bed.

As water splashed down on her head, anxiety for the children who were supposed to be having a wonderful holiday simmered inside her, although it had been subdued for a while by the turbulent emotions Angus's return into her life had caused.

But now he was gone again—his departure unmistakably final, so even if she did see him around the place, they would be meeting as colleagues, not almost-lovers.

She soaped her body all over, rubbing at her skin, actions automatic as her mind followed the trail of Angus.

No, she was damned if she was going to sigh over what had happened. Bad enough that she'd lost sleep.

So what if she and Angus were still attracted to each other?

So what if she'd upset him by her sudden refusal to make love?

Shampoo bubbles cascaded down her face.

She'd upset herself as well—badly—wanting him, aching for him, yet not lost enough in lust to risk what had happened before.

And if he thought she'd pulled away because of what he called her obsession to not have another child, then he could go on thinking that. Better that he thought her a little batty than realised just how much guilt she'd carried over that first pregnancy.

Lifting her head, she let the water stream down her face, hiding tears she wasn't going to admit were there, rinsing out the conditioner from her hair.

By the time she'd dried herself off, combed the tangles from her hair and dressed in clean clothes, she was Dr Beth Stuart again, competent medical practitioner, in charge of the new Wallaby Island Medical Centre.

Mature!

This façade crumpled only slightly when she reached Robbie's bed and found Angus sitting beside the pale, still child.

Beth stood inside the door, wanting to turn away but knowing it was too late.

'I've nothing better to do so I thought I might sit with him for a while. Being in the centre helps me concentrate my mind on what might be happening. I have to consider what else it is, if it's not bird flu.'

'You—' Beth began to speak then realised she didn't have the words she needed, so stared at him instead, disbelief vying with anger.

Anger won and she began again.

'You stalk out of my place, angry because one of us happened to have enough common sense to think about unwanted pregnancies, then come up here to sit beside a child you don't even know. I know I never understood you, Angus, but you sure as hell never understood me either.'

His turn to frown.

'What do you mean?'

Don't sigh! Stay mad!

But mad—angry mad—was something Beth found difficult to sustain, though she did swallow the sigh.

'I didn't stop tonight because of my so-called obsession about not having another child,' she said, hoping she was speaking crisply so he'd realise how maturely she was handling this argument. 'I stopped because I didn't want us back where we were before, with me being accidentally pregnant and you insisting on marrying me—of course you didn't *have* to but your moral code wouldn't allow otherwise. And for your information, I am *not* obsessed about not having another child.'

Angus was doing all right until she got to the 'not obsessed' part. That bit slipped beneath his skin.

Of course she had been. She'd gone ballistic—or as ballistic as Beth could ever go—when, after Bobby's death, he'd suggested it.

'Wasn't that why we parted?' he asked, aware he was treading in the dark and wondering what hidden traps might lie beneath his stumbling feet. 'So, if I wanted a child or children, I could have them with someone else? That's what you said.'

She shook her head—slowly—as if it was very, very heavy. Were her thoughts making it that way?

'We lived on different planets, didn't we?' she said, a note of deep regret in her voice. 'Together but apart because we couldn't understand each other's language. Not that we used language all that often.'

'We talked all the time,' Angus protested, although he knew they were empty words even before Beth raised her eyebrows. They *had* talked but never, ever about emotions.

'Anyway,' she said, sounding ridiculously cheerful and totally unconcerned about their coitus interruptus earlier, 'all that's in the past and it's probably just as well we didn't make love. We'd have ended up having a purely physical affair without giving it a moment's rational thought. Gone into it for all the wrong reasons!'

He stared at her, uncertain that this self-possessed woman, chatting easily and unemotionally about their shared past and purely physical affairs, could possibly be his Beth.

Though that Beth *was* his, he had no doubt! He didn't mean it in a possessive, ownership kind of way but since they'd met again—was it only last night?—he'd felt a deep certainty that they were meant to be together.

And always had been...

Though he could hardly say that now.

He replayed her last comments in his head and found something they *could* talk about.

'Are there wrong and right reasons for an affair where physical attraction is concerned?' he asked, and waited, keen to see just how this new Beth would respond.

She left her position in the doorway, where flight had probably been an option, and sat down beside him in the second chair, her hand reaching out to rest on Robbie's thigh.

'Of course there are,' she said, stroking the child's skin.

As an excuse for not looking at her ex-husband? 'A purely physical affair would be fine if both parties knew and accepted that's all it was—physical pleasure given and received. But if there were doubts, if both parties weren't in agreement or if the outcome of it—the parameters—were never discussed, it's nothing short of dangerous.'

'Experience talking, Beth?' he asked, because he couldn't help himself, though he regretted it the moment she looked up at him, hurt in her eyes.

'My only experience was with you, Angus,' she said quietly. 'So, yes, in a way it *is* experience talking. I know I went into our relationship thinking that's all it was—an affair—and though we didn't talk about it—we've been there, to the not talking, haven't we?—I assumed that's what you thought it would be as well. Two people attracted to each other, enjoying the attraction. We came from such different worlds I couldn't see how it would be otherwise. My pregnancy…' She shrugged. 'Well, who knows what might have happened?'

She'd turned away again, her eyes now fixed on the child. Which was probably just as well, because Angus had no idea what to say—what to reply—or even if a reply was necessary. She'd been right about them being on different planets—that's how it had been when Bobby had died—and that's exactly how he felt now, unable to put into words what he'd felt when he and Beth had begun their affair, unable to remember anything but the need he'd felt to be with her, and the strange melancholy that had followed him around whenever he hadn't been…

'Oh, you *are* here, Beth!' Marcia appeared in the doorway. 'Charles said to tell you, if you were still around, that Lily's conscious and quite lucid. Dreadfully tired and drawn but talking to him and Jill, asking about the bulls, would you believe?'

'That's great news,' Beth responded. 'And with Jack shifted back to a cabin in the camp you have to wonder if perhaps we've raised alarms too early. The two adults were okay earlier when I checked, although little Danny is still quite ill.'

'There's no such thing as too early with a situation like this,' Angus said, happy to switch from muddled emotional thoughts of the past to problems of the present. Problems he could deal with, but emotion—that was a different beast altogether. 'With only one or two people sick plus dead birds, it might have seemed alarmist, but you had five ill, now six, some seriously. No, it was right to put the wheels in motion for quarantine and further investigation.'

'So the mobile lab and decontamination unit will still come tomorrow?' Beth asked, then glanced at the clock on the wall. 'Or today, as it is now?'

'They will,' Angus said. 'Something has been making people sick and if it isn't the birds, what is it? Plus we've got to find out why the birds are dying. It's not as if it's one or two birds. I met a man called Grubby today and he had a bagful.'

'Trust Grubby to be involved,' Marcia said. 'And I bet he wasn't wearing gloves and a mask.'

'He wasn't, but his theory was interesting and I've put in a call to some bird experts on the mainland to see if there's some way we can test it.'

'Not until the containment lab arrives,' Beth said,

annoyed that she should feel such a clutch of panic at the thought of Angus in danger, yet unable to stop it.

So much for maturity! Not to mention parameters!

'That'll be exciting, won't it?' Marcia said. 'Like stuff you see on television when someone sends some white powder through the post and everyone thinks it might be anthrax.'

'I'm not sure "exciting" is the word I'd use,' Beth said. 'Look at Robbie here—he's not excited and neither's his mum, I bet.'

'Oh, she's okay now. I spoke to her tonight and told her the other little boy was already better and that Lily was over the worst and Robbie was resting more easily. I suppose she's so used to him being sick she doesn't get too stressed.'

Had Angus guessed what Beth had been about to say—that she was about to tell Marcia just how stressful every minor ailment or illness was for parents of a child with a disability—that he put his hand on her shoulder?

'He does seem to be doing better,' he said quietly.

And now that Beth turned her attention—all of it—from Angus to the child in the bed, she realised Marcia and Angus were right—Robbie did seem to be sleeping more naturally.

'So you don't need to sit here all night,' Marcia said. 'Either of you,' she added with a smile. 'I'll call you, Beth, if he becomes fretful.'

She disappeared but not before she'd smiled again—a knowing kind of smile that should have made Beth angry but instead made her feel sad.

But only for a moment. Kissing Angus had reminded

her of how good love-making had been between them, and had reminded her body of its needs. Not only reminding her but leaving her aching for the kind of bliss only Angus could bring to it.

Would it hurt to experience it again?

Surely not!

But could she make love with Angus without him realising how much she still loved him?

Of course she could! Hadn't she concealed her love from him throughout their marriage? Hadn't she held back from saying the words she'd longed to say because she'd known how awkward—how unwelcome—he'd have found them?

And wasn't she so much more mature now? Better able to handle such things?

Besides, wouldn't an affair—purely physical, of course—with Angus be a better memory to carry with her into the future than the memory of devastation she'd been left with when they'd parted?

Half-appalled yet totally excited by her thoughts, she took a deep breath and plunged into speech.

'Do you want to come back to my place?' she said, turning to the man she'd been so very angry with only a little earlier.

'Are you crazy?' Angus growled, keeping his voice low so he didn't disturb the sleeping child but still conveying his outrage. 'For what? So we can almost make love again?'

Beth shrugged, took a deep, silent breath, crossed her fingers for luck—or whatever—and said, as calmly as she could, 'More so you could spend what's left of the night there and be closer to the medical centre in the morning.

After all, that was your original idea. And it needn't be *almost* if we make love again, Angus.' Was her voice wavering? Was her trepidation obvious? Keep calm! Just say it. 'I'm the boss of this place. I know where they keep condoms.'

Angus stared at her, sure he should be offended by what she was saying yet so stunned to hear such words coming from shy, unworldly Beth he found them difficult to take in.

'You've just been talking about all the wrong reasons for going into an affair,' he muttered at her. 'Isn't this a prime example of a wrong reason—leftover lust from our marriage?'

To his surprise she smiled, although he suspected the smile didn't reach her eyes.

'I thought it was a prime example of the right kind of affair—no strings attached, like a holiday romance. We're talking about it first, so it's not just impulse. We both know it has no future because you'll be gone when the conference is over or the quarantine lifted and I'll be staying here. Perfect!'

Angus realised he didn't have a clue how to react. His body told him one thing—urging him to agree with Beth's invitation and analysis of the situation—while his mind was quite sure this wasn't Beth at all, just someone else in Beth's body—that delectable, sexy, desirable and utterly tantalising body. Though that last bit was his body talking again…

He opened his mouth then realised he was about to launch into a string of incomplete sentences, things like 'You' and 'I' and 'We'. Not even sentences, just pronouns, with no words to follow them because he had no idea what he wanted to say.

'It's up to you,' Beth said cheerfully, though he suspected he could hear a note of strain beneath the words. Was this all an act, this grown-up, independent, affair-discussing Beth? 'If you want to go back to the resort, I'll drive you back, but you decide. I'll meet you out front.'

And with that she disappeared.

To get some condoms?

The thought excited him—as did this new Beth, act or not! Not that she'd been dependent or clingy during their marriage, more that she'd been a follower—no, not even that. She'd just been there, willing to fit in—her upbringing leaving her with a need to please, but unobtrusively.

His chest tightened just thinking about it. The young foster-child, trying to be so good but invisible as well, hoping if she wasn't noticed, then she might be allowed to stay. He'd only met one of her foster-mothers, who'd explained she'd have been happy to keep Beth for ever, even adopt her, but Beth's maternal grandmother had been her guardian and she'd refused to release the child for adoption, or give her up completely, descending on whatever home Beth might be in to take her for a short time before tiring of the role of mother and giving her back to Children's Services.

Her grandmother, the only relation she'd ever known, had died shortly before he'd met Beth, and though Angus thought the woman had behaved very badly as far as Beth was concerned, Beth, in her gentle, trusting, accepting and unquestioning way, had loved her.

Were these thoughts helping his decision?

Of course not! They were making him even more confused, although if he accepted that the Beth who'd offered him a bed—and an affair—was a very different Beth to the one he'd married, surely that would make the affair okay.

He touched the sleeping child on the forehead, his mind sliding towards what-ifs.

Useless! This was here and now and Beth was offering him a chance at redemption. Oh, she might not know it. She might be thinking of a brief affair—although that suggestion was so foreign to the Beth he knew, he realised there was something he was missing—but he didn't have to agree to that. He didn't have to fit into her so-called parameters.

Did he?

He bent and kissed the little boy on the cheek, hoping somewhere in his sleep he might feel the caress, then he made his way to the front of the new building, night-quiet now the worst was over for the patients within it.

No, the little boy who'd had the seizure was still very ill and according to a doctor called Luke, who had been on duty when Angus had arrived, one of the adults from the resort wasn't much better, being monitored all the time, with respiratory support, fluids and non-steroidal anti-inflammatory drugs the only things they could give him until they knew exactly what had caused the illness.

Angus had heard the murmur of voices as he'd passed the man's room, and been reminded of just why he'd been called to the medical centre.

Not for an affair with his ex-wife, that was for sure, but until the lab arrived there was very little he could do.

Beth was sitting in the driving seat of one of the carts and Angus felt panic clutch at his intestines.

She'd changed her mind—

'I thought you'd need clean clothes, to say nothing of a razor and toothbrush, so I'd drive you over to the resort and you can either stay there or get your things and come back to my place. Up to you.'

Angus got warily into the cart and peered at the woman beside him, visible in the light of the moon they'd intended walking under earlier.

Was there a packet of condoms in her shorts pocket?

Excitement tightened his body and he peered at her again.

She looked like Beth, and her voice sounded the same, it was just—

He had no idea what it was, but it was time to find out. People didn't change this much for no reason and for all she'd said he was the only man she'd had in her life, he was beginning to suspect that might not be true. Someone or something had changed her in some way.

'I'll get my things and come back to your place,' he said, watching closely so he could read her reaction.

Except he couldn't—not even when she'd glanced his way before she started the cart. She steered them onto the narrow track that led into the rainforest, reaching into the shelf below the dashboard and handing him insect repellent.

'Put this on your face and arms. The mossies in the forest could carry you away they're so fierce.'

He took the cream and smoothed it on his skin, hating the smell of it but not wanting to be bitten.

They drove through the dark rainforest, aware from the wailing cries of the shearwaters, the buzzing of insects and the rustling movements in the ferns that the forest was as alive at night as it was during the day.

'The canopy made up of vines and plants—like stag-horns and elkhorns that live high up in the trees—blocks out the moonlight, that's why it's so dark,' Beth said, needing to break the silence that was like a glass wall between them. 'Farther into the park, on the edge of the mountain, the park rangers have built a suspension walkway through the canopy, so you can see all the life that's up there.'

Angus remained silent and she began to wonder what on earth she'd done, asking him back to her place, suggesting he stay—a packet of condoms burning a hole in her pocket…

All to satisfy her lust?

She hoped she could pass it off as that, but in her heart of hearts she knew it wasn't anything to do with lust. What she wanted was some more time with Angus—a little period of togetherness she could enjoy then wrap up like a parcel and tuck away inside her, to be taken out and relived when she felt lonely or depressed.

Like a diamond tucked away somewhere safe, brought out to shimmer in the light from time to time. Better by far a memory like that than the bleak, black stone that had been Bobby's death and the harsh words she and Angus had exchanged so soon after it, before they'd each re-treated into their separate cocoons of grief…

She stopped the cart where she'd parked it the previous morning, suddenly aware of just how long this day had been.

How confusing…

Would Angus go into the hotel and return or was he already regretting his earlier decision?

'Walk in with me?' he said, and Beth's heart leapt because she knew it meant he would return. Then she glanced down at the shorts and shirt she wore and decided walking through the lobby of a five-star resort in this attire wouldn't be the done thing, no matter how late the hour.

Or possibly *because* of the late hour.

'I'll wait here,' she said, and the wall crumbled, Angus leaning right through it to put his hand behind her head and draw it towards him, kissing her with such fierce urgency that desire flooded through her body.

'See that you do,' he said, then he was gone, striding along the path, past the ocean-like swimming pool and up the stairs into the foyer.

Her mobile chirped at exactly the moment Angus reappeared, small overnight bag in hand. Beth answered it, knowing it would be a summons to the hospital.

'The restful sleep didn't last long—can you come?' Marcia said, and Beth knew she would.

Angus saw the mobile held to her ear and asked a silent question.

She nodded in reply, her body tight with tension.

Would he turn and walk away?

Was that it?

The death of the diamond before she'd had it in her hand?

But he threw his bag into the back of the cart and climbed in beside her.

'If it's all right with you—' he began, and Beth, her heart too full for speech, just nodded in reply.

* * *

'You had the chance to go back to the hotel and didn't take it,' Angus muttered to himself as he dried himself, post-shower, in Beth's small bathroom.

He tried to analyse his irritation, deciding in the end it wasn't that Beth wasn't there, but that she *was* so much there in the little cabin she called a home. The soap he'd used in the shower and which had now scented his skin was the smell of Beth, the moss-green mosquito net he was unknotting from above the bed smelt like the little tea candles she'd sometimes lit in their bedroom, a romantic notion he'd looked upon indulgently but had fiercely missed when she had left.

And the bed, with its mountain of pillows and cushions of every size and colour, things he'd flung to the floor before sharing the bed in her little flat, then appreciated when she'd tucked them behind his back in the morning so he could sit and sip the cup of tea she always brought him.

Hell! He must have been the most spoilt, pandered to, pampered and unappreciative mongrel on earth, the way he'd let Beth look after him.

He climbed beneath the net, shifted a million cushions, then settled his head on a pillow.

Which smelt of her shampoo…

He sighed and, accepting the inevitable, breathed it in and, for the first time in three long years, slid peacefully into sleep.

CHAPTER SEVEN

ROBBIE was more than restless, he was crying, uttering little whimpering words that didn't make sense, and twisting in the bed as if his body was racked with pain.

Charles, looking grey and tired, was in the room when Beth entered, close by the bed, talking quietly to Robbie.

'Perhaps we did the wrong thing with the quarantine,' he said to Beth, when the little boy's spasms ceased and he seemed to sleep again. 'We could have airlifted Robbie and Mr Todd, the guest who's in a bad way, across to the mainland.'

'And done what there?' Beth queried.

Charles looked at her and shook his head.

'Watched them both, as we're doing here,' he admitted. 'Control the fluid intake so we're not adding to the pressure on the brain, control seizures with anti-convulsant medication—not that either of them have had seizures—monitor breathing, pulse and oxygen levels in the blood, measure urine output and test it for anomalies. That's what's really bothering me, Beth, the fact that with all our specialised medical knowledge there's nothing more we could be doing for these people on the mainland than we are here.'

He offered her a rueful smile.

'Yet I still feel guilty that they're here. Crazy, isn't it?'

'Not really,' she said. 'We've come to think we can work miracles with machines and drugs. We can put new hearts into tiny babies, even operate on them in the womb, we understand how the human body works and most of the diseases that afflict it, but we're not infallible, and neither is modern medicine. Like doctors always have, we just do what we can.'

His smile this time was even more strained.

'That's true of most things in life, I suppose,' he said quietly, then he wheeled backwards, leaving room for Beth to slip into the chair beside Robbie's bed and take his hand, talking quietly to him, hoping somewhere in his consciousness he'd know she was there and be soothed by her presence.

She was asleep, her head resting on the bed, her two hands clasping one of Robbie's. Angus stood and looked at her for a moment, seeing the shadows of tiredness beneath her eyes, the tangles in the silky dark hair.

He'd slept so well himself, wrapped in the scent of Beth, that he felt guilty, seeing her exhaustion. Not that she'd have slept in her own bed while she was worried about the child.

Although Robbie looked at peace again this morning, his breathing deep and easy. Hopefully, the crisis had passed and he was on the mend. Two of the other children had recovered quickly—well, not fully recovered, they were both tired and listless and would need careful watching for a week or two, but they were certainly well enough to leave the hospital.

Perhaps it was good the quarantine was in place, for with the number of hospital and camp staff and volunteers available it would be easier to keep Robbie on the island while he recuperated rather than sending him home to a harassed mother with four other children.

Children!

He frowned at the memory the word threw up. Last night Beth had denied she was obsessed about not having more children, yet surely the argument they'd had—the only real argument he could remember having with Beth—had been over having another child. He'd been trying to comfort her after Bobby's death and had said there'd be other children and she'd flown at him like a demented banshee—or were all banshees demented?

Anyway, they'd argued, then retreated into their separate cones of silence, held there by some misunderstanding, Angus had felt, as well as grief.

He studied Beth for a moment longer. Fate—and Robbie's setback—had kept them apart last night. If they'd come together, would they have talked?

Really talked?

He shook his head in rueful denial—they'd have made love all night, revelling in the pleasure they could bring to each other. Damn, his body was stirring just thinking about it.

He walked into the room, wondering if he should wake Beth, then walked out again, deciding she needed sleep more than she needed the confusing presence of her ex-husband.

Or he imagined she did, although now he'd realised he didn't know this Beth for all she looked and smelled the same. He wasn't sure what she might or might not need…

'We've had word from AQIS that the two mobile units will be in Crocodile Creek by midday and the army has one of their huge helicopters standing by to airlift them straight to the island.'

A tall man who introduced himself as Cal Jamieson was behind the desk in the office that had become, to Angus, the headquarters of the quarantine.

'I've persuaded Charles to go back to his cabin and get some sleep,' Cal continued to explain. 'This emergency, on top of Lily being sick, has really knocked him.'

'How is Lily?' Angus asked. He'd met the little girl on his first visit yesterday.

Cal smiled.

'Being difficult, would you believe? And "difficult" is a word we've never associated with Lily. She can be naughty, like all kids, but usually she's the most biddable child imaginable. Not this morning, though. She's sitting up in bed like an imperious little duchess, demanding to go home. When Gina, my wife, who was sitting with her, explained that no one could leave the island, she announced she didn't want to leave the island, she just wanted to go home to Jill and Charles because they were her new mummy and daddy and that's where she should be.'

'New mummy and daddy?' Angus queried.

But the phone rang and as Cal reached out to lift the receiver, he said, 'Ask Beth, she'll explain,' before adding a polite, 'Wallaby Island Medical Centre, Cal Jamieson speaking,' to whoever it was on the other end.

At a loose end, Angus mooched around the building, checked Beth was still asleep, then walked outside, slapping at a mosquito as he went, wondering if all the carts had insect repellent in them.

He found some in the first one he checked, and smoothed it onto his skin, noting as he did so it was a sunscreen factor 30 as well.

The mosquito he'd slapped at and missed buzzed around his head, but something else was buzzing inside it.

He walked back inside and found Cal was off the phone.

'What were the original symptoms of the illness?' he asked, and Cal frowned at him.

'Beth could probably list them straight off. I wasn't here when it began—not at the hospital—but from what I know, it was listlessness, a general malaise, achy feelings, headache, some vomiting.'

'Not flu symptoms?' Angus persisted.

'There must have been,' Cal said, 'because we talked of some kind of flu-like virus. I suppose general achiness is often an early symptom of flu—that might have been what set us on that path. Or, with the kids with lung problems, any illness at all is usually accompanied by chest infections. I know Susie, our physio, was involved from the start.'

He paused, studying Angus as if to read his thoughts.

Gave up and asked, 'What are you thinking?'

Angus waved the question aside.

'It's too vague even to be considered a thought at the moment, but my computer's back at Beth's place—I need to check out some stuff. The mosquitoes here—they're fresh-water?'

Now Cal looked downright puzzled.

'I guess they must be—aren't all mosquitoes? This far north we have a long wet season over summer each year and the rainforest is full of places where water can pool or puddle and mosquitoes can breed.'

'And you're how far from the mainland?'

'A half-hour helicopter flight, two hours by fast catamaran—about a hundred k's, I suppose.'

'That's far enough,' Angus said, more to himself than to Cal, thinking if what he suspected proved right, the virus wouldn't spread to the mainland.

Though how had it got to this island?

Thank heavens the island had wireless Internet connection facilities. Back at Beth's cabin, he brought his computer out to the deck table and booted it up, then tracked through all the sites he could find on mosquitoes. Japanese encephalitis was well known—there was even a vaccine available for people travelling to Japan or nearby Asian countries. The disease caused fever, headaches, vomiting and confusion, and there was no antiviral available. All specialists advised was to treat the symptoms.

Next he worked out how far they were from Japan—although the virus had also been found in Southeast Asia. Thousands of kilometres, but tracing the path mosquitoes would take he crossed the big island of New Guinea.

Vague memories surfaced—the miscellaneous file in his head again. The early days of colonisation in New Guinea—people suffering from some form of sleeping sickness. But malaria had raged there and the emphasis had been on finding drugs to deal with that. The sleeping sickness had stayed vague, more a myth than something written up in medical journals.

He switched his research to mosquitoes.

'The problem is,' he said to Beth who'd appeared, a sleep crease in her right cheek, at the bottom of the steps, 'that mosquitoes rarely travel more than a few hundred yards in their lifetimes, maybe a mile, unless, of course, there's wind assistance. But if they breed in the rainforest here, there's no wind—or virtually none…'

He stared at her as he tried to take his thoughts further.

Tired as she was, Beth felt warmth stirring inside her. A different warmth—remembered warmth—the kind she'd always felt when Angus had discussed things with her, using her as a sounding board for his thoughts.

Not that it meant anything to him—he simply found it easier to arrange his thoughts by talking through them. Probably Garf would have done just as well.

'And good morning to you, too,' she said, as she came up the steps, suddenly aware how daggy and sleep-rumpled she must look. 'Have you had breakfast? Would you like a cup of tea?'

The ordinary questions, far removed from how far mosquitoes might or might not travel, seemed to bring him out of his head.

'You sit, I'll get it. I found my way around your kitchen earlier. Went up to the hospital as well. You were sleeping so I didn't disturb you.'

The idea of Angus finding his way around her kitchen was disturbing somehow, although she'd asked him to come—to stay.

But if he could behave as if all this was perfectly normal, so could she. 'How is Robbie today?'

'Sleeping peacefully, but we thought he was over it when he was like that yesterday, so who knows? But Danny is still very ill. They've called in Alex Vavunis, the paediatric neurosurgeon, again.'

She felt the weight of the sick children bearing down on her again and must have shown her feelings, for Angus stood up and came towards her, wrapping his arms around her and giving her a comforting hug.

At least, she thought it was a comforting hug, for all it went on a tad longer than most hugs of that kind.

And reminded her of the packet of condoms in her pocket!

Hell's teeth! Had she really suggested an affair to Angus? Talked calmly about affairs and getting condoms?

Lack of sleep—that was the only possible reason she could find for such bizarre behaviour.

Although—she snuggled into the hug—was it such a bad idea or was it just the daylight making the condoms feel heavy and…tawdry, cheap in her pocket?

'Sit down, I'll get the tea,' he said, condoms obviously the furthest thing from his mind. 'And some cereal?'

She shook her head for cereal but did sit, mainly to get out of the hug. But as soon as Angus walked inside, she stood up and followed, aware how grubby and sleep-stupid she was feeling, needing a shower and clean clothes.

Needing to get rid of the condoms.

Or she could leave them in her shorts pocket in the laundry bin.

Mosquitoes. Focus on mosquitoes—better by far than focussing on Angus.

They'd been bad this year, worse, the rangers said, than previous years, and all island staff and visitors were advised to wear repellent at all times.

Showering quickly, she wrapped a sarong around her body, as she usually did on days off, and brought her thoughts into the kitchen where Angus was making toast, the possible lover of the previous evening having given way to the man of action.

'The camp kids have made a couple of trips into the forest at night—spotlighting. That's what we were doing when Sam spotted you and thought you were a Yowie.'

'And that's when the mossies are at their worst?' Angus said, spreading butter and strawberry jam on the toast then slicing it into fingers.

Beth nodded and smiled to think he'd picked up on her conversation so easily—the warm feeling back inside her.

'So the next thing is a visit to the ranger station,' he said. 'Tea and toast, then you might show me where to go.'

He raised an eyebrow and she nodded, though she'd have to change into sensible clothes. It wouldn't do to be traipsing around the island in a sarong and nothing else.

Although it seemed a shame…

The thought deserved a slapped cheek. How could she possibly be thinking of dallying with Angus when all the people on the island could be at risk of some unknown virus? The familiar throbbing grumble of a helicopter circling overhead again was a further reminder of how serious things were.

'Honestly,' she muttered, 'they're worse than the mossies!'

Then she took a finger of toast back into her bedroom,

eating it as she changed into very proper and practical shorts and a T-shirt.

Clean shorts—no condoms in the pocket—sensible, practical Beth once again.

'We'll take a cart,' she said, when tea and toast were finished and she was walking with Angus back towards the hospital.

But they were no sooner in the cart, when Garf joined them, forcing Angus to move closer to Beth.

'Oh, dear, you really shouldn't come, Garf! How did you get free?' Beth said helplessly to the dog, who was behaving as if he hadn't seen her for a month and was so delighted he might actually turn inside out with glee.

Garf stood on Angus's knee so he could lick Beth's cheek and she gave in.

'All right, but you'll have to stay in the cart,' she warned him sternly.

'Is the whole island a national park?' Angus asked as they drove into the rainforest.

'Technically, no,' Beth said. 'There's been a camp-type of resort at our end for over a hundred years. It started when there was a mutton-bird factory here—making oil— and people used to come over from the mainland to camp. Then some bright person saw a way of making money out of more than campers and built a resort at the other end. When the whole of the Great Barrier Reef was declared a national park, the waters around the island became a national park and not long after that the state government declared the state-owned land in the middle a dedicated park as well. The kids' camp and eco-cabins at our end and the resort at the other end are there on sufferance but what's the use of having pristine rainforest and stunning coral reefs if people can't come to experience and enjoy them all?'

'So Garf can legally live and play at either end of the island but not the middle bit?' Angus said, and the dog, hearing his name, gave him a lick as well.

'That's about it,' Beth agreed, turning onto the narrow track that lead to the ranger headquarters. 'And if he's out of the camp and hospital grounds, right now we're supposed to have him under strict control to keep him away from the dead birds. Last time I saw him he was tied up on the hospital veranda, which is where he's supposed to be. Wicked dog!'

But as she turned she caught a glimpse of white in the jungle-like growth to the side of the track and stopped.

'That must be one of the rangers there,' she said, pointing to where the suited figure had been. 'Let's stop and see if he's finding many dead birds.'

But before they could approach the tree which she was sure must hide the man in the white suit, he broke from cover and plunged into the undergrowth.

Beth made to follow, but Garf, sensing a bit of fun, leapt from the cart and gave chase, barking furiously.

'Hell! Now he'll really be in trouble!' Beth said. She yelled at the dog, who, trained to obey instantly, immediately turned back towards her, although the look he gave her was full of reproach.

'Get in the cart, you bad dog!' Beth ordered, not falling for the soulful-eyes routine.

But when she turned to Angus she was frowning.

'Why did he run?' she said, a shiver of apprehension travelling up and down her spine.

'Scared of dogs?' Angus suggested, but Beth shook her head.

'He ran before Garf chased him,' she pointed out. 'Let's go. Maybe someone at the station can tell us.'

But no one there could shed light on the mystery figure.

'My men and women are working around the perimeter of the park boundary because that's the most likely place the visitors would come in contact with the dead birds. They'll work inwards from there, but I've only six staff available and it will take them a couple of days to get in as far as where you saw the person in white.'

Angus had his own suspicions about the figure but there was no point in worrying either the head ranger or Beth. Besides, he was there for information.

'What types of mosquitoes do you have here?' he asked, and the ranger took them into his office and pulled down a thin book.

'It's years since we've had a specialist entomologist here, but these were the ones discovered last time a survey was done.'

He opened the book, showing illustrations and Latin names of a number of mosquitoes.

'Their family name is *Culicidae*, then the genera comes after that—*Anopheles* is the most well known because it carries malaria in areas where it is still endemic, but we have aedes and culex varieties as well. You're thinking?'

'If it's not the birds, then some kind of arbovirus,' Angus told him. 'These are spreading, and more and more cases of viral encephalitis are now being connected to mosquito carriers. In the United States you have West and East equine encephalitis that can both affect humans, and West Nile virus, then there's La Crosse, which is fairly new in the US as well, affecting mainly children, and Chikungunya fever, first isolated in Tanzania but now found throughout Africa and Asia. At first it was thought *Aëdes aegypti* was the only carrier, but they've now discovered that *Aëdes albopictus* could carry it, and you've that little fellow right here.'

He pointed to a mosquito illustration, running his finger down the abdomen.

'Pointed abdomen with pale bands basally—that's him.'

'And Chika-whatever means?' Pat, the ranger, asked.

'It's a debilitating illness with fever, headache, nausea, muscle and joint pain, and although patients recover quite quickly, it can leave its victims with feelings of listlessness and fatigue. I'm not saying that's what we've got here, but the illness could be a new variant of an arboviral encephalitis.'

'But why now?' Beth asked. 'I imagine there have always been mosquitoes on the island—why now would people be getting sick?'

'Driving along the track, from the resort to the medical centre, and then to this place, I've seen a number of huge trees that were obviously damaged during the cyclone that destroyed the original medical centre. Where they've been uprooted, you get depressions in the ground that fill with water and make ideal breeding grounds. And the cyclone gives us another clue. From the quick research I did before coming here, I know most of these virus-carrying mosquitoes are already prevalent in Asia and in a number of Pacific Islands. And in New Guinea, not that far to the north, there have always been arboviral ill-nesses—malaria and dengue being the most common. So, what if the cyclone blew some new mosquito strains this far—mosquitoes carrying a known or unknown viral encephalitis?'

'And these have bred and now people who haven't been wearing protective clothing or repellent have been bitten and the virus passed on to them?' Beth whispered.

'It makes sense.'

'Are you saying it's definitely not bird flu?' Pat asked, and Angus shook his head.

'We don't know. I've just been exploring other ideas—thinking out loud, really. The lab arrives this afternoon. With luck I'll be able to test some blood from the dead birds and either confirm or eliminate avian influenza from the equation. The fact that the sick children are showing signs of recovery gives me some hope that it's not—or not H5N1 because that has shown itself to be deadly.'

'So my people keep collecting dead birds?'

Angus nodded.

'It's in your interest to collect them anyway, I would think. If there is something wrong with them—some illness—you wouldn't want other predatory birds feeding on them and getting ill themselves.'

'Good grief, no!' Pat muttered, as if this was the first time he'd thought further than the collection stage of this operation. 'And on top of that, we've got your mystery person in the undergrowth.'

He frowned then said, 'Perhaps it *was* one of my staff,

who moved away because he or she knew it wasn't the right place to be.'

'Or an intrepid reporter,' Angus suggested. 'There've been helicopters buzzing overhead—how easy would it be for one of them to land someone on the far side of the island?'

'But would someone risk it?' Beth asked. 'Risk coming to a place where they could be infected by a potentially life-threatening illness?'

'The person was suited up and probably masked,' Angus reminded her, then he smiled. 'Though I doubt he'd get much of an interview dressed like that.'

'A photographer could still take photos while wearing a mask. If he takes photos of dead birds, perhaps people coming and going at the medical centre, the arrival of the mobile labs—wouldn't that be enough for front-page news?' Beth asked, adding, 'As far as I can see, they make up most of the stories that go with photos.'

Angus nodded.

'Photos are much more emotive—think how distressed the families of people on the island will be when they see them. We'll have to find the man.'

'Or woman,' Pat reminded him. 'But how? And is it such a worry? We've got the local paper reporter here already and surely people are already sending photos from their mobile phones.'

'They're always blurred,' Angus pointed out. 'And probably the only people with mobile phones who'd do that are guests at the resort and, believe me, they'd be hard pushed finding a piece of gravel out of place on the paths, let alone a dead bird. No, I can see a news-paper editor wanting photos—maybe even video footage for a television broadcast. The policeman, Beth—what's his name?'

'Harry Blake. He'll be in one of the staff cabins. Grace is on duty this week.'

'Let's find him. And, Pat, tell your rangers to keep an eye out but also remind them about insect repellent. And you might start thinking about mosquito-control measures we can safely take without endangering other animal or plant species in the national park.'

'Great!' Pat muttered. 'Mosquito control. Fish are the best because they eat the larva but that's long term and will only work in the pools of permanent water. Short term's usually poison of some kind and animals in the rainforest drink from the fresh-water holes and from water that collects in the dead palm fronds—we can't poison their water supply.'

'Get on the Net and see what you can find—there has to be some short-term solution,' Angus said. 'I realise it's by no means certain that what we've got is an arbovirus, but if it is we'll have the opportunity to wipe it out before it reaches the mainland. Remember that dengue was unknown there until recent years and look how far south that has spread.'

Pat nodded, said goodbye to Beth then turned to his computer.

'He's a good man,' Beth told Angus as they returned to the cart.

'A good man with a heap of worries on his shoulders,' Angus replied, ordering Garf to move over. 'I want to see out as we go,' he told the dog, who showed him a hurt face again—to no avail.

Angus wasn't looking for the stranger in the rainforest, but for pools of water where mosquito larvae could live.

'How long since it's rained?' he asked, as Beth drove them back towards the camp.

'Two weeks at least—we had a storm but it was well before the kids' camp started.'

'And there's still water lying in palm fronds,' he muttered, as much to himself as to Beth. 'If it's two weeks since you had rain then clearing the forest of water would be impossible. It's everywhere.'

'It's rainforest,' Beth reminded him, and he smiled because, bothered as he was by this viral outbreak, there was something very satisfying in being with Beth again, talking to her, sitting beside her as she competently guided the little cart through the forest. Even the dog made him happy.

'We could get a dog.'

The words had come out before he could stop them, and when he peered past Garf to get Beth's reaction, she was staring at him, eyes wide in disbelief.

'Angus,' she said, very carefully as if the word might burn her mouth. 'There is no we. You live in an apartment, and I already have a dog, or the use of one most of the time.'

She rested her head against Garf for an instant.

'Don't I, Garf?' she said, whispering now—sad, somehow…

She dropped Angus at the hospital where he had to check on the arrival of the mobile laboratories, tied Garf up again, then left the cart in the small parking area and walked home, wondering just how they'd managed to get into such an emotional muddle so quickly.

And it was 'they', not just her—Angus's remark about the dog had made that clear.

Was he, like she, thinking how comfortable it was, them being together?

Beth had to assume so but being comfortable together didn't mean much. Being comfortable together was fine in the good times but come the bad times, when that comfort disappeared, couples needed more.

They needed communication—talking-type communication, not just being good together in bed—and talking-type communication was difficult for both herself and Angus.

Although they could talk about mosquitoes, and arboviruses—it was emotional stuff they couldn't talk about. They couldn't even say 'I love you' to each other but, then, Angus didn't love her—never had...

Her thoughts made her feel ashamed of bringing home the condoms—worse, suggesting an affair with Angus.

For all she longed for that bright, shining diamond of memory, she really wasn't an affair kind of person—she'd known that the first time—and having an affair with Angus would only make her more unhappy when he left.

So?

'I've no idea,' she said to a tiny finch that had fluttered into the tree in front of her then flew to rest on the railing of her deck, leading her home, or so it seemed.

Maybe if she had a proper sleep she'd be able to think it through more clearly.

Maybe!

The pillow smelt of Angus and she wrapped her arms around it and breathed in the smell of him as she drifted into sleep.

CHAPTER EIGHT

VIBRATIONS shook Beth's cabin and a roaring noise made her wonder if a tsunami was about to hit the island, then the shuddering lessened and she realised what had woken her—the big army helicopter delivering a mobile lab for Angus.

She leapt out of bed but could see nothing. Of course not—the labs were to be landed on the mainland side of the island, far from the areas where children camped and tourists strayed.

But Angus would be there, ready, dead birds in hand, so to speak. He would also be testing blood from the victims, though he'd been grumbling that the tests he'd have available would take longer.

A quick shower, shorts and a T-shirt, sandals on her feet, and she was ready to go. He'd need a lab assistant and even if he didn't need one, he'd have one. If Angus was going to be in that chamber, testing things, she wanted to be right there with him.

Not because she had any silly ideas of danger, or romantic notions they should die together—Angus was far too careful to fall victim to the risks inherent in his work—

but because she knew that being there—someone being there—would make things easier for him. It would ease the tension that being in a small, sealed space would naturally bring, and having someone to talk to would help his thought processes.

She grabbed a cart outside the medical centre and drove on the rarely used track to the beach on the far side of the island. The helicopter had departed, leaving a silence that seemed heavy and threatening somehow.

'No bird noises,' she whispered to herself, praying it was because the competition of the helicopter's engines had silenced them, not because the entire bird population of the island was now dying. It was late afternoon, the time the birds were usually coming home, flying back in flocks from their day hunting out at sea.

Then the chattering began again and relief flooded through her. Her beautiful island was still alive.

Charles and Angus were sitting in a cart at the top of the beach, staring at the shiny white cube that had been deposited by the helicopter. Grubby was striding around it, as if searching for a way in, though perhaps he was simply seeing it was positioned safely.

'I'm sorry to leave you on your own here, but we've had to airlift young Danny to Brisbane and I've got to deal with the repercussions of breaking quarantine,' Charles was saying to Angus, who climbed out of the cart as Beth pulled up beside them. 'Beth? Have you come to look at the box that came from the sky?'

Beth smiled at the weak joke.

'I've come to help,' she announced. 'I may not be one hundred per cent up to date on pathology or lab techniques, but I do know most labs have lab assistants. So, one lab assistant, ready and available.'

Charles didn't answer for what seemed like a very long time.

'You don't have to do this.' His voice was low and very serious when he finally spoke. 'I wouldn't ask you to, and I certainly am not asking you to volunteer. Angus knows the risks involved in any situation like this, but you?'

'I'm volunteering without being asked,' Beth assured Charles, more concerned by the weariness in Charles's voice and the strain showing on his face than in the job she was about to undertake.

Not that she could do much, he was her boss and she barely knew him. What puzzled her was that if, as everyone was saying, Charles and Jill were about to marry, the imminent occasion didn't seem to be creating much joy in either of them.

Although she hadn't shown much joy or delight when she'd married Angus—she'd been distracted by feelings of fear and trepidation and a hefty dose of guilt.

She watched the little cart, with Charles in it, head back to the medical centre, and hoped he'd find the joy that seemed to be lacking in his life at the moment.

'You don't have to do this. I don't need anyone to assist.'

The cause of her old guilt was speaking to her in crisp, matter-of-fact Angus tones.

'No, but I can wash the test tubes for you or hold things or do whatever lab assistants do. That's why I came across.'

He studied her for a moment, then said, 'It's a controlled environment and I'll be properly suited. It's not at all dangerous, you know.'

She nodded.

'Of course not. That's why I'm happy to help.'

He looked at her again, then out to sea, towards the mainland, and she knew he was wanting to deny her help, but couldn't work out how to do it without admitting there could be an element of danger in what they were about to do.

'This is the bio-hazard lab. I've told them to hold off delivering the decontamination chamber. If I find it's not bird flu and there's no need for decontamination, we won't need it.'

'So, let's get started,' Beth said, nodding to Grubby who seemed satisfied the unit was sited safely and was now moving a bag of dead birds out of his cart, setting it down at the door of the unit.

Angus hesitated. He longed to tell her to go away, to tell her he didn't want her involved in what he was about to do, but he couldn't without admitting there could be a minuscule element of danger in the process of dissecting the dead birds and testing the blood of infected patients, and he knew her well enough to know she'd insist they share the danger.

So he'd just have to make sure he eliminated that minuscule risk.

'Okay,' he said. 'Inside the door there's a chamber with suits, air bottles and breathing masks. We dress in there, fit the masks, make sure everything's working, then move into another, smaller chamber. It's a positive pressure airlock so nothing from inside can get outside. We shut the

outer door and the inner door won't open until the air
pressure is right in the lock, then we go on into the lab. It
has directed air flow that goes up through a series of filters
in the ceiling which trap and hold all the gases given off.
We're breathing air through our masks, air from the
bottles, not the air in the lab. Do not remove your mask,
your gloves or any other item of clothing, okay?'

Beth nodded, then she smiled.

'Not the place to start our affair, then,' she teased, and
though he knew she'd said it to lighten the tension growing
between them, it made him flinch. His body may be
excited by the thought of the affair she'd suggested, but
the part of his mind not totally focussed on the island's
problems had been toying with the idea and he knew he
didn't like it.

Didn't like the parameters…

Which was probably why he'd made the stupid suggestion about the dog…

'We'll talk about *that* later,' he growled, taking a key
from the leather bag the helicopter had dropped and fitting
it to the door of the unit.

It unlocked easily, and he slid in the bag Grubby had
left, waited until Beth was inside, then followed, bringing
with him the small cool-box with the patients' blood and
sputum samples.

A light had come on as he opened the door and he knew
the solar panels on the top of the unit had kept the batter-
ies fully charged. From the information he'd received from
the army earlier, these batteries would supply power for
four hours, then a generator would kick in, supplying
power for another four hours. But well before that, Grubby

would have run leads across from the nearest electricity supply point on the island and they'd be on mains power.

They dressed in silence, then passed together through the airlock into the lab itself.

It was weird, Beth decided, to be shut in such a small space with someone you knew so intimately yet have no intimacy between them at all. They could have been robots—or was it the distortion of their voices as they spoke through the masks that made her think that way?

Angus had cut through three birds, talking all the time into a microphone above the lab counter, detailing his findings, making suppositions as he saw the wasted muscles on the birds—the way the dark red breast muscles had withered away from the breastbone—taking samples and passing them to Beth to seal and label.

That she was allowed to do, but he wouldn't let her touch the birds, insisting he drop them in the waste container, although he let her seal it when the final bird was set inside it. Neither was she allowed to clean the stainless-steel bench. Angus took care of it, wiping it with paper towels that went into a new waste container, then spraying a heavy duty anti-bacterial agent over it and wiping it again.

'Now bloods,' he said, moving to the opposite bench, examining the new, state-of-the-art machines arrayed there.

'Ah,' he said, the sound conveying satisfaction. 'We have the very best, the very latest—the MChip. It will still take a couple of hours for the tests to run, but with computerisation we won't get a false positive.'

He was busy preparing samples for testing, and Beth stood back, handing him things as he needed them, putting labels on samples when asked, aware he could be doing this on his own yet pleased to be near him.

Mainly pleased. His 'we'll talk about that later' remark still niggled in her head, disrupting her concentration from time to time, puzzling her, for what was there to talk about?

Although hadn't she been thinking they should talk about their feelings? Ho! She and Angus *talk*? That kind of talk? It was an impossible dream—

'Did you hear me?'

She shook her head, startled out of her thoughts.

'I said you should sit down, or you could go—there's really nothing to do.'

Angus waved his hand towards the machines, which were evidently doing whatever they were meant to do with his samples.

'You go out through that door.' He pointed to a door at the other end of the lab from the one they'd entered. 'There's another airlock chamber then a shower room. Strip off, put your gear into a drum and seal it, then shower and go through to the other side of the shower room and you'll find scrub suits.'

She saw his eyes gleam behind the protective glasses he was wearing.

'Hardly summer beach wear on an island but less bulky than our current garb. You look like a fat little caterpillar.'

He sounded gentle—loving—and although she knew it was probably the mask muffling his voice, not emotion at all, her bones felt melty and his name, 'Oh, Angus!', was little more than a sigh on her lips.

Gloved hands touched her shoulder and she stared at him—a tall white-suited figure, no bit of him visible except his eyes through glass. But his eyes seemed to be saying things to her—the eyes she'd never been able to read.

It was the glass, or maybe too much oxygen in the air mix she was breathing—of course Angus's eyes weren't saying that he loved her.

'I'll stay,' she said, holding his gaze, determined not to let him guess at her wild fancies. 'I want to know the results as much as you do.'

'They should have them by now on the mainland—the FluChip takes longer but it still gets there.'

'The samples were lost,' she said, wondering if anyone had told him that. 'It took a while to track them down.'

He nodded. 'And the spinal fluid samples came back negative for meningitis, and with a false positive for encephalitis.'

'False positive?' Beth echoed, both relieved and sorry they'd got back onto scientific talk.

'Something that looks like encephalitis but is unidentifiable as yet. They need to do more tests. The labs are still working on it.'

'It fits with your mosquito theory, doesn't it?' Beth said.

'Enough for Pat to have started putting mosquito traps around in the rainforest and to have asked for an entomologist to fly in as soon as the quarantine is lifted. He needs guidance on how to control them if it is a new arboviral encephalitis—or one that's new to Australia.'

Something beeped behind Angus and he turned away again, leaving Beth to wonder if she really did want to stay locked up with him for the next few hours.

The alternative, she realised, was sitting at home, wondering if he was all right, imagining the worst—he'd fallen and hit his head, run out of air and not realised it, both scenarios having him lying unconscious on the floor of the small lab.

Ridiculous, of course, but she'd accepted years ago that part of loving someone was imagining the worst.

She perched on the bench on the far side of the small room and watched the man she loved manipulating knobs and buttons, tapping information into the computer, feeding samples into machines, his hands sure and steady, as they'd been when they'd made love—as they'd been when he'd held Bobby...

Had she said she didn't want another child?

She was sure she hadn't, and tried to think back to that time of loss and grief and terrible loneliness.

'I didn't want a replacement for him,' she murmured, only realising she'd spoken her thoughts aloud when Angus turned towards her, eyebrows raised behind his protective glasses.

She shook her head and he turned away, hopefully deciding he'd heard her sigh, not speak. But as she dug deeper into her memories she began to realise how easily they could have picked up the wrong messages from each other.

Lack of communication again!

Now she did sigh, leaning her head back against the wall and letting the air come out softly.

'Okay!'

Startled out of her daze by the muffled word of triumph, Beth straightened up and looked across the room, to where Angus was pointing at a screen.

'See that?' he said, pointing at a pattern of dots on the screen. 'Now look at this.'

'This' was a totally different pattern of dots—luminescent dots.

'The second one is bird flu and our pattern definitely isn't that. In fact, it's not a flu virus at all, so we're back to mossies and encephalitis and although that can have severe consequences and debilitating effects, it's not the start of some pandemic. I'll still send the bird samples to the mainland and some whole birds, too. They can go back in the lab, so they're contained. But we're all done here, so let's go and tell folks the good news. Charles can raise the quarantine, people can leave the island—'

'Angus, it's ten o'clock. I doubt if anyone is sitting on a packed suitcase, waiting to leave the island, and hope-fully Charles is sleeping. He's been looking terribly tired and stressed.'

Behind his mask she was sure Angus was smiling when he said, 'You're right about the general raising of the quarantine, but do you want to bet Charles isn't sitting outside the unit, waiting for a result?'

'I do hope he's not,' Beth said, anxious for the man who'd been so kind to her.

Angus was tidying things away, stacking vials into a small freezer.

'Does that run all the time?' she asked, relief that it wasn't bird flu allowing room to marvel at the equipment in the mobile laboratory.

'It has its own battery and inverter running off the solar panels with its own small generator to kick in if the batter-ies fail. But when mains power is on, that tops up the batteries as well, so this has fridge and freezer capacity all the time.'

He closed the door then nodded towards the exit, clearly marked.

'You go ahead and shower,' he said. 'I'll be a few minutes here.'

Which neatly saves any conversation about showering together, Beth thought, remembering his 'talk about it' statement once again.

She went ahead, stripping off her suit and the clothes underneath it, dropping the lot into bins to be taken away.

And no doubt destroyed, but she had other shorts and T-shirts. She showered, then dressed in a scrub suit and stepped out of the unit, finding Charles, as Angus had foretold, sitting in a cart at the top of the beach.

As she walked towards him a light flashed. Had Charles flashed his headlights?

Beth shook her head, too tired to think, although as she drew closer to the cart she smiled and called to Charles, telling him the good news. Behind her she heard the door of the unit close and a key turning in a lock—Angus.

'Angus will explain,' she told Charles, as another light flashed. 'Did you see the light? I guess it's one of the rangers, doing a spotlighting tour for resort guests.'

Charles made a noncommittal noise.

'Are you all right?' Beth asked, driven beyond boss and employee lines by the exhaustion in his face.

'Should I be?' he said wearily. 'We've had an outbreak of a potentially fatal disease on the island—and bird flu or encephalitis are both potentially fatal—I've had my ward—daughter—Lily in hospital, we've had to break the quarantine to fly a desperately ill child to the mainland, and now Susie's collapsed and she's in the medical centre, possibly with the same thing the others have had but Miranda thinks it's ARDS.'

'Oh, Charles, I'm sorry,' Beth managed, wanting to put her hand on his shoulder, to offer the comfort of touch. She knew from listening to the others talk how often Charles had helped or comforted them, but from whom did *he* draw his strength. From Jill?

Beth doubted that Jill had much to offer at the moment. She'd been looking tired and stressed herself the few times Beth had seen her recently.

'Do you want me back on duty at the centre?' she asked, thinking practical help was all she had to offer.

Charles offered her a tired smile.

'You've done enough,' he said. 'I know you're not the type to make a fuss, it's one of the reasons I wanted you for this job, but going into that lab today was a very brave thing to do, Beth. You wouldn't have been human if you hadn't had reservations.'

Beth shook her head. No need to admit she had had reservations—but they'd been more for Angus than for herself.

Angus joined them and Beth stepped aside, returning to the cart she'd driven to the beach. She was finished here. Charles and Angus could work out what happened next— as far as the quarantine and encephalitis was concerned.

What happened next with her and Angus—well, that was a different matter. She was starting to have qualms about her suggestion they have an affair...

* * *

Beth left the cart at the medical centre. Charles and Angus parked beside it, deep in plans. Inside the centre she looked into the room where Susie lay, Alex by her side. He nodded at Beth as if to say, *I have everything under control*, and she moved on to Robbie's room. He was sleeping, so there was nothing for her to do except to walk back through the bird calls of the night towards her hut.

But once inside, what? Crawl naked into bed? Would that look too needy?

And what the hell should she do with the condoms?

Forget about them?

Leave them on the shelf in the bathroom—where Angus couldn't help but see them?

Put them on the bedside table, within reach?

How stupid to be thinking such things. Angus must be exhausted—all he'd want to do was sleep, which was what she should be doing.

But if that's what he wanted, should she pull out the couch—make it up into a bed—at least leave sheets and pillows out?

She reached her hut—the home that had become a refuge—and, not knowing any answers, walked on to where the tide shushed against the coral sand, crystal clear, so she could see the small, flat sand sharks darting in the shallows. She walked into the water, up to her ankles, up to her knees, letting the warm moisture soak into the thin fabric of the scrub suit, then she turned and splashed along parallel to the beach, not wanting to get out, not wanting to go deeper, watching the water she kicked up arc into the air in tiny diamond drops.

Her diamond fantasy was ridiculous.

An affair with Angus would start the pain again—pain she'd barely learnt to erase from her life.

She could pretend she was mature enough to cope with it, probably pretend enough to fool Angus, but she couldn't fool herself.

'We're lifting the quarantine in the morning. I have to give my paper at the convention which means I won't be involved in meetings and press announcements, so I thought I might go back to the hotel and sleep.'

He'd come up behind her while she was splashing water at the silver streak of moonlight that lay across the lagoon.

Close behind her, but not touching.

And in spite of all the things she'd just decided, she heard herself saying, 'You could stay here.'

She didn't turn, though she heard him move, heard the water wash around his legs. Then his hands were on her shoulders and he was turning her towards him.

'Stay for an affair?' he whispered, looking down into her face, his own as unreadable as ever.

Stay for ever, Beth wanted to say—to yell it out loud so there could be no mistake.

But all she did was nod.

'I don't think that would suit me,' he said, then he bent his head and kissed her on the lips. 'Or you either, but I can only speak for myself, Beth.'

He kissed her again, harder this time, so her lips gave way and her mouth welcomed his tongue, taking it greedily inside, wanting more and more of him.

His hands slid around her back, holding her close, so there was no mistaking how his body felt about it.

She snuggled into him, sure all her doubts would be swept away if only—

No, don't think, just kiss. Kissing Angus, being kissed by Angus—was there any better feeling?

The kiss deepened and her thoughts strayed, muddled, drifting, lost in the heat and wonderment of sensation, in the building of excitement in her body. She felt herself trembling in his grasp, her nipples hurting as they pressed against his chest, an ache of wanting deep within her.

Then he wasn't there—cool air washing over her no doubt swollen lips—she could hear his voice but not make sense of what he was saying. Something about not wanting an affair, not liking her parameters, he'd see her, or maybe not, and wasn't it time she was in bed?

'Angus?'

She hated the sound of pleading in her voice but hadn't been able to prevent it.

'Now isn't the time to be talking,' he said, suddenly sounding as exhausted as she felt. 'But we will talk, Beth. Tomorrow I'll be busy in the morning. Later in the day?'

He held her elbow as she walked out of the water— polite to the last.

What was she supposed to say?

Should she suggest a time for them to 'talk'?

Like a dental appointment?

And what had he meant by not liking the parameters?

'We've *never* talked!' she muttered, anger coming to her rescue, pulling her out of the post-kissing daze and the no-affair shock. 'Not about emotional stuff!'

His smile raised the stakes as far as anger went, in-censing her, but before she could react—or find a piece of driftwood and hit him really hard with it—he was speaking again.

'Not really. That's why we should, wouldn't you say?'

She opened her mouth to yell at him, though what she'd yell she didn't know, and while she dithered he stole the initiative again, closing her lips and blanking out her mind with one last kiss.

'Goodnight, Beth,' he murmured against her skin, then he turned her in the direction of her cabin and eased her gently in that direction.

Moving like an automaton, she went, one foot in front of the other, unable to think at all because she had no idea how to untangle what thoughts she had—where to start unwinding them so she could take a good look at them and try to work out what had happened.

Inside the living room she stripped off the scrub suit then made her way to the bathroom, where the packet of condoms mocked her from the laundry basket.

Muttering an oath she'd heard often but had never used before, she picked them up and flung them through the window. It was only as she climbed into bed, in her sensible pyjamas with sweet peas all over them, that she remembered the camp kids walked past that side of her hut to get to the art and pottery room so she had to get out of bed, find a torch and search through the undergrowth for the tell-tale packet.

Prickles spiked her bare feet and she cursed again as she fought the tangle of vines in the undergrowth, thinking now of snakes—night snakes—fear battling the need to find the darned packet.

She picked up a stick that had jabbed into her thigh and threw it deeper into the bushes. Then, out of nowhere, a yellow body hurled itself after the stick. Garf had escaped again and was sensing fun.

'Go away, you stupid dog,' Beth yelled at him, but Garf knew she loved him and ignored her anger, pouncing around in the bushes, then stilling suddenly, head alert, eyes on the darkness of the trees beyond the bushes.

But before Beth had time to wonder what Garf had sensed—please, heaven, it wasn't a snake—she spotted the packet.

There!

She darted forward and thrust her hand into the bushes, then stood up, clutching it, triumphant.

Garf grabbed at it, but she held on, hearing the cardboard tear as she scolded the dog.

'It's not a stick—let go!' she yelled, furious with him now, but he was having too much fun and he kept hold of his end of the small packet, shaking his head to dislodge her grip.

She was beginning to worry about the contents of the packet getting loose and choking him, when light flashed again, but this time there was a scuffling noise and Garf forgot the packet. He gave a sharp yap and dashed into the bushes while Beth wondered what on earth was happening.

She called the dog back, knowing he couldn't go chasing through the national park, but as he reluctantly returned to her side and she gathered up the spilt condoms—how many were supposed to be in the packet?—she wondered about the intruder. Maybe not a ranger spotlighting—maybe a peeping tom.

On the island?

Not with a flashlight!

She dismissed the thought. Kids mucking around with torches—there were a couple of young boys at the resort who'd been plaguing the camp kids. Probably bored with resort life and playing games over here...

She hurried back to her cabin and slipped the torn packet into her rubbish bin, covering it and its now useless contents with the discarded scrub suit.

Much to her surprise, given the tumult of the day, she slept deeply and well, waking in the morning and looking around at the bright sunshine, unable to believe she hadn't stirred.

'Emotional exhaustion!' she muttered to herself, as if she needed to excuse a good night's sleep. 'Not something Angus will be suffering from!'

Good. She still felt very peeved with Angus.

More than peeved—angry!

Hadn't he realised just how much inner strength it had taken for her to suggest an affair—how tongue-tyingly, gut-wrenchingly difficult she'd found it, not only to say the words but to sound so casual and worldly and—yes, mature—as she'd said them?

And he'd turned her down!

Didn't like the parameters—whatever that might mean!

Well, he could go to hell. She was over him. Seeing him again had been good because now she knew he wasn't interested in her she could move on to the next step of her life and find someone who was.

Or who might be...

The pain in her chest suggested she might be fooling herself, but she knew about pains. They faded in time.

They didn't disappear altogether, but they got manageable enough to be put away in a far corner and more or less ignored.

This one, too, would shrink.

Eventually…

'Dr Beth?'

Sam's voice.

'Come in,' she called, hopping out of bed and straightening her pyjamas so she was decently covered.

The little boy sidled across her living room, his face tight with worry.

She hurried to him, kneeling by his side and putting her arm around his skinny shoulders.

'What's wrong, love?'

He nestled against her.

'They took Danny away. They said he was too sick to stay, but Robbie's sick and he stayed. Did Danny die?'

'Oh, Sam, of course he didn't,' Beth assured him, lifting the child and sitting down so he was on her lap, her arms around him. 'It's just that they had to take special pictures of his head and we don't have the right machines here at the medical centre, so he went across to Crocodile Creek, where Bruce comes from, then down to Brisbane to a big hospital.'

Sam turned his head and his dark brown eyes looked steadfastly into her face.

'It's bad to tell lies to children,' he reminded her, and she hugged him as she smiled.

'It's not a lie, darling,' she whispered, rocking him in her arms, sadness flooding through her that a child so young should know so much about death and lies. 'Danny's sick, yes, but he had to go for scans—you know about scans. That's all. Actually, we heard last night that the scans were good—that the operation Stella's dad did on his head made him a whole lot better.'

Sam nodded his acceptance and snuggled closer to her, then changed the subject, reminding Beth how quickly children's moods could swing.

'CJ comes from Crocodile Creek,' he said, mentioning Cal and Gina Jamieson's little boy. 'And Lily. Lily's home now, in the cabin. Did you know?'

Beth agreed she did know, having heard about Lily's insistence on returning.

'She said she'd be my girlfriend.'

Beth had been thinking how fragile Lily had seemed and wondering if letting her out of hospital had been such a good idea, so it took a moment for Sam's words to sink in.

'Girlfriend?' she repeated helplessly. He was, what— eight?

'Like Stella is for Jamie,' Sam explained.

'Ah!' Beth murmured, as if understanding the girlfriend concept for the first time. Perhaps it was the first time— perhaps she'd never understood it any more than she understood relationships.

'I took a flower to her cabin,' Sam continued.

Beth smiled, although she was fairly sure she should be lecturing him on not picking flowers.

'And did she like it?'

'I don't know. The cabin was real quiet so I left it on the deck.'

'That was kind of you. Lily needs to sleep a lot so if she was sleeping, it was best not to wake her. Now, where are you supposed to be? Where are Benita and the other kids?'

'They're walking on the beach before breakfast. We walked up to the point then turned around, but I ran and got here first, because of the flower, you see.'

He'd no sooner explained than Beth heard the chatter of the children returning.

'I've got to get dressed and go over to see Robbie, so how about you join them and maybe after breakfast we can do something?'

'Not today,' Sam told her, recovered enough now to climb off her knee. 'We're going fishing. In a boat. I'm going to catch a king.'

'A king fish?' Beth guessed.

Sam shook his head.

'No. Some other kind of king—it's big and pink and I'll show it to you at lunchtime because we're coming back for lunch.'

And with that, he was gone, a little boy with a tenuous hold on life, but making every second of it count.

While she was wasting hers...

Oh, she'd thought she'd moved on, but one glimpse of Angus had shown her how untrue that was. She'd just moved.

As if moving would make a difference when what ailed her was inside her—when it came with her wherever she went, like an illness in remission.

So! The time had finally arrived when she had to put the past behind her once and for all.

Would talking to Angus help this process or should she phone him—tell him not to come?

Probably.

She dressed and walked up to the medical centre,

switching her mind from personal matters to medical ones, wondering just what the fallout of the lifting of the quarantine would be.

'We're all on telly,' Grace greeted her, waving her into an empty patient room where several staff members were peering at the small screen of a television set.

Beth recognised the mobile lab, sitting on the beach, and there was Grubby, walking around with his bag of dead birds. Then a still shot of someone in scrubs walking up the beach.

'Dr Angus Stuart, prominent epidemiologist, leaving the bio-hazard lab on Wallaby Island.'

'There were flashes of light last night—a photographer,' Beth muttered. 'The figure in white in the rainforest—he or she has been here for a couple of days. Who knows what photos we'll see?'

The news report showed more shots of the island, taken from a helicopter, zeroing in on the medical centre.

The next switch was one that surprised them all.

'That's Charles,' Grace whispered. 'And Jill and Lily when she was still in hospital—how did someone get that shot?'

It was definitely inside the hospital, but could have been taken through a window, and it showed two desperately anxious adults—parents? It certainly looked that way, with one of them on each side of a little girl lying still in a big hospital bed.

Beth was silently cursing the fact that she and Angus hadn't done more to find the figure in the bushes, or found someone to track him or her down, when Grace gave a hoot of laughter.

'Oh, look, there's you!'

Grace's comment diverted Beth and she looked at the screen again, then shook her head in disbelief. The sweet peas on her pyjamas had come out beautifully, as had Garf, but it was the condom drooping out of his mouth that caught the attention, and in case no one recognised it for what it was, the label of the well-known brand was clearly visible on the torn packet. There she stood, knee deep in the bushes, fighting an unlikely-looking dog for the wretched condoms, while a voice over prattled on about her being the doctor in charge of the medical centre.

'Oh, no!' she whispered, unable to believe this was happening. Even Grace had stopped laughing and was looking at her sympathetically. The impression given by the broadcast was that if this was the person in charge, no wonder there'd been an outbreak of bird flu, somehow insinuating further that by having such a person running the medical centre everyone on the island, including vulnerable children, would be put at risk. 'I can't believe it!'

'It doesn't mean anything,' Grace said, but Beth could hear the phone ringing in the office already and knew there'd be an avalanche of calls, not only from the press but from anxious parents.

Needing to escape, she went in to see Robbie, who was sitting up in bed, playing with a small hand-held computer game.

'Hey, Dr Beth, come and see my score. I beat my last one.'

Beth stared at him. Was this the child who'd been so sick? She went over to the bed and sat down to check his score, then asked him how he felt, although the question seemed unnecessary.

'I'm better, a bit tired, but can I go back to camp? Jack went back, and Lily.'

Beth checked his chart.

'Maybe later,' she told him, thinking of the times they thought he'd been recovering and then he'd relapsed. 'I'll come and see you after lunch.'

She wasn't on duty until that night but she checked on Susie—Alex and his daughter, Stella, were both in the room, one on each side of Susie's bed, each holding one of Susie's hands. Susie was going to be all right.

Beth closed the door, not wanting to intrude on what was obviously a private time for all three of them, and made her way to the office. Cal Jamieson was there.

'So, what's happening, apart from the doctor at the new medical centre appearing on TV in her pyjamas?'

Cal smiled at her.

'Quarantine's lifted. Mike's airlifting a lot of the Crocodile Creek staff back to the mainland today and I imagine the resort is putting on extra boat and helicopter trips to take their guests back. Luke's still rostered to be here this week with you—you're on tonight, aren't you?'

Beth eyed him doubtfully.

'If you still want me as the doctor here,' she muttered. 'The way the TV made me look, it might be easier to ride out the waves that follow the bird-flu scare with someone else in charge.'

Cal gave her a stern look.

'Do you think we haven't all been caught in our pyjamas, or in some equally embarrassing situation some time in our lives?' he said, then he smiled. 'Though I'd love to hear the story of the condoms some time.'

Beth felt a blush rising from her toes.

'I didn't want any of the kids walking past there and finding them in the bushes, then Garf came along and he thought it was a game,' she said, stumbling over the words in her haste to get them said.

'Of course,' Cal said, still smiling.

The door opened behind Beth, and Gina breezed in.

'Have you asked her about the condoms?' she demanded of her husband.

'Of course,' Cal told his wife. 'She didn't want any of the kids finding them in the morning.'

'Oh, really!' Gina's eyebrows rose but her smile was warm, and filled with fun. 'Poor you!' she said to Beth, giving her a big hug. 'If I were you, I'd go hide somewhere until tonight. The story will soon get stale, the press will vanish back to wherever they come from, and the island will return to normal.'

She released Beth, then added, 'And I just loved the pyjamas!'

Beth had to laugh, which was much better than wallowing in mortification.

She still had a job, and Gina was right—the press would go and the island would get back to normal.

Though it might never be the same again for her...

CHAPTER NINE

HIDING worked for Beth until lunchtime, when Sam came looking for her.

'I did catch a fish and it wasn't a king but an emperor, a red emperor. You have to come and look at it before Grubby and Bruce cut it up so we can have it for our dinner. Come on!'

He grabbed Beth's hand and led her towards the back of the dining room, Beth wondering just what Angus had meant by 'later' and whether, by going on this expedition to meet an emperor, she would miss him.

Which could well be for the best. After seeing herself on television that morning, all the great maturity she thought she'd managed to achieve seemed to have wilted, and she felt as raw and insecure as an intern.

'See!'

Grubby and Bruce were standing by the stainless-steel bench where fish were scaled and gutted. Beth had wondered whether small children needed to see this process but although most of the girls made noises of disgust, the boys seemed to love watching.

'Wow!' Beth said, for it was a truly wonderful fish. A

pinkish red, with a high snout—exactly the kind of snout an emperor should have. 'That's a great fish!' she told Sam. 'Did you take a picture of it?'

'Benita did and she sent it on her phone to my mum and dad and they texted back to say 'Wow' just like you did. Grubby's going to cut it up and I'm going to give a piece to Lily because fish is very good for getting better when you've been sick.'

'You'd better not leave it on the deck,' Beth said, thinking of the flower.

'Of course not, silly. Malcolm the cook will cook it 'specially for her, and he's going to cook some for me and some for Benita and some for all the other kids. Would you like some?'

Beth shook her head.

'No, you guys eat it,' she told him, 'but thank you for letting me look at it.'

'That's okay. I'm going to lunch now,' Sam told her, and with that he took off, busy as ever, a little boy packing a lifetime of experiences into every day.

Beth wandered back to her hut, not wanting to get into conversations about pyjamas or condoms with any of the staff or volunteers. She'd have a bowl of cereal for lunch, then catch up on some e-mails, maybe have a rest…

It all sounded good but as she climbed the shallow steps to her deck she knew she was returning to her cabin in case Angus came, stupid though that might be!

Immature as it undoubtedly was!

But she did do busy things, keeping herself occupied until mid-afternoon when she heard the noises of the camp children returning along the beach from an exploration of the coral reef that was visible at low tide. Wearing thick-soled sneakers, they were able to walk in the shallow pools and enjoy the sight of the bright coral polyps and vivid waving tendrils of the sea anemones, watching small fish darting around and molluscs moving across the sand in search of food.

She'd joined in the reef walks the previous week, marvelling at the life beneath the water. Now, peering out at where the little group chattered as they walked along the sand beside the translucent blue-green water of the lagoon, she was sorry she hadn't joined them, while the sounds of their talk and laughter reminded her of the joy inherent in this job, and she found herself relaxing for the first time that day.

So the scream didn't mean much at first. Kids often screamed—with laughter or pretend fear, or sometimes for no conceivable reason at all.

The second scream, though, was of pain and terror, and she took off, leaping her steps and racing to the beach, where she could see figures now huddled together.

'Get the kids back,' she said to Benita, who was kneeling on the sand beside a young boy—Sam! 'Do you know what happened?'

Benita shook her head.

'He just screamed and fell down,' Benita said, looking as puzzled as Beth felt.

'Take the other kids back to the camp and phone the medical centre—tell them to send the medical cart.'

Beth was holding Sam's wrist as she spoke, feeling the fast beat of his pulse, but his chest was barely moving. Respiratory arrest?

'I'll take his towel,' one of the children said, reaching for a bundled-up blue towel that had evidently fallen from Sam's hand.

Respiratory arrest!

'Don't touch it,' Beth snapped, bending her head to breathe air into Sam's lungs. 'Just go.'

She didn't want to panic the children and hoped the urgent look she gave Benita would tell her to hurry.

'Breathe, Sam,' she prayed, settling her knees more firmly on the sand, then pinching his nose and breathing into his mouth again, short sharp bursts of air, head turned as she breathed in so she could watch his chest move as she filled it for him. Expired air, not good enough, but all she could offer until the cart arrived with oxygen.

She counted and breathed and prayed they'd get there soon, counting, breathing, praying, warily eyeing the towel from time to time.

'Respiratory arrest?'

The voice broke her rhythm, then Angus was kneeling on the other side of Sam.

'I'll do the breaths, you take a rest,' he said. 'I saw the group near your hut. The emergency cart should be here before long.'

Beth sat back on her heels and watched Angus for a minute, then she looked around, seeking a stick of some kind—a lump of driftwood, though not, this time, to hit Angus with it! Saw a piece a few metres away and went to get it, then, using it, she unwrapped the towel.

'Damn!' she muttered, and as Angus raised his head momentarily, she pointed the stick at the shell.

'That's a cone shell,' a strange voice said, and Beth

turned to see a tanned man in faded shorts and little else standing behind her. 'Poisonous.'

But Beth had no time to be chatting to strangers, although he had confirmed her thoughts. She knelt beside Sam again, remembering where the towel had been lying near his hand, searching his skin for a break where venom might have been injected.

'Here!'

It was on his little finger, and she reached across and pulled a handkerchief out of Angus's pocket. Thank heavens he was a man of habit—of course there'd been one there!

She wrapped it tightly around the finger, and then the hand, not certain what good it would do but remembering, when she'd studied all the dangers on a coral reef, that pressure immobilisation of the affected part was recommended.

'Four hours!' she muttered to herself. 'Clinical recovery has been documented after four hours.'

Angus glanced up at her, but she didn't have her thoughts enough in order to explain to him.

Besides, his attention had to stay on Sam, and on breathing for him.

The cart arrived, and Luke jumped out. Beth used the stick to drag the towel, with the small, innocuous-looking shell on it, out of the way.

'He'll need to be bagged,' she said, as Luke set up the oxygen tank and mask. 'Assisted ventilation and a mild sedative—the pain must be what caused him to pass out, although not breathing wouldn't help.'

But as Luke slid a cannula into the back of Sam's hand

and prepared to give him the sedative, the little boy's eyes fluttered open.

'Hurts,' he said.

Beth held his bandaged hand.

'I know it does, sweetheart,' she whispered. 'But just lie still and Dr Luke will make that better soon.'

The eyelids drooped closed again and Beth looked around. Should they keep treating him here or transport him to the medical centre?

'Do you think he's stable enough to move?' Luke asked, putting her thoughts into words.

'Maybe stay here for a few more minutes,' she said. 'I'd like to see him breathing on his own but if he doesn't then we're better off in the medical centre, where he can go on a respirator.'

'Good thing we've taken Susie off it,' Luke said. 'What happened?'

Beth pointed to the shell on the towel, but although the towel remained, the shell had gone.

'Cone shell. It was wrapped in the towel. A man was here, he knew it was poisonous so I suppose he took it to dispose of it. I saw him pick it up so he knew how to handle it. He should be safe. I don't know them all by name but it looked like the geographus, which is the most poisonous.'

Luke looked surprised.

'I was coming to work on an island where these things live—of course I looked them up. Irukandji jellyfish, seasnake, stonefish and cone-shell envenomation just to name a few. That innocent-looking shell is a cone shell. They shoot out poison through a toothed harpoon in the narrow end of the shell. My guess is Sam picked it up at the fat end and, because all the kids know you're not to touch shells or plants or anything in the national park, he wrapped it in his towel to hide it. It stung him through the towel, which should have further minimised the amount of poison that got into his body, but he's small…'

She stopped talking and started shaking, thinking how close a call it was for the little boy she'd grown so fond of.

'He's breathing on his own,' Angus announced, and Beth looked down to see he was right. He'd stopped bagging and Sam's chest was rising and falling naturally.

'Let's get him up to the centre,' Luke suggested.

'Sit in the cart, Beth.' Angus kept his eyes on the child as he spoke. 'I'll pass him to you.'

Had Angus seen her shaking?

Not that it mattered. She climbed into the cart and watched as Angus lifted Sam gently and carefully, while Luke handled the oxygen bottle and kept the tube from kinking.

Angus bent to put Sam in her arms and their eyes met, so many memories flooding back, so much history, so much pain and sadness flashing between them.

She'd been mad to think they could go back—mad to think having an affair with Angus would give her special memories. More heartache, that's all it would have given her…

'The towel.'

Thank heavens Angus hadn't been distracted by a look between them.

'The towel…' She hesitated. 'I'm concerned about the towel. I don't know if the cone shell barbs detach, in which case one could be in the towel and still be potent.'

'I'll bag it and see it's destroyed,' Angus responded. 'There's a shop at the resort where we can buy Sam a new towel.'

We?

We sounded so good but Beth knew she shouldn't give it any special meaning. It was only a figure of speech. It probably included Luke as all three of them had worked together to save Sam.

But Angus *had* come over to the camp, presumably to see her—to talk…

She could feel the tremors she'd felt earlier returning, but they weren't relief this time.

Stupid thinking!

She held Sam carefully, talking to him, assuring him it would be all right, turning her thoughts resolutely away from Angus, thinking instead how weird it was that the scene that had played out only two days earlier with little Danny being driven up off the beach should be repeated.

Although Sam would be all right, she was sure of that.

Two hours later, feeling unutterably weary and with her shoulders tight from sunburn she'd suffered when she'd knelt on the beach, she made her way slowly back to her cabin.

Settling Sam into bed had taken far longer than she'd anticipated and although Luke was in charge, she had stayed with the little boy, knowing he trusted her and wanted her near. Wanted her to hear his story, how he'd picked up the shell so he could show it to Lily because she'd missed the walk.

Now, with the wound excised and dressed, and with a mild sedative dripping into his veins, Sam was sleeping and she was free—at least until eight when she was due on duty again.

Her cabin was in shadow, the sun already down below the mountain, but not so deep in shadow she didn't see the movement on her deck.

She stopped, remembering the intruder who'd photographed her the night before, but as the figure stood up, she realised it was Angus.

'I'm sorry, I thought you'd have gone back to the resort. I should have let you know I was delayed.'

'You shouldn't have done anything. I knew you'd want to see Sam settled. He's okay?'

Beth nodded, stopped now at the bottom of the steps, not wanting to go up them—to get close to Angus.

But she could hardly stand there for the next four hours and her shoulders were stinging. A hot shower might help.

She came up the steps into the light and heard his oath, looked at him, puzzled, but he wasn't looking at her face but at her shoulders.

'Oh, for heaven's sake, Beth, of all the harebrained ideas I've ever heard, someone with your fair skin coming to live on a tropical island must be one of the worst. Get into the shower, stand under cool water—not too cold, you could go into shock. I'm going over to the kitchen and I'll be right back.'

He strode away—long, angry strides.

So much for diamonds, Beth thought tiredly, unwinding her sarong as she made her way into the bathroom.

Where she saw what Angus had seen—bright red shoulders!

'Damn it all!' she muttered, then she sat down on the toilet seat and thought about having a really, really good cry.

The thought of Angus returning from the kitchen— why the kitchen?—and finding her with red eyes as well as red shoulders put paid to that idea, so she stood up again, started the shower, and did as he'd suggested— stood under lukewarm water, which felt so good she considered staying there.

Until she heard his footsteps on the deck and knew she didn't want to be naked when she saw him. Naked meant vulnerable—very vulnerable.

She dried herself, patting the red bits gently, then wrapped a clean sarong around her body and walked into the living room. Angus wasn't there. He was in the kitchen and, if she wasn't hallucinating, he was peeling cucumbers.

'Come in here and sit on the stool,' he ordered, his voice suggesting she'd better not argue with him right now. 'Let's try this.'

Totally bemused—by the cucumbers as well as this officious, bossy Angus—she went, and sat, then sighed with pleasure as cool inner flesh of the cucumber skin rested on her reddened shoulders.

'I have no idea if there are any scientific benefits in cucumber skin, but once when I was five we had a holiday at the beach and I got sunburnt and my mother put cucumber skin on it.'

Beth sat motionless beneath his ministering fingers. Even if she'd wanted to move, she doubted she could have, for in all the time she'd known him, Angus had never, ever, mentioned his mother.

Let alone suggested the family had ever done anything as ordinary as having a holiday at the beach.

'But as I was saying earlier, Beth, it really is the height of stupidity for someone with your fair skin to live in the tropics.'

He was back to scolding her, yet there was a note of something she couldn't quite put a finger on beneath the cross, hectoring tone.

Something soft—fond almost…

'And running away,' he continued. 'That doesn't solve anything. We both did it, I know that.'

He moved, taking fresh skins and putting them across her shoulders, flinging the used bits in the sink.

'Didn't talk. Stupid, really, because I knew where you were coming from with not talking—not about emotions—but with the way you were brought up, who could blame you? But me—well, you've met my father, know my upbringing. But you'd think intelligence should have made me realise how wrong he was.'

Angus's voice was softer now—far-away somehow—but nothing he was saying was making much sense, although Beth knew, deep down, it was important.

'You've never mentioned your mother before,' she ventured, and felt a piece of cucumber skin slide lower down her back.

Heard Angus sigh.

'Part of not talking,' he said gruffly, moving the skin across her skin, pressing coolness against the heat. 'They fought—that's my only memory of them together—raised voices, bitter with recriminations and hot with accusation and counter-accusation. One morning, I was seven…' His voice faltered and he held the cucumber firmly against Beth's shoulder as if needing to hold on to her right then. 'It was particularly bad. I stayed in my room until the last minute, thinking I could just dash out and up the road to school and not see either of them, but then my father left and as I headed for the door, I heard my mother crying in the kitchen.'

Beth held her breath, not daring to move, wanting so much to hear the rest of the story—wanting even more for Angus to tell her, to talk to her.

'I went in there and she tried to pretend she was all right, but her eyes were red and there were tears on her cheeks. I put my arms around her waist and told her I loved her, then I went to school.'

Long pause.

'When I came home she was gone. I never saw her again.'

Beth bent forward, holding her head in her hands—not crying, but in so much pain for Angus she could barely breathe. Then she stood up, forgetful of the cucumber skins, which cascaded to the floor around her, and moved towards the man who, pale and gaunt, faced her across the kitchen.

'Oh, Angus!' she whispered, and wrapped her arms around him, resting her head on his chest, feeling his hands tentatively settle on her waist. 'Oh, Angus!'

What else could she say?

How could she explain the pain she felt for the little boy he'd been and for the man he'd grown into—the one who dared not say 'I love you' for fear of losing the recipient of that endearment.

His chin rested on her head and she felt so comfortable

and at peace it took her a moment to realise he was talking again.

'It made me over-cautious about love, and as for expressing it—impossible! Then you were pregnant and we married and that's when I should have said it, but you'd never mentioned love and I figured if I said something, I might frighten you away. I was so happy, Beth, and it seemed to me that you were, too, even without words. But deep inside where betrayal lived I couldn't believe someone as alive and vibrant as you could love a dry, emotionless person like me. I had doubts…'

He paused again, but Beth knew there was more, and she stayed where she was, in Angus's arms, listening to him purge the past.

'That was weakness on my part—and further weakness when you went into labour. I hated the thought of seeing you in pain, scared the words I hadn't said to you would be torn from me, and I'd lose you, too. I let you down, not being there from the beginning at Bobby's birth, but I let myself down even more when I walked away from you after Bobby's death, burying myself in my work. When I didn't argue. When I told myself it was what you wanted—that I was doing it for you—but if I'd been half the man I should have been, I'd have fought, Beth. Fought for your love, fought to win it.'

The words brought not understanding but a thousand questions, and as comfortable as she was within the warm circle of his arms Beth had to move.

She pushed away and looked up into Angus's face.

'Did you just say that you loved me—back when Bobby was born?'

Angus nodded, a ghost of a smile on his lips.

'So much I was afraid I'd have to tell you when I saw you in pain—have to say the words that could send you away from me! But how could I not love you, Beth? You were light, and sunshine, and colour, and everything that was ever good that had happened in my life!'

Beth frowned at him. It sounded wonderful, but surely she was missing something here.

'You thought all that and didn't tell me?'

He nodded again, looking less hopeful now—the smile gone.

'And you still feel something for me? This scolding and the cucumbers—that was love?'

Definitely no smile now. In fact, he was looking distinctly uncomfortable.

'It's how I could show you my feelings. Talk is difficult—we'd established that.'

Beth waved away that pathetic excuse.

'Just tell me,' she said, folding her arms across her chest, needing to get everything out in the open.

He paused, moved his shoulders uneasily, then said, 'I love you, Beth.'

She smiled.

'No hug?'

Angus didn't move.

He couldn't.

Tension held him rooted to the kitchen floor, cucumber skins scattered around his feet. He looked at the woman—the second in his life to whom he'd said 'I love you'—and wondered just how big a mistake he'd made in saying it.

Was he too late?

Had there ever been a right time?

He waited until the waiting became impossible, then took a gamble.

'You're supposed to say it back,' he said, surprising himself at how firm and strong his voice sounded, considering the jelly-like mess he was inside.

'Nuh-uh!' his ex-wife said, shaking her head with a great deal of determination. Defying him, his usually biddable Beth! 'Not until there's a whole lot more talk going on. For instance, if, as you say now, you love me, why the business of not having an affair?'

'You should know that,' he said, recovering slightly, wondering if the slightly less reddened skin on her shoulders meant the cucumber had helped.

Ha! That was his mind escaping from the talk he found so difficult—science didn't need a lot of talk.

'Well, I don't,' she told him. 'It doesn't make sense to me at all.'

He took a deep breath, moved closer, put his hands on her waist and, holding her, looking down into her wide-open eyes, he tried to explain.

'What you were suggesting—an affair, holiday romance—that's not what I want with you, Beth.'

He felt the tremor that ran through her body and longed to draw her close, but drawing her close would lead to kissing and kissing would lead to bed, and that's how they'd got into this impossible situation, making love instead of talking, thinking their unspoken communication—body language in its truest form—was enough.

Beth waited, her body aching for closer contact, her head filled with rosy light. Angus loved her—but sex and rosy light weren't quite enough. More words had to be spoken—dragged out of him if necessary.

'What *do* you want, Angus?' she asked, then wondered if she'd gone too far—tempted fate just that fraction too much.

'I want you,' he said, his eyes holding hers, telling her things she'd never seen in them before. 'I want you in my life, for ever. I want to wake up in the morning with you in my bed, in my arms, and I want to go to bed at night with you beside me. I want you sharing all my joys and triumphs and my lows and disasters, and I want to share yours. I want to marry you and stay married to you for ever because without you my life is empty and meaningless.'

He kind of smiled, an expression so uncertain it tugged at something in Beth's chest, then he added, 'Will that do?'

Would it?

Not quite—in spite of the tugging.

'Not quite.'

She said the words this time and saw his startled reaction.

'Beth?'

Her name was a plea but she waited. He was intelligent, he should be able to work it out.

Except that this was all new territory for him, talking about emotions as foreign to him as Icelandic. In fact, knowing Angus, he probably knew some Icelandic.

'Don't you want to know how I feel?'

His face paled and his hands tightened on her waist, then dropped as he turned away.

'You don't love me? Of course, why should you, after the way I treated you, the way I wasn't there for you when you needed me, the way I walked away at the end? Of course! How stupid can a man be? Standing here babbling on about wanting you for ever, embarrassing you no end with all of it, expecting you to say you love me. I'm sorry, Beth.'

She caught his hand and pulled him back towards her, moving so she stood in front of him and now she put her hands on his waist.

'For such an intelligent man, Angus, you are incredibly stupid. Tell me something, why did we get married?'

'Because you were pregnant?'

'Exactly!'

'So, what are you getting at?'

'How do you think I felt?'

'About getting married?' Angus was guessing here, the conversation having gone far beyond his understanding, probably due to lack of practice in this type of conversation.

'Yes,' Beth confirmed, and Angus tried to think. They'd both been happy, he was sure of that. They'd found a marriage celebrant and asked her to marry them in the children's ward, Beth wanting the kids to share the event, he happy because it had been where they'd met.

'I don't know,' he finally admitted, wondering if he'd failed some test, although the vibes between them still seemed as strong as ever.

'I felt guilty, Angus,' Beth whispered. 'So guilty. As if I'd trapped you into something you didn't want—had never wanted. You were so complete in yourself, or so it seemed to me, that you didn't need anyone else. The only thing I could do, I thought back then, was not compound the problem by making silly declarations of love—declarations I was certain would be unwelcome to you.'

'You loved me then?' Angus asked, but even as the words came out he knew the answer. Of course she had, showing him in a hundred ways every day just how much she'd loved him, and he'd accepted it as Beth simply being Beth.

But that had been then and this Beth was someone he didn't entirely know or understand.

'And now?'

She smiled and he felt his heart stir in his chest, expanding to a point where he felt actual pain.

'Of course I love you, stupid. Always have and always will.'

He moved closer, enveloping her in his arms, wrapping her close to his body, finding her lips, kissing her, hands roaming over her satin-soft skin—

'Ow! My sunburn!'

He stepped away from her, searching through the strewn cucumber skins for an unused one.

Beth stopped him with a touch of her hand on his arm.

'I'm sure there's some cream at the medical centre that might work better than cucumber skins,' she said, then she smiled, 'And as the condoms ended up in the bin we may as well go up there and find it.'

He dropped the cucumber skin into the sink and took her hand, drawing her close and kissing her, not touching her sunburnt skin at all…

CHAPTER TEN

THE medical centre was quiet. The press who had come in with the lifting of the quarantine had lost interest when the story turned out to be about mosquitoes, not bird flu. Entomologists had also flown in, suggesting to the rangers that the mossies be controlled with sprays for the moment and people warned to wear repellent at all times.

Luke had discharged Robbie after lunch, and although Sam had been admitted for observation overnight, according to Marcia, who was the nurse on duty, he'd eaten a good dinner—a fillet from the fish he'd caught—and was now sleeping peacefully.

Ben and Mr Woods had both left that morning, but Susie remained, giving Beth, now sensibly clad in long shorts and a checked shirt, a total of two inpatients.

'Huge caseload!' Angus teased, as Beth led him into the small pharmacy.

'More like what I expected to have,' Beth told him. 'The medical centre is necessary as support for the camp, and the resort owners put in money as well, because they like to be able to assure their guests there are medical facilities close at hand. But no one ever foresaw anything like the panic that happened this week.'

'And now?' he said, repeating the question he'd asked earlier.

Beth had found the cream and Angus had pushed her shirt off her shoulders so he could rub it into her skin.

And now? she pondered as his fingers spread the cream, bringing relief to the still tingling burn.

'What do you want?' she asked, her nerves tensing as she realised that for all their talk nothing had been settled. Oh, they'd sorted out the past, but what of the future?

'I've told you what I want,' Angus replied. 'I want you, with me always. I realise you have a job here, and obligations, and I know you have to think about it—think about our future—but it's clear in my mind that I want us to be together—always.'

Beth turned to look at him, but he was concentrating on the tube of cream, carefully putting the cap back on it.

'Just the two of us?' she asked, forcing the words out through the tightness in her chest.

He looked up and half smiled.

'I'd like to have another child with you, or children, but that's up to you.'

He drew closer, touched her cheek.

'Another child wouldn't replace Bobby, not in my heart or mind, and not in yours, I'm sure. Another child would be just that—a person in his or her own right. But think about it, Beth, think what an opportunity it would be for you and me to have a child or children to whom we could give all the love we both missed out on in our childhoods. I sometimes wonder if it was partly that—our own childhoods—that made us love Bobby so much—and made his death so hard to bear.'

Beth rested against his chest and felt his arms enfold her, low down around her waist, pulling her close, holding her safe against his chest—against his heart, which he'd now pledged to her.

Another child?

A child to shower with love?

A child she didn't have to give back when camp finished?

Angus's child!

Or children…

'I was so afraid,' she whispered. 'It hurt so much when Bobby died, I didn't think I could ever live through that again. I didn't want to have to.'

Angus felt her anguish and held her closer.

'And now?'

It was becoming a refrain.

She eased far enough away to look up into his face.

'And now…' She smiled. 'With you beside me, loving me, I—'

'Hey! Oh, I'm sorry! Didn't know I was interrupting anything, but I was looking for you, Beth. Sam woke up, he wants the dog, and I wondered—'

Beth pushed away from Angus, heat in her cheeks rivalling her shoulders for redness.

'It's okay, Marcia. Angus was just putting cream on my sunburn.'

'Exactly!' Marcia said, grinning from ear to ear.

'But Garf!' Beth continued, hurrying her words to cover her embarrassment. 'I don't think we can have Garf in the medical centre.'

'Not Garf,' Marcia explained. 'The dog in the top hat you gave the camp kids. Sam says it will make him happy while he goes to sleep.'

Beth considered that, then shook her head.

'I don't think we can do that. If one child starts to take camp things to help him or her sleep then they'll all want to. I know he's in hospital but it sets a precedent. Oh, dear…'

'I think I've got an answer.'

Beth had been trying to forget that Angus was there, but his voice made her turn.

'An answer?'

He looked very uncomfortable.

'In my things,' he muttered. 'I've got a dog just like it. I could lend it to Sam overnight.'

His eyes met Beth's and she sensed his embarrassment, then he shook his head and shrugged his shoulders.

'You've got his little chair, I noticed,' he said defiantly, and she had to smile, although inside she felt like crying to think that all this time Angus had held on to Bobby's toy—not only held on to it but travelled with it so he, too, always had a little memory of his son.

'Tell Sam we'll be with him in a moment,' she told Marcia, and as the other woman walked away Beth turned back to her ex-husband and put her arms around him, drawing him close.

'Of course we'll have other children,' she whispered. 'We've far too much love to not be sharing it.'

A BRIDE AND CHILD
WORTH WAITING FOR

BY
MARION LENNOX

Marion Lennox is a country girl, born on an Australian dairy farm. She moved on—mostly because the cows just weren't interested in her stories! "Married to a very special doctor", Marion wrote for Mills & Boon under a different name for a while—if you're looking for her past romances, search for author Trisha David as well. She's now had well over ninety novels accepted for publication.

In her non-writing life Marion cares for kids, dogs, cats, chickens and goldfish. She travels, she fights her rampant garden (she's losing) and her house dust (she's lost!). Having spun in circles for the first part of her life, she's now stepped back from her "other" career, which was teaching statistics at her local university. Finally she's reprioritised her life, figured out what's important and discovered the joys of deep baths, romance and chocolate. Preferably all at the same time.

CHAPTER ONE

'YOU'LL have to be married or she's going to someone else.'

Tom's words were a bombshell, dropped with devastating effect into the quiet of Charles Wetherby's office. Jill and Charles stared at Lily's uncle in disbelief and mutual shock.

It was Wendy who filled the silence. Wendy was Lily's social worker. She'd handled the details when the little girl's parents had been killed a year ago. There'd been immediate agreement in the aftermath of tragedy. Charles and Jill would care for her.

'Let's just recap, shall we?' Wendy said, buying time in a situation that was threatening to spiral out of control. 'Tom, the situation until now has seemed more than satisfactory.'

It had. Dr Charles Wetherby, medical director of Crocodile Creek Air Sea Rescue Base, was a distant cousin of Lily's mother and a friend of Lily's father. In this remote community relationship meant family. Jill Shaw was the director of nursing at Crocodile Creek, and it had been Jill who Lily had clung to in those first appalling weeks of loss.

'We've loved having her,' Jill whispered.

They had. Neither Jill nor Charles could bear to think of six-year-old Lily with an unknown foster-family. They'd rearranged their living arrangements, knocking a door between their two apartments, becoming partners so Lily could live with them.

They'd become partners in every sense but one, but that one

was what was bothering Tom now. Tom was Lily's legal guardian. He had six kids by two marriages and he didn't want his niece, but he'd become increasingly unhappy about her current living arrangements.

'Charles and Jill have both loved having her,' Wendy reiterated, taking in Charles's grim stoicism and Jill's obvious distress. 'And it's great for Lily to stay in Croc Creek. She was born here. She's friends with the local kids. Her father's prize bulls are housed locally and Lily still loves them. Crocodile Creek provides continuity of identity, and that's imperative.'

But it wasn't an imperative with her uncle.

'The wife's been onto me,' Tom retorted, sounding belligerent. 'People are asking questions. Why don't we take her? The wife's feeling guilty. Not that we want her, but I'm damned if I'll keep saying she's fostered. I want her adopted, and the wife says whoever gets her has to be married. We've got to be able to say she's gone to a good home.'

Gone to a good home... Like a stray dog, Charles thought bleakly. Lily wasn't a stray. She was Lily, a chirrupy imp of a six-year-old who warmed the hearts of everyone around her.

But there were scars. He remembered the crash. The truck had been a write-off. They'd had to cut the cab open to get to the bodies of Lily's mother and father, and only then had they discovered the little girl, huddled in a knot of terror behind the seats.

'She needs us,' he said roughly. 'Tom, outwardly Lily's a bundle of mischief, cheerful and bouncy and into everything. But she's too self-contained for a kid her age, and almost every night she has nightmares.'

'We're only just starting to get through to her,' Jill added urgently, and Charles looked across at his director of nursing and thought the process was going both ways.

Jill, damaged by a brutal marriage, had escaped to Crocodile Creek and was only now beginning to relax. Jill was starting to give her heart to this waif of a little girl.

And Charles...

He'd been a loner for twenty years. It had been no small thing for him to knock a hole in his living-room wall and let Jill and Lily into his life. To give Lily up now…

'We want her,' he said, watching Jill, and he knew by Jill's bleak expression that Jill was expecting the worst.

'Get married, then,' Tom snapped.

'We can't,' Jill whispered.

'Yes, we can,' Charles said, spinning his wheelchair so he was facing Jill directly. 'For Lily's sake…why can't we?'

It seemed they could. When the shock of the question faded, Wendy was beaming her pleasure, seeing in this a really sensible arrangement that meant she didn't have to relocate a child she was still worried about.

Tom was satisfied.

'But do it fast,' he growled. 'I want her off our hands real quick. A month's legal? I'll give you a month to get it done or she's gunna be adopted by someone else.'

He bade them a grim goodbye and departed. No, he didn't want to see Lily before he went. He never did. He might be her uncle but he didn't care.

'This is wonderful,' Wendy said as the door slammed behind him. They were sitting in Charles's office at the Crocodile Creek medical base. The hospital was wide and long and low, opening out to tropical gardens and the sea beyond. Wendy looked out the big French windows to where Lily was swinging on a tyre hanging from a vast Moreton Bay fig tree. 'This is fantastic.'

'It'll mean she can stay here,' Charles said, casting an uneasy glance at Jill.

'It means more than that,' Wendy said warmly. 'What Lily needs is commitment.'

'We are committed,' Jill said, startled out of her silence, but Wendy shook her head.

'No. You're doing the right thing. Neither of you give yourselves. Not really.'

'What the hell do you mean by that?' Charles demanded.

'I mean you two are independent career people. Both of you have been hurt in the past. I'm no mind reader but I can see that. You've gone into your individual shells and you've figured out how not to get hurt. Both of you are lovely people,' she said, gathering her notes with an air of bringing the interview to a close. 'Otherwise I'd never have let Lily stay with you. But both of you need to learn to love. That's what that little girl really needs. Children sense—'

'We do love her,' Jill interrupted hotly.

'Yes, you do,' Wendy said, smiling. 'Enough to marry. It's come as a surprise to me—a joy.' She stooped to kiss Charles on the forehead and then she hugged Jill. Jill stood rigid, unsure.

'You'll figure it out,' Wendy said. 'You and Charles and Lily. It's fantastic. Get yourselves married, learn to expose yourselves to what loving's all about and then I can rip up Lily's case file. Oh, and invite me to the wedding. Tom's not leaving you much time—I guess you'd better start organising bouquets and wedding cake now.'

She left them, skipping down to say goodbye to Lily with a bounce that was astounding for a sixty-year-old, grey-haired social worker.

Jill and Charles were left staring after her.

Not looking at each other.

'What have you done?' Jill said finally into the stillness, and the words sounded almost shocking.

'I guess I've just asked you to marry me,' Charles said.

'I… We can't.'

'Why not?'

'In a month?' she whispered, and he nodded. But he was frowning.

'It's a problem,' he agreed. 'We've got so much on.'

They did. Six months ago a tropical cyclone had ripped a swathe of destruction across the entire coastline of Far North Queensland. The damage had been catastrophic, and only now were things starting to get back to normal. Here on the mainland things were reasonably settled, but their base out at Wallaby Island—a remote clinic plus Charles's pet project, a camp for kids with long-term illnesses or disabilities—had been decimated. With government funding, however, and with the sympathy and enthusiasm of seemingly the entire medical community of Queensland, they had it back together. Better. Bigger. More wonderful. The first kids were arriving this week, and the official opening was on Saturday.

'I guess it doesn't take long to get married,' Charles said cautiously. He wheeled out to the veranda. Jill followed him, unsure what else to do. They stood staring out to sea, lost in their own worlds.

'I shouldn't have said it without asking you,' Charles said at last, and Jill shook her head.

'It doesn't matter.'

'You do want Lily.'

'Of…of course.'

'And this seems the only way.'

'I guess.'

'You *are* divorced?' he asked suddenly, and she bit her lip on a wintry little smile.

'Oh, yes. You think I'd have stayed married…'

'Jill, if you ever want to marry anyone else…' Charles spun his chair again. He was as agile with his chair as many men were on their feet. Shot by accident by his brother when he'd been little more than a kid, Charles had never allowed his body to lose its athletic tone. The damage was between L2 and S1, two of the lowest spinal vertebrae, meaning he had solid upper muscular control. He also had some leg function. He could balance on elbow crutches and move forward, albeit with difficulty. He had little foot control, meaning his feet dragged, and his knees refused to respond, but every day saw him work through an exercise regime that was almost intimidating.

Jill was intimidated. Charles had a powerful intellect and

a commanding presence. Tall, lithe and prematurely grey, with cool grey eyes that twinkled and a personality that was magnetic, he ran the best medical base in Queensland. He might be in a wheelchair, he might be in his forties, but he was one incredibly sexy man.

And he'd asked her to marry him.

No. He'd said they'd marry. There was a difference.

'You don't want to marry me,' she whispered, and he smiled.

'Why would I not? You're a very attractive woman.'

'Yeah, right.'

'No, but you are.'

She stared down at her feet. She and Lily had painted their toenails that morning. Crimson-tipped toes peeped out from beneath faded jeans.

She was wearing ancient jeans and a T-shirt with the sleeves ripped out. She'd pulled her thick chestnut hair back into an elastic band. She left her freckles to fend for themselves. Make-up was for kids.

She was thirty-seven years old. The young medics who worked in Crocodile Creek hospital looked fabulous, young, glowing, eager. In comparison Jill felt old. Worn out with life.

'You know you can trust me in a marriage,' Charles said gently. 'It's in name only. If you hate the idea…'

She turned to face him. Charles. Wise, intelligent, astringent. Funny, sad, intensely private.

How could she think of marrying him?

'O-of course it w-would be in name only,' she stammered. 'I… You know I wouldn't…'

'I know you wouldn't,' he said, sounding suddenly tired.

'Tom won't let Lily stay with us if we don't marry,' she said, turning away from him. Fighting for composure. 'And…and you do want Lily?'

'You want Lily, too,' he said. 'Don't you?'

She stared out across the garden at Lily, swinging higher and higher. Did she want a daughter?

More than anything else in the world, she thought. Until Lily's parents had died her life had been…a void.

Her life had been a void since she'd walked out on her marriage. Or maybe it had been a void since she'd married.

'What the hell did he do to you to make you so fearful?' Charles demanded suddenly, and Jill shook her head.

'I'm not fearful.'

'Not in your work, you're not. Put bluntly, you're the best nurse it's ever been my privilege to work with. But in your private life…'

'I'm fine.'

'You've kept yourself to yourself ever since you've been here.'

'And you've kept yourself to yourself for even longer.'

'Maybe I have more reason,' he muttered. 'Hell, Jill, do you think we can make a marriage work?'

'I… How different would it be from what it is now?'

'I guess not much,' he conceded. 'I'd need to buy you a ring.'

'You don't.'

'No, that much I do,' he said. 'Let's make this official straight away.' He glanced at his watch. 'But things are tight. We've got Muriel Mooronwa's hernia operation in half an hour, and I've promised to assist Cal. If things are straightforward we might catch the shops before closing.' He grimaced. 'And the paperwork…that'll take time and I need to go to the island tomorrow.' He frowned, thinking it through. 'You know I've told Lily I'll take her with me. Why not rearrange the roster and come with us? We could sort out the details over there.'

'I can't,' she said flatly. 'Someone senior has to stay here.'

'I can ask Gina and Cal to stay. Cal's so much second in command here now he's practically in charge.'

'He's not a nurse. Doctors think they know everything but when it comes to practicalities they're useless.'

'You don't want—'

'No,' she said flatly, and would have stepped away but Charles's hand came out and caught her wrist. Urgent.

'Jill, this doesn't have to happen. I'm not marrying you against your will.'

'Of course not,' she said dully, and a flash of anger crossed Charles's face.

'You'll have to do better than that,' he snapped. 'I want no submissive wife.'

'What's that supposed to mean?'

'It means I employ you as a director of nursing and I get a competent, bossy, sometimes funny, sometimes emotionally involved woman who keeps my nursing staff happy. It's that woman I'm asking to marry me—not the echo of what you once had with Kelvin.'

'I'm over Kelvin.'

'You're not,' he said gently. 'I know you're not. I'd like to murder the bottom-feeding low-life. More than anything else, Jill, I'd like to wipe the slate clean so you can start afresh. Find some great guy who can give you a normal life—kids, dancing, loving, the whole box and dice. But I can't. OK, I can't have them either. We're stuck with what life's thrown at us. But between us we want to give Lily a great home. She makes us both smile, we make her smile, and that counts for everything. It's a start, Jill. A need to make a kid smile. Is it a basis for a marriage?'

She took a deep breath. She turned and leaned back on the veranda rail so she was looking down at him.

'I sound appallingly ungrateful,' she whispered.

'You don't. You sound as confused as I am.'

'You're burying your dreams.'

'I don't do dreams,' he said roughly. 'We've both been there, Jill. We both know that life slaps you round if you don't keep a head on your shoulders. But what we have... Friendship. Respect. Lily. Is it enough to build a marriage?'

'For Lily's sake?'

'Not completely,' he said, and he looked out to where Lily was swinging so high she just about swung over the branch. 'Just a little bit for our sakes.'

'Because we love Lily,' Jill whispered.

'And because the arrangement suits us.'

'I guess we already have a ruddy great hole in our living-room wall.'

'We may as well make it permanent,' Charles said. He'd released her hand. He put his hands on the arms of his wheel-chair as if he meant to push himself to his feet, but Jill took a step away and he obviously thought better of it. 'What do you say, Jill? For all our sakes…will you marry me?'

'As long…as long as you don't expect a real marriage.'

'Outwardly at least it has to be real. Lily needs to know that we're marrying and we're her adoptive parents.'

'She calls us Jill and Charles,' Jill said inconsequentially.

'Wendy says that's OK.'

'Yes, but I'd really like her to call me…' She faltered. 'But I guess that's something I can get over. Charles, if you really mean it…'

'I really mean it.'

'Then I'll marry you,' she whispered, and despite the enormity of their decision Charles's eyes creased into laughter.

'I'm supposed to get down on bended knee.'

'And I'm supposed to blush and simper.'

'I guess we make do with what we've got.' He caught her hand again and before she guessed what he intended he lifted and lightly brushed the back of her hand with a kiss. 'It makes sense, Jill. There's no one I'd rather marry.'

The sound of laughter echoed from the pathway. Across the lawn was the doctors' house, a residence filled with young doctors from around the world. Doctors came here and gave a year or two's service to the remote medical base.

Two young women were coming along the path now, in white coats, stethoscopes around their necks.

They were young and carefree and gorgeous.

There was no one Charles would rather marry? Jill doubted that. He was gorgeous, she thought. His disability was nothing.

But it wasn't nothing in his eyes. It would always stop him giving his heart.

If he couldn't give his heart, she may as well marry him, she thought. And, hey…

A tiny part of her…just a tiny part…thought marriage to Charles Wetherby might be…well…interesting?

Quite simply, Charles was the sexiest man ever to be stuck in a wheelchair, voted so by every single female medic who ever came here.

'OK,' she said, and managed a smile. The smile even felt right.

'OK, what?'

'I'll marry you.'

'Fine,' he said, and grinned and let her hand go. 'Let's get this hernia organised and go into town and find us a ring.'

'A ring…'

'A ruddy great diamond,' he said. 'If we're doing this at all, we're doing it properly.'

'Charles, no.'

'Jill, yes,' he said, and spun his wheelchair to the end of the veranda where the ramp gave him access to the outside path. Decision made. Time to move on.

'Let's tell Lily,' he said. 'She needs to approve. But, hell, we only have a month to make this legal. We may as well stop wasting time.'

'Don't…don't tell Lily yet.' It seemed too fast. Too sudden.

'Tonight, then, when we tuck her into bed,' Charles said. 'But it has to be done. Let's get a move on.'

CHAPTER TWO

HE NEVER wasted time. Charles Wetherby didn't know what it was to stand still.

Jill stood beside Cal and handed over instruments as Cal carefully repaired Muriel Mooronwa's inguinal hernia. It should have been repaired months ago. It had been seriously interfering with her life for over a year, but that Muriel agreed to have the operation at all was a huge achievement.

It was down to Charles, Jill thought. Ten years ago women like Muriel would have become more and more incapacitated, and probably ended up dying needlessly as the hernia strangulated. Muriel, like so many of the population round Crocodile Creek, was an indigenous Australian who'd been raised in a tribal community. She distrusted cities and all they represented. She distrusted white doctors. But Charles had brought these people a medical service second to none.

From the time Charles had been shot, his wealthy farming family had deemed him useless. Their loss had been the greater gain of this entire region. Charles had gone to medical school with a mission, to return here and set up a service other remote communities could only dream of. He'd had the vision to set up a doctors' residence which attracted medics from all over the world. He talked doctors such as Cal, a top-flight surgeon, and Gina, an American cardiologist, into staying long term. His enthusiasm was infectious. Wherever you went, people were caught up in Charles's projects.

Like Wallaby Island's kids' camp. As soon as his remote air sea rescue service was established Charles had got bored, looking for something else to do. The camp for disabled kids, bringing kids from all over Australia for the holiday of a lifetime, was brilliant in its intent. It brought kids to the tropics to have fun and it provided first-class rehabilitation facilities while that happened.

He acted on impulse, Jill thought as she worked beside him. What sort of impulse had had him asking her to marry him?

'You're daydreaming,' Charles said softly. The main part of the procedure was over now. Cal was stitching, making sure the job was perfect. There was time for his helpers to stand back. Or, in Charles's case, to wheel back. He had a special stool he used in theatre. He'd devised it himself so he could be on a level with what was going on and swivel and move at need. As director of the entire base it was reasonable to assume he didn't need to act in a hands-on capacity, but the day Charles stopped working…

It'd kill him, Jill thought. The man was driven.

'You're dreaming diamonds?' Charles said, teasing, and Jill gasped.

'What…? No!'

'Diamonds,' Cal said, eyes widening. 'Diamonds!'

'Maybe just one diamond,' Charles said. 'Jill, seeing Gina and Cal are our babysitters-in-chief, I figure maybe Cal should be the first to know.'

'You guys are getting married?' Cal said incredulously.

'Only because of Lily,' Jill said in a rush, and the pleasure in Cal's eyes faded a little.

'Why?'

'If we don't get married Lily gets adopted by someone else,' Charles said. 'We're sort of used to her being around.'

'You mean you love her,' Cal said gently, and the smile returned. 'You want to tell me how it happened?'

'Her uncle wants her adopted,' Charles explained. 'He's her legal guardian. He wants a married couple.' He turned to the tray of surgical instruments and focused on what needed attention.

Nothing needed attention.

'We can't let her go,' Jill said warmly, life returning to her voice. 'We all love her.'

'Of course we do,' Cal said. Lily was playing with Gina and Cal's small son, CJ, right now. CJ and Lily were best friends. They were in and out of each other's houses, they slept over at each other's places; in fact, sometimes Charles thought Lily regarded Gina and Cal as just as much her parents as he and Jill.

It was a problem, he thought. Oh, it made life easy that Lily transferred her affections to whoever she was with, but Wendy worried that the child's superficial attachments were the result of trauma.

It didn't matter, Charles thought. It'd settle.

'So when's the date?' Cal asked, and Charles looked questioningly at Jill.

'I... We need to do it within a month.'

'Hey, it's a magnificent excuse for a party. It'll be headline news...'

'Private ceremony,' Charles said before he thought about it. 'No fuss.'

'No fuss,' Jill agreed, and Charles looked sharply up at her. Kicking himself. He'd done it again. He'd made the decision without consulting her.

'And no photographs,' she said. Her voice was flat, inflexionless. No joy there.

Of course not. She'd had the marriage from hell the first time round. Marriage could never be something she approached with joy.

He knew few details of her past, and those he hadn't gained from Jill. His friend Harry, the Crocodile Creek policeman, had passed on information to Charles when he'd become involved with Jill that he'd thought might be important.

Married absurdly young and with no family support, Harry reported that Jill's marriage had been a nightmare of abuse. She'd tried to run, but she'd been hauled back, time and time again. Her final attempt to defy her husband had nearly cost her life. Only the fact that there'd been a couple of tourists on the jetty as Jill had staggered from her husband's fishing boat had saved her life.

But despite her appalling marriage, Jill Shaw was a woman of intelligence and courage. She'd still been young enough to start a new life. Cautiously, and with the encouragement from women she met at the refuge she'd ended up in after she'd been discharged from hospital, she'd applied for a nursing course as far away from the scene of her marriage as she'd been able to. She still feared Kelvin and had changed her name to keep hidden, but she'd moved on. She'd lived on the smell of an oily rag to get what she wanted.

She'd graduated with honours, she'd embraced her profession and when she'd applied to Crocodile Creek—it had to be one of the most remote nursing jobs in Australia—Charles hadn't believed his luck.

But she wasn't happy. Normally bossy and acerbic, with a wry sense of humour, the events of the afternoon seemed to have winded her. Was she afraid? Of more than her ex-husband finding her? Hell, she had to know he'd never hurt her. And she'd agreed. She did love Lily, he thought. She wanted this.

He was going to Wallaby Island tomorrow without her. He had to have her smile about this—he had to have her feeling sure before he went.

'Cal, we're finished now,' he said, maybe more roughly than he intended. 'Do you think you and Gina can hang on to Lily for a few more hours?'

'Of course,' Cal said easily. 'We're packing to go to

Wallaby Island tomorrow. Having Lily will get CJ out of our hair while we organise ourselves.'

'Fine,' Charles said. He had his own packing to do but it'd have to wait. 'Don't mention what's happening to Lily—we want to tell her ourselves tonight. But Jill and I are going out to dinner and we need to leave now.'

'It's only four now,' Jill said, startled. 'What's the rush?'

'We need to get changed,' Charles said. 'And we need to get into town before the jeweller shuts. I've never been engaged before and if we're going to do this...Jill, let's do this in style.'

He wouldn't listen to her objections. She didn't need a ring. She didn't need...marriage.

What was she doing?

Jill stood in her bare little bedroom and gazed into her wardrobe with a sense of helplessness. She was going out to dinner with Charles. She should wear clean jeans and a neat white shirt.

'A dress,' Charles called from his bedroom, and she winced.

A dress. The outfit she'd bought for the weddings?

It was an occupational hazard, working in Crocodile Creek, she thought ruefully. So many young medics came here to work that romance was inevitable. They'd had, what, eight weddings in the last year? So much so that the locals laughingly referred to the doctors' house as the Wedding Chapel.

She'd never lived in the doctors' house. She valued her independence too much.

What was she doing?

She wanted Lily. It was like an ache. From the time she'd held her, the night her parents had been killed, her heart had gone out to the little girl. Even Lily's fierce independence, the way she held herself just slightly aloof from affection... Jill could understand it and respect it.

'Dress?' Charles called again, and she smiled. He was as

bossy as she was. But not…autocratic. Never violent. She'd seen him in some pretty stressful situations. There'd been a family feud. His brother had been responsible for his injury, yet his father had vented his fury on Charles. He'd considered his injured son useless.

Charles had never railed against the unfairness of fate. He'd taken his share of a vast inheritance—a share which his father hadn't legally been able to keep from him—and he'd proceeded to set up this medical base. He'd funnelled his anger and his frustration into good.

He deserved…

A dress.

OK. She tugged her only dress from its hanger—a creamy silk sliver of a frock that hugged her figure, that draped in a cowl collar low around her breasts, no sleeves, a classy garment Gina had bullied her into for Kate and Hamish's wedding. She slipped it on, and then tugged her hair from its customary elastic band.

Her glossy chestnut curls had once been a source of pride. She brushed them now. They fell to her shoulders. She looked younger this way, she thought as she stared into the mirror. There was no grey in her hair yet.

She was a woman about to choose her engagement ring…

It was nonsense. She shoved her feet into sandals, grabbed her purse and headed for the door.

And stopped and returned to the mirror.

She stared at her reflection for a long moment, then sighed and grabbed a compact and swiped powder over her freckles. She put on lipstick that had been used, what, eight times for eight weddings?

Hers would be the ninth?

'It's nonsense,' she whispered, but as she put the lid back on her lipstick she caught sight of her reflection and paused.

'Not too bad for thirty-seven,' she whispered. 'And you're going to marry Charles.'

It was a sensible option. But…Charles.

She couldn't quite suppress a quiver of excitement. He really was…

'Just Charles,' she said to herself firmly. 'Medical director of Croc Creek. Your boss.

'Your husband?

'Get real,' she told her reflection. She stuck her tongue out at herself, grinned and went to meet her fiancé.

He liked it. She emerged from her bedroom and Charles was waiting. His eyes crinkled in the way she loved.

'Hey,' he said softly. 'What's the occasion? An engagement or something?'

Charles had made an effort, too. He was wearing casual cream trousers and a soft, cream, open-necked shirt. Quality stuff. Clothes that made him look even sexier than he usually did.

He hadn't lost muscle mass, as many paraplegics did, Jill thought. His injury could almost be classified as cauda equina rather than complete paraplegia—a damage to the nerves at the base of his spine. He pushed himself, standing every day, forcing his legs to retain some strength. It'd be much easier to stay in the wheelchair but that had never been Charles's way—taking the easy option.

He was great, she thought. The most fantastic boss…

But a husband?

'Lily's OK?' she asked.

'Settled at Cal and Gina's.'

Her face clouded. 'You know, I wish—'

'That she wasn't quite as happy to go to strangers,' he said softly. 'I know. It's what Wendy says. Tom's right in a way. She needs permanence. Even commitment. That's what we're doing now. Let's go buy us an engagement ring.'

The jeweller was obsequious, eager and shocked. He tried to usher them into the door, tugging Charles's wheelchair sideways in an unnecessary effort to help, and came close to upending him in the process. By the time Charles extricated himself from his unwelcome aid, the man had realised the potential of his customers.

'Well,' he said as he tugged out trays of his biggest diamonds. 'Never did I think I'd have the pleasure of selling an engagement ring to the medical director of Crocodile Creek. And you a Wetherby. I sold an engagement ring to your brother. He runs the farm now, doesn't he? Such a shame about your accident. Not that you haven't done very well for yourself. A healthy man could hardly have done more. You're still a Wetherby, though, sir. Now, your brother purchased a one and a half carat diamond when he got engaged. If you'd warned me... I don't have anything near that quality at the moment, but if you'd like to choose a style, I can have a selection flown in tomorrow. As big as you like,' he said expansively. 'You're a lucky lady, miss.'

'Yes,' Jill said woodenly. The way the jeweller looked at Charles was patronising, she thought. She'd spent enough time with Charles to pick up on the way people talked to him. This guy was doing it wrong. He was talking to Charles but keeping eye contact with her. He was making her know he was being kind to the guy in the wheelchair. And the way Charles had looked when he'd mentioned his brother...

She hated this shop. She hated these ostentatious diamonds. How big was the man saying this diamond should be?

Would Charles like her to have a bigger diamond than his brother's wife?

'What would you like, Jill?' Charles asked gently, and she shook herself out of her anger and tried to make a choice. She had to do this.

'Any diamond's fine,' she said. 'I guess....however big you want.'

'However big *I* want?'

He was quizzing her. He had this ability to figure what she

thought almost before she thought it herself. The ability scared her.

Maybe Charles scared her.

'You don't really want a diamond, do you?' he said.

'If you think—'

'I don't think,' he said with another flash of irritation. 'It's you who gets to wear the thing. Some of these rings are really….'

'Ostentatious?' she said before she could help herself, and Charles's face relaxed. He smiled wryly, though the touch of anger remained.

'I'm right, aren't I? You hate these as much as I do.'

'I suspect we do need an engagement ring, though,' she said. 'If you're planning on telling everyone we're engaged.'

'I *am* planning on telling everyone we're engaged.' He hesitated and then held out his hand to the jeweller. 'Sorry, Alf,' he said bluntly. 'I've a lady with simple tastes. I'm thinking it's one of the reasons I've asked her to marry me, so we'll not go against that. Thank you for your help and good day. Coming, Jill?'

'We're not…?'

'No, we're not,' he said forcefully, and propelled his chair out the door before she could argue.

By the time Jill caught him up he was half a block away. She had to run to catch up.

He realised, slowed and spun to face her.

'Sorry,' he said, rueful. 'Telling me the size of my brother's engagement ring pushed a few buttons I don't like to have pushed.'

'I can see that,' she said cautiously. 'And the way he treated you…'

'I don't care about the way he treated me. I'm used to it. But you… You don't really want a three-carat diamond ring?'

'I don't want any ring.' She hesitated, looking down at her hands. They were work hands, scrubbed a hundred times a day in her job as a nurse. They were red and a bit wrinkled. The nails were as short as she could cut them.

'I'd look ridiculous with a diamond.'

'How about an opal?' Charles asked, and she hesitated. 'If you don't want one, just say so.'

'I love opals,' she said cautiously. 'But—'

'But nothing. George Meredith's in town. Have you met him? He's a local prospector—he spends his time scraping in dirt anywhere from here to Longreach. What he doesn't know about opals isn't worth knowing. I know he's in town because I saw him for a dodgy back this morning. I told him no digging for a week, to stay in town, get himself a decent bed and put his feet up. He'll be down at the hotel. I also know he has some really decent rock. Let's go and take a look.'

He had more than decent rock. He had ready-made jewellery.

'I don't normally make it up,' he told them. A big, shy man, quietly spoken but with enormous pride in the stones he produced to show them, he stood back as they fingered his fabulous collection. 'I sell it on to dealers. But a mate of mine's done some half-decent work and while the back's been bad he's been teaching me to do a bit. These are the ones I'm happiest with. When me back's a bit better I'm heading to Cairns—I reckon the big tourist places will snap this lot up. Hang on a sec.'

They hung on. George had spread his stones out on the coverlet of his hotel bed for them to see. Now he delved into a battered suitcase and produced a can of aftershave. He glanced suspiciously at his visitors, then grinned as if he'd decided suspicions here were ridiculous, but all the same he turned his back on them so they couldn't see what he was doing. He twiddled for a bit and then spun back to face them. The aftershave can was open at the base and a small, chamois pouch was lying in his open palm.

He opened it with care, unwrapping individual packages. Laying their contents on a pillow.

Four rings and two pendants. Each one made Jill gasp.

'They're black opal,' George said with satisfaction. 'You won't find better stuff than this anywhere in the world. You like them?'

Did she like them? Jill stared down at the cluster of small opals and thought she'd never seen anything lovelier.

She lifted one, drawn to it before all the others. It was the smallest stone, a rough-shaped opal set in a gold ring. The stone was deep, turquoise green, with black in its depths. But there was fire, tiny slivers of red that looked like fissures in the rock, exposing flames deep down. The opal looked as if it had been set in the gold in the ground, wedged there for centuries, washed by oceans, weathered to the thing of beauty it was now.

She'd never seen anything so beautiful.

'Put it on,' George prodded, and as she didn't move Charles lifted it from her, took her ring finger and slid the ring home.

It might have been made for her.

She gazed down at it and blinked. And tried to think of something to say. And blinked again.

'I think we have a sale,' Charles said in satisfaction. Both men were smiling at her now, like two avuncular genies.

'It ought to go on a hand like that,' George said. 'You know, that stone… I almost decided to keep it. I couldn't bear to think of it on some fancy woman's hand, sitting among half a dozen diamonds and sapphires and the like. If you don't mind me saying so, ma'am,' he said, 'your hands are right for it. Worn a bit. Ready for something as lovely.'

'Not a bad pitch,' Charles said appreciatively.

'I mean it,' George growled, and from the depth of emotion in his voice Jill knew he did.

But…

'I can't,' she whispered. 'This is black opal.' She hadn't lived in a place such as Crocodile Creek without knowing the value of such a stone. 'You can't…'

'I can,' Charles said solidly. 'Jill, why don't you go down to the bar while George and I talk business?'

'I—'

'Go,' he said, and propelled her firmly out the door.

They went to dinner at the Athina. They were greeted with pleasure and hugs and exclamations of delight before they so much as made it to their table.

Word was all over town.

'Oh, but it's beautiful,' Sophia Poulos said mistily, looking at the ring and sighing her happiness. 'If you two knew how much we hoped this would happen…'

'We're only doing this for Lily,' Jill said, startled, but Sophia beamed some more.

'Nonsense. You wear a beautiful ring. You wear a beautiful dress. You are a beautiful woman and Dr Wetherby…he's a very handsome man, eh? And don't tell me you haven't noticed. You're doing this for Lily? In my eye!' She gave a snort of derision and headed back to her kitchen. 'Hey,' she yelled to her husband. 'We have lovers on table one. Champagne on the house.'

It was silly. It was embarrassing. It was also kind of fun. But as the meal wore on, as the attention of the restaurant patrons turned away, there was a sudden silence. It stretched out a little too long.

It's just Charles, Jill told herself, feeling absurdly self-conscious. It's just my boss.

'What's happening tomorrow?' she asked, and it was the right thing to ask for it slid things back into a work perspective. Here they were comfortable. For the last eight years they'd worked side by side to make their medical service the best.

'There's three days' work happening tomorrow,' Charles growled. In the project ahead Charles held passion. The kids' camp on Wallaby Island had been a dream of Charles's since he'd returned to Crocodile Creek. Jill had been caught up in his enthusiasm and had been as devastated as Charles when the cyclone had wreaked such havoc.

But tragedy could turn to good. With public attention and sympathy focussed on the region, funding had been forthcoming to turn the place into a facility beyond their imagination. Charles was heading there tomorrow to welcome the first kids to the restored and extended camp. It was a wonder he'd found time to talk to the social worker about Lily, Jill thought ruefully, much less take this evening off to wine and dine a fiancée.

And give her a ring.

As they talked about their plans—or, rather, Charles talked and Jill listened—her eyes kept drifting to her ring.

She'd never owned anything so beautiful. Despite what George said, it didn't look right on her work-worn hand.

But Charles had always known what she was thinking. She had to learn to factor that in. 'It's perfect,' he said gently, interrupting what he was saying to reassure her, and she flushed.

'I'm sorry. I didn't mean…'

'It's me who should be sorry. This is no night to be talking about work.'

'We don't have a lot more in common,' she said bluntly, and then bit her lip. She hadn't meant to sound so…tart.

Maybe she was tart. Maybe that was how she always sounded. She'd stop pretences years ago.

One of the reasons she'd relaxed with Charles over the years had been that he seemed to appreciate blunt talking. He asked for her opinion and he got it.

She needed to soften, though, she thought. He wouldn't want a wife who shot her mouth off.

'We have Lily in common,' he reminded her, and she nodded.

Of course. But… 'I'm not sure why you want her,' she said cautiously. 'I know your reaction when her parents died was the same as mine—overwhelming sadness. But you do already have a daughter.'

'I have Kate,' he said. 'A twenty-seven-year-old daughter I've only known for the last few months.'

'You must have loved her mother.'

'We all did,' he said ruefully. 'Maryanne was gorgeous. She was wild and loving and did what she pleased. I wasn't the only one in love with her. You know that's what caused the rift in my family? Philip, my brother, shot me by accident, but he put the blame on a mate of mine who also loved Maryanne. The repercussions of that can still be felt today. Anyway, that's what happened. I was injured and was sent to the city. Apparently Maryanne was in the early stages of pregnancy but didn't tell anyone. Certainly not me. A rushed marriage to a young man who was little more than a boy, and who was facing a life of paraplegia...that would never be Maryanne's style.

'By the time I was well enough to return here she'd disappeared down south. Apparently she had Kate adopted and then proceeded to have a very good life. The first I knew of it was when Kate arrived on the scene just before the cyclone.'

He said it lightly. He said it almost as if it didn't hurt, but there was enough in those few words to let Jill see underneath. A young man wildly in love, deserted seemingly because of his paraplegia. Knowing later he'd fathered a child, but Maryanne had not deemed it worth telling him. It was more of the same, she thought. More of the treatment meted out by the jeweller.

Charles as a young man would have been gorgeous. She knew enough of his family background to know he was also rich. Maryanne might well have chosen another course altogether if she hadn't classified the father of her child as something...

Well, it was all conjecture, Jill thought harshly. Charles must have done his own agonising. It wasn't for her to do his agonising for him.

'But it does mean you have a daughter,' she said gently into the silence.

'I do,' he said. 'But I missed out on the whole damned lot.

With Lily it's a bit like being given the chance again.' He hesitated. 'OK. Enough. What about you?'

'Me?' she said, startled.

'All I know of your background is from other people,' he said. 'Maybe if we're to be married I ought to know a bit more.'

'You don't want to know about Kelvin.'

'Harry told me he was in jail.'

'He had a five-year sentence for…for hurting me. I'm still…'

'Afraid of him?'

'He used to say he'd kill me if I left him,' she whispered. 'He demonstrated it enough for me to believe him.'

'You think he's still a threat?'

'He doesn't know I'm here. You know that. You know I've changed my name. Judy Standford, dumb, bashed wife of a fisherman down south, to Jill Shaw, director of nursing at Croc Creek. But he'll still be looking.'

'Surely after so many years…'

'What Kelvin owns he'll believe he owns to the end,' she said bleakly. 'He'd want me dead rather than see me free.'

'Why the hell did you marry him?' he asked savagely.

'The oldest reason in the world,' she said. 'Like you and Maryanne, only maybe without the passion. I was sixteen. A kid. Kelvin was a biker, a mate of my oldest brother, Rick. Rick agreed I could go with them to a music festival. I was way out of my depth and I ended up pregnant. My dad…well, my dad was as violent in his way as Kelvin. Kelvin agreed to marry me and I was terrified enough to do it. Only then I lost the baby. And when I tried to leave… It just…' She stopped, seeming too distressed to go on.

'You don't have to explain to me,' Charles said gently. 'But, even after you left, you never thought you'd marry again? You never thought you'd like a child?'

'Of course I'd like a child,' she said explosively. 'I was seven months pregnant when I lost my little girl. I hadn't realised…until I held Lily…'

'So Lily's a second chance for both of us.' He reached over the table and took her ring hand, folding it between both of his. The warmth and strength of his hold gave her pause.

She'd been close to tears. Close to fury. His hold grounded her, settled her. Made her feel she had roots. But it also left her feeling out of her depth.

'D-don't,' she said, and tugged back.

'We need to show a bit of affection,' Charles said wryly. 'If we're to pull off a marriage that doesn't look like a sham.'

'It doesn't matter if it is a sham.'

'You see, I'm thinking that's where you might be wrong,' he said. 'We've been given Lily. It's a huge gift.'

'We should be home with her now.'

'She doesn't need us now,' Charles said. 'That's the problem. Oh, she needs us in that we're providing security whether she knows it or not. But if we said she was to live with Gina and Cal…'

'She'd be upset,' Jill said. She tugged her hand away and stared down into the depths of her ring. 'Or she'd be more upset,' she amended. 'She's traumatised.'

'She won't let the psychologists near.' Charles sighed. 'Well, you know the problems as well as I do. Do we tell her tonight that we're getting married? That she can stay with us for ever?'

'Cal knows. Gina knows. Sophia Poulos knows. We'd better do it or she'll be the last in Croc Creek to find out.'

CHAPTER THREE

CHARLES settled the bill and they went out into the balmy night. On another occasion they might have walked here—or wheeled here, Jill corrected herself. Charles never let being in a chair stop him going places. The strength in his arms was colossal and he could push his chair long after those around him were tired from walking.

But there was packing to do tonight and they needed to collect Lily before it got too late. So they'd driven. Or Charles had driven. He was almost as fast getting into the car as a normal driver, opening the door, sliding into the driver seat, clipping his chair closed and swinging it into the rear seat behind him. By the time Jill had adjusted the drapes of her dress they were already moving out onto the road.

He was a normal guy, Jill thought as she tried to focus on the road ahead, and she swallowed. A normal husband. Did he realise what that did to her?

It terrified her.

She'd agreed to this marriage why? Because she loved Lily. Because she couldn't bear that Lily be further dislocated.

Because Charles was in a wheelchair and would make no demands on her as a wife?

Maybe that had been a factor, she conceded. Up until now Charles's paraplegia had made this marriage seem…safer? A sexless marriage.

But maybe that was dumb. His injury was so low that maybe…maybe…

Maybe nothing. It didn't matter, either way. She trusted Charles. It'd be OK.

But she glanced sideways at his profile in the moonlight. The lean, angular features of a strongly boned face. The crinkles around his eyes where years of laughter had left their mark. And pain. He'd never admit it but you didn't suffer the type of injury he'd endured without pain.

She loved the way his hair crinkled at the roots and then became wavy—just a little. She loved the silver in it. Premature grey was so damned sexy in a male…

Sexy. See, there was the thing. Charles didn't see himself as sexy so neither should she. She was right to think of his paraplegia as her security. She had to keep thinking of him as disabled, because if she kept thinking of him as sexy this marriage of convenience would never work. She ought to run rather than risk it.

But she was tired of running. She wanted a home. A home, a husband, a daughter.

Charles.

If Kelvin found out, he'd kill them all.

Was she being paranoid? The logical part of her said yes. The part of her that had been controlled by Kelvin said she wasn't being paranoid at all.

'What are you thinking?' he asked, his voice a little strained. Maybe he was finding this as hard as she was.

'That maybe it's good for you that you're going to Wallaby Island tomorrow,' she said, and for the life of her she couldn't stop her voice from sounding faintly waspish. 'This place is going to be awash with gossip, and you and Lily will have escaped.'

'Just snap their noses off when they ask to see your ring,' he said. 'That'll sort them out.'

'You think I'm…prickly.'

'I *know* you're prickly.'

'Charles, why do you want to marry me?' she burst out. 'I'm plain and I'm bossy and I'm old.'

'Now, that,' Charles said solemnly, 'is ridiculous.'

'Is it?'

'So why do you want to marry me?' he demanded. 'I'm in a wheelchair.'

'That's just as ridiculous.'

'You don't think you want to marry me *because* I'm in a wheelchair?'

'Because I feel sorry for you?' she muttered. 'Fat chance.'

'You don't feel sorry for me?'

'Anyone feeling sorry for you gets their heads bitten off.'

'So you're scared of me.'

'I'm not,' she said, and then decided to be honest. 'Or not very much.'

'So let me get this straight,' he said slowly. 'You're thinking you're plain and bossy and old, you're scared of me but you've decided to marry me anyway.'

'It does sound dumb,' she admitted.

'Yeah,' he agreed. 'With all the romance in the air around Croc Creek, the place practically sizzles.'

'It's just as well it doesn't sizzle near us, then.'

'Not even a bit?'

'Of course not. I mean, look at us. We've discussed this sensibly. We've bought an engagement ring. We haven't even kissed.'

'I kissed your hand.'

'You did,' she said. 'Um…yeah. Very nice it was, too.'

'You want to be kissed?'

'No!'

'We ought to,' he said thoughtfully. 'I mean…we do intend to make a marriage out of it. We could just try.'

'Charles, don't.'

'Because you're plain and old and bossy?'

'No, because…'

'Because I'm in a wheelchair?'

'No!'

'Then why?' he demanded, and there was suddenly frustration in his voice. 'Why the hell not?'

'Because we don't…'

'Deserve it?' He glanced over at her. She was staring straight into the night, trying to figure out what to say. What to do. She was fingering her engagement ring like it was burning.

'Jill, don't look like that.'

'Like what?'

'Hell,' he said again, and before she knew what he intended he'd steered the car onto the verge. They were at the foot of the bridge beside Crocodile Creek. There was a sloping sandbank running down to the water.

In other circumstances a romantic couple might get out and wander down to the water's edge to admire the moonbeams glimmering over the water's dark surface.

Yeah, in other circumstances a couple might get taken by a crocodile. Getting out here was for fools.

Stopping here was for fools.

'Jill, I'm not marrying any woman who's afraid of me,' Charles said steadily into the darkness.

'I'm not…'

'Look at me and say it.'

She turned and looked at him. He gazed steadily back, serious, questioning.

She knew this man. She'd worked with him for years. He was the best doctor in Crocodile Creek.

He loved Lily. He was doing this to give her a daughter.

'I'm not afraid of you,' she said, and it was true. She trusted him. She knew it at every logical level. It was only the thought of marriage that had her terrified.

But this was Charles. Charles!

'It'll be OK,' Charles said softly, and he caught her hands

and tugged her toward him. 'Jill, I don't think you're plain or bossy or old.' Then he smiled, that crinkly, crooked smile that transformed his face. The smile she loved. 'OK, maybe bossy,' he conceded. 'But bossy's good for a director of nursing. Maybe bossy's even good for a mum, and that's what you're going to be. It'll be fine. It might even be fantastic. Let's give it our best shot, eh?'

And he tugged her close—and he kissed her.

She hadn't been kissed for how long?

Years and years and years. Her kissing skills had lain dormant, forgotten. Buried.

But not dead.

She'd last kissed with passion when she'd been a teenager. She'd forgotten…or she'd never known…

Strong, warm hands holding her face, centring her so he could find her mouth. Lips meeting lips. Warmth meeting warmth.

Not warmth. Fire.

That was what it felt like. A rush of heat so intense that it sent shock waves jolting through her body. She felt her lips open, she felt his mouth merge with hers…

It was like moving into another dimension.

Her hands lifted involuntarily, her fingers raking his hair, firming their link. Not that there was a need for such firming. She couldn't back away from this.

This magic.

It was a feeling so intense it seemed she was almost out of her body. Transformed into something she'd never been, or if she had she'd long forgotten. A girl, a woman who could melt with pure desire.

For just a moment she let herself fall. She let herself be swept away, feeling how she could feel if she were a girl again and life was before her and she didn't know what happened to women who surrendered control.

Kelvin had called her an ugly cow—over and over until she'd believed it totally. But maybe…just maybe he was wrong.

This was delicious, delectable, dangerous… Seductive in its sweetness. Overwhelming in its demands. For he wasn't just kissing her; he was asking questions she had no hope of answering; he was taking her places she had never been and had no intention of going.

But she was going there.

No. She was Jill Shaw, solidly grounded nursing director of Crocodile Creek hospital. She recalled it with a tiny gasp of shock. Her hands shoved between Charles's chest and her breasts and she pushed back.

He released her immediately, leaning back so he could see her in the moonlight. He looked as surprised as she did, she thought shakily. As out of his element. The great Charles Wetherby, shocked.

'I don't think…' She tried and then had to try again for her voice came out a squeak. 'I don't think this is a good idea.'

'Kissing?'

'Anything,' she managed. She was still squeaking. Oh, for heaven's sake… She was a mature woman. It had just been a kiss.

Yes, but what a kiss. If a kiss could wipe a woman's logic away as this one had… If a kiss could make her feel beautiful…

She wasn't beautiful. She had to get her bearings. She had to be sensible.

'We don't want anything to happen?' Charles queried, and she bit her lip.

'Certainly not.'

'Any particular reason?'

'We're too old.'

'Hey! Speak for yourself.'

'I didn't mean…' She swallowed. 'Charles, maybe I need to say… I just don't want…' Another swallow. Another attempt. 'I'm not going to be what you might call a jealous wife. I don't know what you do now…'

'For sex, you mean?' he asked, and affront had given way to bemusement.

'I don't need to know,' she said hurriedly. 'I mean… I don't even know…'

'If I can?' he said, still bemused. 'I can.' Damn him, he was enjoying her discomfiture.

'That's…that's good. I guess. So if you want to…'

'If I want to then you'll permit it? But not with you?'

'Just because you kissed me doesn't mean I'm expecting…'

'What if I want to?'

'You don't want to,' she said flatly. 'Or, at least, I don't. Look, it was a very romantic evening, for which I thank you. I love my ring.' She glanced down at it, a moonbeam caught it at just the right angle and she saw fire. 'I really love my ring. But what we're doing is practical.'

'You don't find me—'

'Don't ask,' she snapped. 'It's ludicrous.'

'Of course it's ludicrous,' he said, and the trace of laughter died from his voice as if it had never been.

What…? Oh, God. 'I didn't mean that,' she whispered, mortified.

'Of course you didn't.' He turned back to the wheel and flicked the engine into life. 'Don't worry. I won't touch you again. It's time we were home.'

'Charles…'

'It's OK,' he said wearily. 'As you say, we're too old. Let's go and pick up Lily and tell her she has two very respectable prospective parents.'

Jill shrank back into the passenger seat and felt about six inches tall. She'd never meant to infer she found Charles's disability offensive. Or even a bar to…well, to anything.

It was just that she didn't want anything. She didn't want contact at all.

She surely didn't want to risk those sensations coursing

through her that threatened to undermine the control she'd fought like a wildcat to regain after her marriage. She never wanted to be exposed again.

She should apologise to Charles. His face was set and grim, and she could lighten it. She could make him smile.

But…but…

Did she want him to smile? Not when they were alone, she thought frantically. Not when she was dressed like this, when she was wearing his ring. Not when his smile made her feel vulnerable and exposed and terrified.

No. Better to sit here, rigid, on the far side of the car, to school her expression into passive nothingness.

Like a cold fish.

She'd heard one of the younger nurses call her that once, and she'd thought, Good. That was how she wanted to be thought of. Emotional nothingness.

But she had a daughter. Or she'd have a daughter once this marriage took place. How could she be a cold fish with a daughter?

'Keeping ourselves only unto ourselves except for when we're with Lily,' Charles said.

'You understand,' she whispered, humbled.

'We're birds of a feather,' he said.

'Charles, I am sorry.'

'Don't be sorry,' he said. 'It was me who kissed you. I was overstepping the boundaries. It won't happen again.'

Lily was asleep when they arrived at Cal and Gina's. Cal heard the car and brought her out to them. She was slight for her age, a wiry, freckled imp with a tangle of brown-gold curls and a smattering of freckles, just like Jill's. She woke as Jill buckled her into her car seat but she made no demur. She was accustomed to this. Even when her parents had been alive, their love affair with rodeos meant she was very adaptable.

'Goodnight, sleepyhead,' Cal said, ruffling her tousled curls before he stepped back from the car. Then he smiled at Jill. He lifted her ring hand and whistled.

'Congratulations.' He hugged her and kissed her on the cheek. Jill found herself flushing.

'It's nothing.'

'It's fabulous,' he said. He looked into the car at Charles and grinned. 'Congratulations to you, too.'

'Thanks,' Charles said. 'But we're only doing it for Lily.'

'Right,' Cal said, sounding dubious. He looked back into the car at their sleepy little daughter. She was wearing her favourite pink pyjamas with blue moons and stars, her curls were tied up—or they had been tied up—with a huge, silver bow and there was a smudge of green paint on her nose.

'We did give her a bath,' he said ruefully. 'With CJ. And Gina did her hair.'

'I'll give her another one before she leaves tomorrow,' Jill said.

'You're not coming across to the island for the opening?'

'I'm in charge here.'

'Alistair can take over. You know he'd like—'

'I'm in charge here,' she said flatly.

'But you're telling Lily tonight, right?'

'Telling me what?' Lily asked sleepily.

'What we've been doing tonight,' Charles said bluntly from inside the car. 'Come on, Jill. I need to go back to the hospital before I go to bed. I have two patients I want to see tonight and there's packing to do afterwards. We need to move.'

So move they did. They took Lily home and tucked her in as they'd done a score of times before this night and Jill thought, Where do we start?

Lily started for them. She snuggled into her little bed, checked that her toys—two teddies, one giraffe, a bull like her favourite real bull, Oscar, one duck and a doll with no hair—

were all lined up in their appropriate places. Then she said, 'It's a really pretty ring. Did Charles give it to you?'

'Yes,' Jill said, and felt helpless.

'Why?'

'We've decided to get married,' Charles said. 'You know your uncle came today? He says he wants you to live with a real mother and father. For some reason your Uncle Tom thinks that we can only be a real mother and father if we're married. Jill and I want to look after you until you're old enough to take care of yourself. So we've decided to get married so your Uncle Tom will let us keep you.'

She regarded them both, her eyes wide and interested.

'So you'll look after me all the time?'

'Yes,' Jill said firmly. 'If it's OK with you we'll sign papers that say no one can take you away from us.' She took a deep breath. 'And, Lily…if you wanted to call us…well, maybe you wouldn't want to call us Mum and Dad. Your mum and dad were your special, real parents. But if you feel you'll like to maybe call us something like Mama and Papa…'

'Your names are Jill and Charles,' Lily said flatly.

'That's right,' Charles said, and he flicked a strand of Lily's hair back behind her ear. 'We're Jill and Charles, or whatever you want to call us. And you're Lily. But we're family from now on. Right?'

'OK,' Lily said obligingly, and hugged her teddies and closed her eyes. 'Goodnight.'

And that was that. A mammoth, life-changing decision converted to a few simple sentences. They returned to Jill's living room and Jill felt deflated.

The door from her living room led through to Charles's living room. This was what they did every night. They said goodnight to Lily. Charles wheeled through to his apartment. He closed the door behind him.

Contact over.

'You know, we could knock this whole wall out,' Charles said thoughtfully, and she stared at him.

'What?'

'This used to be an old homestead before the hospital was built. It was too big for me so I cut it into two apartments. But this room… It was the original sitting room. It had huge French windows looking over the cove. I had to sacrifice the windows to convert it into two rooms. We've knocked a door through. Why not go the whole hog, knock the entire wall down and put the windows back in? You know we almost always have the televisions on the same channel. Or we could have stereo televisions. Or,' he said, warming to his theme with typical male enthusiasm, 'one really big television.'

'I might have known,' she said tightly. 'Boys with technology. Is this the entire motivation behind the proposal?'

'Hey, you get an opal,' he said, aggrieved. 'I reckon I ought to get a big screen. How big do you think, if we make it one room?' He hesitated. 'A family room,' he said cautiously. 'Where we can be a family.'

'But I need my privacy.'

His smile died. 'I'm not talking combining bedrooms, Jill.'

'No,' she said, and faltered.

'So marriage doesn't mean watching telly together. It doesn't mean family?'

How to explain that that was dangerous in itself? Closeness? Familiarity? She didn't do it.

As it was, it sometimes felt too close. Lily popped back and forth between the apartments. She slept in her bedroom on Jill's side, but if Jill was caught up at the hospital Charles would check on her. Jill would occasionally get home and discover Charles on her side of the beige door.

It shouldn't matter. But she'd spent so long building her defences that to breach them now…

Kelvin was there. He was still in her head. A shadow, waiting to crash down on her. She should see a therapist, she thought dully, but then a therapist would tell her she was imagining her terror, and she knew she wasn't.

She was risking enough with this marriage. If she could just keep it…nothing, maybe the sky wouldn't fall on her head.

'OK, we won't knock down the wall,' Charles said wearily. 'We go on as before.'

'Maybe I could buy you a bigger television,' she said, striving for lightness.

'I guess I can make that decision on my own,' he said flatly. 'I need to get over to the hospital.' He hesitated. 'Jill, I'm intending to be on the island for two weeks. I've agreed to take Lily and she's looking forward to it. But Cal's right. You could come over. Come to the opening ceremony at least.'

The opening… Half the press in the country would be converging on the island. Photographers. Media. No and no and no.

'I said I'd take over here.'

'We can cover you. Hell, Jill, you can organise the roster for you to be gone. You've done half the planning for the new rehabilitation centre anyway. You've cut all the red tape. You've negotiated with the Health Commission. It's your baby.'

Should she explain it was because she was still afraid of Kelvin? After eight years? He'd say it was crazy.

It was crazy.

'It's your dream, Charles,' she said at last.

'We're allowed to share dreams,' he snapped, and she blinked at the anger in his voice.

'I… Yes,' she whispered. 'But there's no need for me to be there.'

'You can stay in the damned resort if you want,' he snapped. 'It's on the far side of the island from my bungalow.'

'That's dumb.'

'It is dumb, isn't it?' he said. 'But it's what you seem to want. Jill, I'm not going to pressure you, but if you act like I'm an ogre…'

'You kissed me.'

'So what?' he said explosively. 'You're an attractive woman, you've just agreed to marry me and I kissed you. Obviously it was a mistake. I've agreed it won't happen again. But Lily needs a mother and a father. As far as I can see it, that's not going to happen if we live on separate planets.'

'Charles—'

'Just work it out,' he said wearily. 'Figure out the rules and let me know what they are. Meanwhile I have patients to check. Go to bed. I'll see you in the morning before I leave.'

He spun his chair and pushed it through the dividing door, back into his side of the house.

He closed the door behind him.

CHAPTER FOUR

WHY had he kissed her? Had he learned nothing? Charles wheeled himself through the silent corridors of the hospital and decided he was worse than a fool.

This was an eminently sensible solution as to what to do for Lily. To stuff it with emotion...

It was just that she was so damned kissable.

See, that was the problem. He hesitated at the nurses' station. He needed to get the patient notes for old Joe Bloomfield. He lifted them from the rack but then sat with them on his knee and stared down unseeingly at the closely written information.

Jill was gorgeous.

Under that prickly exterior he'd always suspected there was a woman of passion. He knew her past had never left her. He knew she was fearful to the point of paranoia.

That she'd agreed to marry him was extraordinary. She'd let him put his ring on her finger and the pleasure in her lovely grey-blue eyes had made him forget momentarily that she had years and years of carefully built defences in place.

And then he'd kissed her and for a moment she'd responded. For a moment he'd felt the woman he'd suspected she could be. Warm, vibrant, passionate. A woman to cherish.

Only then...remembrance had flooded back and the shutters had slammed down. How the hell he'd thought he could get through her reserves… He was a paraplegic, for God's sake.

He swore. There was a rail running the length of the corridor, used so patients returning to mobility could practise their walking with something to grab. He spun his chair up to the rail, flipped up his footrests, grabbed the rail and hauled himself up.

He stood, gripping the rail fiercely with both hands. Slowly, his left hand gripping so hard his knuckles showed white, he released his right hand and turned slightly so he was facing forward. Hell, his legs were useless.

But not completely. He had some feeling. He had some strength. He pushed his right leg forward, steadied, and then brought the left one through. His toes didn't pull up on command so it was more of a shuffle. He could do this on the walking frame or on elbow crutches but to do it one-handed…

He was going to do it.

He took another step and then another. Beads of sweat were standing out on his forehead. Dammit, he'd get to the storeroom.

Another step. Another. Another.

He reached the boundary of the door where the rail gave out. He swung in and allowed himself the luxury of gripping the rail with both hands.

Applause came from behind him. He turned and Susie, the hospital physio, was watching him.

'If all my spinal patients had your determination I'd be out of a job,' she said cheerfully. 'How long have you been doing that?'

'Do you mind?'

'Sneaking up on you? Not at all.' She beamed. 'It's your specialty, I know, so it's nice to catch you out at your own game. Do you want your chair?'

He'd intended to walk back, but that would involve turning his left hip outward. His left hip wasn't as obliging as his right.

'Yes, please,' he said, and she pushed his chair forward. He sank into it with relief.

'You've already done an hour and a half in the gym today,' Susie said mildly. 'Plus swimming. You don't think maybe you're pushing it?'

'No.'

'And you're thinking of getting married.'

'I'd imagine they know it in London by now,' he said sourly.

She chuckled and leaned back against the rail. 'Charles, do you ever see a specialist any more?'

'No,' he said, revolted.

'You treat yourself, huh?'

'There's nothing they can do for me.'

'Hey, there's stuff I've done for you,' she retorted. 'Isn't there? Go on, admit it. Since you started working on the exercises I've recommended you're a lot more mobile.'

'Blowing your own trumpet…'

'If I don't, no one else will,' she retorted, still smiling. Then her smile faded. 'You damned near snapped my head off when I suggested it, but the exercises I've given you have worked. And you'll probably snap my head off now, too.'

'Then don't suggest anything.'

'Well, I won't,' she said. 'It wouldn't be appropriate. I'm your employee, I'm several years younger than you are, and I'm a single woman. But I am a trained physio. You know, if you're about to be married—'

'Susie!'

'There's things that can help,' she said, speaking fast and backing away. By the look on Charles's face she *needed* to back away. 'I know there are. Exercises that can make things much more fun for you and Jill.'

'It's a marriage of convenience.'

'I know that,' she said scornfully. 'The whole town knows you're doing it for Lily. But we also know that you guys are lovely people. A real live marriage would be fantastic for both of you and if it's for want of a few exercises…'

'You want to be turned off without a reference? Shipped

off to Weipa on the next plane out of here, with instructions to send you down the deepest mine? Susie, butt out.'

'I'm butting,' she said, but she grinned as she turned and headed back the way she'd come. 'I've said what I want to say. I know names and I can give you contact details. In fact, you might find them on your desk even without me asking. You employed an interfering, bossy physiotherapist who always wants the best for her patients. That's what you got, Dr Wetherby, so live with it. See you on the boat tomorrow.'

She headed out the nearest exit as a jar loaded with pencils came flying down the corridor after her.

Packing for Lily took ten minutes. Jill managed to stretch it out to half an hour.

Her brain was on empty. It was like she'd been shocked into a stupor. How many pairs of knickers? She stared into the depths of Lily's bureau and her brain didn't come up with an answer that made sense.

She'd agreed to marry Charles.

He'd kissed her.

Her fingers kept drifting up to her lips as if they were bruised. They weren't. It hadn't been a punishing kiss. It had been a kiss of exploration. A kiss of questions.

And she'd answered those questions. She thought back to the look on Charles's face as she'd said it was ludicrous.

Of course it's ludicrous.

He'd thought she'd been backing off from him because his legs didn't work properly. As if that could possibly make him less than sexy.

And that was the whole problem. If he wasn't so sexy maybe she could give a bit. She thought about Charles's suggestion that they knock the wall out between them. They could sit here like some aging Darby and Joan, watching their telly into their twilight years.

Now, there was a ludicrous suggestion. Charles with a

crocheted rug over his knees, twiddling with the remote control? No and no and no.

Charles.

She lifted her hand so she could see her ring. Its flames flickered in the light cast by Lily's bedside lamp, seemingly almost a living stone.

He'd known she didn't want a diamond. He'd given her this.

Involuntarily she raised the ring to her lips. To be given something so beautiful… It was as if she had worth.

She did have worth, she told herself harshly. For heaven's sake, of all the miserable, self-indulgent thoughts… She was really competent at her job. She ran the nursing administration with a skill she was proud of.

She'd make a good mother to Lily. She knew she would. She had to stop Kelvin's ugly taunts messing with the rest of her life.

She crossed to the bed, stooped and lifted a strand of dusty curls from across Lily's eyes. From across her daughter's eyes.

'You have us both,' she whispered to the sleeping child. 'It'll be good.'

It'd be better if she let Charles knock down a wall.

She couldn't. She just couldn't.

She went back to staring at the knickers drawer but nothing was happening. Finally she shrugged and went out to the phone.

Mrs Grubb answered on the first call.

'Dora, can you do your knitting in front of my telly instead of yours for an hour?' she asked. Dora Grubb was the hospital cook and babysitter to any child she could get her hands on. She had five grown sons, not one of them had produced a grandchild and she was suffering. She was also a lady who lived on snatches of sleep, regarding eight hours in one hit as a waste. For two medics with a little girl who needed company at a moment's notice, Dora was a blessing.

'Sure,' Dora said expansively. 'I'll be there in two minutes. I wanted to get this sleeve finished tonight. And this is special after all.' Jill could practically hear her beam. 'Grub's telling me you and the doc—'

'We're engaged,' Jill confirmed hastily. 'For Lily's sake.'

'But you and Doc already went out tonight, yes?'

'I… Yes.'

'I guess you want to take a walk in the moonlight or something,' she said, sounding hopeful.

'Something,' Jill said. 'It's a full moon. The road will be clear. I'm going to run to the bridge and back.'

'Run…tonight… Are you out of your mind?'

'If I don't run I will be out of my mind,' Jill said firmly, and she put the phone down on Dora's romantic imaginings and went to put her trainers on. Running was what she did when her brain was threatening to explode. It was threatening to explode now.

Hopefully Charles would come back while she was out. He'd look through and find Dora. That'd be the end of any romantic imaginings as far as tonight was concerned.

Hopefully he wouldn't look through again. And tomorrow he was going to the island. Without her.

Maybe her brain wouldn't explode just yet.

The boat was due to leave at eleven. Jill was on duty from seven. She was up at dawn, finishing Lily's packing. Lily woke just as she finished and she sat down on the bed and hugged her, keeping her voice low. Charles would be up already, doing his admin stuff in his living room next door. Or packing himself.

Their normal routine was that he worked here until it was time for Lily to go to school. This morning Lily wasn't going to school—she was heading to the island with Charles. Jill could stay here until she left—the hospital was quiet enough for her to take a few hours off—but she wanted to be out of here.

'I'll come and wave to you at the boat,' she said. 'You get up now and have breakfast with Charles.'

'I thought you said he was my daddy now.'

'OK,' she said, regrouping. 'You go in and have breakfast with Daddy.'

'I'll go in and have breakfast with Charles,' she said contrarily, and submitted to Jill kissing her goodbye.

OK. Work.

Maybe she should say good morning to Charles, too. She didn't usually. But…she was wearing a ring.

She stuck her head round the dividing door. As she'd thought, Charles was up and working already. He was sitting by the small window where he could get a glimpse of the sea. It really would be sensible to haul this whole wall out. If they did that…

She looked at him before he raised his head. He was intent on what he was doing, his intelligent face focused. He worked so hard for this place.

He should have his view if he wanted it.

But…

'I didn't think you'd be working this morning,' he growled, and she jumped a foot.

'Hell, Charles…'

'What?'

'You scared me.'

'It's my principal skill,' he said, and smiled at her, but his smile didn't reach his eyes. 'You're not walking us down to the boat?'

'I thought I'd go through the checklist with Gina one more time,' she said. They had some really sick kids going to Wallaby Island this time. Usually they selected their kids with care so there would only be one or two high-risk participants, but the newly vamped kids' camp was set up with a state-of-the-art medical facility. The influx of doctors into the region over the last few years meant they could rotate enough doctors out of Crocodile Creek here to have a skilled team on the island at all times.

They had three precarious asthmatics going this time, a

couple of kids with advanced cancer, two brittle diabetics...
Each kid had to be given a good time, not cosseted but allowed
to enjoy the tropical experience to the full. But they also had
to be covered every medical eventuality.

Jill and Charles had gone over the equipment lists so many
times they must have covered all bases.

'It'll be fine,' Charles growled. 'You know that.'

'I just want to check.'

'You mean you're feeling weird being here. With me.'

'You kissed me,' she said, not accusing. Just a statement
of fact.

'I did, didn't I?' he said, and this time the smile did reach
his eyes. 'And very nice it was, too. OK, go check your drugs.
But be down at the chapel at nine-thirty.'

'The chapel?' she said, startled.

'I should have asked you that, too,' he said, but he didn't
sound apologetic. 'You were out running when I came back
last night and I had to get this set up. We need to be married
in a month. That means we have to give four weeks' legal
notice. The only person around here I know who does marriages is the local vicar. If we want a civil ceremony we need
to go to Cairns and we can't get to Cairns today to sign our
statements of intent.'

'You've found this out...when?'

'By talking to Bill McKenzie this morning,' he said. 'As it
happens, Hannah Blake died in the night. I went over to say
goodbye and Bill was already there.'

He would be, Jill thought. Bill McKenzie was Crocodile
Creek's only clergyman. Little and round and overwhelmingly
kind, pushing seventy, he beamed at the world over his too-
thick glasses. He welcomed all comers, regardless of religious affiliation, and if there'd been a death and a need Bill
would have sensed it before being asked.

'He said to come over before the boat leaves and he'll get
it sorted.'

'Bill's going to marry us?' she said cautiously.

'He'll do the paperwork. If you won't want a church wedding we can take our paperwork down to Cairns.' He hesitated. 'I don't mind. But then...' He smiled again. 'It's my first wedding. I wouldn't mind doing it here. Maybe I should even wear white.'

'Where I should wear purple as a tainted woman.'

'That's a bit melodramatic,' he said. 'But if you want purple...'

'Charles...'

'Whatever you want, Jill,' he said, becoming serious. 'But we do need to get these legalities sorted.'

They did. Fine. But...signing this morning...

'You can always pull out later,' Charles said. 'You're not marrying this morning. You're simply signing a document of intent. And I swear I won't sue if you don't go through with it.'

'Your white bridegroom gear might be really expensive,' she said, struggling for lightness. 'I hear veils for men cost a fortune.'

'You reckon I should hold in reserve my right to sue?'

'Let's both hold it in reserve,' she said. 'Meanwhile, I'm heading over to check medical lists.'

A document of intent. That was all it was, Charles thought. But sitting in the vestry of Crocodile Creek's little chapel, waiting for Jill, he suddenly felt as nervous as a bridegroom on his wedding day.

What if she pulled out?

She had every right to pull out. And why should he mind?

Because of Lily.

This was more than Lily.

He felt his fingers dig involuntarily into his palms. He wanted this.

Damn, his palms were sweating.

'She'll come,' Bill said, smiling sympathetically at him. 'This is Jill we're talking about.'

'She's terrified of marriage.'

'She is,' the elderly priest agreed. 'She's been on the outside looking in for a good while now. But, then, so have you.' He smiled. 'And here she is. Running. She's always running, your bride. Maybe the pair of you will slow down a bit now.'

'I hardly run,' Charles said, but the priest simply smiled again and crossed to open the door for Jill.

She was wearing her work gear. Plain black trousers and a sleeveless white shirt. Plain black sandals. She'd tugged her hair back, as she always did, into a tight bunch at the back.

But she was beautiful, Charles thought. She was mature and assured and lovely.

Sure, she'd had it tough. She had life lines round her eyes. She was smiling, grasping Bill's hand, warm and friendly. Charles had seen her with patients in distress. Sure, she was matter-of-fact and practical, but patients responded to her. What you saw was what you got. A woman of integrity and courage and...

Beauty.

She deserved someone better than him.

She glanced across at him and her smile died. They stared at each other for a long moment while Bill looked on with bemusement.

In the end it was Bill who broke the silence.

'Well, my children,' he said gently, 'they tell me there's a boat about to leave. And they also tell me you want to get married.'

In the end it was relatively painless. Forms, forms and more forms. Legal stuff.

The emotional stuff could be put aside.

'You know, at this stage I normally give my couples a spiel about what marriage is all about,' Bill said as he collected the forms together.

'We know it,' Jill said.

'Do you?' Bill asked.

'As much as we need,' Jill said grimly. 'It's a marriage of convenience.'

'Is it a marriage before God?' Bill asked. 'You know, if you're intending to dissolve the marriage the moment Lily's of age then I can't marry you. Yes, I'll send the forms in and I'll organise for you to have a civil ceremony elsewhere. But if you're to have me marry you, then you're marrying for ever.'

'I...' Jill faltered and looked at Charles.

'I'd like to be married by Bill,' Charles said, and he met her confused gaze steadily. 'And I've no intention of marrying anyone else. As far as I'm concerned, it's for ever.'

'You won't want me hanging round you for ever.'

'I'm pretty used to you now,' Charles said softly. 'I'd miss you singing in the shower every morning.'

'I don't...' She paused. Oh, wait. Maybe she did.

'It's great,' Charles said, and he smiled.

She wished he wouldn't. He took her breath away. That she was agreeing to marry a man who smiled at her like that...

'Is it for ever, Jill?' Bill was asking gently, and she gave herself a mental shake. So what if it wasn't? She'd made these vows before. Sure, she'd had her father standing behind her with a metaphorical shotgun, but she'd made the vows and she'd broken them. What was different now?

Was she going into this intending to divorce?

Not yet.

'There's no one else I want to marry,' Jill said, almost in a whisper, and Bill looked at her sharply.

'Things change. People change. If you meet the man of your dreams...'

'I don't have dreams,' she said flatly.

'Neither do I,' Charles said dryly. 'So there you have it, Bill. Two pragmatic people without dreams, marrying to keep Lily safe. It seems we're both happy to have it in church—if you'll have us.'

'So you'll be promising to love, honour and obey?'

'Honour,' they said in unison, and Bill grinned.

'Well.' He considered them both, with affection and years of wisdom. 'I guess there's worse start-off points than that. You'll need to work out your own vows.'

'Can we do that?' Jill said cautiously.

'Sure,' he said, ready to be expansive. 'The way I'm looking at this—love comes in all shapes and sizes. I'm thinking love might be edging into the equation here, like it or not.'

'Not,' Jill snapped.

'We'll see,' Bill said, still smiling. 'Now, let's get these forms signed so you can catch the boat. Jill, I gather you're not going across to the island?'

'I need to work here.'

'You're promising to be a family,' he said, sounding disapproving for the first time.

'After the wedding.'

'So be it.' He sighed, and then smiled again. 'Lots of marriages have started with less and gone a lot further. Let's get you started and see where you end up.'

CHAPTER FIVE

MAYBE she should have gone. Jill stood on the jetty and she could still feel the warmth of Lily's small hand in hers. She could still see Charles's smile. If he hadn't been on elbow crutches as he boarded the boat he might have even kissed her goodbye, she thought, but she'd been able to back away.

She wanted no more kissing.

'You take care of yourself,' he'd said as he'd left her. 'You're my affianced wife. You're not to work too hard, you're to delegate anything you don't want to do, and if I come back and find you're tired I'll sack the entire Croc Creek medical team.'

He'd said it loud enough for everyone on the jetty to hear. There'd been grins and laughter from everyone and Jill's colour was still fading. For Charles to make such a public statement of affection...

It warmed her inside, but it also made her feel disoriented. People were watching her as if she was different. She wasn't different.

She couldn't be different.

'You take care of yourself—and of Lily,' she'd managed, and Charles had smiled at her with a tenderness that had been a caress all on its own.

And then they'd gone.

She watched them until they'd rounded the headland out of the cove. Two distant figures in the stern of the boat.

Charles seated, Lily standing beside him. They waved to her just before they disappeared from view.

Her husband and her daughter.

She let the words seep into her head, waiting for the familiar sense of panic to reassert itself. Strangely, it didn't.

It was because they weren't here, she thought. They were away for maybe two weeks.

She should join them.

That did make her panic. Marriage...families...were all very well in the abstract. But reality...

Charles was so different to Kelvin.

That made her flinch. The thought of Kelvin.

Where was he? If he knew what she was doing now, what she intended...

Kelvin was no more to her now than a distant nightmare, she told herself. A bad dream. He was so far out of her world that he should no longer exist.

But he'd always said...

No. She didn't have to listen to the echoes of her past. This was the future.

A future she was scared to embrace.

There was a roar of an engine behind her. A motorbike came down the jetty's service road, leaning over so far Jill flinched again. Georgie. The town's obstetrician. Biker extraordinaire.

'Have I missed them?' she yelled, dumping her bike and striding along the jetty to meet Jill. 'Damn. I wanted to say goodbye but the Langley's baby wouldn't co-operate. Charles must be feeling so proud.'

'He is,' Jill said.

'And not just because of the island,' Georgie said, and grinned and tucked her arm into that of her friend's. 'Another wedding! Hooray.'

'Yeah.'

'Hey, you don't sound like a blushing bride.'

'I'm a bit old to be blushing,' Jill said bluntly, and Georgie hesitated. Like Jill, Georgie had had it tough in her early years. Now blessedly in love with her ultra-conservative Alistair, the look she gave Jill said she understood a bit of what she was going through.

'Charles is a lovely man,' she said gently.

'He wouldn't thank you for saying it.'

'Yeah, he likes us to think he's omnipotent and crabby,' Georgie agreed, and chuckled. 'But you know he's a pussy cat.'

'Right,' Jill said faintly.

'You *do* want a pussy cat?' Georgie said cautiously. 'Women like us…it's so easy to think we can never be happy unless we're with someone who knocks us round.'

'I don't—'

'No, but my Alistair's a case in point,' Georgie said, pushing on. 'If he hadn't turned into hero material the day of the cyclone, I might never have seen what he was.'

'I don't need Charles to be macho.' Jill sniffed. 'I mean… maybe he already is.'

Georgie paused. She released her friend, turned and faced her square on.

'Hey! You think he's a hunk?' she said on a note of discovery. 'Don't you?'

'I… Of course. I mean, don't we all?'

'Maybe not in the way I'm seeing in your eyes,' she said thoughtfully. 'Wow.'

'I don't want to think of him like that.'

'Why?'

'It scares me to death,' Jill said flatly. 'As if I can ever get away from my past.'

'You're still frightened of your ex?'

'He always said…' She shook her head. 'No. It's crazy. After so many years…'

'Follow your instincts,' Georgie said urgently. 'Talk to someone if you're frightened. Talk to the police.'

'There's no need.' She shook herself. 'No. This is stupid.

No policeman would ever agree I have reason to be afraid. It's paranoia and it's dumb. I'm a really practical person and we're going into this marriage for purely practical reasons. Stop distracting me. I need to get on.'

'Fine,' Georgie said, and linked arms again. 'Let's get on. But this is very exciting. Something tells me Sister Jill Shaw's armour plating might not be as impermeable as once supposed. And now he's left. Absence makes the heart grow fonder, they say.' And then as Jill shoved her friend sideways on the jetty, pushing her inexorably towards the water, she broke free, laughing.

'Enough. There's crocodiles in this creek and I have babies to deliver. And you have a wedding to arrange. Can I be bridesmaid?'

'No.'

'I'll ask Charles,' Georgie said, refusing to be squashed. 'This is a wedding, after all. You guys need to get a consensus. I think I want to wear red.'

Wallaby Island was fantastic.

The work that had gone into this place since the cyclone was truly astounding. Charles had been back on the mainland for the last two weeks. He'd hoped the final stages could be done without him.

They had.

The contractors had done him proud, as had his medical staff. Beth, his newly employed doctor in charge, showed him through the facilities as soon as he arrived. Charles was mostly silent as he wheeled his way through the ten-bed hospital, the individual bunkhouses, the family units, bungalows with every facility for looking after an ill child.

Everything was ready. His team was in place, even down to the wildlife guides and recreational officers who had been recruited specifically to give ill children a wonderful time. They all had first-aid qualifications and they'd spent the last few weeks increasing that training. If a child started feeling wheezy on a nocturnal wildlife hunt, it would never go unnoticed with these leaders.

'It's fabulous,' he told Beth.

'It is, isn't it?' she said. Then, as a crazy, woolly mutt of a dog came bounding out from the bushland behind them, she chuckled. 'And here's Garf, to greet you.'

'Garf,' Lily yelled, delighted. Garf was the camp dog, a great golden labradoodle with a grin the size of a house. He'd been purchased because of his friendly nature and his hypo-allegenic fur. He went happily from kid to kid, seeming almost to sense which kids needed him.

But Lily loved him best of all. Maybe they could get Lily her own dog, Charles thought as he watched Lily hug and Garf lick. If the wall came out…

Dumb thought.

'I need to be getting back,' Beth said, glancing at her watch. 'One of the rangers rang in to say he's coming down with flu. I agreed to meet him at three.'

'Can I help?'

'No,' she said, and smiled. 'The one thing I don't need at the moment is medical help. Every medic who's ever worked at Croc Creek seems to have taken the grand opening as an excuse to visit. There's a huge medical conference over at the eco-resort as well, and they're all aching to check out the new facilities. I have doctors coming out of my ears. If I'm not careful I'll find myself sacked because I'm redundant. I'm only going back now to assert my rights to treat the odd patient myself.'

So he wasn't needed.

He was needed. It was just…his role here was administrative. That was what he did.

But he watched Beth until she disappeared from view and thought that's where he wanted to be. In the middle of the action.

'When are the kids coming?' Lily asked, and he forced his attention back to his daughter.

'Tomorrow.'

'That's good 'cos I need someone to play with.'

Ditto, he thought, and then gave himself a metaphorical sideswipe to the head. One kiss and he'd been thrown right out of kilter.

Jill wasn't coming over.

He had a ceremony to organise.

He might resent his administrative role, but it produced results. As soon as the kids arrived—disabled and chronically ill kids from all over Australia—his team swung into action like a well-oiled machine, a machine with heart. The island came alive with the sound of kids having fun.

For the privileged few staying at the five-star eco-resort at the far end of the island, this must seem a normal camp for normal kids. It was only when you got closer and saw the prostheses, the wheelchairs, the oxygen cylinders, you might suspect things were not quite right.

This was the culmination of Charles's dream. It should feel fantastic. It did feel fantastic, Charles thought as the camp settled into its intended rhythm. So why did it feel empty?

Lily had been on Wallaby Island a dozen times already. She blended in with the camp kids like she belonged. Too easily, Charles thought as the days wore on. She should have roots.

She should have Jill.

Hell, Jill should be here.

On the third night the camp recreational officers set up a campfire and barbecue on the beach. It sometimes seemed more trouble than it was worth, getting onto the sand—dry sand was incredibly difficult to negotiate, even on elbow crutches—but there was no way he'd stay isolated while the rest of the camp had fun. Besides, it was something of a tradition and several of his staff had come over to attend from the mainland.

Jill was the isolated one, he thought as he watched the kids toast more marshmallows than they could possibly eat. Claire

Harvey was eating her third. That mightn't seem a great deal, but nine-year-old Claire had become anorexic after the death of her mother. By the look on her father's face, the third marshmallow was a very big deal indeed.

They were getting through to Claire. Could he get through to Jill?

He was seated a way back from the fire—far enough to make a phone call without being disturbed. On impulse he made the call. Jill answered on the third ring.

'Charles.' Her voice lifted in apprehension. 'Is something wrong?'

'What should be wrong?' he asked. Normally when he phoned she slipped straight into business mode. Why the change?

The kiss?

'I… Sorry,' she said, sounding flustered, and he knew that indeed it was the kiss. 'What can I do for you?'

'We're missing you,' he said. 'Lily and me.'

There was a sharp intake of breath. Whatever she'd expected, it hadn't been that.

'Don't,' she said sharply.

'Don't miss you?'

'Say things you don't mean. Lily doesn't miss anyone.'

He winced. Maybe it was the truth, though. Lily was having fun down by the shallows, romping with Garf, surrounded by kids and carers. But as he watched…

'I think she does need us, Jill,' he said softly. 'I think she surrounds herself with people and activity as a form of defence. Like you surround yourself with work.'

'I'm not marrying a psychologist,' she snapped, and he chuckled.

'I wouldn't be a very good one. Jill, come over.'

'I… I can't.'

'You can,' he said inexorably. 'I'm your boss. I know every detail of every staff roster and I say you can.'

'I don't want to.'

'Now, that's a different matter,' he said gravely. 'Do you want to tell me why not?'

There was a drawn-out silence. He let it lie. In the course of years of being medical director he'd learned the importance of not rushing to fill the silence. And Jill, of all people, mustn't be pushed.

'Charles, I need a bit of time to get my head around what's happened,' she confessed at last. 'When Wendy suggested this…'

'I believe it was me who suggested marriage.' That seemed suddenly important. He wanted no marriage at the instigation of a social worker.

'Well, it seemed a good idea. It seemed logical.'

'It is logical,' he agreed. 'I do think we needed to make a decision. We've kept everything in limbo for too long, and that's not good for anyone, let alone a child.'

'You know I agree,' she said, sounding suddenly desperate. 'And it still does seem logical. But then…the ring…and you kissed me…and then you suggested we knock down the wall…'

'We can take the ring back,' he said gravely. 'We can keep the wall. There's not a lot we can do about the kiss.'

'I'm being dumb,' she said miserably.

'Jill, I'm not coercing you into this against your will.'

'Of course you're not,' she said hotly. 'You're a good man.'

He didn't feel like a good man. He felt like throwing the damned phone into the sea.

Hell, what was happening here? Talk of a wedding and suddenly he was seen as noble.

What was he doing, marrying like this? He didn't want to. When the hell had what he wanted ever come into it?

'Charles, I need to go,' Jill said, sounding distracted. 'Jack Blake's come in bleeding all over my nice clean tiles. I need to find someone to put a couple of stitches in.'

'Do you want to end this?' he asked. He knew Jack. Jack

required stitches approximately once a month. He really did have to learn how to whittle something other than his fingers.

Jack's stitches could wait for a bit. This was important.

'N-no.'

'You're still wearing the ring?'

'Yes.' Her voice firmed. 'It really is beautiful. Thank you, Charles.'

'I don't want your gratitude,' he said savagely. 'I need your commitment. Think about it and let me know.'

He left Jill to Jack's stitches, and he was left to his thoughts. They weren't great. All around him were kids and parents and carers. They were having a good time or giving a good time. They had roles here.

He hated the reality that he couldn't join in. He had the reputation for being aloof, and of knowing things almost before they happened. That wasn't hard. He was always on the fringes, looking on. He could see tension between people. He could see people simply living.

He let his mind drift back to when he'd been a young man, to when he'd still had legs that had held him up. He'd always been in the thick of things. He'd loved life. Hell, he still did. That was part of the reason he'd worked so hard to build this place. To show kids with disabilities that they could join in.

A great example he was being, he thought morosely, giving himself a mental shake and looking around for Lily. It was time they headed back to the cabin.

She wasn't with the other kids, playing down by the water's edge.

Great. Here he was, being a parent, caught up with intro-spection and not watching his daughter.

He grabbed his elbow crutches and pushed himself to his feet so he could see further. She was nowhere in sight.

'Luke,' he called to the closest doctor he knew. 'Where's Lily? She was here just a minute ago. Dammit, I hate it when she runs off in the dark.' She did it too often, he thought. She'd be with the other kids and then simply disappear. Like she didn't need people.

But she hadn't gone far. Luke walked into the shadows, calling, and she re-emerged almost at once. She came toward him, carrying something with care.

She seldom went far, Charles thought. It was simply that she was independent. Too independent, he thought grimly. Maybe that went for the three of them. Jill and Lily and…and maybe him, too. Could three isolated units become a family?

'I need to show Charles,' she was telling Luke. 'He'll help.'

'I don't think…' Luke said doubtfully, but she shrugged him off and came running over the sand toward him. He sank back into his chair and turned his attention to what she was carrying.

A dead bird.

'Look. It's sick.'

'It's dead,' he told her.

'Can you make it alive?'

'Lily, no.' It lay limp in her hands. When he put a tentative hand on the bird's soft neck he felt the last faint traces of warmth. 'It's still warm. That means it's only just died, but it is dead. Put it down on the sand, Lily.'

'But can't you make it come back alive?'

'Lily, I'm a people doctor, not a bird doctor, and anyway it's dead. I can't bring it back.'

'But I saw it move.'

'You probably did,' he agreed. 'It must have been its last flutter. It hasn't been dead for long. But it is dead now, I promise, and there's nothing we can do. Luke?' Again he had to turn to his fellow doctor, and again he didn't like it.

'Bury it?' Luke suggested. 'I think we'd better. We don't want the kids playing round with it.'

It was a wedgetailed shearwater. Charles lifted it from Lily's hands and gave it to Luke with a feeling of regret. The shearwaters were beautiful birds, migrating all the way from Siberia during the Australian winter and coming back every year to breed on the island. He handed it over to Luke with a feeling of vague disquiet.

'Go and wash your hands in the sea,' he told Lily, 'and then we'll do them properly with soap when we get back to the cabin.'

It was time to go. He and Lily had this down to a fine art. He got back on his elbow crutches. Lily turned his wheelchair back to front and towed it across the sand to firmer ground. He followed as fast as he could, but Lily was patient. She didn't mind waiting.

Strangely he didn't mind Lily helping him. A six-year-old...his daughter.

She was subdued, and she stayed subdued when they reached their cabin. Still uneasy about the bird, he insisted she have a bath. She allowed him to tuck her into bed but she was obviously still concerned about her bird.

'Why couldn't you make it alive again?' she asked. 'You're a doctor.'

'There are some things doctors can't make better.'

'Like your legs?'

'That's right.'

She thought about it. 'So when you and Jill get sick and die...I'll have to live with someone else?'

That was one to give him pause.

'Lily, you were very, very unlucky that your mum and dad were killed.' He didn't know where to go with this. He wanted, desperately, for Jill to be there. 'I think you can be pretty sure we'll be around until you're grown up.'

She wasn't convinced. 'Can I live with Gina and Cal if you die?'

Maybe now wasn't the time for probabilities. 'We won't die.'

'You're in a wheelchair. You're already sick.'

'I've explained that to you. I even showed you the model of the spine I have in my office. I have a small damaged part of my spine that controls my legs. The rest of me's fine.'

'Yes, but you'll get worse,' she said, definite. 'I think Gina and Cal will look after me.'

'Gina and Cal would look after you if we did die,' he said, stumped for anything else to say. 'Anyone in Croc Creek would. But they won't need to.'

She wasn't hearing reassurance. She was focused on security. 'They're all my friends,' she said doubtfully. 'But Uncle Tom didn't want me. Maybe they won't want me either.'

'Jill and I want you. We love you, Lily.'

'Yes,' she whispered, as if it made no difference at all. 'I'm going to sleep now.'

She wiggled over in bed and turned her face to the wall. He had been dismissed.

He went and sat on the veranda and stared out to sea. He hadn't got that right.

What were he and Jill doing? he thought bleakly. How could they make a family from three such troubled pasts?

Jill rang just before midnight. He was still sitting on the veranda. Filling time. If Lily wasn't there, he'd be at the hospital, getting things done. It drove him nuts to be still.

If Jill were there, he could be gone.

'Don't tell me,' she said as he answered his phone on the first ring. 'You're sitting on the veranda, bored out of your brain, I knew it. I thought I'd check but I knew it.'

'I'm about to go to bed.' But he was absurdly—disproportionately—pleased she'd rung before he had.

'You live on four hours' sleep a night and now you're stuck caring for Lily. You'll be going stir crazy.'

'I'm fine,' he said. No one else gave him a hard time like Jill did. No one knew him as Jill did.

'A bit of enforced idleness will do you good,' she said. 'You've been pushing yourself.'

'Is that another reason for you not coming over?'

'I don't need another reason. I'm busy.'

'You're still on duty?'

'I told you—yes.'

'And no one else can work instead. Jill, I need you here.'

There was a moment's silence. 'Why?' she said at last.

'Hell, Jill, we're getting married.'

'That's no reason for you to need me. What else has happened?'

'Lily found a dead bird.'

She didn't respond. She was like him, he thought ruefully. He'd learned not to fill silences—to wait for others to jump in. Jill was turning his trick neatly on him.

'It led to a discussion of who'll look after her when we die,' he explained at last, giving in to the inevitable. 'She's pretty sure we'll end up dying. Tomorrow, if not sooner.'

'Do you think that's why she's so eager to be friends with everyone?'

'I don't know.' He raked his hair with his fingers, exasperated. 'I'm in uncharted territory here, Jill.'

'Which is why you want me to come over?'

'Yes,' he admitted bluntly.

'And to get you off the veranda and back into the hospital.'

Was he so transparent?

'I'm taking thinking time,' she said into the silence.

'You feel you've been rushed?'

'Maybe.'

Anger washed across him like a vicious slap. Anger and frustration. 'Look, if you really don't want this then put the blasted ring in the rubbish and get on with your life,' he snapped, and this time the silence was loaded.

'Charles, can you please try and understand?'

'I'm trying. But I'm being played the villain here. Coercing you into marriage against your will. Adopting Lily when I've already got one foot—or one wheel—in the grave.'

'Are you sure that's what she thinks?'

'I don't know what she thinks. I don't know what you think.'

'I'll try and come over for the opening.'

'That's big of you.'

'It is,' she said abruptly. She paused, obviously fighting for control. 'Look, I know, I'm being unfair, but there's baggage I need to sort out. I hoped you'd be understanding.'

'I'm trying,' he snapped back. He took a deep breath. 'I'm sorry. I know you do have issues but I have the odd one or two myself. This seemed pretty clear cut when we first discussed it. If it's not then we need to pull back. Lily's been messed around enough. Neither of us want pressure, but both of us want what's best for Lily. Maybe...' He hesitated.

'Maybe what?'

'Maybe given both our backgrounds we're not what Lily needs. Maybe we should face it.' He stared out to sea and what he was saying seemed to be forced out of him, a leaden fog of reality. 'Maybe Lily needs parents who know what loving's all about. Maybe she needs parents who can reach her.'

'You're saying it's unfair of us to adopt her?'

'I don't know,' he said heavily. 'It seems, however, that we both have time to think about it.'

He clicked his phone closed.

'Thinking sucks,' he added to the silence. 'Who wants to think?'

But in the end the thinking stopped. In the end, Jill came. Not because Charles wanted her to, but because Lily was ill.

The Friday before the opening Lily woke up lethargic and not wanting breakfast. Actually, Lily seldom wanted breakfast but that was because she was aching to get outside and see what the day had to offer.

On Friday morning she fiddled with her cornflakes, wandered over to the settee and curled up, uninterested in anything.

Alarmed, Charles checked her out. She seemed OK. Maybe she was coming down with a cold.

She stayed listless. He spent most of the day with her,

aching to be at the hospital, aching to be working instead of reading Lily stories or simply watching her watch television.

'You can go and look after the sick kids,' she said mid-afternoon, and he thought he'd been summarily dismissed.

'I like being here.'

'No, you don't,' she said wisely. 'You keep looking out the window.'

'But it's my job,' he said. 'To stay here and look after you. That's what dads do.'

'You're not my dad.'

'I'd like to be.'

'Mmm,' she said, noncommittal. She watched a bit more television, then drifted off to sleep.

Charles called in one of the hike leaders to sit with her while she slept. There was a mass of stuff happening down at the hospital in preparation for tomorrow's opening. He should have been down there all day.

What sort of medical director was he?

A medical director with a kid of his own.

There was a drama with a teenager with a split chin. He reacted with gratitude—any medical need helped keep him from thinking about the personal issues battering him from all angles. Sadly—or fortunately, depending on whose angle you looked at it from—the parents refused to allow him to take care of it. They were hyper-caring parents, they wanted a plastic surgeon on the job, and amazingly there was a plastic surgeon available among the parents and dignitaries.

When Charles returned to the cottage Lily was awake.

She was feverish and beginning to be obviously unwell.

It wasn't just a cold.

He examined her with care. She was running a temperature of thirty-nine, she had swollen lymph nodes, she was dry and fretful.

She curled into herself as she always did when she was hurt. She wanted no comfort.

'Lily, you need to drink,' he told her, but she'd have none of it. Neither would she tolerate him giving her a sponge bath. 'I think you should get someone to fly Jill over here.'

Beth, the permanent doctor in charge of the Wallaby Island clinic, had come across to check on Lily when Charles had been caught up in the chin drama. As Lily whimpered into her pillow, a picture of abject misery, Beth placed her hand on the little girl's forehead and frowned across at Charles, sending him a silent message of concern. 'You'll be OK, sweetheart,' she said. 'It'll be just a nasty virus that's made you feel bad. But what if we ask Jill to come?'

'Jill won't come when Charles is here,' Lily whispered.

Was the conflict between them so obvious? Or… Charles thought back to the months Lily had been living with them. This was the pattern, he thought. One of them did the caring while the other worked.

Other families spent their spare time together, he thought with a flash of useless insight. Not them.

'The boat won't get over here until late tomorrow,' he told Beth, feeling useless.

She fixed him with a look. Hell, what was it with the women here? The minute he'd put the ring on Jill's finger he'd lost his authority.

'You know, you *are* the medical director and founder of this entire set-up,' she said now. 'You call the shots. There's a helicopter parked here right now. Mike Poulos is here for the opening and he's more than ready to fly back to Croc Creek. The only reason the chopper's here is that Mike's using this as a base for his runs because he wants to attend the opening. You know that. Jill could be here in little more than an hour.'

'It's just a virus.'

'You're her dad, Charles,' Beth said gently. 'You're the only dad she's got. What do they say about doctors' kids getting worse treatment than any other segment of the population? Do you think Lily might feel better if Jill was here?'

Maybe not, Charles thought. He could set up a drip if needed. He could do anything Lily required.

But...

But he'd feel better if Jill was there. He'd feel better if they made the attempt to make this family unit work. Even if Lily didn't need it.

Maybe she did need it, though, he thought, watching Lily as Beth smoothed a curl back behind her ear. She reacted to everyone but clung to no one. Maybe it was time to teach her to cling.

Maybe that clinging had to start now.

'OK, we need Jill,' he said in a tone that startled both Beth and Lily. He knew it and he grimaced. It was his medical director tone—the voice he used when he wanted things done. But now the decision had been made, he needed to get on with it. 'Lily, possum, drink your lemonade while I phone your... While I phone Jill.'

'You called me possum,' Lily said, puzzled.

'Do you mind?'

'You always call me Lily.'

'I guess. Sorry.'

'I like Possum,' she said, and then she sighed. 'My neck hurts.'

Her neck. He gave Beth a startled glance and wheeled across to the bed. 'Is it stiff?' he asked. He ran his fingers gently down the sides of her neck and watched as she winced. But surely it wasn't the stiffness that might be a sign of meningitis. Surely it was only her glands, swollen even more than when he'd last felt them.

'We'll give you some medicine to make it stop hurting,' he told her. 'And then you can go to sleep. If we're lucky, by the time you wake up Jill will be here.'

'Where will she sleep?' Lily asked, but Beth was lifting her so she could drink her lemonade. Lily spilt a little and it distracted her enough for Charles not to have to answer the question.

But it was a good question, he thought as Beth bade them goodnight and headed back to the hospital. The island accommodation was booked to capacity.

This was a one-bedroom cabin. Lily was sleeping on the settee in the living room. The settee was tiny. There was a bedroom at the clinic used by visiting specialists. Charles usually used that when Jill came across, or when their cabin was needed, but it was being used tonight by visiting dignitaries.

Maybe he shouldn't ask her to come.

But he was asking her. If they were to be a family…family started now.

He tucked the sheet around Lily, frowning as he felt the heat of her skin. She was only in her knickers and he'd covered her in a sheet and nothing else, but still she was hot.

He wanted Jill.

CHAPTER SIX

SHE arrived three hours later. He heard the chopper come into land. Not wanting to leave Lily, he simply wheeled out to the veranda to wait.

Ten minutes later she came hurrying up the bushland path, carrying her overnight bag. A tiny wallaby grazing in front of the cabin stopped its feeding and moved a generous two feet to the left to let her pass. Wallaby Island was aptly named. The wallabies thought they had right of way.

But Jill wasn't focused on wallabies. She climbed the steps two at a time, her face tight with anxiety.

'How is she?'

'We're looking at a cold,' he said, frowning. He hadn't meant to scare her. He thought he'd outlined exactly what was wrong.

'No,' she said tightly, reaching the top step and looking down at him. 'You said it was just a cold, but you wanted me to come.'

'Lily wanted you to come,' he said, and then could have bitten his tongue as he heard the echoes of his words and saw them resonate. Jill's face tightened. 'I didn't mean that,' he said swiftly. 'It was just… Yeah, she's ill and miserable. She's running a fever, her glands are swollen. She's a sick little girl. But she's still drinking and the blood test Beth ran shows her electrolytes are fine.'

'So why—?'

'I asked her if she wanted you. She said you wouldn't be

here if I was here,' he told her. 'I thought…' He paused, unsure where to go from here. But suddenly, dammit, he was going on. 'We need to be a family, Jill,' he said gently. 'I know you're unsure but that decision has to be made and I guess I'm asking you to make it now. Though maybe you have already made it. When I phoned and said Lily was ill, you weren't asking how ill, you were already thinking about how to get here. You're her mother in every way but legally.'

'I am,' she said uncertainly. She flipped her hair back behind her ears in a gesture he recognised as pure nerves. 'I need… I need to see her.'

'Of course you do,' he said, and smiled, trying to lighten things. He wheeled across to the screen door and hauled it open. 'She's asleep but I think we should wake her. Families start now.'

'Let's not make this heavy,' Jill retorted.

'Let's not.'

Lily woke when Jill touched her. That in itself was unusual. Lily usually slept the sleep of the angels. She had two gears, Charles thought, full throttle or at a dead stop, but now she was in between, exhausted enough to sleep but too feverish to sleep deeply. She opened her eyes as Jill stroked her hair, and her eyes widened with astonishment.

'Jill.'

'Hi, sweetheart,' Jill said softly. 'I'm sorry you're feeling bad.'

'You came.'

'I came. I hated thinking you were sick without me.'

'Charles said I have a virus. He said I have to keep drinking lemonade.' Her voice was a thready whisper, and Jill lifted her wrist and held it.

She glanced across at Charles and Charles wondered if she was getting worse.

'Lemonade's good,' Jill said.

'Mrs Grubb made it.'

'It's lucky the Grubbs are here,' Jill said, stroking her hair.

'Everyone's here for the opening,' Lily whispered. 'Do you think it was the bird that made me sick?'

'I don't think so,' Jill said, startled.

'Charles said I had to wash my hands 'cos we didn't know why the bird died. But it did die.' Her eyes widened again, flaring in panic. 'I might die.'

'Well, you won't,' Jill said solidly. 'The sad thing for the bird was that it didn't have a bird doctor to care for it. You have a people doctor right here—you know Charles is a lovely doctor and he makes people better all the time.'

'And you're the boss nurse,' Lily said, her panic fading.

'I am,' Jill said. 'And what I say is what happens. So I'm saying I need to give you a sponge bath. We'll see if we can stop you shivering. And then we'll give you some more medicine and you can go to sleep while we wait for you to get better.'

'You'll both look after me?'

'Yes.'

'You'll both stay here?'

The implications hit her. Charles saw the moment Jill realised what had been gnawing at him since he'd decided to ask her to come. She glanced through to the bedroom. Charles's gear was on the left-hand side of the big bed. There was nothing on the right.

'We're both staying here,' Charles said strongly, before she could answer. Dammit, he'd sleep in his wheelchair on the veranda if he had to. But they were both here for Lily and nowhere else.

Lily submitted to Jill's sponge bath. She even seemed to enjoy it. The paracetamol took hold and before Jill had finished her eyes were drooping closed.

Charles had been sitting in the background, watching. As Lily slept he wheeled across to the kitchenette, made a couple of mugs of tea and carried them out to the veranda.

Jill settled Lily to her satisfaction and came out to join him. There were two cane chairs out on the veranda, one at each end. Charles had pushed his wheelchair to rest by one, the mugs of tea on the table in front of him. Jill cast a fleeting glance at the other chair and Charles thought if she had a choice, that's where she'd sit.

She was like a frightened kid.

'I'm not going to jump you, Jill,' he said softly, and she flushed and came and sat in the chair beside him.

'I know. I'm being dumb. I'm sorry.'

She was still wearing the ring. That was a good sign. A very good sign.

'It…it seems more than a cold,' she ventured.

'I know. I'm starting to worry.'

'You don't think we should put her in hospital tonight?'

'She's still drinking. As long as we keep her cool and hydrated, there's not a lot of point.'

'You're sure it's viral?'

'There's nothing to explain a bacterial infection. I've given her a thorough check.'

'It's come on fast.' She hesitated. 'You're sure it couldn't be connected with the dead bird?'

'I doubt it,' Charles said, thinking it through as he spoke. In truth he was starting to get edgy. Lily had brought one dead bird to camp. So far today Charles had seen more than a dozen dead birds on the beach and a couple on the paths leading up to the bungalows.

It'd simply be nature taking its course, he told himself. The shearwaters' normal migration patterns might have been interrupted by something similar to the cyclone. Their nesting burrows might have been destroyed, and for ill and struggling birds, coming back to a burrow that had to be rebuilt might well mean physical exertion they were simply not capable of.

'You're worried about the bird,' Jill said.

'I'm worried about Lily.'

'No one else is ill?'

'We've got a couple of kids down with colds. And one of the rangers.'

'Just colds?'

'It was just a dead bird, Jill.'

'Yes, but this isn't just a cold.'

'Let's see how she is in the morning,' he said uneasily. 'If she's still unwell, I'll run some more blood tests.'

'You have the opening tomorrow night.'

'Yes.' He grimaced. It promised to be a glittering black-tie occasion at the resort hotel. It wasn't something he'd planned but there were so many firms eager to be corporate sponsors for such a worthy cause that it had been impossible to keep this low key.

'So did you bring your tux?' she said, teasing.

'My dinner suit,' he growled. 'Bloody thing.'

'You look great in it.'

'Right,' he said dryly. 'Seeing the only time I'm in it is for weddings… You want me to wear a dinner suit to ours?'

'No!'

'That's unequivocal.'

'It is,' she said, biting her lip.

'So what do you want me to wear?'

'Charles…'

'You want to call the whole thing off?'

'I… No.'

'What do you want to do?'

'Just leave everything as it is.'

'It's not going to happen, Jill. We'll lose Lily.'

'Maybe Tom will change his mind.'

'Will you go down to Brisbane to ask him?'

'He won't change his mind,' she said miserably.

'I guess he won't.' He hesitated. 'So what are you afraid of?'

'I'm not afraid.'

'Is my paraplegia a plus or a minus?' he asked bluntly.

'What do you mean?'

'Are you not wanting to marry me because I'm in a wheel-chair? Or is the fact that I'm in a wheelchair making it seem safe for you to marry me?'

'I guess…mostly the second,' she whispered.

'That's honest at least.'

'I know you well enough now to figure I need to be honest.'

'You also know me well enough now to cut it out with the whispering,' he retorted. 'The Jill Shaw I asked to marry me is a feisty, strong-minded woman who doesn't suffer fools gladly, who doesn't put up with rubbish and who knows what she wants in life. She'll be a great mother for my daughter. The Jill who's emerged since I put a ring on her finger, though, is a pale imitation of that. For heaven's sake Jill, you're almost a trembling virgin.'

'I can hardly be that,' she said, startled.

'It's what you sound like.'

'I didn't mean—'

'Then cut it out,' he snapped. He set down his mug with a decisive thump. 'I'm going to bed. This is the time you start whimpering with fear and insisting I sleep on the veranda or decide to sleep in an armchair by Lily's bed. But there's a per-fectly comfortable bed which is big enough for both of us. Whimpering aside. You want to share a bed with me?'

'I…'

'No whimpering.'

'I wouldn't whimper.' And indeed the whimper had faded. She sounded affronted.

'Good. You want me to sleep on the veranda?'

'Where?'

'In my chair,' he said. 'It's not the first time I've done it.'

'Of course I don't. But I should…'

'You can if you want,' he said cordially. 'Stretched between two cane chairs. You'll be as uncomfortable as hell, and I'll think you're even more wimpish. But go ahead.'

'Charles—'

'And, no, I'm making no more promises about not jumping you,' he said. 'No more reassurances. You either trust me or you don't.'

He left her. He wheeled inside. She heard him in the bathroom, brushing his teeth. Ordinary. Mundane.

The problem was, though, she thought fearfully, that Charles was none of those things. From the time she'd first met him she'd been mesmerised by the power of his personality. And by his physical power, too, she thought. The sheer strength of the man... She watched him day after day as he hauled himself out of his chair and forced his body through the exercise routine he imposed on himself. A lesser man than Charles would have given in to his disability. Not Charles.

He wasn't the giving-in type.

He was waiting for her in the bedroom.

If she had been in her twenties again... If she had been young and gorgeous...

Maybe she'd jump him, she thought ruefully. Maybe she could show him just what a fantastic marriage they could have.

But she was just Jill. The practical one. Nurse administrator, oldest nurse in the hospital, plain and even a bit saggy next to the gorgeous young medics Charles worked with every day.

He was stuck with her because he wanted Lily. So to be afraid of him...

It wasn't that she was afraid of him, she thought. But she was afraid of showing him just how attracted she was to him. Dammit, she didn't want him feeling even more sorry for her.

He'd finished in the bathroom.

They were getting married. There was one bedroom. One bed.

What were her fears? That Kelvin would find them? That somehow by loving she put Lily and Charles at risk?

That she wasn't good enough for them?

'Ugly cow.' She heard Kelvin's taunt echoing over and over.

Well, she thought, maybe she was and maybe she wasn't. But the lights could always go off. Charles didn't have to look at her. If she could give him pleasure...

Maybe...just maybe...

Come on, you ugly cow, don't be a wimp, she told herself. Just for tonight...just for Charles, try and be beautiful.

As if.

But it was a thought and it wasn't a bad thought. In fact, it wasn't bad at all.

A wallaby was watching her from below the veranda.

'Can I do it?' she asked him.

He didn't say no. That was enough.

'I'll do it if he wants,' she told the wallaby. 'I can't say fairer than that.'

She took a deep breath and headed inside.

He was already in bed. Or on the bed. He was wearing plain, blue pyjama pants and nothing else.

The man was in his mid-forties. He should be showing signs of wear and tear by now. A trace of flab.

There wasn't the slightest sign of flab about him. He looked... What did the younger nurses call it...ripped? Buffed, in the old parlance.

Sexy in anyone's vernacular.

How did they describe it in the penny dreadfuls? In walked Doctor Sex-On-Legs. Nurse Ditzy took one look at the hunk in the white coat, her knees turned to jelly, her heart pounded wildly and she had to lean against the wall to stop herself from swooning.

She grinned.

'So what's funny?'

'The changing face of medicine,' she said obliquely. 'You don't wear a pyjama top?

'I'm wearing pyjama bottoms in deference to you. I'm hoping you have a flannel nightgown to match.'

'T-shirt and knickers,' she said. 'I travel light. Close your eyes, roll over and face the wall, and I'll put them on.' She hesitated. 'No. I'll put them on in the bathroom. But face the wall anyway.'

'On account of T-shirt and knickers would inflame my senses.'

'There'll be no inflaming of senses in my bedroom,' she said primly.

'I seem to recall it's my bedroom.'

'What's yours is mine. It's in the wedding vows. Face the wall.'

'Yes, ma'am.'

It was all very well facing the wall. It was another thing entirely going to sleep.

Charles wasn't a great sleeper at the best of times. If Jill hadn't been there he'd probably still be out on the veranda, catching up on clinical journals, or over at the hospital, making himself useful. Or, hell, even reading a decent whodunit.

Instead of which he was facing the wall while his intended bride lay three feet away.

As far to the other side of the bed as she could get.

Was she asleep?

He lay and listened to her breathing. Strong and even, strong and even...

Nah. She was as wide awake as he was.

'Should we tell each other bedtime stories?' he asked, and she gasped.

'I...'

'I knew you weren't asleep,' he said in satisfaction. 'No one breathes as regularly as that unless they're really concentrating.'

'It's my way of going to sleep,' she said with dignity. 'I feel my breath.'

'You feel your breath?'

'You know Gabby? She teaches relaxation classes to our expectant mums. Our insurance doesn't cover her unless there's a trained health professional in attendance so I've sat in a few times. She teaches the mums to focus on each breath. In. Out. If I can't feel my breath above my lip I'm doing it wrong.'

Charles breathed in and out a few times. Harder.

'Nope,' he said. 'It's not doing it for me.'

'So how do you go to sleep?' She sighed. 'No, you don't have to tell me. You don't. You disappear about bedtime and then appear again and scare the living daylights out of unsuspecting night staff.'

'If they work in my hospital they pretty soon aren't unsuspecting,' he said in satisfaction, and she relaxed enough to chuckle.

'No. Your reputation is truly fearsome.'

'Is that why you're scared of me?'

'I'm not scared of you.'

'See, that's what I don't understand.' Despite her previous orders he rolled over in bed so he could see her in the moonlight. 'I would have said you were the only member of my staff who's never been in awe of me. No matter how grouchy I get.'

'Which is pretty grouchy.'

'See what I mean? You give cheek.'

'I can't help myself.'

'So where's the cheek disappeared to?' he asked gently. 'Why have you turned into a trembling kid?'

'Hey!'

'A trembling kid,' he said firmly, 'who looks as if she'll flinch if I raise my hand, rather than raise her hand right back.'

'If I thought you'd ever hit anyone, I'd never come near you.'

'You do believe that?'

'I...I guess I do. Did I tell you that you were allowed to turn over?'

'I decided I was allowed to turn over all by myself,' he said proudly. 'I'm a big kid.'

'You're no kid,' she whispered into the dark.

He didn't know what to say to that.

A trembling kid...

Did he really think that of her? She needed to get a grip, she thought. Here she was, lying in bed with the man of her dreams...

Hey, she was! The thought was suddenly mind-blowing in its intensity. It was like she'd been creeping round the edges, not seeing, and suddenly the sky had opened, revealing all. Or, more like, slapping her over the face like a wet fish.

Wow, she thought suddenly. And then, more awesomely, Wow!

She was in bed with Charles.

She should go back to concentrating on breathing techniques.

But why?

A tiny little voice had started shouting from inside her head when she'd been out on the veranda. Her inner voice was getting louder by the second.

You're in bed with Charles, the voice was saying. Just shut up with your dithering, you idiot, and do what you really, really want.

Was there a reason why not?

Probably there were lots of reasons. Millions of reasons. Control, for one thing, but then again, maybe that was fear as well. More of the trembling-kid thing.

He wouldn't cross her boundaries. She knew that. And she also knew that she'd implied those boundaries were there because he had a damaged spine.

Which was dumb. But if he thought it...hell, she hated that he could think it.

So what to do about it?

She knew what she could do about it. But...

But don't think about it, she decided, squashing her dumb scruples way back into the furthest recesses of her brain. Thinking turned her into a bag of nerves.

Just do it.

What was happening? He was lying staring into the dark, tense as hell, trying to figure where to take it and how, and—

'How long since you've had sex?' Jill suddenly asked into the stillness.

The stillness suddenly got…well, suddenly a lot more still.

'Did you ask what I just thought you asked?' he managed.

'Yep.'

The rising moon was sending soft light washing across the bed. Jill was staring up at the ceiling, her face almost expressionless. But not quite. There was a tiny upward quirk of her lips, as though she knew the shock her words would cause. It was almost a look of…mischief?

Jill?

'I can't see that it's your business,' he started, and there it was again, that definite quirk. Like she'd decided, Dammit, she'd crossed some line and she wasn't going back.

'We're getting married, aren't we?' she said. 'So maybe it is my business.'

'But you said…'

'That we had to keep our distance. I did think that. Maybe the sensible part of me still does. But there's a tiny, non-sensible part of me that's saying if we're going to cross boundaries anyway… If you're going to knock out that wall…'

'I said we didn't have to.'

'So you did,' she said cordially. 'And then you invited me into bed with you.'

'Because we had no choice.'

'So you don't want to make love with me?'

'I didn't say that,' he managed. Just.

'You inferred it.'

Silence fell again. Charles stared across at her, baffled. Surely she didn't mean…

'I can, you know,' he said, as if goaded, and she nodded.

'You said you could. Your injury's below L2. What sort of sensation do you have?'

'Most.' He hesitated. 'Or I assume most. I forget…'

'What it was like to be nineteen and blind with lust?' she queried, as if this was a totally normal conversation, as if she was speaking to a teenage patient about his physical difficulties. 'I'd imagine back then you weren't thinking, Oh, I must remember how it feels when someone's finger runs the full length—'

'Jill!'

'Hey, I'm just talking,' she said, and rolled over and propped herself up on her elbows so she could look down at him in the moonlight. The mischief was there in full now. Her eyes were alight with laughter.

He couldn't believe what he was hearing. Jill. Prim, proper, self-contained Jill, who kept herself to herself.

'It is a blur,' he admitted. 'Not a bad blur…'

'See, the problem for me is that it is a bad blur,' she confessed. 'I haven't made love to anyone but Kelvin in my life. How appalling is that for an admission? He owned me body and soul. I was so much younger than him—the first few times I was desperate to please him, and after that I was simply trapped and he used me as he willed. But there were bits…' She paused, almost as if she couldn't believe she was about to say. 'There were bits I think could have been better. Things I wouldn't mind just trying…'

'But your boundaries…' To say he was hornswoggled was an understatement.

'I learned a long time ago that sex isn't a total loss of emotional control,' she said.

'You kept yourself apart in marriage?'

'Of course I did.'

'So you're saying we could…'

'Only if you want.'

'I guess I do want,' he said cautiously. Hell, of course he wanted. She was propped up on her elbows, smiling at him. Her beautiful curls were cascading softly around her shoulders. Her lovely grey-blue eyes were twinkling down at him, the laughter lines at the edges creasing, deepening the sense of surety, maturity.

Maturity? He wasn't feeling mature right now. He was feeling like a kid who'd been offered the moon.

'I'm not sure…'

'If you remember how? I'm not sure if I remember either. But if you want, we could give it a really good shot.'

'I want,' he said, suddenly definite, and she chuckled. It was a sound he'd very seldom heard. Sister Jill Shaw laughing. Sister Jill Shaw leaning forward to kiss him lightly on the lips.

Her curls fell onto his chest. They barely touched, a light feather brush. It was the most erotic feeling he'd ever known.

She let her head fall to rest on his chest. Her hands moved.

His whole world seemed to still.

'You're a very sexy man, Charles Weatherby.'

Yeah, right. But this wasn't the time to argue. 'You're pretty damned sexy yourself,' he managed—but only just. For lightly, so lightly that at first he thought surely he must be dreaming, her fingers were drifting down, along his chest, lower, across the flatness of his stomach. Lower still. To touch…

His whole body shuddered in response and there it was again, that lovely, throaty chuckle.

'You are interested, then.'

'Are you kidding?' he breathed, and suddenly it wasn't Jill who was calling the shots. He had her in his arms, lifting her high so he could see her, all of her in the moonlight, then tugging her down against him. His body felt alive, strong, young. And so did she. She felt amazing. The loveliest thing… His hands slipped under her T-shirt. She was wearing no bra.

Her skin was silky smooth, so smooth that to touch her sent erotic shivers shooting through his body, and it was as if he was being jolted awake after years of sleeping. His hands cupped her breasts, marvelling at the perfection of her. She was lying on his chest. He rolled and she rolled with him so they were side by side. Her breasts moulded softly under his hands. Her nipples were proudly upright, making their own statement.

She was as aroused as he was.

She'd instigated this. She wanted it.

She was in his arms, a warm, vibrant woman. Jill. He'd suspected there was this under her controlled, almost fearful exterior, and he'd been right.

'You're beautiful,' he whispered into her hair. 'Jill, you're magnificent.'

'There's no need to get carried away,' she said, sounding embarrassed. And then... 'Mind, you're not bad yourself.'

'You've seen worse things come out of cheese?' he teased, and she chuckled again and looped her hands around his neck and tugged his face toward her.

'There's not a lot of things come out of cheese I'd kiss like I'm intending to kiss you,' she whispered. 'Or the next bit either, come to think about it. Charles, I'm fed up with this talking bit. Do you want to take me?'

'More than anything in the world,' he murmured and she smiled in the moonlight, a tiny cat-got-the-cream smile that did things to his body he hadn't known his body was capable of. The way he was feeling... It was like life was opening before him. Gates that had been slammed shut years ago were opening in the face of this woman's smile.

'I want you so badly I'm on fire,' she whispered, and that was enough. He found her mouth. He took her body tight against him and swung her over him. She lay atop him, her T-shirt soft against his skin.

She was struggling to get her hands free and he knew what

she wanted. He seized both sides of her T-shirt and it disappeared somewhere onto the floor.

She still had knickers on but she was attending to that herself. Dammit, if his legs worked properly he could kick off his pyjama pants.

He needn't have worried. Her knickers came off in one swift kick and then her fingers tugged his pants clear.

'Years and years of dressing patients,' she said smugly. 'I knew it'd come in handy one day.'

'You're playing nurse?'

'And you're playing doctor. Examining my breasts for lumps?'

'There seem to be two,' he said. 'Two magnificent…lumps. They need close examination.' He rolled sideways to flick on the bedside lamp but she was before him, pushing the lamp out of reach.

'No!'

'You don't want…'

'I do want. But dim is better.'

He frowned but she was having none of it.

'There's a lot here that needs close examination, and I can perform whatever examination I need to in the dark,' she whispered, her fingers closing in against his groin, making him groan in pleasure. 'As dedicated health professionals I suggest we get on with it. Right, Doctor?'

'Anything you say, Nurse,' he whispered, and chuckled and held her tight, glorying in the warmth of her, the smell of her, the taste…

Jill. This woman had promised to be his wife.

'I think I'm falling in love with my fiancée,' he murmured into her hair, and she chuckled and wriggled so her hair was brushing against his chest, over and over, in a motion that was unbelievably erotic.

'It's a pretty nice ring,' she whispered. 'It deserves a little love in the equation.'

'Are you saying—?'

'I'm not saying anything,' she said serenely, and her fingers moved again, searching, finding, sending sensations through his body that rendered him incapable of anything but the most primal needs. This woman in his arms, right now… This woman giving herself in a way he'd never dreamed she would. 'And why the hell are you?' she murmured. 'Talk, talk, talk. Charles, I don't want talking. I don't want thinking. I just want…you.'

CHAPTER SEVEN

JILL woke just before dawn. For a moment she struggled to remember where she was. All she knew was that she was enveloped in a cocoon of such intense pleasure that it was almost an out-of-body experience.

She'd made love to Charles.

She'd wanted to make love to Charles for years. She acknowledged it to herself now as she lay half-asleep, not wanting to open her eyes, not wanting this sensation to end. From the first time she'd seen him, when he'd interviewed her for the job, she'd thought simply that he was the sexiest man she'd ever met.

For those years she'd watched as medics—young men and women from around the world—lived and worked at Crocodile Creek. As romances happened around him. She'd watched Charles hold himself in rigid containment. She'd seen him at weddings, his eyes still. Perfectly disciplined.

He didn't want. He didn't allow himself to want.

As she had. But last night she'd relaxed the rules. Last night...

It had been so good. More than good. There wasn't a word for how he'd made her feel.

She'd read abut orgasms, but in truth she'd always believed they were something the popular press made up. A myth, promulgated by generations of women to please their men. *Yes, of course I came, dear, just like you.*

But it was no myth. Her lips curved into a smile of delicious remembrance. It was reality. Her reality.

She wiggled deliciously, loving the feel of the sheets against her bare skin. Hugely daring, she edged backward, thinking she'd curve against his body.

He wasn't there.

Her eyes flew open. She wiggled around, and Charles's side of the bed was empty.

The disappointment was almost overwhelming. For an appalling moment she thought, Had it all been a dream? But the indentation of his head was in his pillow. She touched the place where he'd been sleeping and it was still warm.

Maybe that's what had woken her. Charles getting up.

At least he hadn't seen her naked, she thought, but then... that was only a part of it.

His wheelchair was gone. She glanced round to the door. They'd left it open during the night so they could hear if Lily stirred. It was now shut.

She relaxed, just a little. She was familiar enough with Charles's routine to know he'd never sleep as long as she did. He'd have risen but he'd have wanted to leave her sleeping.

Self-consciously she tugged on her T-shirt and knickers and crossed to the door to see what was happening.

Charles was dressed. He was in his chair, seated by Lily's bed. Watching her sleep. He hadn't heard the door open. He was simply watching Lily.

His face said it all, she thought. No wonder he'd asked her to marry him. This was the child he'd never thought to have.

He wanted Lily as much as she did.

It should make her feel good. Strangely it didn't.

Last night...last night had been pure fun. Fun was something she had never had. The idea of loving as fun was novel and exciting. But it had been more than fun. Last night she'd given a part of her she'd never thought to give.

But Charles didn't really want to marry her. Oh, he'd enjoyed last night. She could keep giving him that, she thought. She could even take enjoyment herself. But she must never lose sight of the fact that he was marrying her for Lily's sake.

'How is she?' she whispered as he turned, his face snapping into a frown.

'I wanted you to sleep for longer.'

'I slept for longer than you.'

'About two minutes.' He smiled at her, and his smile raked her from the top of her head to the tips of her toes. 'I believe we were both very tired.'

'We worked very hard yesterday,' she said primly, and then gave in and smiled back. Wham. To allow herself to smile as she wanted to smile... She could see that she'd even surprised Charles. Well, she'd surprised him the night before. Why not keep on surprising them both?

'Lily's not great,' Charles was saying, dragging his eyes from hers with obvious difficulty. 'She's still running a fever.'

'You think we should wake her and get her to drink?'

'Let's leave her to have her sleep out,' Charles said. He ran his finger over the back of Lily's palm, pushing forward and watching the skin fall back into place immediately. It was a simple test but effective. If dehydration was a problem the wrinkles in the skin took a while to resettle.

There was a light knock on the door. Jill looked ruefully down at her bare legs, shrugged and went across to answer it. She'd be less respectable in a bikini, she thought, and anyone knocking at this hour had to be a friend.

It was. Beth was on the other side of the door, smiling a greeting.

'Hi,' she said. 'I was worried about waking you, but I was sure Charles would be awake.'

Only just, Jill felt like retorting, but she didn't. The whole hospital staff knew Charles survived on four or less hours of sleep a night. Last night he'd had, what, seven? In between interruptions. It was a piece of information she couldn't give Beth, but she did feel a trifle smug.

'I popped by to see how Lily was,' Beth said.

'No better,' Charles said, wheeling over to the door so he could be included in the conversation without risking waking Lily.

'We've got a couple more kids showing similar symptoms,' Beth said, looking worried. 'Fever, swollen glands, lethargy.'

'Our kids?' That was a worry. Normal kids like Lily could shake off a virus but the camp kids had other, deeper health problems. For Lily a virus was a hiccup. For kids with cancer or severe asthma, a virus could be a death sentence.

'All ours,' Beth confirmed. 'Their camp leaders rang me during the night on the report-any-symptom rule. I checked them out and ordered them to have a quiet day.' She hesitated, glancing over at Lily. 'Lily's the sickest.'

'She got sick first,' Charles retorted. 'Hell.'

'Look, let's not worry about it now.' Again Beth glanced from Charles to Jill. Noting Jill's bare legs. Noting the open bedroom door. Noting whatever else she fancied.

Jill's face was turning pink. She knew it was, but there wasn't a thing she could do about it.

'Would you guys like to go for a swim?' Beth asked, deliberately looking away from the bedroom door and making her voice bright and a bit too impersonal. So impersonal Jill knew she'd added up the evidence and was reaching her verdict.

'I might,' Charles growled, and Jill knew he was thinking exactly what she was thinking. That rumours were about to fly around the entire island.

'The day's going to be frantic,' Beth said. 'We've got the opening tonight. You'll be over run with every sponsor who's donated so much as an inch of newspaper space. You have a sick little girl and we have a couple of other sickies who may or may not prove to be worries. I'm coming off duty now. I need to eat breakfast and wind down before I go to bed. Your refrigerator is stocked with exactly the same ingredients as mine. I can eat breakfast here, listen to the dawn chorus from your veranda and keep an ear on Lily while you guys go swim off your energy.'

'I could go for a run,' Jill said, dubious.

'Or you could both go for a swim,' Beth said strongly. 'You know I'm the doctor in charge of this island. You also know the danger of swimming alone. I know, Charles, that you break the rules all the time, but I'm not aiding and abetting you. My offer is for you, Charles, to go for a swim while you, Jill, do what you want as long as it's within rescue distance of Charles.'

'I won't need rescuing,' Charles said, annoyed.

'Everyone needs rescuing some time or other,' Beth said enigmatically. 'I reckon you two are doing a pretty good job already. So my offer's on the table. Take it or leave it.'

Of course they took it.

Hard physical exercise was the best mental curative in the world, Jill thought as they made their way to the cove. On the flat paths around the camp Charles's wheelchair could go faster than she could walk. He'd slowed down. She wanted to run. He could keep up, she knew.

But running… She might not stop, she thought.

But the decision she'd made last night had been that she'd try to make this a marriage. That meant that somehow she had to leave the loner Jill behind. It meant she had to stop running.

Just a bit. Just when Charles was by her side.

'You don't want to go swimming,' he growled, and she jumped. The man was omnipotent. It was going to be unnerving spending a lifetime with a man who could read her mind.

'I don't mind swimming.'

'Run if you want.'

'I'm happy to swim with you.'

'I don't want you to be good to me,' he said grumpily, and

pushed his chair faster, forcing her to either break into a run or let him go.

She let him go. This was uncharted territory. She didn't have a clue how to react.

She walked on slowly, feeling foolish. When she emerged from the bushland to the little cove, Charles was already out of his chair, making his way to the water.

His chair wouldn't work on the soft sand. He was forced to use elbow crutches to get himself to the water.

He'd been incredibly lucky, she thought, to have been left with enough power in his legs to give him this much mobility.

She thought of last night and, despite her confusion, she felt herself smile. In that department he'd also been incredibly lucky. Or she'd been incredibly lucky. She was marrying him.

Last night could be the first night of many, and the thought was enough to take her breath away.

She felt herself blush. It was weird. She was out of her depth, losing control, but she wasn't panicking. In a sense it was like she was on the outside, looking in. Wondering what this strange, new Jill-person would do next.

She needed to swim. With Charles.

She hadn't seen him swim before. She knew that he did, but she also knew that he was a man who valued his privacy. She wasn't sure that he wanted her there now, watching him.

She should join him, but instead she tugged her T-shirt off, leaving only her bikini, then stood, feeling exposed and self-conscious. But distracted by Charles.

He used his elbow crutches until the waves were almost to his knees. The crutches were sinking into the soft sand but they were enough to give him the support he needed.

As the water reached knee depth he let himself drop into the shallow-breaking waves, then simply hurled the crutches up onto the beach. Then he sank full length into the sea and used his arms to pull himself out to deep water.

He was like a seal. He took less than a minute to reach the buoys marking the boundaries of the netted cove, slicing through the small, incoming waves with the ease born of long practice.

The power of the man took her breath away.

She hesitated, feeling unsure. This was so much his private territory. But he was beyond the breakers now, floating, looking back to the beach to see what she would do.

What did he think she'd do? Retreat?

What had he said? *I don't want you to be good to me.*

Sympathy was so far from what she was feeling that she almost laughed. Almost.

Her fiancé was waiting in deep water.

She was getting into some pretty deep water herself, she thought. But the time for retreating was past.

What the heck. Charles was waiting.

She tossed her T-shirt onto the sand and ran into the water.

In the water he was alive. He was free.

Every morning back at Crocodile Creek, Charles swam. There were so many small bays around Crocodile Creek that he could always find a private place to swim. Crocodiles usually only went to sea to transfer from one inlet to another, so as long as he stayed away from the mouth of the creek he was safe.

For the rest of the day his chair chafed him. He should be used to the restrictions by now, and mostly he was, but there were still many times when standing would be easier, walking would be faster, running would be fantastic.

But in the water his legs didn't hold him back at all. He had enough strength in them so they didn't drag, and the extra strength in his arms more than compensated.

Jill was watching him.

He wasn't sure what had happened with her last night, he thought as he swam. He'd accepted it with joy, but he wasn't sure that it was anything that could last.

He'd had so many people be good to him. Especially women. Men were gruff and taciturn and often embarrassed, but there'd been more than one woman in the past who'd approached him thinking…

Well, enough. He could feel sorry enough for himself without some damned do-gooder aiding and abetting the sympathy vote.

Had Jill made love to him out of sympathy?

He wasn't sure, he thought, not yet, but if she had then she'd done a good job of disguising it. Her turnaround had been astonishing. Magnificent.

Jill was magnificent.

He watched her run into the water. Her body was as taut and lithe as a teenager's. Years of running had toned her so there wasn't an inch of spare flesh on her.

What the hell was she doing, refusing to let him see her naked? But maybe…maybe it was because she didn't want to see him. Making love in the dark was possible.

No matter. He'd take Jill any way she offered herself.

She dived into the first small wave, and emerged spluttering. She didn't swim as often as he did. The waves here were tiny, the island sheltered from the bigger surf by miles of coral reef. But even this small wave was enough to make her splutter.

He smiled and stroked forward to meet her, sliding his body into a wave and riding it forward. He surfaced right by her legs and she was still wiping the water from her eyes.

He gripped her leg and she yelped.

'I'm not a shark,' he said, rolling over lazily and smiling up at her.

'You look like one to me,' she retorted, and then as the pressure on her leg grew greater she toppled forward into the shallows. 'Oi. Unhand me, sir.'

'Why would I?' he asked, teasing, and tugged her leg harder so she slid forward into his arms. Another wave broke over them. He lifted her high so she was clear of the water, and then brought her down again to kiss her.

'Charles…' she said, breathless.

'Yes?' He kissed her again, on the mouth, deeply, then sliding her upward so he could kiss the swell of her breasts.

'This is scaring me,' she managed.

'You don't seem scared.'

'No, but…'

'But what?'

'I didn't think… You must know I never intended last night to happen.'

'And I never allowed myself to hope it could happen,' he told her gravely, then had to lift her again to allow another wave to roll past. 'You know, if we're to make love here, we need to head further into the shallows. Or find ourselves snorkels.'

'We can't make love here,' she said, shocked.

'I guess it is more public than my little cove back at Croc Creek,' he said. 'How soon do you think we can go home?'

'You think…you really think we might…?'

'Why not?' he said, and tugged her down and kissed her again.

If she'd died and gone to heaven she couldn't feel any better than she did right now, she thought. He was kissing her, lifting her, kissing her again, laughing up at her, holding her in his arms so strongly she felt loved, protected, cherished. It was a surge of emotion so strong she could hardly take it in.

Another wave caught them, bigger than the rest. Charles's lifting techniques failed. He'd been holding his breath as the waves had passed but this one was too deep.

It submerged her. He let her fall. She fell into his arms, and they both emerged with noses and eyes full of water.

'Hey, you're no lifesaver,' she managed as she choked and choked again.

'Beth said you had to save me.'

'I can't save you if you try and drown me.' She chuckled and then looked at him through a mist of water and thought it was too much. She didn't deserve this. Even if he was doing it for Lily… To have this much happiness…

He was doing it for Lily. He had to be. But for now…

'Race you out to the buoy,' he said, and she stared at him in bemusement.

'Excuse me? You swim every morning. You'd beat me hands down.'

'Then give me a handicap.'

'One hand,' she said, and it was the right thing to say. People had been nice to him about his disability for so long that to insist on rules like this…

'Hey, I have no kicking power.'

'You have so,' she said serenely.

'I'd have to swim sidestroke.'

'Yep.'

'You'd have two good legs and two arms.'

'To your one arm. That might make us almost equal. Are you going to race or are you planning on thinking up more excuses?'

He stared at her. She stared back, challenging.

'Right,' he said. 'Ready, set, go.'

She beat him, but only just.

That required a re-race.

She beat him again, so she was handicapped. No kicking. That meant her two arms against his one.

He beat her for the next three races.

'OK, running tomorrow,' she gasped as they did the last of best out of five. 'Me against your wheelchair.'

'I'd beat you in a minute.'

'In a minute on sealed tracks, sure,' she said. 'I want all round the island on the unsealed tracks.'

'Hey! What about obstacles?'

'What's a few obstacles to you?' she teased, and watched with delight as his eyes lit up with laughter. She could make this serious man smile. She'd never tried. No one had. Everyone had always been in awe of him.

It was a shock. He didn't quite know how to take it. She wasn't sure if he'd keep on enjoying it, but it was working now and she intended to give it her very best shot. She'd keep on trying.

But he was glancing at his wristwatch, grimacing.

'We'd best get back,' he said regretfully. 'Lily...'

Of course. Lily. She'd almost forgotten.

How had that happened? Lily was the only reason she was marrying Charles. Wasn't she?

'Of course,' she said, and turned her face toward the beach.

'Jill? One kiss before we go,' he said, and her body quivered in delight.

'Just one?' she whispered, and he chuckled and tugged her close.

Only, of course, happy endings were for fairy-tales. Dreams had a habit of turning into nightmares.

This one did almost the moment they hit the beach. For they were no longer alone.

There were two boys further up the beach. They were tossing stones at seagulls, obviously bored, their body language overtly aggressive.

Showing off to each other. Proving their adolescent macho stuff.

'Hey, there's two from the cripple camp,' one yelled.

They'd be from the resort, Jill thought warily. It was the one problem that Charles hadn't yet been able to solve. The tip of the northern island was home to a resort that was unaffordable to normal people. That meant most guests wanted privacy, but occasionally the super-rich brought their families. This island may be a fabulous eco-resort, famed throughout the world, but indulged adolescents found it boring.

These two looked like trouble. Left to her own devices, Jill would have left the beach fast, pre-empting problems.

But Charles's crutches were up the beach a little, just out of reach of the waves. It'd take him time to reach them.

She ran out of the shallows and grabbed them, then took his arm as he staggered upright. He didn't like it.

'I can manage,' he growled.

'I know you can. But I don't like the look of these two.'

'Zach and Dom Harris,' Charles said, steadying himself as the boys approached. 'I've met them. Their father's Cray Harris, a trucking magnate. They upset one of our kids yesterday. Stella. She's lost a leg from cancer. I wouldn't mind…'

'Confronting them? Please, don't.'

'You don't like a fight?'

'No!'

'I guess you've had enough of that to last a lifetime.' He shrugged and started up the beach. It was a struggle, even for a man of Charles's strength. The sand here was soft and drifted into piles that shifted under his crutches.

'Hey, it must be catching,' one of the boys sneered, edging closer. 'Bloody cripple. I'm going to tell my dad to get us off this place. There's cripples everywhere.'

'I need to have a word with your father myself,' Charles said grimly.

'Yeah, well, he wouldn't want to talk to you,' the oldest of the boys jeered. 'He might catch something.'

Charles closed his eyes. Jill put her hand on his arm, urgent. Don't react, was her silent message. Sticks and stones…

'That's right, hold him up,' the smaller kid yelled.

'He doesn't need holding up,' Jill retorted.

'Maybe you're holding each other up,' the bigger kid yelled. 'What's wrong with you? You got cancer or something?' He was walking closer now, holding something in his hand. It was a sand bomb, Jill saw. A round, hard ball of packed sand, about as big as a baseball.

'Ancient cripples,' the younger boy yelled, and laughed as if he'd said something uproariously funny. 'Put your shirt on, you ugly cow. You're too old for a bikini.'

Ugly cow. The name hit her like a physical blow. She wasn't Jill again. She was a sixteen-year-old kid, losing her baby, losing everything she cared about.

For one awful moment she thought she might be sick.

'Leave it, Charles,' Jill said urgently, as she felt him stiffen in fury. 'Let's get off the beach.'

But he'd stopped. He was facing them square on.

'Do you know how much your words can hurt?'

It was supposed to defuse the situation. It was supposed to be calmness in the face of rage.

But these two didn't want calm. They were out for trouble. If Jill and Charles had tried to keep going up the beach, they would have followed them all the way, taunting them as they went.

Charles had stopped that by facing them. They eyed him uncertainly.

'Cripple,' the younger one said again, as if he was trying to get the older one's approval.

'Don't,' Jill said savagely before she could stop herself, and it was enough. The older boy's face creased into an expression of pure vitriol.

'Don't tell us what we can and can't do, you stupid cow,' he yelled. 'You get off the beach with your crippled boyfriend and take this for good measure.' And before either of them could react he'd lobbed the sandbomb straight at her.

It wasn't just sand. It had a stone in its centre. It hit her hard on the cheek, so hard she staggered back. She would have fallen but Charles's hand came out and gripped her. Hard. One of his crutches fell uselessly to his side but he didn't need it. He hauled her against him and held her.

'Jill…'

She had her hand to her cheek. She could feel a faint warm trickle.

'Jill!'

'I… It's OK.' This was minor. She was used to it.

'Hell!' He turned her to him. 'Hell!' He turned savagely toward the boys.

But the boys had scared themselves. One glance at the blood oozing down Jill's face had them running up the beach like the hounds of hell were after them.

'It was just a stone,' Jill said, but Charles was pushing her hands away, checking for himself.

'Little—'

'Don't.'

'If I could…'

'You can't,' she said flatly. 'And neither can I.'

'What do you mean?' he demanded.

'I mean leave it.'

'We don't have to.'

'I thought you'd have accepted that long ago,' she whispered.

'Being a victim?'

'I…' She faltered. Her face hurt. Her lovely morning was smashed.

She felt about a hundred years old.

'Look, this is OK,' she whispered. 'I just need a sticking plaster and we need to get back to Lily. Beth will be waiting.'

'Jill, we don't have to take this.'

'So what would you have us do? Run after them? I don't think so.' She shook her head, stepped back from his hold and retrieved his crutch from where it had fallen. 'No. Lily's waiting. Thank you…thank you for wanting to…' She shook her head. 'No. We need to not want. I learned that a long time ago.'

CHAPTER EIGHT

THEY returned to the bungalow in silence. Garf met them just off the beach. He greeted them with joy, pushing his great body between them and acting as a goofy buffer.

The big dog was normally a comfort but not now. Jill felt sick.

Charles had withdrawn. He hated it that he hadn't been able to defend her, she thought, but, then, that was what she wanted. She didn't want anyone to fight on her behalf.

No fighting. Ever.

Her cheek stung, but worse was the aftertaste of the aggression she'd seen in those kids.

This was minor compared to what had happened to her in the past. She glanced over at Charles and saw his face was set and stern. And angry.

Angry at her?

Maybe he was, she thought.

She wanted him to be passive.

'I won't do it,' he said as they reached the ramp up to the bungalow, and she stared.

'What?'

'You know damned well,' he growled. '*You* expect me to play the invalid...'

'I don't expect anything.'

'Then start expecting,' he snapped. 'Don't you dare keep playing the victim.'

'I'm not—'

'Let's get off the beach,' he mimicked, and it was so much like her voice that she winced.

'Charles, I only wanted—'

'To run away.'

'What's wrong with that? We can't—'

'We can,' he snapped back at her again.

'Charles? Is that you?' The screen door swung open above them. Beth was standing in the doorway, looking worried.

'Lily,' Charles and Jill said together.

'I can't wake her,' Beth said. 'She's having a nightmare.'

Charles reached her first. Lily was thrashing round on the bed, incoherent.

'Lily,' he said peremptorily, and she stared blindly up at him.

'They're here,' she whimpered. 'They're here. Everywhere.'

'What are, sweetheart?' He leaned forward and lifted her onto his knees. 'What's here?'

'The birds,' she whimpered. 'Daddy, don't let them near. Daddy, the birds…'

It was too much. For Jill, crouching before him, gazing up into his face, she saw the point where things broke.

The events of this night were too much. His rigid control was crumbling.

He'd called Lily sweetheart. He never did. He didn't approve of nicknames. Frivolity.

Lily had called him Daddy.

Lily was delirious.

It didn't matter. The emotions the word had engendered couldn't have been stronger if Lily had been in full control of her senses.

He was fighting back tears.

'I've been sponging her,' Beth said. 'It's not working. I can't get her cool. Charles, we need to admit her.'

'To do what?' Jill whispered, but she already knew the answer.

'This isn't a cold,' Beth said. 'We need to get some fluids on board, we need to get that temperature down and we need to rule out meningitis.'

Meningitis… The word was enough to make her world stop. She tried frantically to think. 'But meningitis… We need a lumbar puncture… We need a paediatrician…'

'We have a paediatric neurosurgeon here on the island,' Beth said. 'Alex Vavunis. His daughter's one of our camp kids. He'll help, I know. If you agree, I'll set it up now. Can I phone for a buggy?'

'Of course,' Jill whispered. She couldn't take her eyes off Lily. The little girl was still struggling with her nightmare. Charles was holding her against him, trying to calm the worst of her struggles.

Lily. Her daughter.

'What are we waiting for?' Charles asked abruptly. 'Beth, make that phone call and see if you can find Alex. Tell him half my kingdom if he'll help. All. Jill, get dressed. Put some anti-biotic cream on that face, though. I don't want it being infected.'

'What happened to your face?' Beth asked.

'My face doesn't matter,' Jill whispered. 'Oh, Lily…'

Beth left to make preparations for Lily's admission. Charles held Lily while Jill dressed and stuck a plaster over her cheek, then Jill held Lily while Charles dressed. The buggy arrived before they were ready. The driver was Walter Grubb, hospital handyman. Walter and Dora were permanently based in Crocodile Creek but they'd been desperate to be come over for the opening.

Walter looked just plain desperate now. Charles rolled down the ramp with Lily in his arms. Walter stared down into her white little face and his own face lost colour.

'Oh, no,' he whispered. 'Not Lily. Not our Lil.'

'She's going to be fine,' Jill said strongly, trying to make herself believe it.

'Get in, Jill, and I'll lift her up to you,' Charles said. 'Get out, Garf.'

She hadn't even noticed the dog was in the buggy. Of course. Where there was a buggy, there was Garf.

They didn't need him now.

But Lily had other ideas. She opened her eyes and a trace of normality edged back.

'Garf,' she said and smiled, and that was that. Jill sat in the back of the buggy with Lily in her arms. She wouldn't let Garf lie on top of her as he clearly intended—she needed to keep Lily cool—but Garf took up half the seat.

Charles brought up the rear in his wheelchair, clearly unhappy the buggy wouldn't go as fast as his chair would.

They were an oddly assorted family.

But they were family, Jill thought. Any way she could make them.

Marcia, the clinic nurse, met them at the entrance, pushing a trolley. 'I'll carry her in,' Jill said, but Marcia simply lifted Lily from her arms and laid her on the cool sheets and pillows.

'You can hold her hand,' she said. 'But Beth says we need her cool and you holding her won't help that. Dr Wetherby, Jill, you guys are the parents from this point on. Beth says.'

Jill cast a helpless glance back at Charles. He nodded grimly and Marcia pushed the trolley forward.

There was a medical team waiting for them. Beth and this new doctor Jill hadn't yet met. But Charles obviously had.

'Vavunis,' he said, in a strange, grim voice Jill had never heard before. 'Jill, this is Alex Vavunis. It's good of you to do this for us.'

'I wish I could say it was a pleasure,' the man said. 'I'm just glad I was here.'

'He was here looking for Susie,' Beth said, with an attempt at lightness, and Jill looked sharply up at the big Greek doctor and thought of Susie, their resident physiotherapist. Here we go again, she thought. Crocodile Creek romance. For everyone but Charles and herself?

Marriage and children.

Oh, Lily, please...

She wanted to help. She wanted to be doing what Marcia was doing, helping Beth with equipment, taking obs. She glanced at Charles and saw the same rigid tension in him.

'Can you hear me, Lily?' Alex asked.

'No,' Lily whispered, and they all smiled. But not very much.

Alex had his fingers on her carotid artery, feeling her pulse. He lifted her eyelids, checking pupil reaction. She didn't protest. She seemed almost drugged. Lethargic and uninterested. The total opposite to their normally livewire Lily.

'You've got a bug, Lily, is that it?' Alex asked, and Jill's almost unbearable tension levels eased a notch. Alex was using the same tone Charles used when he coped with sick or injured children.

There was no one more competent in a crisis than Charles. It was inappropriate—dangerous even—to treat a child when your emotions were severely compromised, but if Charles couldn't be in charge she was glad this man was here to take his place.

'You've certainly done the right thing admitting her,' Alex said, and the terror washed back threefold.

'Not...? We're not overreacting?'

'Not,' he said bluntly. He was testing Lily's reflexes now, tapping her knees, watching her reactions. The little girl's eyes were closed, as if the light hurt. Alex put down his hammer, but kept Lily's leg bent at the hip, supported by his arm. 'Can you straighten your leg for me, Lily?'

She could. She did. Jill felt her breath rush out in a tiny sob of relief. This was a negative Kernig's sign, one of the major pointers for meningitis.

'She started showing these symptoms yesterday, is that right?' Alex asked them.

'Yes.' The word was almost a growl from Charles. He was

staring fixedly at Lily, as if concentration alone could make her better. 'But it looked like any run-of-the-mill viral illness. She was a bit sniffy. That's all.'

He sounded defensive. For a moment Jill wanted to go to him, hug him, but his body language said not to. His face was set like stone. Expecting the worst?

So was she. She couldn't help him.

'Beth says she was having nightmares.'

'More like hallucinations,' Jill whispered.

'It was a nightmare,' Charles snapped. It seemed that for Charles it was important to get the distinction right. 'I told you, she was upset by the dead bird she found the other day.'

'But she saw it flying around the room,' she whispered.

'She's running a temperature,' Charles replied. 'She's in a strange place.'

They were arguing, Jill thought dully. Why? She couldn't figure it out. She could only figure out that the fingers under hers were hot to the touch. That this was Lily. *Lily.*

As if thinking her name had brought her back to them, Lily opened her eyes. She looked up at Jill, and then over to Charles, and her bottom lip trembled. 'I want to go home.'

Jill was trying hard not to cry. She was being useless, she thought savagely. She was just like any other distraught parent.

She glanced across at Charles and saw he was feeling exactly the same. The urge to go to him…to hold him…was almost overwhelming. But Lily was gripping her hand tightly, and Alex was trying to get her to listen.

'We've got you here so we can take extra-special care of you,' he said. 'Do you remember my name, Lily?'

She shook her head, but barely, however. She was drifting toward sleep, Jill thought, and then, more terrifying, she thought, She's drifting toward unconsciousness.

'How's your neck, poppet?' Alex's voice was insistent. He slipped his hands behind Lily's head. 'In here.'

'It hurts.'

'It's just her glands,' Charles said sharply, but Alex looked over at him and shook his head.

'Let's not take that as read.' He straightened. 'Let's step outside so Lily can go back to sleep. Marcia, can you stay with Lily, please? She could have that dose of paracetamol now.'

They left. It nearly killed Jill to release Lily's hand, but Lily was drifting toward oblivion. She didn't protest as Jill disentangled herself, and if decisions were to be made about what happened now, Jill wanted to hear.

Charles would do her listening, she thought. She trusted Charles. But…this was her daughter.

She walked blindly toward the door. Charles reached it before she did. She put out a hand toward him. Hoping… hoping what? She didn't know. It was a dumb gesture that achieved nothing.

He didn't even acknowledge it, just wheeled through and waited for Alex to start talking.

'Beth's right,' Alex said without preamble. He seemed to know already that neither she nor Charles would tolerate platitudes. 'On the positive side we've got no rash and a negative Kernig's sign, but we can't rule out meningitis without a lumbar puncture.'

Jill closed her eyes. This was the worst of all nightmares.

'I'll do it,' Charles said, and her eyes flew wide. What was he saying? But the strain behind his eyes… He was as terrified as she was.

'No.' Beth's tone was gentle but firm. 'You can't. You know you can't. You have one of the country's top paediatric neurosurgeons right here. How many lumbar punctures have you done on children, Alex?'

'I can't say. A lot.'

'I'd be guessing it's a lot more than Charles or I have done,' Beth said. 'I'm sorry, but it's a no-brainer. You're her daddy, Charles. You get to hold her hand.'

'I'm staying with her,' Jill said, suddenly terrified she'd be left out.

They'd both be with her. They had to be a family. They were all Lily had.

Lily was all they had. She stared down into Charles's frozen face and thought that without Lily they didn't even have each other.

She'd helped with this procedure a hundred times or more in the course of her career. She always hated it.

She hated it so much now she felt sick.

They needed enough staff to position Lily correctly if she struggled. Susie, the physiotherapist, was in the corridor, the first person to hand, and she was appalled to find out why she was needed.

'Not our Lily,' she whispered, hugging Jill.

'Don't worry,' Alex said gently. 'Let's assume this is a needless test, taken to be on the safe side. I'll use plenty of local anaesthetic and make it virtually painless. With so many people around who know and love her, she'll be just fine.'

Dammit, he should be doing the test himself. He should have organised it last night. He should have…

Been of more use.

He felt like lifting the surgical tray and hurling it against the far wall. Instead, all he could do was watch as Alex did what he should be doing.

He did it in his head. He was watching every move of Alex's fingers, as jealous as hell. Helpless. Sick.

'What gauge needle have you got there, Beth?' Alex was asking.

'A twenty.'

'Does the stylet fit the barrel?'

'All checked. We're good.'

'Right. Lily, let's get you lying on your side, sweetheart.

We're going to do a test on your back that'll help us find out what's the matter with you. It'll tell us which medicine is right for you. OK?'

'O-OK,' Lily whispered but it clearly wasn't. Dammit, he was close to tears, Charles thought.

'Jill, you stay close to her head and hold her hand. Charles, can you keep a hand on Lily's hip and legs? Marcia? Legs for you, too, and, Susie, I'll get you beside me with extra support for Lily's chest and arms.'

Alex was OK, Charles thought. He was ensuring Lily would stay still. He knew what he was doing.

It didn't make him feel any better.

Beth was swabbing Lily's lower back with antiseptic and Alex pressed along the spine, counting carefully, looking for the space between the third and fourth vertebrae. He was talking but Charles wasn't hearing. If he could go through this himself in Lily's stead...

He glanced along at Jill and he knew she was feeling exactly the same.

His feeling of helplessness intensified. What sort of parent was he? What sort of husband?

There was still a smear of blood on Jill's cheek, running down from her sticking plaster. The sight of it made him feel even worse.

'Small scratch,' Alex warned Lily, and Charles felt Lily stiffen in terror. She whimpered at the feel of the needle. Jill, too. It was a tiny sound, almost inaudible, but he heard it nonetheless.

'Talk to her, Jill,' he said urgently, and Jill cast him a frightened glance. He met her eyes with a silent, strong message. Children sensed fear.

She swallowed. He saw her take two, three deep breaths, and then crouch and whisper to Lily. He couldn't hear what she was saying.

He wanted to hear. But he needed to watch Alex.

There was no faulting Alex. It was a textbook procedure, skilfully executed. But still Charles watched every single move.

Angling the needle with care, Alex moved slowly and surely, withdrawing the stylet often to check for the drip of any cerebrospinal fluid. The decrease in the resistance to the needle would mean he'd know precisely when he was in the right place. And in seconds he was. Clear fluid dripped easily, and Beth had the required tubes ready. The stylet was replaced, the system withdrawn and a sterile swab pressed to the puncture site.

Charles hadn't been aware that he'd stopped breathing. But maybe it was just as well he was sitting down. He couldn't have done this for Lily, he acknowledged. He felt sick.

'All over,' Alex said into the stillness. 'You were a very brave girl, Lily. Well done.'

Charles wasn't sure she could hear. Jill was nose to nose with her, still whispering. There it was again, that stab of jealousy. He wanted it. He wanted this closeness.

He was useless.

'What about blood tests?' he demanded, trying to get his mind back into gear.

'Let's get an IV line in and collect the bloods at the same time.'

'Antibiotic of choice?' This was Beth's job, asking these questions, he thought, but he couldn't help himself. And everyone seemed to understand his need.

'Benzylpenicilin IV,' Alex said, talking to Beth as well as to Charles. 'She's going to need half-hourly neurological checks. Responses to light and verbal commands, hand grip on both sides—Beth, you know the drill. Fluid restriction for the moment as well until we get a better idea of what we're dealing with.'

'We'll get the samples away on the first ferry or flight,' Beth said.

'Mike can take them now,' Charles snapped, and then, as

everyone looked at him he gave a shame-faced grin, he added, 'I know. But this is my kid. I help fund the service; it cares for my kid.'

Beth smiled at him, her smile saying she understood. 'That's great. It'll mean we should get the first results back later today.'

She hesitated, looking from Charles to Jill and back again, as if trying to think of something she could say to reassure them. 'It's so good you're both here with Lily,' she said softly. 'Poor little Robbie Henderson's come in with a bug, and his mother's a single mum. There's no way she can leave four other children to be here.'

'What's wrong with Robbie?' Lily whispered. Now the adults around her had started to relax she seemed to have stirred a little. 'Is he sick, like me?'

'Kind of,' Beth said, and glanced toward her friend. 'Susie, you know Robbie? Is he one of your patients?'

'Robbie? Ten years old. Cerebral palsy?'

'That's him.'

'I do know him. There were no requests for any special programme for him. He did join in with my swimming-pool group once but camp activities have been enough to keep his joints mobile. Has he got flu?'

'He started vomiting in the night. He's running a temperature and complaining of a headache and sore eyes.'

'I've got sore eyes,' Lily whispered, 'but I haven't vomited.'

Jill was so glad it was over. So relieved she felt dizzy. Now all she wanted was the results. She was with Charles every inch of the way. If all fast results required was money, she'd have mortgaged her soul.

She glanced up at Charles but he was frowning, staring at Beth with a pucker between his brows that he always had when he was worried.

He was distracted, Jill thought. Worried about something else? About Robbie? 'I'll see you later, Lily,' he told her. 'I've got to go and get things ready for our big opening this afternoon. Jill's going to stay with you, aren't you, Jill?'

'Of course.'

He nodded abruptly and Jill knew for sure then that he was worried about something else. This mind reading worked both ways, she thought. But he wasn't sharing.

'Maybe it's the same thing,' Alex said thoughtfully. 'You want me to take a look?'

'If he gets any worse, yes, please,' Beth said gratefully.

'If you have an influenza virus doing the rounds it's not that uncommon to get meningoencephalitis. It should be self-limiting and only require supportive measures.'

'But I want to know straight away if we have any more cases,' Charles said. 'There's been a couple of staff off colour over the last two days. If there's a flu bug—'

'The last thing we want is for it to spread to our sick kids,' Beth finished for him.

Charles nodded. He wheeled over to Lily's bed and took her hand. Leaning over, he kissed her lightly on the forehead. So much for barrier nursing, Jill thought.

'I love you, sweetheart,' Charles whispered, and Jill blinked.

So much for any barriers at all.

'I need to go,' he told her, and wheeled away. Without saying goodbye to her.

OK. There were definitely still some barriers.

It was the longest day of her life.

All day Jill sat by Lily's bed, watching her little girl grow sicker. Maybe they should ring her uncle, she thought. She mentioned it to Charles mid-morning. Charles made the phone call and came back, grim-faced.

'He says kids get sick all the time. If we're going to adopt her, get used to worrying.'

'He doesn't care,' Jill whispered.

'We're her parents,' Charles said.

He couldn't be with them all the time. There were urgent pressures outside. The gala dinner was taking place tonight over at the resort. Major sponsors had contributed megabucks. They were expecting to be thanked in style, and not just in the short few moments of speechmaking tonight.

He was trying to keep the worst of the pressure away from her, Jill thought. He wheeled through into Lily's ward every half-hour or so and she saw the effort it cost him to stop the wheels spinning, to slow as he entered the room, to pause by Lily's bedside and be still.

The official opening—the ribbon cutting—was at four. She didn't leave Lily. Charles came in soon after, looking grey.

'Can't someone else take over out there?' she asked him.

'I've talked half these people into contributing,' he said grimly. 'I've twisted arms, I've hauled in favours; in some cases it's pretty much close to blackmail. If I don't keep thanking people—if I'm not at the official dinner tonight—there's no saying that some of that money won't be forthcoming. We've promised this island to too many kids…'

'It's a wonderful thing…'

'Yeah,' he said bitterly. 'It's so damned important that I have to go dress up in a penguin suit.'

'It is important,' she said solidly. 'I'll be with Lily every minute.'

But she wanted to be with him. The strain on his face was well nigh unbearable. All these people surrounding him tonight…they wouldn't know Charles's daughter was ill. Even if Alex told them what was happening, well, Lily was just his adoptive daughter after all, and not really even that yet.

They wouldn't know how much he cared.

He was looking down into Lily's face now. She was drifting in and out of sleep, feverish, fretful.

'We've done everything we can,' he said. 'We've hit her with everything we can. She wouldn't get better treatment if we evacuated her to the Children's Hospital.'

'She'd be worse,' Jill said stolidly. 'There'd be the flight, the strangeness. Here she knows every single member of the medical team apart from Alex, and she's already starting to recognise him.'

'He's good, isn't he?' Charles said, momentarily diverted.

'He's been in twice again, just to check.'

'Good of him.' He stared down at Lily's pallid face and a muscle pulled at the corner of his mouth. 'You'll buzz me the minute she gets worse.'

'She won't get worse.'

'She might before she pulls the corner,' he warned. 'Twelve hours before the antibiotic takes hold.'

'That's if she has meningitis. There's still no rash.'

'The test results should be back soon.' He glanced at his watch. 'Hell. I have to go. I need to—'

'What else is wrong?'

He stilled. 'What do you mean, what else is wrong?'

'I know you, Charles,' she said softly. 'Yes, you're worried about Lily, but you're worried about something else.'

'We have three sick kids now. And a couple of adults. Isn't that enough to worry about?'

'So it's flu?' She said it almost eagerly.

'I'm thinking yes.'

'But what?' she said, still watching his face.

'Nothing.'

'I know your face,' she said. 'This is something bad. What's wrong with them all getting flu? We could relax if it's just flu.'

'Not if it's bird flu,' he said heavily.

CHAPTER NINE

FOR a moment she couldn't take it in. She stared at him in disbelief, and then, involuntarily, she turned back to Lily.

Lily's eyes were closed. There were dark smudges under them, her pale little face looking almost bleached. The fingers tucked into Jill's hand were hot and dry.

Bird flu. The deadly flu virus that had the world terrified.

'She picked up the bird on the beach,' Charles said heavily. 'I've been going over and over it in my head. There are dead birds all over the island. The shearwaters arrive here as part of their regular migratory pattern—they come to breed. But this year they seem to be coming to die, and there's confirmed cases of bird flu just north of us.' Then, at the look on her face, he swore. 'Hell, Jill, I didn't want to scare you with this. I didn't want to tell anyone. But I'm going nuts.'

Was it then? Afterwards she thought maybe it was. She'd been so caught up with Lily—she still was—she was terrified for her small daughter. But in that instant something changed.

Up until then Charles had seemed aloof, distant, even hero material. She'd admired him enormously. She'd watched as he'd fought to build this medical service so it was second to none. She'd been in awe of him.

But now…he seemed lost. This threat alone he could cope with, she thought, but he kept looking at Lily. He wanted all his attention to be on Lily.

Even this morning…she'd been hit and he hadn't been able to prevent it. His control was shattered.

He needed her, she thought with a flash of insight that was almost overwhelming. He needed her right now almost as much as Lily did.

Lily was asleep. Her priority right now had to be Charles.

She carefully disentangled herself from Lily and pushed her chair round so she could take both Charles's hands in hers.

'Birds die,' she said softly. 'Come on, Charles. Every time I'm on a beach I see a decomposing bird or two. It's nature. When birds die we don't have undertakers coming round to put them in mahogany coffins. Who's to say there wasn't a bit of a baby-boomer swell in numbers, say, five years ago— how long do birds live? And now there's a vast geriatric population creaking their way back to the island to die?'

He smiled but his smile didn't reach his eyes. 'There's far more dead birds than usual. I've been talking to the rangers. They're worried, too.'

'So this afternoon…'

'I've been on the internet. The strain of avian bird flu that's been threatening the countries north of here is called H5N1. The symptoms match Lily. And Robbie. And…'

'And any other flu,' she said stoutly. Then her voice faltered a little. 'But it doesn't react to treatment…'

'She's holding her own, Jill.'

'Do you really think…?'

'I can't be sure,' he said, tugging his hands away so he could rake his hair. 'I'm ordering blood tests. I've been onto a couple of epidemiologists from the mainland. The symptoms are non-specific. A lot depends on whether Lily's meningitis test comes back positive.'

'So we're hoping for meningitis?'

'No! Hell, Jill, I don't know what I want. Look, I shouldn't be saying this even to you. There's only a tiny chance I'm right. But if I am…I need to have everything in place. No one's leaving the island tonight. We've got priority on all blood testing. A decision will be made in the morning.'

'To close the island down?'

Marcia came in then, to check Lily's drip. They stopped talking and Marcia saw the look of strain on both their faces and felt the need to stay and chat and reassure them.

Jill was screaming inwardly for her to leave. Charles was glancing at his watch. There were so many pressures…

That he'd shared this with her was huge, she thought. Whether he wanted it or not, she reached out and took his hand again. And held it. He stared down at their linked hands as if he wasn't quite sure how to respond.

'You're thinking quarantine?' she said as Marcia buzzed out again, and he nodded.

'Yes.'

'Is there vaccination?'

'I'm organising it now. Provisionally. There's no flu vaccine specific to H5N1 but there are antivirals we can give that make it much less leth—harmful.'

'It is lethal,' she whispered, turning back to Lily.

'From what I've read, if this was a bad case Lily would be even sicker than she is now,' he told her. 'She's a strong little girl. She has the best possible care.'

'We have to keep her,' she whispered.

'We will.' He lifted her ring finger, and his mouth twisted into a crooked smile. 'Our engagement's still on, then?'

'Of course.'

'I'm no catch.'

'You are,' she said solidly, and her grip on his hands tightened. 'Look at you. You've got everyone on this island wanting a piece of you right now. You're worried sick about Lily. You're worried sick about bird flu. Have you told anyone else on the island?'

'No.'

'Because you don't want panic. You only told me because

I wouldn't let you off the hook. You keep it all to yourself. And tonight…you have this damned dinner…'

'I have to go.'

'You don't. If people there knew the reason—'

'If they knew I wasn't there because I was figuring out how the hell to enforce quarantine, we'd have people trying frantically to get off the island tonight. If they thought I wasn't there because I was desperately worried about Lily then we'd have every one of the Croc Creek staff over here in a bedside vigil. It's bad enough that you won't be there.'

'I can't be,' she whispered.

'Of course you can't,' he told her, and then suddenly he tugged her forward so she was leaning into him. He pushed himself to his feet, pulled her up and against him and hugged her. It was a weird, un-Charles-like gesture. It was a gesture of pure physical comfort, nothing else. He released her, but as they both sank back into their chairs he put his fingers out to touch her face and run them across her cheekbone. Gently pausing at the sticking plaster on her cheek.

'You will look after her for me?'

'Of course I will.' She was feeling choked, close to tears.

'I do need to go.'

'And put your dinner suit on.' She managed a smile. 'You look fabulous in a dinner suit.'

'I need my fiancée beside me,' he said, but she shook her head.

'Of course you don't. You don't need anyone.'

'I wish that was the truth,' he said. 'For your sake…' He grimaced. 'Enough. You will ring me if anything changes.'

'Of course.'

'And what we just talked about…'

'Is nonsense talk,' she said. 'Bird flu. Ridiculous.' But she met his eyes and their gazes held. He really believed it, she thought.

'I know,' she said softly. 'It'd cause major panic. I won't say a word. You go off and strut your tail feathers to all the corporate sponsors and I'll keep the home fires burning.'

'There's a bit of a mixed metaphor there.'

'Probably,' she admitted. 'Mixed is the least of how I'm feeling. But, Charles…'

'Yes?'

'See if you can enjoy yourself, just a bit,' she said. 'This opening…you've worked so hard for it. You deserve this night.'

'Then I'm getting what I deserve,' he said, and his voice was suddenly as grim as death.

The official dinner was a glittering occasion, a who's who of Australian corporate money plus anyone who'd been in on the construction of the kids' camp from the beginning. There were corporate bankers, with their wives wearing designer outfits worth thousands. There were doctors from around the world, and politicians. There were the likes of Dora and Walter Grubb in their Sunday best, rubbing shoulders with wealth and loving every minute of it.

Charles moved through the crowd with care, spending time with whoever needed personal attention to ensure further sponsorship, and also making sure anonymous donors, those who'd come because they wanted to see what their money had achieved rather than make a splash themselves, also got attention. The people who'd donated in a small way, like the Grubbs who'd worked tirelessly for this, had to be thanked as well.

He was good at it now. He could almost do it in his sleep.

He could watch the door at the same time. Harry, chief police officer from Crocodile Creek, was working through what needed to be done if the tests came back inconclusive. They were assuming the worst. Like Charles, Harry was wearing a dinner suit so his coming and going was inconspicuous. The messages he was passing on to Charles weren't good.

Neither were the messages he was getting from Beth. 'Two more cases,' she texted him just before the speeches started, and he felt sick.

Then, just before he was due to speak, he received another text. From Jill.

'Lily's awake. We both send our love. Knock 'em dead, Daddy.'

He stared down at the screen of his cell phone and his rigid self-control almost deserted him.

They were great. Jill and Lily.

They deserved a proper family.

He stood up to deliver his speech, holding the sides of the lecturn to steady himself. There were flashlights all around— this camp had the right ingredients to make news all by itself in tomorrow's press. Halfway through his speech he thought, What if it is bird flu? The media will go nuts. It was almost enough to give him pause.

He didn't pause. His rigid self-control held him in good stead. He finished speaking, to thunderous applause. A politician made a longer speech to slightly less applause.

It was over. The formalities were done. The Crocodile Creek Kids' Camp was open.

To be shut tomorrow?

It wasn't a great thought. There were people milling around, congratulating him, wanting to shake his hand. He was starting to seem preoccupied, he thought. 'He's worried about Lily,' he heard Dora say to Grubby.

How soon could he get back to them?

The night dragged on, interminable. He smiled until his face ached. He was back in his wheelchair now, and his left hand stayed in his pocket. He had his phone on vibrate. Willing it to ring? Willing it not to ring. Jill would tell him the minute things changed. He knew she would.

Dammit, he wanted to be there so much he felt sick.

Finally, just when he was about to lose it, tell these people they weren't wanted, to get the hell out of there, Beth appeared at the door. He was talking to Rick Allandale, the father of one of the camp kids. Rick was overbearing and pompous and had been telling him all the things that should be improved in the camp.

Beth slid easily into the conversation, smiled charmingly at Rick and intercepted an elderly man with a vast pot belly.

'Sir Henry... I'm not sure if you know Rick Allendale. Lauren, Rick's daughter, is one of our very favourite camp kids. Rick, Henry is head of Scotsdale Packing. You were saying we needed more recreational facilities? I'm betting if you told Henry exactly what we needed you might both be able to work something out to the benefit of everyone.'

She smiled sweetly at them both, then turned her back on them, effectively getting Charles for herself.

'See,' she said, grinning at the look on his face. 'It's not only you who can play the politician. Want some good news?'

'Yes!'

'The test result's come back clear. No meningitis.'

He closed his eyes. Of all the scenarios, meningitis was the worst. But then...

'And her temp's dropped,' Beth said. 'Not much but enough to think that maybe she's turning the corner. She fell asleep about an hour ago. It seems a lovely, natural sleep.'

So even if it was bird flu, she might recover. The consequences of bird flu would be appalling, but for now all he could think was that Lily was improving.

How could he worry about the greater good when his kid was threatened? It was an impossible ask.

'Do you want to tell Jill it's not meningitis?' Beth asked.

'You haven't told her?'

'Nope. If you go through to the ward now, you'll see why not.'

'I can't leave here.'

'Yes, you can,' she said forcibly. 'If anyone dares question it I'll say Lily's test results have come through negative for meningitis and you need to tell Jill. There's not a soul in this room—even the ghastly Allendales—who'd question that. Go, Charles.'

'But—'

'But you have a dozen or more Croc Creek doctors working this room,' she said. 'You've done your duty here. Your duty now is to your family.'

She sounded so stern that he almost smiled.

'Yes, ma'am,' he said, and he went.

It wasn't just Lily who was sleeping. It was Jill as well.

Barrier nursing? He didn't think so. Jill had slid onto the bed and held her little daughter close. Lily was curled in against her in a pose as old as time itself.

They slept.

Charles wheeled across to the bed and stared down at the pair of them. The tension in Jill's face had eased in sleep. She looked younger, he thought. She looked...vulnerable.

The contrast between the women he'd just been with was stark. This morning Jill had hauled on a T-shirt and shorts. Maybe she'd brushed her hair but it surely hadn't seen a comb for the rest of the day. Her curls were tangled out onto the pillow behind her.

The sticking plaster on her cheek looked almost shocking.

He wheeled to the bottom of the bed and fetched the thermometer. Carefully, so he wouldn't disturb either of them, he slid it into the fold under Lily's arm.

And waited.

Thirty-eight point one.

It was down a point and a half since he'd last been here. It was down half a point since Beth had checked half an hour ago.

He closed his eyes in thankfulness and when he opened them Jill was watching him.

Blankly. Expecting the worst.

'Not bad,' he whispered, and because he couldn't help himself he reached over and touched her nose. It was a feather touch, a simple way of grounding him to her. 'Don't look like that, love. The test results have come back. No meningitis.'

'No?'

'No.'

'And…' She swallowed. 'And bird flu?'

'Those tests will take longer,' he said gravely. 'But Lily's temperature is dropping. Beth thinks, and I concur, that she's coming out of the woods. Even if it is bird flu, she's looking like she'll be OK.'

'Oh, Charles.' She didn't move. She couldn't. She was on her side, facing him, but Lily was curled in against her. A slow tear trickled down her cheek and Charles grabbed his beautifully starched handkerchief from his dinner suit pocket and wiped it away.

Something flashed outside the window. Lightning? He barely caught it and it was gone.

No matter. Jill was choking back a chuckle. 'I don't think those handkerchiefs are meant for real wiping.'

'It's damned useless if it isn't,' he growled. He sighed. 'Jill, I need to go.'

'Of course you do,' she whispered, though her face clouded. 'There are other sick children.'

'Of course.' She took a grip. 'I'm sorry. That was really selfish of me. How did your dinner go?'

'Interminably.'

She smiled. 'Your favourite thing—making speeches.'

'Yeah, well…' He was smiling at her too damned much. He caught himself and tugged the wheels of his chair away from the bed. 'I…I'll see you later.'

'You need to go to bed.'

'Not yet.' He hesitated. 'Will you…?' There was a host of questions in these two little words but Jill didn't feel competent to answer any of them.

'I need to stay here,' she said.

'Of course you do.'

'Not because…'

'I understand that, too,' he assured her, and maybe he did and maybe he didn't. On a logical level he understood. On a gut level he hated it.

'Goodnight, then.'

'Charles?'

'Yes?'

'You're not going to kiss us goodnight?'

He stared at them both. His mouth twisted again, as if there was dark humour in what he was thinking.

'Barrier nursing,' he said at last, and he wheeled away and left the ward.

He'd called her love.

'Don't look like that, love.'

He hadn't even known he'd done it, she thought. It had been an involuntary figure of speech.

He was calling Lily sweetheart. He'd called her love.

It was enough.

There was a long way to go, she thought sleepily. She thought back to Charles's reaction on the beach, his hatred of the fact that he couldn't defend her. There'd always be a barrier, she thought.

It didn't matter. He'd called her love. He'd touched her nose.

She was behaving like a moonstruck teenager.

She didn't care, she thought suddenly, defiantly. She was in bed with her daughter and all the signs were that Lily would recover. The appalling threat of meningitis had been lifted.

Other kids were sick.

They were, and she'd worry about them in the morning. She promised herself that. But for tonight... Tonight she had Lily in her arms and Charles had called her love.

It was enough to be going on with, she thought dreamily.

Lily stirred in her sleep and Jill hugged her closer. Usually Lily pulled away. She didn't much like cuddles.

Not now. She was huddled against Jill like a kitten needing warmth.

Tonight she'd take this as a happy ever after, Jill thought. She'd ignore Charles's comments about barrier nursing. This was time out.

It was a time for believing that love could really work.

CHAPTER TEN

'YOU'VE got to close the island.'

It wasn't what he wanted to hear. He hadn't slept. The bungalow had seemed cold and empty without Jill and Lily. The big bed had seemed...well, too damned big. At dawn he'd come back to the hospital. Lily had been fast asleep and Jill had gone to find a change of clothes and take a shower. And now this...

He'd talked to Beth. He'd talked to the rangers and to Harry, as representative of the state's police force.

Even then he'd been unsure, but Beth had suggested consulting her ex-husband. Angus Stuart was a pathologist with an interest in epidemiology. He'd been over at the resort at the medical conference.

Fifteen minutes after he arrived at the medical centre he was telling Charles what he didn't want to hear.

'You must have had similar thoughts yourself, given the number of dead birds,' Angus told him. 'We have to quarantine the whole island until we know more. It's a thousand to one chance that it's anything sinister, but lower odds than that are still too big a chance to take.'

The implications were enormous. Charles was struggling to take them in.

'It has to be done and it has to be done now,' Angus said, in a voice that brooked no opposition. 'It'd be criminal to allow even one person who could be carrying a deadly virus to leave the island. We'll have to get the police and health authorities to trace anyone who's left in the last week and isolate them as well.'

That'd be the easy part, Charles thought. But convincing people to stay...especially if there was a deadly disease around...

'I need to talk to Harry again,' he said heavily. 'There's so much...' He took a deep breath. 'It needs to be me who breaks the news. I'll set up a briefing room. I'll contact Harry.'

He hesitated. 'But first I need to talk to Jill.'

She was just out of the shower. She was sitting in the chair beside Lily's bed, towelling her hair dry. She looked up as he entered and smiled, nodding toward the sleeping Lily, signalling that she was better still. And then her smile faded as he glanced briefly at Lily and returned his gaze directly to her.

'What is it?'

'Nothing more than last night,' he said quickly. Damn, he hadn't meant to panic her. 'But we've decided to close the island.'

'We?'

'Beth's ex-husband is here. He's at the resort, giving a paper at the conference. He's an epidemiologist.'

'He says it's bird flu?' The fear in her eyes was still there. He wheeled forward and took her hands. They were wet from her hair. They felt great, he thought. She had the best hands. Lovely, practical, caring hands. Seductive hands. Spine-tinglingly sensitive hands. A man could fall in love with those hands.

He had a flashback of what those hands had been doing...had it only been the night before last?—and he had to concentrate fiercely on what needed to be said.

'Angus says it's a thousand to one it's not bird flu,' he said. 'But whatever the virus is, it's nasty, aggressive and spreading. Given we have dead birds, given how sick Lily and Robbie grew, and how fast, we have no choice.'

'People will panic,' she whispered.

'They will. I need you not to panic.'

'I won't panic.'

'Thank you,' he said, and went to pull away. But she held on.

'You look exhausted.'

'I'm fine.'

'You're not.'

'You look after you and Lily,' he said. 'I've looked after myself so long now I don't know any other way.'

The hardest part was breaking the news. As many staff as could be spared, from the camp, the clinic, the national park and from the resort, were asked to attend the lecture theatre at the convention centre.

Thank God Angus was here, Charles thought. The man spoke informatively, in a way that was intended not to spread alarm.

'It's highly unlikely to be bird flu,' he told them. 'But because it's similar to a flu virus, we believe flu vaccine might stave off infection in people not already infected. A number of you are hospital staff or in related medical fields so you'll have already had flu shots this year, but we're flying in more stock and will vaccinate everyone on the island who isn't already covered. There are also antivirals which will help ease symptoms. We believe we have things under control. The quarantine is a precaution only and the last thing we need is panic.'

Charles was watching faces. There were resort guests here, too. How had they found about this? Damn, this lecture wasn't meant for them. He'd meant this to be for staff, with tactics worked out here to minimise alarm.

It was too late now. There was definite alarm.

'We should have tests results within forty-eight hours,' Angus was saying. 'That means in forty-eight hours you'll probably all be able to go home. But in the meantime we must act as if bird flu is a possibility, however remote. We know that more than ninety-nine per cent of bird flu cases have

come from direct contact with infected birds, so it's imperative we warn guests and staff to keep away from all birds,
whether alive or dead. We've already ordered full body suits
with rebreathing masks to be flown to the island. As soon as
they arrive we'll roster people to collect and dispose of any
remaining dead birds.'

He didn't say the cull might end up including all birds,
Charles thought bleakly. The bird life on Wallaby Island was
fantastic. A cull was unthinkable.

It had to be thought of.

There were questions coming at them from all sides
now. He had to concentrate as he and Angus fielded question after desperate question. Then, just as he thought the
questions were at an end, there was a stir at the back of the
room. A thick-set man and his two sons. Cray Harris, Zach
and Dom.

The two thugs from the beach yesterday, with their father.

Almost the moment he saw them he saw Jill. She'd come
in late, and was standing at the back, almost hidden in the crush.

Why had she come? To support him? The thought was a
shot of warmth in an atmosphere of chill fear.

'You can't stop us leaving,' Cray Harris was saying—
shouting.

'We can.' It was Harry, dressed in his official police
uniform. He'd been standing quietly to one side, not wanting
to make this seem any greater a threat than it already was.

His words caused a deathly silence.

'How?' the man said belligerently.

'Quarantine rules granted to me by the Department of
Health mean I have jurisdiction to arrest anyone trying to
leave the island,' Harry said, strolling to the front of the
small stage and meeting Cray's belligerence head on.
'Angus and Charles here have been telling me that this quarantine is likely to be short—probably only for two days.
Chances are this isn't bird flu. We're probably overreacting.

When the testing comes through negative everyone will be allowed to leave—except for those people who've attempted to break quarantine regulations. Those people will find themselves in jail for the two years' maximum sentence the law allows. You try and leave the island, I'll lock you up. As simple as that.'

It put things in perspective. There were people who'd been clearly about to ask the same question. Charles had seen the beginnings of plans forming—private boats, a bribe in exchange for a blind eye.

Harry's statement stopped that in its tracks.

'We'll keep you informed every step of the way,' Harry assured everyone. 'Thank you. But, Mr Harris, can I ask you to stay behind? I need to talk to you and to your sons.'

That was the end of the briefing. Their audience filed out, muttering among themselves in subdued tones. Jill looked as if she might leave, too, but Charles beckoned her down to his side.

'I need to get back to Lily,' she said as she reached him. She felt odd here. She'd only come because, well, because Lily was asleep and it seemed right to be here. Charles shouldn't have to bear everything on his broad shoulders.

'Yes, but you need to hear this,' he said. 'Harry was thinking he'd do this later, but we're all together now.'

'What?' She gazed around, puzzled. Everyone was gone barring Charles, Harry and Cray Harris, and Zach and Dom, standing uncertainly at the top of the tiered seating.

'Come on down,' Harry said cordially.

'Why the hell?' The man looked furious.

'I need to explain why I'm not planning to arrest your sons,' Harry said.

There was a sharp intake of breath. Cray swung round to face his boys. 'What the—'

'Come down,' Harry said again, his voice turning steely.

'We're going back to the hotel,' Zach muttered, but his

father put a large hand in the small of his son's back and propelled him down the steps with force.

'Thank you,' Harry said, but he didn't smile.

'What the hell's going on? I've got things to do,' Cray said angrily. 'I've a hundred phone calls to make.'

'And so do your boys have things to do,' Harry said gently. 'Boys, this is Sister Jill Shaw, our director of nursing. Do you recognise her?'

'She's the... She was swimming yesterday,' Zach muttered, not looking at her.

'Charles tells me you threw a stone at her. You cut her face.' Harry's voice had changed completely now. His tone was almost frightening. It was so soft they could hardly hear it, but for Jill, who'd had no idea what had been coming, it sent a shiver down her spine.

'We didn't,' Zach spat, but his face said he had.

'You know, both Charles and Jill say you did,' Harry said. 'And one of our groundsmen, Walter Grubb, saw you as well. They all say you threw the stone, deliberately intending to hurt her.'

'It was an accident,' Zach muttered.

'Then I'm sure you want to make up for it.'

Jill's gaze flew to Charles. This was his doing, she thought. How had he managed...?

'We have protective suits arriving here in two hours,' Harry went on. 'Then we'll be asking for volunteers to spread out over the island and collect bird carcasses. I expect you two to be our first volunteers.'

The boys gasped as one. It wasn't a prospect that would attract anyone. For these two, the indulged sons of a very rich man, it must seem unthinkable.

It was unthinkable. 'In your dreams,' Dom jeered.

'Then I have no choice but to arrest you for the assault on Sister Jill Shaw,' Harry said implacably. 'You do not have to say anything but anything you do say—'

'Hey,' Cray said, and held up his hand. 'Hang on there!'

'Yes, Mr Harris?'

'You guys threw stones at a nurse?' he demanded incredulously of his sons.

'We didn't know she was a nurse,' Zach whined. 'I mean, she was with a cripple.'

The big man stared at his sons, truly appalled. 'You guys threw stones? To hurt someone? Why the hell?'

'We were bored.'

There was a moment's stunned silence.

'I'll give you bored,' Cray roared, embarrassed, humiliated, close to apoplectic with fury. 'Of all the stupid, dumb, mindless... Right. That's it. Your mother's indulgence stops now. As does mine. To think I let you out of school for this holiday... First you can apologise. Right here. Right now. If there's anything else Sister Shaw wants you to do, you'll do that, too. And then, of course, you're volunteering. You're volunteering until this bird thing clears,' he said furiously. 'Even if it takes a year.'

They were left alone.

Jill felt...winded.

'You set that up,' she said at last, wonderingly. 'With all you had on your mind, you set that up.'

'If you thought I'd have let those little thugs get away with it...'

'You're still angry about it?'

'Of course I'm angry.' Charles looked at her steadily. 'You would have liked it if I'd been able to chase them and knock their heads together?'

'I would have liked it if I'd been able to chase them and knock their heads together.'

'But you never would. Pacifist Jill.'

'Is there something wrong with that?'

'Not if it's what you want,' he said, and she flushed.

'Of course I want it.'

'Which is why it's OK to marry me,' he said softly. 'You don't think I'm capable of violence.'

'I didn't say that.'

'You didn't have to.' He said it bleakly but then caught himself and smiled. 'I'm sorry. It's unfair. We are what we are. Damaged goods.'

'Hey, speak for yourself.' She tried to smile back but her smile didn't reach her eyes.

'That's how you see yourself.'

'Look, there's nothing wrong with not wanting violence,' she retorted.

'Of course there's not. But you're frightened of it. Not normally frightened. You're expecting it. All the time. You see it as the norm.'

'I don't.'

'Do you see marriage to me as safe?'

'I don't see any marriage as safe,' she confessed, and then pushed her hair wearily back from her face. 'I'm sorry. Charles, we can make a go of this. We can have fun.'

'When you forget that you're frightened.' He looked at her steadily. 'You're still terrified of Kelvin. But you're not frightened of bird flu. You slept all night with Lily. When you need to be, you're brave.'

'I am, aren't I?' she said mockingly. 'It's only loud voices that turn me to jelly. A little bit of bird flu is nothing.'

'So we need to avoid loud noises.'

'It'd be good,' she whispered. She hesitated. 'I'm sorry. That sounds wimpy. I decided that I don't want to be wimpy. It was only the stone that brought it all back.' And the words. *Ugly cow...*

'Damn.' He swore harshly into the stillness and pushed himself to his feet. He'd braked his chair so he could use it to steady himself but he didn't hold it. Instead, he reached out and took Jill's hands, drawing her into him. 'If I was—'

'Don't,' she muttered, distressed. 'There's too many ifs.'

'There are, aren't there?' he said ruefully, stroking her hair. 'If we could turn back time… But we can't. What we can do is make this as good as it gets.'

'That's a movie,' she whispered. 'As good as it gets.'

'Did they live happily ever after?'

'Probably not,' she admitted. 'But better than apart.'

'That's what this will be for you?'

'I… Maybe.'

'Jill, sex with you…'

'It was good, wasn't it?' she whispered, and the smile came back into her voice.

'As good as it gets?' he said. 'Or better?'

'Maybe we need to work on it,' she suggested, and she tried to keep her voice prim but failed.

He held her at arm's length and smiled at her. 'You're laughing.'

'Not me. Sex is a serious business.'

'Really?'

'Maybe not,' she said. 'Maybe that's why people do it in the dark. So they don't have to see that it looks ridiculous. All those wobbly bits.'

'There speaks a true medical professional,' he said, and grinned. 'Wobbly bits. Which particular pieces of our anatomy would you be referring to?'

'You'll never know while the lights are out,' she said, and then thought, Whoa, what had she said? She wasn't asking. She wasn't even suggesting.

But Charles was looking at her with a gleam that said he thought she had been asking, she had been suggesting.

'Tonight?'

'Lily's ill.'

'I'm thinking Lily may well have turned the corner.'

'I won't leave her in the hospital by herself.'

'She'll be fine.'

'She might be fine. I don't want her to be fine without me.'

'It's OK for us to be fine without each other?'

'Of course it is,' she said, startled. 'We don't want dependency.'

'Of course we don't.' But he didn't sound sure.

He'd been stroking her hair, sifting her curls with his long, lean fingers. It did lovely things to her. More than lovely. It was making her feel… Melting.

Was the head supposed to be an erogenous zone? She'd have to look it up. Later. After he'd stopped. There was no way she was stopping him now.

But he stopped himself and she could have wept with loss.

'I need to get back to work,' he said reluctantly. 'We need to get this quarantine sorted. The powers that be are sending in a biohazard lab we need to set up. There's a million protocols. I need to get antiviral therapy started.'

'Plus you'll have hysterical people wanting to get off the island.'

'That's Harry's job,' he said seriously. 'He's the policeman. He copes with the scary stuff.'

'You just cope with the deadly disease.'

'*We* do,' he said. 'Jill, I can't tell you how much it means to me that you're here.'

But his voice was formal again. What was it? she wondered. What had shifted the mood? Her saying she didn't want dependency?

Surely he didn't want a clinging vine.

She didn't understand. All she knew was that he'd suddenly taken a step back, emotionally as well as physically. She watched in silence as he dropped back into his chair and released the brake.

Emotion over. Time to move back into medical mode.

And she needed to get back to Lily. Of course she did. There was no other choice.

'I'll see you soon,' she whispered.

'I guess you will,' he said, and his voice was even more formal. 'Keep Lily safe for me.' He took a deep breath. 'OK, now let's watch as all hell breaks loose.'

He'd been good to her, and it felt wrong.

He was in control, she thought as she made her way back through the hospital to Lily's ward. He'd stroked her hair, he'd raked her curls with his fingers, he'd set her back away from him, deciding they both needed to move on, he'd made her feel…protected.

She didn't want to feel protected, she thought suddenly, savagely. She wanted to feel…

Hot.

It was such an unexpected emotion that it had her stopping dead in the corridor and Beth, coming swiftly along the corridor behind her, almost bumped into the back of her.

'Whoops, sorry,' Beth said, and then she paused as she saw Jill's face. 'What's wrong?' And then, more urgently, 'Lily?'

'No,' Jill said, fast, though she tugged open Lily's door just to make sure. But Lily was just as she'd left her, sound asleep. The high colour in her cheeks had faded. Even from here she looked more normal. 'I think…'

'We all think,' Beth said solidly. 'We're all sure she'll be OK.'

'Robbie's not.'

'No,' Beth agreed gravely. 'He's not. Is that why you were looking like you were about to cry?'

'I wasn't.'

'Or is it Charles?' she said, more gently still.

'I… No.'

'I guess it's Charles,' Beth said softly, and then as Jill couldn't think of a reply, Beth caught her hand and lifted her ring to the light. 'It's a lovely ring,' she murmured, still watching Jill's face.

'It…it is.'

'You don't sound so sure.'

'It's just…' But she couldn't say. In truth, she didn't know. What was wrong with her? This was all just too complicated.

On the surface it had seemed easy. But when it got deeper it got hard. Too hard. And Beth was watching her, her eyes compassionate, waiting for a response.

'I think I want a husband,' Jill said at last, as if compelled to answer an unasked question. 'Not a medical superintendent.'

'Really?' Beth grinned. 'I can see you two playing doctors and nurses.' But her smile faded as she caught the fear in Jill's eyes. 'So what's wrong with that? I thought when I saw you yesterday morning…'

'I seduced him,' Jill said, and suddenly her voice was almost a wail. 'Of all the stupid, immature…'

'Wow!' Beth's eyes widened. Marcia came up behind them with an armload of linen. Beth grabbed Jill's arm and tugged her sideways into the tiny theatrette. 'Medical team meeting,' she said to a bemused Marcia. 'See that we're not disturbed.' She closed the door behind them.

'So you seduced him,' she said, leaning on the door in case Marcia couldn't resist joining in. 'And he submitted, kicking and screaming all the way.'

'Of course not. I shouldn't be saying…'

'No, that's just it,' Beth said. She left the door, put her hands on her friend's shoulders and pushed her back to sit on the examination couch. 'You never say. Neither of you. Look, I'm a newcomer here. A month working in Crocodile Creek and two weeks on this island is hardly enough for me to figure everything that's going on. But you two…everyone holds you in respect. You hold each other in respect. Here's Charles being so damned paternalistic…'

'He is, isn't he?'

'While you'd like him to take you to his lair, ravish you with red-hot kisses, smoulder you with molten desire…'

Jill blinked. 'Pardon?'

'Romance novels,' Beth said. 'I love 'em.'

'I don't think…'

'Come on, Jill, admit you wouldn't mind a bit of molten passion.'

'I did admit it,' she wailed. 'But now I feel stupid.'

'Because he's gone back to being paternalistic?'

'Yes!'

'Any particular reason?'

'I… Maybe I've brought it on myself,' she admitted. 'I mean…he knows I hate violence.' She shook her head. 'He's so kind. He was really kind to me just then. But I don't know…' She pushed her hair back from her face, trying to make her confused mind think.

She'd lost her hairband some time in the night and she hadn't had time to find a new one.

Lily was still asleep. She had time to fix her hair now. Get herself together. Stop being needy.

'He's a proud man,' Beth said thoughtfully.

'Yeah, and I'm a stupid woman,' Jill said. 'Beth, sorry. You were in the wrong place at the wrong time. Can we forget we had this conversation?'

'Sure,' Beth said, and her face softened. 'No. I'm not sure. I think you should keep talking. To Charles, if not to me. Tell him what you'd like.'

'See, that's just it,' Jill said, pushing herself to her feet. 'I don't know what it is that I would like.'

On the other side of the building Charles was having almost exactly the same conversation with Garf. Garf was confined to quarters and was bored enough to lie still and listen while Charles alternately barked orders into the phone and bellyached to the dog.

On the surface he was organising the logistics of the biohazard lab. A Black Hawk helicopter was on its way, loaded with gear designed to turn this place into an efficient, effective quarantine station. He had to be ready.

So he worked. In the gaps between phone calls he told Garf about Jill.

'I don't want her being kind,' he told the dog, and Garf made a strenuous effort to look intelligent.

'It's not that I don't want her, though.' He needed to say that, even though it was only to Garf. He wouldn't want even a dog to be getting the wrong idea.

For he definitely wanted her, he thought over and over as the arrangements for quarantine fell into place. Hell, he wanted her.

But on any terms?

She'd made love to him. Out of kindness?

Did he want that sort of loving?

Yes, a part of him shouted. He'd get what she was offering under any terms she cared to name.

But he knew it wasn't true. Even Garf was looking at him as if he knew it wasn't true. Gratitude... The last thing he wanted to think of when he was making love was how much he owed her.

It left a sour taste in his mouth which grew and grew.

How long could he stay married when the woman he loved felt sorry for him?

'And don't you feel sorry for me,' he told the soulful-eyed dog at his feet. 'Feel sorry for yourself. You're stuck within the campgrounds unless you're under supervision, to keep you away from the birds. Me...I'm just stuck.'

They were waiting for him outside, trying to decide on the site for the temporary lab. He had to go. He shoved his chair forward so hard that he misjudged the distance and hit the doorjamb. The metal from his chair's footrest took a neat wedge out of the skirting board.

'Good,' he said in grim satisfaction, and Garf eyed him with care, edged forward to his visitor's chair and gave the leg a tentative chew.

'Don't even think about it,' Charles warned him. 'I can be

destructive. Not you. Jill hates violence but me…I'm feeling more and more like violence. If I were you, dog, I'd be very good indeed.'

He shoved the door open. Garf gave a joyous leap toward freedom, only to be caught up by the length of rope round his neck.

'See,' Charles said grimly. 'Me and you both. Get used to it.'

Lily was definitely on the mend. By late that night she was sitting up in bed, sucking on flavoured ice, snuggling into Jill's arms and able to summon a smile when Charles wheeled through to see how she did.

'I've been really sick,' she whispered.

'You have,' Charles said, and his gut wrenched at the sight of how gaunt she'd become, and so fast. There was little enough of her at the best of times, but forty-eight hours of fever and no food had made her almost skeletal. 'Would you like something to eat?'

'No,' Lily said. And then, cautiously, she went on, 'Jelly beans?'

'Your wish is my command,' Charles said, thankful her request was something they always had at hand. He wheeled out to the nurses' station and came back with a handful.

'Not black ones.'

'I'll eat the black ones,' Jill said.

'They make your tongue go black.'

'So I'll have a scary tongue.'

He wanted them. Jill was sitting on the bed, smiling down at her little daughter, and he wanted them both so badly it was a physical pain. But Lily still had her IV line up. It wasn't safe to let her go back to the cabin yet, and Jill wouldn't go back to the cabin without Lily.

Maybe he could discharge her. For his own dishonourable reasons?

Of course he couldn't. Beth was Lily's doctor. He and Jill

needed to let Beth be in charge, do what she said, be parents instead of doctors.

'I want to go home,' Lily whispered.

'Not until Dr Beth says so,' Jill decreed, echoing his thoughts.

'Can Garf come and visit?'

'Not yet.'

'But he always visits the sick kids in camp.'

'You've got an illness that people might be able to catch,' Charles said. 'People can wash their hands and be careful about catching things. Garf would probably lick your face.'

Lily giggled. It was a tiny giggle but it sounded great. She snuggled against Jill, even closer than she had been. Possessive.

He put his hand out to stroke her cheek.

And then he flinched as light flooded the room. He turned to the window, just in time to see a blur of white—a man?—backing fast back into the darkness.

A photographer? What the hell…?

Media, he thought bitterly. They'd get photographs every way they could. This was huge. The possibility of bird flu would be on the front of every newspaper in the country.

'What was that?' Jill asked.

'I'll find out,' he said grimly, knowing his chances of stopping such intrusions were tiny. They needed security guards. They needed… Hell, they needed more resources than he could envisage. Quarantining a whole island…

'Will you sleep with me again tonight?' Lily asked Jill, and Charles knew her answer before she'd formed it.

'Of course.'

'That means you have to sleep all by yourself,' Lily said to Charles, and she sounded worried. 'Will you be scared?'

'No.'

'Will Garf sleep with you?'

'Of course he will,' Jill said soundly. 'Garf's the best dog in the world for stopping Charles being scared.' Her gaze met Charles's and held.

'He's Daddy,' Lily whispered, her eyelids drooping and the hand holding her jelly beans drooping as well, forcing Charles to wheel forward and take them from her. 'He's not Charles. He's Daddy.'

'That's right,' Jill said. 'Not Charles. Daddy.'

Was it a start? Maybe, but he sure as hell didn't want to be Daddy to Jill.

He lay in the too big bed that night and tried to concentrate on all the things that had to be done the next day. He was surrounded by chaos—furious guests from the resort, panicked camp parents, bureaucrats wanting answers, the media… There was so much for his mind to sort that the last thing it should be doing was sorting trivia.

Daddy.

It wasn't trivia, he thought. It was a fantastic start by Lily.

One down and one to go? He wanted to be Daddy to Lily. He wanted to be Charles to Jill. Not boss Charles or protector Charles or even friend Charles. He knew what he wanted.

He wanted the world.

CHAPTER ELEVEN

MONDAY was a blur. A crazy mix of high drama, bureaucracy, paperwork and personal involvement.

Even normal flu could be fatal in this set-up, Charles thought bleakly as he worked his way through everything the day threw at him. Like five-year-old Danny… Struggling to recover from cancer, infection led to almost lethal build-up in cranial pressure. Danny proved to be the exception to the quarantine rule—he had to be evacuated if he was to live. The protocols for getting that done proved a major headache.

Susie, their physiotherapist, was hit hard, the virus turning into potentially lethal pneumonia almost instantly. That shook the entire medical staff. Charles's job was to hold the team together, but watching Susie fight for her life shook even his steely control. Luckily the crisis was as short-lived as it was intense, but who knew who'd get ill next?

At least his own personal drama was lightening. Lily woke feeling better. As Charles wheeled in on his regular rounds she snuggled tight against her adoptive mother and peered at him with caution. And hope.

'Dr Beth says I can go home,' she whispered.

'To Croc Creek?'

'No, silly, to our bungalow,' Lily whispered, and snuggled against Jill some more. Jill kissed her hair and held her close, and Charles saw the glimmer of tears behind her tired eyes.

This self-contained woman was cracking inside. Opening to love?

Maybe, he thought. Maybe, he hoped. How far could she go?

'Maybe Charles can take us all home,' she whispered.

Lily considered. 'With Garf?'

'Maybe with Garf,' Charles said, and thought this felt great. Negotiating deals with his little daughter when two days ago he'd held grave fears for her life.

If only they could get past the acute stage with everyone. He'd heard from the hospital down south that Danny was starting to improve, but there were still two critically ill patients in the clinic and there were three more kids showing symptoms.

Dammit, there had to be a cause. Was it the birds?

'At least the biohazard lab's here now,' he told Jill. She'd been watching his face and he knew she was worrying about the same thing he was. 'Angus is starting tests on blood samples already. He's saying we might even have a result tonight.'

'As soon as that?'

'It'd be great,' he said. 'As long as…'

'As long as it's not bird flu?'

'There's a possibility it might be some sort of encephalitis,' he said. 'That's what Angus is thinking.'

'Isn't that caused by mosquitoes?'

'I've got a mosquito bite on my arm,' Lily said, and poked a skinny arm out to be inspected. 'It's itchy.'

They both grinned at one red bump on one skinny arm— a medical imperative where the imperative had been much, much more frightening. And suddenly they were grinning at each other.

Only Jill backed off. Her smile started wide and free, but suddenly it was like she remembered she had no right to feel like that.

What would it take to have her relax with him again? It was like she'd taken one huge step over her boundary, scared herself stupid and retreated.

Well, if she thought he was staying on his side of the wall…

He had to, he thought grimly. Rushing her… There was no way he could.

'Dr Wetherby?' It was Marcia, calling from the corridor. 'Robbie's mother's on the phone from Melbourne. Can you speak to her?'

He winced. Robbie's mum had four other children, all younger than Robbie. She was desperately frightened to have Robbie ill and so far away.

'I'll ring her back in five minutes,' he told Marcia. 'Meanwhile ask her if she can get on to the Internet. Beth's with him—right? She's being almost a surrogate mother to him. I'll grab the digital camera. A picture of Beth cuddling him might do his mum more good than any reassurance I can give.'

'It should,' Marcia said, smiling her agreement. 'We have so many doctors we can almost have one-on-one attention. Robbie has Dr Beth. Susie has Dr Vavunis. Our Lily here has you two.'

'They're my mum and dad,' Lily said firmly.

Charles smiled. But then he glanced at Jill and his smile faded.

She looked fearful.

She wouldn't believe in happiness, he thought. Would she spend the rest of her life not believing she could move out of the shadows?

Even though they had an over-supply of doctors, there was still a mass of work that only he could do. But he did manage to go with Jill and Lily late that afternoon when Beth decreed Lily could return to the bungalow. She'd lost her bounce, he thought as he watched Jill carry her up the steps. In all the time they'd cared for her, Lily had refused to be carried. Even when she'd fallen off her swing and given herself a greenstick fracture of the arm four months ago, she'd refused to be held.

Now she was clinging so tightly to Jill that he was worried

all over again. And when he said he had to return to the clinic her face crumpled into tears.

'I want you to stay.'

'Charles has to go,' Jill said, trying to sound firm.

'I'll be back tonight,' he said.

'When tonight?' Lily demanded fiercely. 'To read me a bedtime story?'

'I'll try.'

'It's not fair,' she whined.

'We're fine alone,' Jill said, and they all had to regroup after that.

This family business was getting complicated.

Be careful what you wish for, Charles thought ruefully as he wheeled back along the path leading to the beach. The bio-hazard lab was just up from the cove. He'd just check with Angus to see how things were going.

Things weren't going. 'It'll be some hours,' Angus told him. 'I'll let you know. Will you be in your bungalow?'

'I might be. Or I might be sitting outside this damned lab, just waiting.'

And in the end that's where he was. For medical imperatives took over and by the time he returned to the bungalow both Lily and Jill were asleep.

Together in the big bed.

We're fine alone.

They didn't stir as he wheeled silently into the bedroom. Stealth on wheels—that's how his junior staff described him. He wheeled in and looked across the bed at his future wife and his daughter, their heads just touching on the one pillow.

What would a normal father do? Wake them up? Ask them to shove aside, climb in beside them, cuddle them both and fall asleep? It was so far out of his orbit that it seemed unimaginable.

There was an empty room in the clinic now Danny had

been evacuated. He'd sleep in there. If anyone asked he'd tell them he wanted to be around when the results came through.

He did want to be around when the results came through.

He gazed for another long moment at the woman and child peacefully sleeping and his mouth twisted. So near…

It was an impossible ask. The familiarity of family. Where the hell did one start?

Not here. Not now.

'Goodnight,' he whispered, but they didn't stir.

He turned and went out into the night. To sit outside a lab and wait.

It was better than waiting for what might never happen.

And as he went Jill's eyes opened. She stared bleakly out through the darkened doorway.

What sort of stupid cowardice had kept her silent?

What sort of cowardice was driving her forward?

The results came through at ten. The door of the lab opened. Angus came out, leading Beth by the hand. Joyous.

Charles was sitting back a little so he could look out over the moonlit sea as he waited. Their body language spoke of triumph. And more.

Here was another one, he thought bleakly. Another Croc Creek romance.

But at least the news they carried was good. Great!

They approached him with concern. 'Are you all right?' was the first question Beth asked as they approached him, and he thought he must seem a figure for sympathy. Sitting alone late at night, waiting for test results. He normally slept little but he'd slept so little in the last few days that he knew his face must be showing signs of strain. And Beth was a doctor who saw beyond the surface.

'Should I be?' he said wearily. 'We've had an outbreak of a potentially fatal disease on the island. I've my ward—my daughter—Lily in hospital, we've had to break quarantine to fly a desperately ill child to the mainland…'

She didn't believe his reasons. He watched her face and he knew she was thinking of Jill. That was his penance for employing good doctors, he thought. He should try employing a few who treated outward symptoms and didn't go fishing where they weren't wanted.

'At least we can take one load off your shoulders,' Angus said gently. 'It's not bird flu. I can show you the screens if you like—I've left them up. The genetic make-up of whatever we have here is totally different to bird flu. In fact, it's not flu at all. We're back to mosquitoes and encephalitis, and even though that has severe consequences it's not the start of some pandemic. We can raise the quarantine—people can leave the island.'

Encephalitis. A blood-borne virus carried by mosquitoes.

'It makes sense,' Charles said slowly, thinking it through. 'Even though we had to take precautions over bird flu, we've been thinking further. We had a vast number of trees uprooted in the cyclone. Where they came out we've got depressions in the ground that have filled with water and made ideal mosquito breeding grounds. Also, with the fierce winds of the cyclone… If it's encephalitis I'm guessing there's been some different strain of mosquito blown down from the northern islands.' He shook his head. 'Too easy. We can get the depressions filled. It's such a contained area we can do a spray. The dry season will get rid of the last of them… We just have to weather this patch.'

'And we'll all live happily ever after,' Angus said.

'Yeah,' he agreed and tried to look cheerful. 'Thank you both,' he said. 'Doing the lab work was dangerous.'

'It had its compensations,' Angus said, and Charles glanced at Beth, who blushed and grinned.

'Right,' he said dryly.

'Will you tell Jill now?' Beth asked, and once again he had the feeling that Beth saw too much. His staff accused him of having second sight. Here he was on the other side of the fence, and he wasn't enjoying it one bit.

'I guess. If she's awake,' he said brusquely. 'But there's a thousand phone calls to make before then. I need to get on.'

And he wheeled away, leaving them to their happiness.

He spent an hour on the phone contacting all relevant authorities. He also contacted Mike Poulos, the helicopter pilot, who was here with his wife Emily. Mike had been going quietly nuts, worrying that Emily could catch whatever this was. In the first trimester of pregnancy, treating her would be really problematic.

Even though the need no longer seemed urgent, Charles knew the only way Mike would relax would be if he could get her off the island. He made the call and twenty minutes later watched the helicopter take off.

Emily was still protesting. 'This is crazy. I can wear insect repellent. It's the middle of the night. I'm not an emergency.'

But Mike's face said it all. He loved Emily so fiercely that a middle-of-the-night flight meant nothing.

Here it was again. Gut-wrenching envy as Charles watched them go.

The media was next but he was so tired he couldn't think straight. He could go to sleep in Mike and Emily's bungalow, he thought, but maybe, just maybe, Jill was worrying.

So he went. The cabin was in darkness. He wheeled through into the bedroom and Jill and Lily were curled up together in the big bed.

Were they asleep? He hesitated but Jill's eyes opened. She gazed across at him in the moonlight. Soundlessly she slipped out of bed and padded over the bare floorboards.

She was gorgeous, he thought, and the ache that had been in his gut for the past few days grew even fiercer. In her T-shirt and knickers, her curls tangled around her shoulders, her feet bare... She was the woman of his dreams. She'd given him a taste of paradise but had then withdrawn. How to get her back? Was it fair to even try?

They mustn't disturb Lily. He turned the chair and wheeled outside. She followed him out onto the veranda.

'Lily wanted to sleep with me,' she whispered, sounding defensive.

'Of course.'

'I'll…I'll move her onto the settee now.'

'But she might wake up,' he said, and waited for her to disagree.

She didn't.

'It's OK,' he said gently. 'There's a cabin spare. Mike flew Emily out tonight—you know she's in the early stages of pregnancy? We've confirmed it's not bird flu.'

'Oh, Charles,' she whispered. 'That's wonderful.'

'It's not bad,' he said, and managed a smile. 'But Mike still wanted to get her off the island as fast as possible. It may not be bird flu but it's still a nasty bug.'

'What do you think it is?'

'Angus is saying some sort of encephalitis caused by mosquitoes. We won't wait for confirmation—we'll have an eradication team start tomorrow.'

'You'll take Zach and Dom off dead-bird duty?'

He gave a wry smile. 'If I didn't think their father would get the hell out of here the minute he gets the news that quarantine's been lifted, I'd have them culling mosquitoes by hand.'

'Thank you,' she said simply.

'I think I've told you before,' he said, almost roughly. 'I don't want your thanks.'

'What do you want?'

'You,' he said, so savagely that he startled them both.

'You can't want me,' she whispered, sounding awed.

'What the hell do you mean by that?'

'I'm not…' She bit her lip. 'Just because you're in a wheelchair…'

It was the wrong thing to say. The words hung in the stillness, a tangible, awful truth. There was a moment's appalled silence.

'It always comes down to that,' Charles said, and even though he'd lowered his voice the savagery was even more intense. 'It always comes down to the bloody wheelchair.'

'I didn't mean that.' She could barely get the words out. Her face was blanched of all colour and she shrank back against the balustrade.

'You said it.'

His phone buzzed. It had been buzzing non-stop all night. He shouldn't be here, he thought savagely. There were a million things he should be doing.

He glanced at Jill's distressed face and thought even more definitely that he shouldn't be there.

It was the head of one of the nation's largest media outlets.

'My journalists are having trouble getting through to you,' the man snapped. 'I need an in-depth interview before we roll the presses, Charles. There's rumours flying everywhere that you've got something worse than bird flu.'

'I'll be in my office in ten minutes,' he said wearily. 'I'll do a teleconference if you want to set it up. Not just you, though, David. The opposition as well.'

'I want an exclusive.'

'Don't we all,' Charles snapped, more harshly than he'd intended. Looking at Jill.

He replaced his phone in his pocket. Jill was looking distressed and confused and…frightened? It took only that, he thought bleakly. She was frightened of him?

'How's Robbie?' she whispered. 'And Susie?'

OK. If she wanted to move back to medicine—safe ground—then maybe he had no choice but to follow.

'No one's worse,' he told her. 'We're thinking they'll be OK. We're figuring this bug out now. Fluids, fever control and antivirals on first symptoms. Those who showed the first signs yesterday aren't getting sicker. Mosquito repellent will be compulsory as of first thing tomorrow and hopefully the scare will be over. I have to go.'

'Of course you do,' she whispered. 'Charles…what I said…about the wheelchair…'

'Forget it,' he said roughly. 'I just wish to hell I could.'

She hadn't meant it. She sat on the balustrade and stared out into the night, replaying the conversation over and over in her head.

He'd said he wanted her. And she'd said, *Just because you're in a wheelchair…*

He'd taken it to be some sort of rejection. And in a way it was, she thought bleakly. Just because he was in a wheelchair he was restricted to the likes of her.

Only…he hadn't been thinking that. She knew that. Her words had been meant to be an apology. Instead he'd taken them as a slap.

She should go after him. Set it right.

She couldn't, of course. Lily was here. Lily was asleep in her bed.

She could have lifted Lily onto the settee and taken Charles into her bed. Exposed her neediness again…

It was just as well he was needed elsewhere, she thought as she returned to her too big bed to face the demons of the night. She wanted… She wanted..

What did she want?

She wanted him to be well, she thought fiercely. She wanted him to be whole and wonderful and able to choose a mate worthy of him.

Because she loved him.

She hugged her arms across her breasts and shivered, even though the night was warm and still.

How could she figure this out? How could she possibly make herself someone he deserved?

* * *

'Someone's left a flower for Lily.'

It was Marcia, cheerfully pushing the screen door wide to find Jill and Lily having breakfast. Lily was propped up on pillows and Jill was feeding her toast fingers dipped in egg. For a fiercely independent little girl, this was an admission of need indeed, and Marcia's eyes widened.

'Wow! I wish someone would feed me toast fingers. And leave me flowers.' She set the flower on the bedside table and grinned down at Lily. 'I think you might have a boyfriend.'

'I have lots of boyfriends,' Lily said serenely. 'Which one?'

'I saw Sam running back toward the camp,' Marcia told her, grinning at Jill.

'I like Sam,' Lily said. So did they all. The little boy was in his second remission from acute lymphoblastic leukaemia, but no amount of medical battering could conquer his indomitable spirit. 'He isn't sick?'

'No more sickies this morning,' Marcia reported. 'But Charles has called a meeting of all staff. Jill, he'd like you there. Lily, is it OK if I sit with you while Jill spends a little time in the hospital?'

'She's not Jill,' Lily said, and dropped her spoon and lunged forward to grab Jill round the waist. 'She's my mum.'

Jill blinked. She now had egg all over her T-shirt. She had a clingy little girl to contend with and Lily had never clung.

She was a mum.

'Hey,' Marcia said, and smiled, a trifle mistily. All the Crocodile Creek staff knew Lily's story. More people than Jill and Charles had worried about her fierce independence. This was a new Lily.

Maybe it wouldn't last past convalescence, but maybe...just maybe there'd been a breakthrough.

'I'll be gone for an hour at most, poppet,' Jill murmured, and Lily pulled back and glared.

'Promise?'

'I promise.' She glanced apologetically at Marcia. 'If I can be spared.'

'You're officially on leave, starting now,' Marcia said. 'We've decided. You were never meant to be here anyway. You need to stop being Director of Nursing for a bit while you learn to be a mum. But after Charles's meeting,' she said apologetically. 'Now, I think you need to change your T-shirt and I need to make your daughter another egg.'

They were in contact with the outside world. Jill walked into the meeting room and was assailed by news.

The big screen television was on, and Wallaby Island was the news of the day. There were pictures of Beth on the screen, with Angus. And Garf, being ridiculous. 'Medical authorities in charge of the suspected bird flu epidemic,' the voice-over was saying, and Jill looked at Beth's image in gorgeous blue pyjamas and smiled in sympathy. The media took whatever angle they wanted.

But then the image changed. 'Dr Charles Wetherby, Medical Director, with his fiancée and child,' the voice-over was saying, and there they were, framed as a family by Lily's bedside. Charles was touching her cheek. Jill's cheek. She remembered him touching her. Her hand flew involuntarily to her cheek now, remembering.

He looked like he loved her.

She swallowed hard while those around her turned and smiled in sympathy.

She glanced away, down at the table. Newspapers... Mike, she thought. He must have returned this morning after taking Emily off the island and had brought back the world's news.

And on the front cover...

This was yesterday's newspaper, she thought, dazed. A photograph taken—by who? She didn't remember. She was cradling Lily in her arms. Lily looked ill almost to the death. Jill was holding her close, looking down into her face with despair.

The photograph was huge, almost bigger than real life.

'The Human Cost of a Pandemic', the caption read.

Fear gripped her. Cold and hard and terrible. This was what she'd spent the last eight years trying to avoid.

Kelvin.

She'd changed her name. She'd spent the last eight years hiding. But there was no hiding this. She lifted the paper and underneath was another newspaper. A daily national broadsheet. A different caption.

Same photograph.

He had to see this.

He'd never let this go.

'Jill?' She dropped the newspaper and turned. Charles.

'What is it?' he said. And then more urgently, 'Jill?'

'I...'

'What?' He glanced down at the table and saw what she'd been seeing. 'The papers?'

'Kelvin,' she whispered.

'Hey.' He understood, she thought. One fast glance at the headlines brought comprehension. 'Jill, don't look like that,' he said. 'It's been eight years. He's in jail.'

'He isn't any more. At least, I don't think so.'

'You don't know. You're on a remote island.' And then, more urgently, 'You have me.'

'You don't know what he's like,' she said dully. 'I have to leave.'

'Of course you don't have to leave.'

'He'll hurt Lily. He'll destroy us.'

'Jill, this is paranoid.'

'It's not. I have to go. For Lily's sake.'

'It's OK,' he said, sternly. 'Let's not overreact. I'll talk to Harry.'

'He won't be able to stop him.'

'Jill, he can't be that bad.'

'He is.'

'Then we'll talk to Harry,' he said. 'Harry can move heaven and earth for the people he cares about, and he cares about you. We all do. He'll find out where he is and we'll go from there.'

The terror lessened. Just a fraction. If she could know where he was...

'He'll do that?'

'Let's ask him,' Charles said strongly, and took her hand. 'But you're not to look like that. Jill, I need to talk to the staff about what's happening, and the nursing questions about encephalitis would be better directed to you.'

'Of course. I shouldn't have worried you.'

'Of course you should have worried me,' he said strongly. 'If I'm to be your husband... Hell, I'm worried already.'

Harry took her seriously as well.

'We'll put a track on him straight away,' he said. 'With his criminal record, even if he's out he's likely to be subject of a parole order. Meanwhile you concentrate on getting your little girl well again. Leave Kelvin to Charles and to me.'

'But—'

'We won't let him hurt you,' Charles said, softly but with quiet assurance. 'I promise.'

She had to be content with that.

She listened while Charles outlined the precautions staff were to take to prevent any more cases of encephalitis. Bush walks were off the agenda until the waterholes were filled. Insect repellent was to be worn by everyone. But now they knew, the island could be made safe. The camp staff could go back to the job at hand. Which was making sick kids feel great.

'Which means this is a beach day,' Melissa, the activity director, decreed. 'There's no mossies near the beach. We'll set up shade sails, with a few camp beds for those who need a rest. We'll have beach games, a reef walk and a barbecue. Let's get these bad few days behind us.'

She didn't say what everyone here knew. For many of these kids life was precarious. You didn't wait around until everything was perfect before having fun. Perfect might never happen.

'Now we know the kids with the virus aren't contagious, they can be included if they're well enough,' Melissa went on. 'Some of the kids have been frightened. They've watched Danny and Lily and Robbie get sick. We need reassurance. Jill, what if we brought you and Lily down to the beach in a buggy for a couple of hours? Lily could lie on a camp bed and watch. She wouldn't have to join in. I could tell the kids she was resting and she could watch from a distance.'

'That'd be great,' Charles said warmly, smiling at Jill, and she knew he was thinking it'd be great for her as well. It'd get her out of the bungalow. Away from her fears.

'Fine,' she said weakly.

'We'll both be there,' Charles said. 'Life gets back to normal. Starting now.'

They'd had enough dramas. They should have been able to relax for the next few days.

It didn't happen.

Charles worked until after lunch and then came back to the bungalow just as Lily woke up. The little girl was pale and weary but when Jill suggested they take the beach buggy down to the sea, she reacted with pleasure.

'With both of you?'

'Yes.'

'With my mummy and my daddy,' she said, and smiled a secret smile.

Jill felt like crying. It was so good. It was almost perfect. Except for the fact that she and Charles were still absurdly formal.

And out there somewhere was Kelvin.

But she was able to forget that on the beach. Almost every kid in camp was there, and most of the staff as well. There were also guests from the resort. Normally the resort guests kept to their part of the island, but Benita Green, the cancer nurse had invited resort kids to share in the reef walk if they wanted.

They did want. For everyone on the island, it felt like a holiday, a release from the threat that had hung over them briefly but terribly. Even the few photographers snapping in the distance didn't feel like a threat.

For they stayed apart. Benita had set up a shade sail solely for their use, tucked discreetly to the side of the first of the sand-hills so the rest of the kids couldn't see Lily was there. Lily wasn't up to joining in just yet, and neither did she want to. Here they could lie side by side and watch everything on the beach without Lily tiring.

That was another blinking moment for Jill as she saw the set-up. Benita, Beth—everyone in camp knew the pressure they'd been under.

This was a gesture to their embryonic family.

'I'm in the middle,' Lily said importantly so they lay on the lounges on either side of their daughter, and Jill caught Charles's gaze over Lily's head and they shared a smile that took her breath away.

It felt so good. Just to lie here as a family… Maybe it could work, she thought as they soaked up the sun. Maybe it just needed time. Maybe—

A scream broke the stillness. She looked toward the sea, startled. Benita, the cancer care nurse, was in the shallows, surrounded by a gaggle of assorted kids. Sam had broken away from the group, running up the beach as if terrified, a skinny little kid in scant bathers, holding his towel like it contained something precious.

But his run faltered. As she watched, he screamed again. The towel fell at his feet and he stared at it in horror.

And crumpled where he stood.

Sam!

'You stay. I'll go,' Charles snapped. She'd hardly reacted before Charles was in the buggy.

'They might need—'

'The beach is covered with medics.' Charles was already shoving the buggy into gear. 'Take care of Lily while I see what's happening.'

Charles moved fast but in this crowd from the medical camp and the medical conference, it was inevitable that other medics got there before him.

Beth reached Sam first, falling onto her knees beside him, moving into reflex airway check.

'Get the kids back,' she snapped as Charles got within hearing range. 'Do you know what happened?'

'He just screamed and fell down,' Benita said, appalled.

Beth was holding Sam's wrist. His chest was barely moving. How could he go from a laughing, running child to this in seconds?

'I'll take his towel,' one of the kids said uncertainly, and Beth and Angus, and Charles, too, speeding along the beach to join them, had the same thought at exactly the same moment.

'Don't touch it.'

Respiratory arrest? It had to be.

At least there were enough doctors here, and then some. Sam was in the best of hands but Charles felt helpless. Beth was already breathing for the little boy, pinching his nose and breathing into his mouth, short, sharp bursts of air, her head turning as she breathed so she could watch his chest move as she filled it for him. It was expired air but it was the best they could offer until they could get oxygen. Angus was by her side, ready to assist.

What had caused this? Charles turned his cart toward Sam's towel. But once again he and Beth were thinking alike.

Angus had taken over Sam's breathing and the moment he did, Beth grabbed a piece of driftwood and poked at the towel. It fell open, and a shell rolled sideways onto the sand.

'That's a cone shell.' It was an onlooker—a stranger. There were too many people on the beach but at least this one seemed sensible. The stranger strode forward and stood protectively over the shell, as if to stop anyone else being inadvertently stung.

A cone shell… Dear God.

This was the geographer cone. Charles had read about them. He'd seen pictures but he'd never seen one in real life. Neither had he ever wanted to. A thing of exquisite beauty, the fish inside shot poison through a series of toothed harpoons in the narrow end of the shell. The venom could kill almost instantly. The fine harpoons could even be directed backwards toward the fat end of the shell, and a direct sting could kill a man.

What was it doing on this sheltered, netted beach? It was extremely rare in these waters. It must have been washed here in the storm. For Sam to find it…

It was a nightmare.

And there was nothing Charles could do. Angus was working as well as any doctor could, a big, competent doctor moving into emergency mode with practised precision, pinching Sam's tiny, snubbed nose and breathing into his mouth, over and over, short, sharp bursts of air.

Where was the medical cart? He lifted his phone and barked orders, telling Luke that fast wasn't fast enough. They had to have oxygen. Now!

Beth was examining Sam's hands, searching for what they knew had to be there.

'Here!' It was a tiny red welt on his little finger. There was no doubting it now. One of the barbs had dug right in.

Charles turned and glanced up the beach. Jill was holding Lily, and he could see Lily's distress as well. The body language of everyone on the beach told its own story.

Sam had to live. It was too far for him to see Jill's expression from here—or to listen to Lily's distress—but they both knew Sam.

Sam was almost family. Charles's embryonic family was too small as it was.

Sam had to live.

Jill had to take Lily home. There were too many people on the beach already. She couldn't see what was happening. She wasn't needed. Charles would do what needed to be done. Charles and his team. And if the worst happened...

Lily was sobbing in distress, having heard enough from the shouting, from the terrified yells of the kids, to know that Sam was in danger. She was frantic for Sam, desperate to know what was happening.

'I think something's stung him,' Jill told her, cradling her in her arms, wanting to know herself but fearing that taking Lily closer might be—would be—crazy. 'But the doctors are taking care of him. I think we should go home.'

'Will Sam die?'

'Charles is looking after him.'

'My daddy is looking after him,' Lily corrected her, sounding suddenly stern, and the fear in her voice faded a little. 'Daddy will make him better.'

Luke arrived faster than could reasonably be expected, barrelling down the track from the camp in the medical cart, bringing much-needed equipment. Oxygen. Analgesics. It must have been pain that had caused Sam to collapse so dramatically, Charles thought as he watched his team in action. Shock would have sent him into incipient cardiac arrest, thankfully now reversed.

Sometimes it was hard to be the boss, he thought bleakly. These young doctors were great. He'd hand-picked his team and he trusted them, but sometimes it'd be easier to get in there and do the work himself.

But Sam looked as if he was coming out the other side. There was no need for him to intervene.

As Angus slid a cannula into the back of Sam's hand and prepared to give him morphine, the little boy's eyes fluttered open.

Just momentarily but enough to give them all hope.

Now they had oxygen going and breathing established they could afford to take their time—in fact, it was better to try and stabilise him before they moved him. With the immediate medical imperatives covered there was now time to take in the whole scene. To one side lay Sam's towel, discarded. The stranger was still standing over it—seemingly protective. In its midst lay the cone shell, a cylindrical whirl of beauty. Tangerine and cream and black, perfectly patterned. Deadly.

How the hell…? He'd had divers go over every inch of the cove before he'd let the kids swim here. The nets had been broken in the storm, but he'd had the cove checked again afterwards.

He closed his eyes. Not securely enough, obviously.

'You want me to take care of it?'

The stranger was a thick-set guy in his forties or fifties. Unlike most of the people on the beach he was fully clothed and wearing thick boots and hat. Charles took in his appearance in some surprise. This guy looked as if he worked outdoors. His hat was battered and grubby. He didn't look like a tourist.

'I'm a fisherman here on holiday,' he said, answering Charles's question before he uttered it. 'I make my living fishing for abalone. I know how to cope with this.'

'My rangers will—'

'Do your guys know what range these things will sting from?' the man said. He walked across to the nearest shade sail, tugged it out of the ground and brought it over. 'They can stay alive for hours out of water, but a few layers of canvas'll do it,' he said. 'I'll wrap it up so tight nothing can get near it. Tell me where to take it.'

'We have a medical disposal unit at the back of the hospital,' Charles said, grateful for the man's practical assurances. 'I'll send a ranger down to help you.'

'I'll be right here.'

He nodded, grateful. Hell, he'd had enough drama. He was feeling sick. But Sam's colour was returning. They had the best medical staff on the island and he knew that it was sheer skill that had saved Sam's life.

Maybe they'd got past this threat, too.

Please.

Jill took Lily back to the cabin. They were silent on the way back, awed and frightened by what they'd seen.

'But he won't die,' Lily kept saying. 'He won't die.'

'Of course he won't die.'

'It's lucky we have Daddy.'

'It is.'

They paused when they reached the bungalow. There was a small brown dog sitting on the doorstep. A stuffed toy. Ritz. This cute little dog with his top hat and cane played his crazy song and did a little dance every time someone pressed his foot. He was the camp mascot.

'Someone's trying to make you feel better,' she told Lily, and Lily picked up the little dog and smiled and pressed his foot.

'But I don't need him,' she said softly as Ritz danced. 'Lots of kids at camp don't have mummies and daddies here. They need Ritz more than I do.'

'That's lovely,' Jill whispered, feeling choked. She set the little dog on the bench by the door. Even though he was gorgeous, he wasn't a toy to take to bed and cuddle. The heavy musical mechanism in his base made him more of a paperweight. 'I'll take him back later.'

She'd show Charles first, though, she thought. She'd tell him what Lily had said.

Lots of kids here don't have mummies and daddies.

Lily had moved on.

Maybe…maybe…

She wanted him to come. Maybe all her fears were irrational.

Lily was asleep almost as soon as her head hit the pillow. It was a skill of childhood—moving from being awake to the deepest of sleep in an instant. Jill was almost jealous.

She couldn't sleep. She was left alone with her thoughts.

How soon till Charles came?

The screen door swung open behind her in the living room, and she smiled. She left the sleeping Lily and walked out to meet him. 'Charles, you'll never guess what Lily said—'

It wasn't Charles.

It was Kelvin.

'Sam's going to be OK?' Harry, like everyone at the resort, was appalled by what had happened. The big policeman met Charles as he walked out of the treatment room, his tanned face drawn and worried.

'He's looking good,' Charles told him. 'He must have only got a tiny sting through the towel. The barbs didn't stick. But when I think of what could have happened… It's my job to keep this place safe. How the hell—?'

'It's what happens,' Harry said, gripping his friend's shoulder in concern. 'You know that. It's life. You can keep these kids in cotton wool for the rest of their lives or you can give them a camp like this one. With risks.'

'I had no right—'

'The risks were tiny,' Harry said. 'The encephalitis was dead unlucky and so was the cone shell. I just did a search on the Internet, finding out about them. They're rare as hens' teeth on this coast. It must have been blasted down during the cyclone. There's been one recorded death in all of Australia's history. Sam had better odds of being abducted by aliens than of being stung by one of these.'

'Don't say it,' Charles begged. 'The way I'm feeling, you're tempting fate. Any minute aliens will land.'

'If they do, we'll pick them up on the way in,' Harry assured him. 'I've got the base covered. Any arrivals get vetted before they set foot on the island.'

'Kelvin?'

'Jill's not a woman to scare easily. From what I'm hearing, she's right to be scared.'

'Hell.' He was starting to feel overwhelmed.

'We'll keep her safe,' Harry said. 'I've had his photograph faxed through and I've just taken copies down to the jetty. The ferry staff will notify me the minute they see him—well before he gets near the island. We'll saturate the district with his image. I left one in your office. Can you show Jill and tell her what we're doing?' He gripped Charles's shoulder once more. 'It's OK. The run of bad luck ends here.'

He left him, striding out of the hospital looking purposeful and competent. He was a good man to have on side, Charles thought. Jill could relax with Harry taking care of her.

Harry rather than him? Yeah, he thought grimly. He was feeling sick with frustration. No matter what Harry said, he'd failed to protect the people who were depending on him.

He had to phone Sam's parents.

Who'd want to be a medical director? Not him. Not now. He felt weary to the bone.

He wheeled forward into his office and lifted the receiver. While he dialled he glanced idly at the photograph Harry had left on the desk.

He dropped the phone.

CHAPTER TWELVE

IT WAS the nightmare she'd known must finally happen. If she ever left he'd kill her. He'd said it so often she heard it in her dreams.

It had hung over her, even as she'd built her career, as she'd fallen in love with Lily. As she'd fallen in love with Charles.

'I told you I'd come,' he said, almost pleasantly, and she saw what he was carrying and she almost fainted.

He was wearing gloves. Thick leather gloves that covered his arms to the wrist. She remembered he'd worn them when the winches had got stuck, when he'd had to haul fishing lines in by hand.

He must have his boat here, she thought, feeling sick. Somehow he had his fishing gear. So he had his protective gloves.

He was holding Sam's cone shell with all the reverence in the world.

'Just lucky, eh?' he said. 'I saw your picture in the paper and I had the boat in Cairns. It was dead easy to bring the boat into one of the coves along the coast. So I was watching you playing happy families on the beach. With the cripple. I sat there on the beach away from the crowd, trying to figure it out. I've done enough years behind bars on your account. There's no one going to point the finger at me for your murder—or even if they do, they won't be able to prove it.'

'What…what do you mean?'

'Natural causes,' he said sardonically, and he tossed the shell a couple of inches in the air and caught it with casual care. 'Yeah, people will have seen me on the beach. I know that. So I took the shell and came inland to dispose of it like a good little citizen. On the way I met my ex-wife—after all, you were the reason I was here. I wanted to apologise for all that past rubbish. Anyway, you wanted to have a look and I was so dumb I showed it to you and you just touched it—'

'No!'

'Nothing to it,' he said mildly. 'I wonder if the kid touched it, too?'

'No!'

'Ugly cow,' he said. He was walking steadily toward her, forcing her to back into the bedroom. Blessedly Lily was deeply asleep, exhausted with the combination of illness and shock from the scene on the beach. Please, God, she wouldn't wake up.

'Kelvin, don't do this,' Jill whispered, trying to keep her voice steady. 'There's nothing to gain and everything to lose.'

'I won't lose anything,' he said. 'I spent five years in the slammer over you. Five years! You think you should get off scot-free?'

'I didn't.'

'No,' he said, staring at her, taking in how she looked now. 'Look at you. Ugly as sin. Even uglier than you were when your old man forced me to marry you. Women get old faster than men and you're getting old faster than most. It's a wonder you can get any man to look at you, even the miserable cripple you've finally latched on to.' And he moved toward her with the shell.

'Jill could have any man she looked at,' Charles said strongly from the living room, and Jill's gaze flew past Kelvin. Shock piling on shock. Charles had come in silently. He was in his wheelchair, just inside the living-room door, maybe fifteen feet from Kelvin.

He was simply sitting, watching the events in the bedroom with his usual calmness.

'H-he's g-got the shell,' Jill stuttered, and Charles nodded.

'I can see he's got the shell. What I want to know is, how on earth can he aim it at you if he's blind?'

'What the hell do you mean by that?' Kelvin snarled.

Charles didn't pose a threat, Jill thought. Kelvin had moved sideways a little so he could see them both, but his face showed no alarm. In fact, there was almost a hint of satisfaction.

He'd kill Charles, too, Jill thought in panic. He could. He was a big man, at the height of his physical powers. He was armed with something as lethal as a gun.

'I mean Jill's the sexiest, most desirable, most wonderful woman I've ever had the privilege to meet,' Charles said, as if this was a normal conversation, with a normal man, and he was telling the world of the woman he was to marry. He lifted Ritz, the crazy little dog, from the bench by the door and looked down at him with affection. 'She's given me a family. Jill, Lily, friends, dogs, toys... I have a family now, with Jill at its heart.'

The pride in his voice was unmistakable and Jill's eyes widened in shock.

'Don't...' she whispered.

'Don't tell Kelvin what a fool he was for having you and losing you? For not knowing what a gift he had, if only he'd treated you as you deserved to be treated? He has a whole body. He was capable of giving you the loving you deserved and he squandered it.'

'Oh, Charles,' she whispered. 'As if you're not capable—'

'Shut the hell up,' Kelvin yelled, clearly rattled by a conversation he didn't understand. And then he laughed. 'Sorry. I should be more generous. Any last words, or something like that?'

'Don't be a fool,' Charles said. 'I've called the police. They know what you intend. Your only chance is to lay the shell down and walk away. Fast.'

'Right,' Kelvin jeered, and took two fast steps toward Jill and grabbed her by the hair. He tugged her hard against him and raised the shell in his free hand. 'Her first and then you. She's touched the shell and it speared her; you came in and were so upset you just grabbed her, like they did with the kid on the beach. I tried to warn you the shell was under her—'

'Leave her,' Charles said sharply.

'Watch me,' he said, and he raised the shell slightly higher, its lethal end poised and ready to fall...

But then...

It came from nowhere, a brown blur of fur and metal, Ritz, hurled across the room with all the force of Charles's strong arm. Years of pushing his wheelchair, of holding himself up on his elbow crutches, of depending on his arms for everything, had given him strength that was almost uncanny.

And deadly accuracy.

The shell was exposed, in the palm of Kelvin's hand, held high, and Charles didn't miss. The shell smashed where it was held, with a cracking thud, spattering shell and fish fragments everywhere.

And Charles was there. His wheelchair followed through with savage ferocity, smashing into Kelvin's legs, hurling him backward beside the bed.

His hand was still grasping Jill's hair, hauling her down. Charles grabbed her arm and wrenched her away with such force he must have come close to dislocating her shoulder, and Kelvin had no chance to hold her.

'Get back,' he yelled at her, but there was no need, for the force of his pull had her stumbling behind him, sprawling to the floor.

And Kelvin didn't follow. Instead he screamed. His gloved hand clutched his face—and he screamed again.

'Don't touch anything,' Charles barked at him. 'Stay still.'

But Kelvin was clutching his face as if it burned, crumpling to his knees. The broken shell must have spattered against his face, piercing the skin. The geographer cone was one of the most deadly of sea creatures and if it smashed, even a tiny scratch would let venom in. Kelvin's hands had been protected by the gloves. Involuntarily he was clutching his face with his hands, pushing smashed shell against his skin, spreading more of the venom.

Jill staggered upright, appalled. 'I'll get—'

'Get in the shower,' Charles snapped at her, hauling back from the man on the floor, shoving his chair between Jill and Kelvin. 'Now. Use a towel to open the shower door and to turn on the tap. You'll have stuff on you. You don't know if you've got scratches anywhere. Don't touch your clothes. Don't touch anything. Get in and stand under the water until I tell you to get out.'

'But—'

'Go,' he barked in such a tone that she fled without a word.

She stood under the water for fifteen minutes. Twenty minutes. Minutes while the world shifted.

She shook the entire time.

People came to check on her. Harry first, hauling open the bathroom door, staring in with fear, but his face sagging in relief as he saw she was alive, upright, not hurt.

'Lily?' she whispered.

'She's fine. We've got her out. Stay there,' he said. 'Charles says it's safest.' He left again.

So she stayed there. She couldn't think of anything else to do. She knew exactly why Charles had ordered her to do what she was doing. If there were fragments of broken shell on her clothes and she touched them…

She mustn't.

She stood, numbed and shocked, while the water streamed over her. She let her mind go blank. She couldn't imagine what was happening in the other room.

She didn't want to imagine.

Marcia came in then, white-faced, terrified.

'Are you OK?'

'I... Yes.'

'I can't stay,' she said, sounding apologetic. 'I need to—'

'I know.'

'Charles says keep your hands away from your sides. Don't attempt to get your clothes off. We'll do it with gloves as soon...'

She faltered.

'I'm OK,' Jill whispered.

Marcia gave her a scared glance and left.

There was noise coming from the other room. Appalling noise. She turned the water up and put her head under water, trying to block it out.

Dear God.

The noise subsided. The sound of horror gave way to the sound of subdued voices.

And finally he came. Charles. Pushing the door wide. Wheeling into the room.

Looking like death.

'Oh, Charles...'

'He's dead,' he said bluntly, and she cringed back against the tiles.

'Kelvin...'

'He never stood a chance,' he said. 'He went into cardiac arrest but with venom on his face there was no way we could give him mouth to mouth. Not without a mask. Even if—'

'Don't say it.'

'No,' he said, and looked at her. 'You're alive,' he said, as if he couldn't quite believe it. 'You know how long it took to get from the hospital to here?'

'You knew?'

'Harry had his photograph faxed through and left it on my desk. I'd seen him on the beach. God, help me, I'd accepted his offer to dispose of the shell. I hit the panic button for Harry but—'

'You got here first.'

'If he'd killed you, I think I would have died,' he said simply, and she stared out through the shower screen at the man she loved and felt her world shift all over again.

'Charles...'

'You want to come out?' he said, opening the screen door. 'I have gloves.'

'Gloves?'

'You think I'd let anyone else undress you?'

She smiled at that. It was a poor excuse for a smile but it was a smile for all that. She could hardly see him through tears.

'L-Lily?' she managed.

'Marcia's taken her over to the hospital. Would you believe she didn't even wake up? Our bedroom's a crime scene now, roped off for the coroner. I've done a fast change, I'm clean. But you were right there when it smashed. Marcia's brought you a robe. We'll go over to Mike and Emily's bungalow.'

'But—'

'All the stuff in the bedroom has to be cleaned before it's touched,' he said roughly. 'There's shards of shell everywhere. Come here.'

She stepped out onto the bathmat. He wouldn't let her help. Wearing heavy gardener's gloves and armed with a pair of scissors, he simply sliced her clothes off her.

He wrapped her in a towel, propelled her onto the bathroom stool and combed her hair. Over and over.

Then he had her put her head over the basin while he rinsed her hair so thoroughly that no trace of shell could remain.

'Stand up,' he said at last, and she did. He tugged the towel from her and held out another.

She went to take it from him, but he took her hands and he pulled her into him so she was cradled against him, cradled like a child, wrapped in a clean, dry towel, her hair still dripping, but safe.

Safe.

'I thought I'd lost you,' he whispered, and he held her close with something akin to wonder.

'It was the best throw,' she managed, still struggling to believe it was over.

'You realise we're going to have to get Ritz decontaminated?' He was striving from lightness but she could still hear the raw emotion in his voice.

'We could throw him out,' she said. 'Buy another one?'

'Are you kidding? He saved your life.'

'You saved my life,' she said, turning into him and hooking his face in her hands. 'You. My hero. My wonderful, sexy, fantastic Charles. My love.'

He stilled. 'You say that now…'

'How can I not say it?' she demanded. 'What did you tell Kelvin? That he had a whole body, he was capable of giving me the loving I deserved. Oh, Charles, as if you're not.'

'You're so beautiful,' he whispered, his face in her hair.

'I'm not beautiful. Once…'

'What the hell are you talking about?' he demanded, and put her away from him. 'Look at you. Look at you!' He turned her, swinging the chair so they were both staring into the bathroom mirror. She was curled on his knee. Before she could stop him he'd tugged the towel away so she was naked. She made a grab for the towel but he smiled and tossed it to the far side of the bathroom.

'No. Why cover it up?' He gazed into the mirror, soaking in every inch of her. 'What a waste, to cover it. You're every inch a woman, the most beautiful woman I know. From the moment I first saw you I wanted you.'

'You can't have done.'

'Don't tell me what I can and can't have done,' he said roughly, grasping her still tighter. 'Not while I'm holding you. Not while I have you. Not when I thought I'd lost you. But you're alive and wonderful and I have you in my arms and you're wearing my ring.'

'You wanted me?' she whispered, awed.

'For years,' he said simply. 'Only every time I approached you, you reacted like you didn't want to know me.'

'Oh, Charles,' she managed. 'I wanted you, too.'

'Excuse me?' he said in a strange voice, and she tugged back still further so she could see his face.

'I wanted you,' she said simply. 'The first time I met you I thought you were the most gorgeous doctor—the most fabulous man—I'd ever met. But you were rich and powerful and you could have any woman you wanted.'

'You're saying you wanted me?'

'I want you,' she said simply, still not believing. 'I love you, Charles. I love you with every inch of my being. Yes, I want a daughter. Yes, I agreed to marry you so we could adopt Lily. But I would have taken you on whatever terms I could get. I—'

'No,' he said, the awe in her voice echoed in his. 'My turn. I love you, Jill. I always thought…'

'Then stop thinking,' she said, half laughing, half crying. 'Let's both stop thinking. This is crazy. Oh, Charles, Kelvin's just died…'

'Do you mind?'

Her smile faded. 'I wouldn't have wanted him dead,' she said.

'But now he is, you're free to choose your life,' he said. 'Without fear. You're free to choose your own path.'

'I have,' she said simply. 'I choose you.'

'Jill…'

'Yes?'

'This is not going to work,' he said, goaded. 'Your clothes have contaminated the floor. There's a crime scene outside. I can't…'

'Yes, you can,' she said serenely. 'You can do anything you want, Charles Wetherby. Let's see a bit of that great improvisation you're famous for. I depend on you, my love. Starting now.'

* * *

It was the wedding to end all weddings. The chapel in Crocodile Creek was far too small to hold all the people who'd decided they wanted to attend. Jill and Charles had no control over their guest list.

'We've been waiting for this for eight long years,' Dora Grubb decreed. 'Do you think it's your wedding? It's our wedding.'

They came from all around the world. Doctors, nurses, paramedics who'd worked in Crocodile Creek and on Wallaby Island since the inception of the medical service. Patients Charles had cared for. Farming families who owed their ability to stay on the land to the medical service Charles had set up.

So many people.... The locals built a mini-chapel on the beach, an altar, an arch the bride had to walk through, paving set down specially so Charles could stand...

He stood, with Walter Grubb by his side. So many people to choose from for his best man... It had to be Grubby, caretaker of Crocodile Creek hospital.

Dora was matron of honour, gorgeous in purple taffeta, swelling fit to burst. Georgie had been asked but she'd pulled out at the last minute.

'Sorry, sweetie, even though I'm an obstetrician I have no control over what's happening to me at the moment. I'd have to carry a bucket instead of a bouquet.'

She was in the front row, wearing scarlet, looking pale but serenely happy with her Alistair. Alistair was carrying a bucket adorned with red bows.

Lily was flower girl. Of course. She wore a lacy confection of the palest pink with a huge pink satin bow at the back. She had silver and pink ribbons in her hair. There was no hint of tomboy Lily on this, the wedding day of her parents. She was determined to do this right.

As they all were. The crowd of friends clustered close, gasping their pleasure as Jill appeared.

She had no one to give her away.

'I'll be giving myself to you,' she told Charles with a hint of the austerity she'd been renowned for. 'As you'll be giving yourself to me.' And who could argue with that?

And she walked steadily down the beach toward her love. First came Dora, then Lily, scattering rose petals.

After her came four little boys, CJ, Danny, Robbie and Sam. They were there to hold her train. They were also there to celebrate the end of a nightmare and the moving forward into a future full of hope.

Six attendants. One labradoodle, tailing wagging furiously, bringing up the rear.

One bride.

Charles had eyes only for his bride.

His Jill.

She'd dressed simply. Her ivory silk gown had a low-cut bodice and tiny capped sleeves. The dress fitted perfectly to her waist, then flared out to lovely sweeping folds of soft silk, shimmering around her.

He'd never seen anything more beautiful in his life.

Where was the prickly, defensive woman of the past bleak years now? In the last four weeks she'd blossomed, flowered. She smiled at him mistily through tears, and it was as much as Charles could do not to weep himself.

This woman… His Jill…

He stood before her. Her Charles. He'd abandoned his wheelchair and his crutches for the day. There was a slim handrail near the makeshift altar and it was enough. Planning for later, when they'd walk out through the throng of well-wishers as man and wife, he'd said simply, 'I'll lean on you.'

And she'd lean on him, she thought. For ever.

Her Charles. Impossibly handsome in his black dinner suit. Impossibly wonderful. Impossible to believe he'd be her husband.

She reached him. He took her hand and held it.

He smiled into her eyes, and his smile was declaration enough before any vows could be spoken.

Man and wife. From this day forth.

And then there was the wedding gift from the town. Organised by Harry.

They hadn't wanted to go far away tonight, for there were so many friends from overseas that they intended this party to end all parties to go on for all the weekend. But as their wedding day faded toward dusk they disappeared, promising their guests they'd see them tomorrow but tonight they had things to do, places to go...

Their guests all knew where they were going. Even Lily had serenely granted them leave of absence to get this honeymoon over with. For it was planned. The carpenters were busy knocking walls out of their apartments. The town had therefore arranged alternative accommodation.

A tiny cove, just north of the town. A secluded beach. One of the loveliest places in the world.

Their friends had been at work and as Charles and Jill arrived, knowing only they'd been ordered to come here, not knowing what to expect, they gasped in wonder.

A marquee had been erected just past the high-tide mark. It was a beribboned confection of a honeymoon palace.

They made their way down the beach in wonder.

The marquee was set up as a honeymoon suite. Inside were rich silk rugs covering the sand. There was a vast, king-sized bed festooned with silk hangings, pillows and quilts, like something out of an Eastern harem.

There was a portable bathroom to the side. With a full-sized bath! A tank of fresh water was connected through the wall.

There was a refrigerator brimming with a feast fit for royalty.

The flaps on the far side of the marquee were open to the sea, the high-tide mark right there. The moonlit beach beckoned.

There was a notice attached to the tent wall.

'Welcome to your honeymoon. The cove's been searched and netted so thoroughly not even a tadpole can get through. The access road was cordoned off by the police the minute you went through, and security's in place. Nobody, nothing gets into this cove for however long you want it. With love. CC.'

Crocodile Creek. Their friends. Their family.

'It's perfect,' Charles said.

'You're perfect,' Jill whispered.

'Maybe not,' he admitted, cautious still. 'Do you remember what you said back at Wallaby Island? That we'll never get to know our wobbly bits while the lights are out? I guess this is the perfect time to examine our wobbly bits.'

'So it's time for an anatomy lesson,' she said softly.

'I'm thinking it might be.' He smiled at her, that heart-melting smile she loved so much. 'It seems a shame to take off that beautiful dress.'

'It seems a shame to take off that gorgeous suit.'

He nodded. His eyes darkened with laughter and with something else.

'I'm ready when you are,' he said.

'Right,' she said, and grinned and threw reserve and caution and everything else she could think of to the wind.

MILLS & BOON®

Want to get more from Mills & Boon?

Here's what's available to you if you join the exclusive **Mills & Boon eBook Club** today:

✦ *Convenience – choose your books each month*

✦ *Exclusive – receive your books a month before anywhere else*

✦ *Flexibility – change your subscription at any time*

✦ *Variety – gain access to eBook-only series*

✦ *Value – subscriptions from just £1.99 a month*

So visit **www.millsandboon.co.uk/esubs** today to be a part of this exclusive eBook Club!

MILLS & BOON®

Why shop at millsandboon.co.uk?

Each year, thousands of romance readers find their perfect read at millsandboon.co.uk. That's because we're passionate about bringing you the very best romantic fiction. Here are some of the advantages of shopping at www.millsandboon.co.uk:

* **Get new books first**—you'll be able to buy your favourite books one month before they hit the shops

* **Get exclusive discounts**—you'll also be able to buy our specially created monthly collections, with up to 50% off the RRP

* **Find your favourite authors**—latest news, interviews and new releases for all your favourite authors and series on our website, plus ideas for what to try next

* **Join in**—once you've bought your favourite books, don't forget to register with us to rate, review and join in the discussions

Visit **www.millsandboon.co.uk**
for all this and more today!